For Adults

ALFRED HITCHCOCK PRESENTS:
My Favorites in Suspense
Stories for Late at Night
Stories My Mother Never Told Me
Stories Not for the Nervous
Stories That Scared Even Me
A Month of Mystery
Stories to Stay Awake By

For Juveniles

ALFRED HITCHCOCK'S
Haunted Houseful
Ghostly Gallery
Solve Them Yourself Mysteries
Monster Museum
Sinister Spies
Spellbinders in Suspense
Daring Detectives
Supernatural Tales of Terror and Suspense

ALFRED HITCHCOCK PRESENTS:
STORIES TO BE READ WITH
THE LIGHTS ON

ALFRED HITCHCOCK

Presents

STORIES TO BE READ WITH THE LIGHTS ON

Random House, New York

Library of Congress Cataloging in Publication Data

Hitchcock, Alfred Joseph, 1899–   comp.
Alfred Hitchcock presents.

1. Detective and mystery stories, American. 2. Detective and mystery stories, English. 3. Horror tales, American. 4. Horror tales, English. I. Title. II. Title: Stories to be read with the lights on.
PZ1.H53Ald [PS648.D4]   823′.0872   73-5059
ISBN 0-394-48720-6

Manufactured in the United States of America

9 8 7 6 5 4 3 2
First Edition

Acknowledgments

WHO'S GOT THE LADY by Jack Ritchie. Reprinted by permission of Larry Sternig Literary Agency. Copyright © 1964 by Renown Publications, Inc. First published in *Mike Shayne Mystery Magazine*.

THE MOTHER GOOSE MADMAN by Betty Ren Wright. Reprinted by permission of Larry Sternig Literary Agency. Copyright © 1959 by H.S.D. Publications, Inc. First published in *Alfred Hitchcock's Mystery Magazine*.

HEY YOU DOWN THERE by Harold Rolseth. Reprinted by permission of Larry Sterning Literary Agency. Copyright © 1971 by Yankee, Inc. First published in *Yankee Magazine*.

SOCIAL CLIMBER by Robert J. Higgins. Reprinted by permission of the author and Larry Sternig Literary Agency. Copyright © 1967 by Leo Margulies Corp. First published in *The Man From U.N.C.L.E. Magazine*.

SHADOWS ON THE ROAD by Robert Colby. Reprinted by permission of the author. Copyright © 1971 by Robert Colby. First published in *Alfred Hitchcock's Mystery Magazine*.

TOO MANY SHARKS by William Sambrot. Reprinted by permission of Curtis Brown, Ltd. Copyright © 1956 by Dee Publishing Corp.

The editor gratefully acknowledges the invaluable assistance of Harold Q. Masur in the preparation of this volume

Contents

Death Out of Season · *Mary Barrett*   3

Witness in the Dark · *Fredric Brown*   11

Shadows on the Road · *Robert Colby*   33

Mr. Mappin Forecloses · *Zena Collier*   49

Granny · *Ron Goulart*   63

The Landlady · *Roald Dahl*   75

Three Ways to Rob a Bank · *Harold R. Daniels*   85

No Loose Ends · *Miriam Allen deFord*   95

Goodbye, Pops · *Joe Gores*   105

Pin Money · *James Cross*   113

Social Climber · *Robert J. Higgins*   127

I'd Know You Anywhere · *Edward D. Hoch*   133

The Pile of Sand · *John Keefauver*   143

Payoff on Double Zero · *Warner Law*   151

The Bitter Years · *Dana Lyon*   173

Man's Best Friend · *Dee Stuart*   183

Killer on the Turnpike · *William P. McGivern*   191

Payment Received · *Robert L. McGrath*   241

Agony Column · *Barry Malzberg*   247

Guessing Game · *Rose Million Healey*   255

The $2,000,000 Defense · *Harold Q. Masur*   265

The Man in the Well · *Berkely Mather*   281

Crawfish · *Ardath F. Mayhar*   295

The Strange Case of Mr. Pruyn · *William F. Nolan* 301

Ludmila • *David Montross*   309

The One Who Got Away • *Al Nussbaum*   315

It's a Lousy World • *Bill Pronzini*   321

Only So Much to Reveal • *Joan Richter*   339

Who's Got the Lady? • *Jack Ritchie*   353

Hey You Down There • *Harold Rolseth*   367

Too Many Sharks • *William Sambrot*   379

Christopher Frame • *Nancy C. Swoboda*   387

Obituary • *Paul Theridion*   397

Random Demand • *Jeffrey M. Wallmann*   401

The Mother Goose Madman • *Betty Ren Wright*   407

The Green Fly and the Box • *Waldo Carlton Wright*   415

The Blue Rug • *Mitsu Yamamoto*   425

Introduction

Good morning.

I say good morning instead of my customary good evening by way of warning. These stories should be read at night only if you are an incurable insomniac and cannot fall asleep anyway. Of course, if you work during the day then you have no choice, unless your employer is remarkably tolerant. In any event, you may read them whenever you can spare the time and yearn for relaxation.

Correction. I do not wish to mislead you. The contents of this volume are hardly relaxing. Startling, horrifying perhaps, certainly entertaining. I know because I am considered an expert. With a characteristic lack of modesty I have allowed myself to be billed as a Master of Suspense. The description is indeed accurate, and you must admit, fully justified.

As with all so-called experts my counsel is often solicited by interviewers seeking definitions. Just what is this business of suspense, they inquire. Well, years ago I consulted one of those massive unabridged dictionaries one lifts only with the aid of a derrick. It defined suspense as uncertainty accompanied by apprehension.

Fair enough. In my films I try to intensify this apprehension to a point where it becomes unbearable. That is the name of the game. And I believe the authors in this collection have achieved a similar result with notable success. All of them are practiced craftsmen in this sinister profession and here is a heady sampling of their dark art.

A word of caution. Before turning the next page, please check with your cardiologist. I accept no responsibility. The risk is yours. After all, you must like this sort of thing or you would not be here in the first place.

ALFRED HITCHCOCK PRESENTS:
STORIES TO BE READ WITH
THE LIGHTS ON

Death
Out of
Season

Mary Barrett

Miss Witherspoon crouched low to the ground and with her little trowel turned over some earth in her herb garden. She silently reminded herself not to cultivate too closely lest the tender roots of the herbs be damaged. Miss Witherspoon was a very careful gardener, as results testified. Her flowers and herbs were the most luxuriant in town; they were, if her neighbors had had the grace to confess it, the envy of everyone.

Britomar rubbed herself against Miss Witherspoon's ankle, purring. Miss Witherspoon idly patted the black cat with her gloved left hand.

"Hello, Miss Witherspoon," a woman called from the sidewalk beyond the white picket fence. It was Mrs. Laurel, the stylishly dressed divorcée who had recently moved into the neighborhood. "Are you fixing those little May baskets I've heard so much about?" she asked, her mock-friendly tone failing to hide her disdain.

Miss Witherspoon straightened from her task. "Yes, I am," she said with cool politeness. Mrs. Laurel smiled condescendingly and went on her way. Miss Witherspoon continued her work, hardly acknowledging the interruption. She had more pressing matters to attend to than Mrs. Laurel's impertinence.

In any case, Miss Witherspoon was accustomed to mockery; for over the years she had become famed as the town eccentric. It is true that other people in town deviated from the usual in various ways—

3

drunkards, feeble-minded people, even one murderer if you counted Jake Holby's beating the life from his skinny wife when he discovered her in the barn loft with his hired hand. Yet none of this aberrant behavior was considered nearly as peculiar as old Miss Witherspoon's insistence on total privacy. Not one person had ever been inside her little house; and only the most reckless boys, egged on by absolutely irresistible dares, ventured through the gate or over the white picket fence onto her well-manicured lawn, and then only in the dark of night after the old woman was asleep.

Years before, the town children had made up a taunting chant which was still being sung with glee: "Miss Witherspoon/Is a goon." Although the children thought this was hilariously witty, few of them ever dared to intone it in the old woman's hearing; for, though they hated to admit it to themselves or to each other, the children were frightened of her.

Never in the memory of anyone living had Miss Witherspoon spoken spontaneously to any person she passed on the sidewalk; nor had she ever called neighborly greetings across her fence. She had never brought soup to the ailing or cakes to the bereaved. In short, she observed none of the usual social rituals. If anyone had ever dared to ask her why, and if she had chosen to respond, she would have said that she preferred plants to people, primarily because plants did not sin, were incapable of evil. Furthermore, by preserving her solitude, she was better able to observe, objectively, the misdeeds of those around her.

However, Miss Witherspoon did have one more or less social ritual of her own which she faithfully performed once a year, on Walpurgis Night. It was that annual event to which Mrs. Laurel had referred, but Mrs. Laurel did not know, nor did anyone else for that matter, the ritual in its entirety. This year, for the first time, Miss Witherspoon entertained the thought of altering her pattern slightly. She was, after all, growing old, and the arthritis in her fingers was becoming increasingly a handicap. There might not be enough years left for her to carry out her entire program. Perhaps this year, just for once, she should take care of two people rather than one. But no, she finally decided. Once a pattern was successfully set it was best to stick to it.

Walpurgis Night was the only date in the year which had any significance for Miss Witherspoon, the only one which she marked on her calendar. It was the eve of May Day, named for an English missionary and abbess who had won renown by driving out witches. As everyone who has read Sir James Frazer knows, that night above all others is the one when witches are most likely to be abroad.

On Walpurgis Eve each year Miss Witherspoon prepared exactly ten May baskets. And every year, on that night, she stealthily hung them on the doorknobs of ten houses. It was never the same ten houses, although over the years she had been forced to repeat occasionally. And every year one, and only one, May basket was especially chosen to contain a particularly interesting lagniappe.

Of course, the townspeople knew the identity of their May Day benefactor. Only Miss Witherspoon's garden could provide such an abundant variety of flowers and herbs.

It was a game among the townspeople to speculate who would be favored by the little baskets of flowers and herbs, which were inevitably accompanied by a verse or a saying penned in Miss Witherspoon's careful hand. Everyone tittered over this annual proof of the old woman's eccentricity. What they failed to notice was that each year the recipient of one basket met with a strange and unexpected fate.

Well, no matter. Miss Witherspoon sought no fame or credit for her work.

The sun shone warm and comforting on her back as she carefully chose and picked the flowers for each basket. She savored in her mind their lovely Latin names—*Lathyrus odoratus* (sweet pea), *Lobularia maritima* (sweet alyssum), *Convallaria majalis* (lily of the valley), and, of course, the fabled hyacinth which sprang from the blood of Apollo's dying friend—"that sanguine flower inscribed with woe."

At last the baskets were filled and she set them in the cool shade of the maple tree. And now for the final, the most important, decision. Which herb would be chosen for the favored tenth basket? Miss Witherspoon could use the rootstock from the May apple; but that was not, perhaps, pretty enough to capture interest. Larkspur might serve; but that would mean drying the seeds, and perhaps that entailed more trouble than was necessary.

For the sake of symbolism she was tempted to use the "beautiful lady" flower, belladonna, or, for the same reason, monkshood. But no. The best choice was *Digitalis purpurea*, foxglove. It was true that her garden held only the American variety, *Phytolacca americana*, and she hated the ugly sound of its American name, pokeweed. But still, the dark purple berries were pretty and they would serve her purpose well. So into the tenth basket they went, along with a verse from Rudyard Kipling which she had copied in her neat handwriting:

> Excellent herbs had our fathers of old—
> Excellent herbs to ease their pain.

She had added, as if in afterthought, "The purple berries, served in any form, will make even a laggard in love become ardent, and an ardent lover passionate beyond belief."

Miss Witherspoon regretted having to resort to such an outright lie, for she was a true artist and would have preferred her annual ritual to be perfect in all its parts. However, she would have to forgive herself this one false detail in the interest of her larger plan.

That night Miss Witherspoon set out, accompanied only by Britomar. The moonlight was bright, and there was the feel of spring in the warm moist air. Miss Witherspoon happily quoted to herself from *The Merchant of Venice*:

> "In such a night
> Medea gather'd the enchanted herbs."

Nine baskets were hung, and then the tenth—on Mrs. Laurel's door.

Two days later, Edward Johnston, the tailor, died a painful and inexplicable death, the victim of some violent emetic accidentally ingested and apparently served to him in some food prepared by the attractive divorcée. For, strangest fact of all, he died not in his own home, with his wife and four children, but in the house of Miss Witherspoon's glamorous neighbor. Only Miss Witherspoon, in all the town, was not surprised that he should die there; for only she had observed the tailor's frequent clandestine visits, and only she had surmised which of the ten commandments was being broken within the walls of Mrs. Laurel's house.

The morning after this shocking news had spread throughout the town Miss Witherspoon was working peacefully in her garden, as usual, when a highly unusual visitor arrived. The sheriff picked his way toward her across the stepping stones.

"Good morning, Miss Witherspoon," he called across the close-clipped lawn.

She looked up from her flowerbed. "Good morning, Sheriff," she said calmly. "You wish to talk with me?"

"Yes, I do." The sheriff's uncertain tone of voice betrayed his discomfort and his doubts. Now that he looked at her she seemed innocent beyond question, incapable of harming anyone. And yet, when his theory had finally jelled that morning, it had seemed sound to him—in a strange way.

"Let's go indoors," Miss Witherspoon suggested, "where we can have a nice talk."

The two went into her cool, dimly lit living room and sat down in chairs facing each other across a tea table. Britomar jumped into Miss Witherspoon's lap and the old lady caressed the cat as she spoke. "I have been expecting you for years," she said.

"You have?" the sheriff exclaimed, clearly taken aback.

"Oh, yes. I knew that you were not a stupid man, and that some year you would realize the truth about my little rituals."

"You mean you have—uh—done this before?"

Miss Witherspoon nodded.

"You knew that you'd be found out and yet you kept right on doing it?"

"Of course I kept right on. You would not easily give up your work, your mission in life, would you, Sheriff?" The old lady paused, although the question was obviously rhetorical. "Of course you wouldn't," she answered herself, "and neither would I. We are in the same work, after all, and neither of us could honorably give it up. The world needs our efforts."

The sheriff, beginning to understand, asked gently, "And what do you think our work is?"

"Why, ridding the town of evildoers, of course," she stated matter-of-factly. "There are far too many of you to dispose of alone, and not all of them come to your attention. That is why, each year, I select a single candidate for extinction."

The sheriff had no ready response.

Miss Witherspoon brushed the cat from her lap and rose to her feet. "Excuse me. I shall make us some tea."

In a few minutes she returned from the kitchen with a tray full of the items necessary for serving tea. In her absence the sheriff had decided what his next question would be. "How did you choose your—er—your candidates for extinction?" he asked.

"I simply took note of which people were breaking which one of the ten commandments and disposed of them, in order. This year I had reached the seventh commandment." She looked down at her hands, folded in her lap, somewhat embarrassed to mention the word aloud, to a man. "Thou shalt not commit adultery."

"Do you mean to say," the sheriff asked, "that you have—uh—eliminated six other people?"

"Yes, I have." Miss Witherspoon's pride was apparent. "Beginning with the person who most blatantly broke the first commandment—John Leger, the money-worshiping bank president—and going right down the list to Number Seven."

She paused a moment as if waiting for praise. None was forthcoming and so she continued, "My greatest difficulty came last year—finding a candidate for Number Six. You yourself do a fairly efficient job at apprehending those few who actually kill." She was now taking the tone of one professional speaking to another. "But finally I succeeded. You see, it doesn't specify *what* not to kill, and it was common knowledge that Edna Fairbanks put out poisoned meat for the cats to eat."

"So that was it!" the sheriff exclaimed, relieved to have that year-old puzzle solved. And then he asked, "But what about you, Miss Witherspoon? Haven't you been breaking Number Six yourself?"

"No, not really," the old lady answered, her eyes twinkling with the pleasure of finally being able to reveal her cleverness to someone. "I've thought that through most carefully. I don't actually kill anyone. I simply put within their reach the instrument of death. There's no commandment against doing that."

The old woman is even nuttier than I realized, the sheriff thought. Aloud he said, "But you made fairly certain they would use that instrument, didn't you? It was that note in Mrs. Laurel's May basket that put me wise to you."

"It's true that my notes encouraged those people to use my herbs; but I succeeded only because the messages which I gave them appealed to the worst in the persons who received them—to the very sinfulness for which they were being punished."

"Well, now," the sheriff said, with grudging admiration, "you've done a thorough job. But even so, of course, we can't let you go free."

"Oh, I quite understand that," Miss Witherspoon said cheerfully. "You have your job to do."

The sheriff sighed with relief. This was going to be easier than he had feared. He said, "Take a little time to get your things in order and I'll come back later with a warrant."

"That will be quite satisfactory," Miss Witherspoon said as she showed him to the door.

After all, the ground-up poison parsley with which she had laced his tea would be quick and effective. It was as deadly as hemlock—Socrates' drink.

She did regret that this one death was out of season. But, after all, it was an emergency. Also, she had not told the sheriff that she had been forced to skip one commandment in the list. So far as she knew, the sheriff had not stolen anything. But he certainly was very close to breaking Number Nine, for what was he planning to do but to bear false witness against her? She had perceived that immediately.

Witness in the Dark

Fredric Brown

I

Even reading about it in the papers gave me a mild case of the willies. For some reason I had a hunch, right off, that I was going to be put on the case and that I wasn't going to like it. Of course they might have it cleaned up by the time I got back; it was the evening of the second to last day of my vacation. But I didn't think so.

I put down the paper and tried to forget what I'd read by looking at Marge. Even after four years of being married, I like to look at Marge.

But this time it didn't drive what I'd been reading out of my head. By a roundabout way, it brought me back to it. I got to thinking how bad it would be to be blind and never be able to see Marge again. The story in the paper had been about a blind man—a blind man who was the only witness to a murder.

Marge happened to look up; she asked me what I was thinking about and I told her. She was interested, so I told her the details, what there was of them in the paper:

"The blind man's name is Max Easter. Until three days ago he was the bookkeeper at the Springfield Chemical Works. Until three days ago he wasn't blind—and they're not sure now whether his blindness is permanent; it's from an industrial accident at the plant. Some acid splashed in his face while he was collecting time slips out in the

11

plant. They think he'll recover, but right now he's completely blind, and with his eyes bandaged.

"So yesterday evening he was in his bedroom—he's still in bed—talking to a friend of his named Armin Robinson, who'd dropped in to see him. Their wives—Easter's and Robinson's—had gone to a movie together downtown. The two men were alone in the house—except for the killer.

"Armin Robinson was sitting in a chair near the bed, and the bedroom door was ajar. Max Easter was sitting up in bed and the two of them were talking. Then Easter heard the door squeak and someone step into the room. He heard Robinson move and thinks he may have stood up, but nothing was said. Then all of a sudden there was a shot and the sound of a fall, from Robinson's direction. And then the footsteps came farther into the room and Easter sat there in bed, waiting to be shot too."

Marge said, "How awful."

I said, "Then comes the odd part. Instead of being shot, Max Easter felt something land on the bed, on the mattress. He groped for it, and he had a gun in his hand, a revolver. Then he heard the killer move and pointed the gun in that direction and pulled the trigger—"

"You mean the killer gave him the gun? Tossed it on his bed, I mean? Wouldn't he have known a blind man can shoot at a sound?"

I said, "All I know is what's in the papers, Marge. That's the way they tell Easter's story. But it could be. Probably the killer didn't realize that the bounce of the mattress would tell Easter where the gun landed and that he'd get it in his hand that quickly, the first grab. Probably he thought he could be out of the room before Easter would find the gun."

"But why give it to him at all?"

"I don't know. But to go on with Easter's story: as he swung the gun around to aim at the sound, he heard a noise like a man's knee hitting the floor and he figured the killer had dropped down to be under the shot if he fired. So Easter lowered the gun to aim a couple of feet above the floor and pulled the trigger. Just once.

"And then, suddenly, he says, he got scareder of what he was *doing* than of what might happen to him, and he dropped the gun. He was shooting in the dark—literally. If he'd misjudged what had happened, he might be shooting at Armin Robinson—at anybody. He didn't even know for sure that there'd been a murder, or *what* had happened.

"So, anyway, he dropped the gun and it hit the edge of the bed and clunked onto the floor. So he couldn't get it back even if he changed his mind. And he just sat there sweating while whoever it was moved around the room awhile and then went out."

Marge looked thoughtful. "Moved around the room doing what, George?"

"How would Easter know? But Armin Robinson's wallet was gone, so taking it was probably one thing. And Easter's own wallet and watch were gone off the dresser, where his wife said later they'd been lying. And a small suitcase was gone."

"A suitcase? Why would he take a suitcase?"

"To put the silverware in. That was gone from downstairs and a few other small articles a burglar might take along. Easter says the man moved around his room for what seemed a long time, but was probably only a minute or two. Then he heard him walk down the stairs and move around a while down there, and then the back door opened and closed.

"He hadn't dared get up until he heard the killer leave the house and then he got up and groped his way to Robinson and found he was dead. So he felt his way down the stairs to the telephone and called police. Period. End of story."

"But that's horrible," Marge said. "I mean, it leaves so many loose ends, so many things you can wonder about."

"Which is just what I've been doing. Particularly, I get the picture of that blind man shooting in the dark and then getting scared because he didn't know what he was shooting at."

"George, don't blind people get special senses? I mean, so they can tell who a person is by the way he walks—things like that?"

Very patiently I said, "Max Easter had been blind all of three days. He might have been able to tell a man's walk from a woman's—if the woman wore high heels."

"I guess you're right. Even if he'd known the man—"

I said, "Even if it had been a friend of his, he wouldn't have known. At night, all cats are gray."

"All cats *be* gray."

"You're goofy," I said.

"Look it up in Bartlett's *Quotations*."

Marge and I are always quibbling over things like that. I got Bartlett's out of the bookcase and looked it up and this time she was right. I'd been wrong on the "at night" part, too; it read "When all candles be out, all cats be gray."

When I'd admitted to Marge that she was right—for a change—and we'd batted that around for a while, her mind went back to the murder again. She said, "What about the gun he left, George? Can they trace him from it? The serial number, or something?"

I said, "It was Max Easter's own gun. It was in the drawer of a desk downstairs. I forgot to mention that. The killer must have rifled that desk before he came upstairs."

"Do you think, George, that it was just a burglar?"

"No," I told her.

"Neither do I. There's something about it—a false note."

"More than a false note. A whole damn discord. But I can't guess what it is."

She said, "This Max Easter. Maybe he isn't blind at all."

I snorted at that. "Woman's intuition! A guess like that is as silly—unless you've got a reason for saying it—as saying that what he shot at was a gray cat, just because I happened to mention the proverb about one."

"Maybe he did," Marge said.

That wasn't even worth answering. I picked up the paper again and turned to the sports section.

The Sunday papers, the next day, had a lot on the case, but none of it was new. No arrests had been made, and apparently no one was even under suspicion. I hoped I wouldn't get put on it. I don't know why, exactly. I just hoped so.

II

I was on it almost before I got inside the door. Before I got my raincoat off, I was told Captain Eberhart wanted me in his office, and I went in.

"Have a good vacation, George?" he asked me, but he didn't wait for my answer; he went on, "I'm putting you on that Armin Robinson murder. Have you read about it in the papers?"

"Sure," I said.

"Then you know as much about it as anybody else, except one thing. I'll tell you that, but outside of that, I want you to go on it cold, without any preconceived ideas. We haven't got anywhere and you just might hit something we missed. It's worth a try."

I nodded. "But how about lab reports, ballistics? I can tackle the people cold, but I'd like to have the physical facts."

"Okay. The coroner's report is that Robinson died instantaneously from a bullet through his head. The bullet was in the wall about three feet behind where he'd been sitting and about five and a half feet up from the floor. Went into the wall almost straight. It all checks if he stood up when the killer came through the door and if the killer stood in the doorway or just inside to fire the shot and held the gun at eye level."

"Bullet matches the gun?"

"Yes, and so does the other bullet, the one Max Easter fired. And there were two empty shells in the gun. No prints on the gun besides Easter's; the killer must have worn gloves. And Mrs. Easter says a pair of white cotton work gloves is missing from the kitchen."

"Any way Max Easter could have fired both shots instead of just one?"

"Absolutely not, George. He *is* blind—at least temporarily. The doctor treating him guarantees that; there are tests—reaction of pupils to sudden light, things like that. The only way a blind man could hit someone dead center in the forehead would be to hold the gun against him—and there weren't any powder burns. No, Max Easter's story sounds screwy, but all the facts fit it. Even the timing. Some neighbors heard the shots. Thought it was backfires and didn't investigate, but they noticed the time; they were listening to the radio and it was at the eight o'clock change of programs—two shots about five seconds apart. And Easter's phone call to us was at twelve minutes after eight by our own records. Twelve minutes just about fits what he says went on between the shooting and his getting to the phone."

"How about the alibis of the two wives?"

"Good as gold. They were together in a movie at the time of the murder. Eight o'clock was just about the time they were going in, in fact, and they saw friends in the lobby, so it's not only their own word. You can take the alibi as okay."

"All right," I said, "and what's the one thing that didn't get in the papers?"

"Lab report on the other bullet, the one Easter fired at the murderer, shows traces of organic matter."

I whistled. "Then the killer was wounded?" That ought to make it a lot easier.

Cap Eberhart said, "Maybe." He sighed. "I almost hate to tell you this, George, but if he was, he was a rooster wearing silk pajamas."

"That's fine," I told him. "My wife says Easter was shooting at a gray cat, and my wife is mostly right. About everything. But now would you mind talking sense?"

"If you can make sense out of it, swell. We dug the second bullet out of the wall near the door, about a foot and a half up. The microscopist who examined it says there are minute traces of three kinds of organic matter on it. Infinitesimal quantities; he can identify them only up to a point and he's not sure *that* far. But he thinks they're blood, silk and feathers. A chicken wearing silk pajamas would be one answer."

"What kind of blood?" I asked. "What kind of feathers?"

"No dice. They're minute traces, and he won't stick his neck out any farther than that, even on a guess. What's this business about a gray cat?"

I told him about our argument over the quotation and Marge's kidding remark. I said, "Seriously, Cap, it does sound as though the killer was wounded. Just a scrape, probably, since he went about his business afterwards. That takes care of the blood on the bullet, and the silk isn't too hard. Silk shirt, silk shorts, silk tie—anything. But the feathers are harder to figure. Only place a man's likely to wear a feather is in the band of a new hat."

Eberhart nodded. "Pajama-wearing roosters aside, that's the best suggestion we've had to date. Could be like this—the killer sees the gun swinging toward him and drops down low, throwing up his hand toward the gun. Hands don't stop bullets, but people often do that when they're going to be shot at. The bullet grazes his hatband, which is silk and has a feather in it—but not hard enough to crease him or stun him—and goes in the wall. Then the killer wraps a handkerchief around his hand and goes about his business, after Easter drops the gun off the bed and he sees he's safe."

"It could be," I said. "Anybody connected with the case wounded?"

"Not where it shows. And we haven't got enough on anybody to drag them in and strip them. In fact, dammit, we haven't even found anybody with a motive. Screwy as it seems, George, we've almost decided that it really was a plain and simple robbery. Well, that's all I'm going to tell you. Go at it cold and maybe you'll get something we missed."

I put my raincoat back on and went out.

III

The first thing to do was the thing I hated worst—talk to the widow of the murdered man. I hoped, for both our sakes, that she'd be over the worst part of the shock and grief.

I didn't enjoy it, but it wasn't as bad as it could have been. Mrs. Armin Robinson was quiet and reserved, but she was willing to talk, and able to talk unemotionally. The emotion was there, but it was two layers down; it wasn't going to come to the surface in hysteria.

I got the matter of her alibi over first. Yes, she and Mrs. Max Easter, the blinded man's wife, had met at eight o'clock in the theater lobby. She was sure it was eight exactly, because both she and Louise Easter had commented on the fact that they were both exactly on time; Louise had been there first, but had said she'd been waiting less than a minute. Louise had been talking to two friends of theirs whom she'd met—accidentally, not by appointment—in the lobby. The four women had gone in together and had stayed together in the movie. She gave me the names of the two other women, and their addresses. It sounded, as Eberhart had said, as good as gold. The theater they'd gone to was at least twenty minutes' driving time from the Easter residence, where the murder had occurred.

I asked, "Did your husband have any enemies?"

"No, definitely not. Possibly a few people may have disliked him, but no more than that."

I asked gently, "Why would some people have disliked him, Mrs. Robinson? What traits in his nature—?"

"He was pretty much of an extrovert. You know, the life of the party, that sort of thing. When he had a few drinks, he may have grated on some people's nerves. But that didn't happen often. And, too, some people thought him a little too frank. But those were little things."

They certainly didn't sound like something that would lead to premeditated murder. I said, "He was a C.P.A., an auditor. Is that right?"

"Yes, and he operated independently. He was his own boss."

"Any employees?"

"Only a secretary, full time. He had a list of people he sometimes called on for help in an audit that was too big a job for one man."

"How close friends were you and your husband with the Easters?"

"Fairly close. Probably Armin and Max were closer friends than Louise and I are. Frankly, I don't like Louise *too* well, but I get along with her because of the friendship between my husband and hers. Not that I have anything against Louise—don't misunderstand me— it's just that we're such different types. For that matter, I don't think Armin liked Louise especially either."

"How often did you see them?"

"Sometimes oftener, but at least once a week regularly. We're— we were—members of a bridge club of four couples who took turns meeting at one another's homes."

"Who were the others?"

"The Anthonys and the Eldreds. Bill Anthony is editor of the *Springfield Blade*. He and his wife are away on vacation right now, in Florida. Lloyd Eldred is with the Springfield Chemical Works—the same company Max Easter works for. He's Max's immediate superior there."

"And Max Easter is bookkeeper there?"

"That's right, bookkeeper and paymaster. Lloyd Eldred is the treasurer of the company. That's probably not as much of a difference as it sounds. I think Max probably makes about ten thousand a year and Lloyd about twelve thousand. Springfield Chemical doesn't pay very high salaries to its officers."

"Your husband ever do any auditing for Springfield Chemical?"

"No. Kramer and Wright have done their auditing for years. I think Armin could have had the account if he'd gone after it, but he had all the business he could handle by himself."

"He was doing well, then?"

"Well enough."

"This is an unpleasant question, Mrs. Robinson. But does anyone gain by his death?"

"Not unless you'd consider that I did. There's ten thousand in insurance and title to this house is clear. But almost no savings; we bought this house a year ago and used our savings to buy it outright. And Armin's business can't be sold—there's nothing to sell. I mean, he just sold his own services as an auditor."

"Then I wouldn't say you gained," I told her. "Ten thousand in insurance doesn't compensate for the loss of ten thousand a year in income."

"Nor for the loss of a husband, Mr. Hearn."

That could have been corny except that it sounded sincere. It made me remember I wanted to get out of there, so I got down to brass tacks by asking her about Friday evening. "Had your husband planned in advance to go to the Easters'?" I asked. "Would anyone know he was going to be there?"

"No, except Louise and myself. And then, only just before he left. Here's what happened: Louise and I had made the movie date before Max's accident at the plant. About half past six that evening, when Armin and I were just starting dinner, Louise phoned. She said she'd better not leave Max home alone, that he was feeling pretty low.

"Armin heard my end of the phone conversation and guessed what it was about. So he came to the phone and talked to Louise and said she should keep her date for the movie, that he'd just as soon go over and sit with Max for the evening."

"When did he leave to go there?"

"About seven, because he was going by bus and wanted to get there by half past seven so Louise would have time to make the date. He told me to take our car and pick him up after the show to bring him back home."

"And he got to the Easters' by half past seven?"

"Yes. That is, Louise said so. She says he went upstairs right away to Max's room, and that she left about ten minutes after that. She drove their car. We had two cars between the two of us, which wasn't very good planning, I guess."

I asked, "Was there anything unusual about the way your husband acted Friday evening, before he left? Or, for that matter, any time lately?"

"He'd been a bit moody and preoccupied for two or three days. I asked him several times if he was worried about something, but he insisted that he wasn't."

I tried prying a little deeper on that, but couldn't find out whether she had any guess as to what he may have been worrying about. She was sure it wasn't financial troubles.

I let it go at that and left her, telling her I might have to come back later to talk to her again. She was pleasant about that and said she understood.

I thought it over after I got in my car. The alibis of both wives sounded solid. Neither of them could have been at the theater at eight and still have killed Armin Robinson. But I didn't want to take anything for granted, so I drove to the addresses of the two other women who'd seen Louise Easter and Mrs. Robinson in the movie lobby. I talked to both of them and when I left the second, I was sure.

I got back in my car and drove out to the Springfield Chemical Works. I didn't see how Max's accident there—his blinding—could have anything to do with the murder of Robinson, but I wanted to get that angle out of the way before I went to the Easters'.

Springfield Chemical must have had an efficient office system; their office quarters were small for a plant that hired over a hundred men.

I asked the receptionist, who was doubling in brass on a typewriter and had a telephone switchboard in front of her, for Mr. Lloyd Eldred. She made a call and then directed me to his office.

I went in. There were two desks, but only one of them was occupied. A tall, slender, almost effeminate-looking man with rumpled curly black hair looked up from the occupied desk and said "Yes?" in a tone that meant, "I hope this won't take long; I'm awfully busy." And from all the stuff stacked on his desk, he was.

I said, "I'm George Hearn, Mr. Eldred. From Homicide." I took the chair in front of his desk.

He ran his fingers through his hair, thereby explaining why it was so rumpled. He said, "About Armin Robinson again, I suppose," and I admitted the fact.

"Well—I don't know what more I can tell you. But Armin was a friend of mine and if there *is* anything—"

"He was a close friend of yours?"

"Well, not exactly. We saw each other at least once a week, at a bridge club that met around at our houses. The Easters, the Anthonys, the Robinsons, and my wife and I."

I nodded. "Mrs. Robinson told me about that. Are you going to continue the club?"

"I don't know. Maybe we'll find another couple—but not until after Max Easter's eyes are all right again. Right now we'd be missing two couples—three, until the Anthonys get back from Florida."

"You think Easter's eyes will get all right again?"

"I don't see why not. The doctor says they will—he's a little puzzled that they've been bad for this long. We gave him a sample of the acid, and he says it definitely should not cause permanent injury to the eyes."

He ran his fingers through his hair again. "I hope—for selfish reasons if no others—that he's back soon. I'm swamped here trying to handle both our jobs."

"Can't your company get another man?"

"They could, I suppose, and would if I wanted them to. We discussed it, in fact. The catch is it would take weeks to break someone in to the point where they'd be a help instead of a hindrance. And the doctor says he thinks Max *should* be back in another week at the outside. Anyway, it won't be so bad after Wednesday, day after tomorrow."

"Why Wednesday?" I asked him.

"Semimonthly payroll. That's Max's main job, keeping payroll and time records. This time I'm having to do them besides my own work, so it'll be tough until the payroll's done. But if Max isn't able to be back by next payroll, we *will* make other arrangements. I can't work twelve hours a day indefinitely."

I nodded. Apparently the guy really was plugging, and I liked the fact that he gave it to me diplomatically instead of telling me to hurry up and get it over with.

So I asked the one routine question I had to ask about Armin Robinson—whether Lloyd Eldred knew any reason anyone would have for wanting Robinson dead—and got a flat, unequivocal no. Also a no as to whether Eldred knew what Robinson might have been worrying about for a few days before his death; Eldred hadn't noticed that he was as of the last time they'd played bridge together and that was the last time he'd seen him.

So I switched to the other matter. "Will you tell me about Max Easter's accident?"

"Max can tell you about it better than anyone else, because he was

alone when it happened. All I know is that he was out in the plant—
in the plating room—collecting time slips during the men's lunch
hour. He takes a later lunch period himself so he can collect slips
while they're off. He can go through the whole plant in an hour that
way; it'd take twice as long when there's work going on."

I asked, "But didn't he tell you how it happened?"

"Oh, sure. He went in one of the little vat rooms off the plating
room to get a slip off a shelf there, where the man who works that vat
always leaves it. When he took down the slip pad he knocked down a
jug from the shelf into the vat below it. It's a bad arrangement, having to reach across the vat to get something on the shelf, especially as
that shelf is slightly above eye level. We changed the arrangement
there since then."

I asked, "Was the acid that blinded him in the jug that fell, or in
the vat?"

"In the vat. But landing smack in the middle of the vat, the jug
splashed acid all over him."

"Any damage except to his eyes?"

"No, unless you count damage to clothes. Probably ruined the suit
he was wearing. But the acid wasn't strong enough to hurt the skin."

"Does the company assume responsibility?"

"Of course. At any rate, he's on full salary and we're taking care of
medical expenses."

"But if the injury is permanent?"

"It can't be; we have assurance from the doctor who's treating
him. In fact, he tends to believe that the blindness may be hysterical.
You've heard of hysterical blindness, haven't you?"

I said, "I've heard of it. But for something like that there is supposed to be a deep-rooted psychic cause. Would there be in Max's
case?"

I thought he hesitated slightly before he said, "Not that I know
of."

I paused, trying to think of further questions, and I couldn't. From
the way Lloyd Eldred looked at me, he was wondering why I'd been
asking so many questions about Max's accident and about Max. I was
wondering that, too. And I looked again at the piles of work on his
desk and I thanked him and excused myself.

It was nearly noon. I was only a ten minutes' drive from home, so I
decided to have lunch with Marge. Sometimes I go home for lunch

and sometimes not, depending on what part of town I happen to be in when lunchtime comes around. Marge always keeps stuff on hand that she can rustle up quickly if I do get home.

IV

"I'm on it," I told her, as soon as I got in. She knew what I meant; I didn't have to tell her.

While we ate I told her the little I'd learned that hadn't been in the papers. I said, "So you see it *wasn't* a gray cat Max Easter was shooting at in the dark. It was a rooster in silk pajamas. For once you're wrong on a hunch. And on your other wild idea, too; Easter is really blind."

She turned her nose up at me. "Bet you a dime he isn't."

I said, "That's one dime I'll collect."

"Maybe. I won't bet you on the gray cat, but it's no sillier than Captain Eberhart's rooster in pajamas. Or than your silk hatband with a feather in it."

"But if it was that, he'd have worn it out with him. If it was a gray cat, what happened to it?"

"The killer carried it out in the suitcase he took from the closet, naturally."

I threw up my hands on that one.

Just the same, Marge had been serious in regard to her hunch that Max Easter wasn't really blind, and when Marge takes one of her hunches seriously, I do too. At least to the extent of checking as thoroughly as I can. So before I left home I phoned Cap Eberhart and got the name and address of the doctor who was treating Max Easter's eyes.

I went to see him and was lucky enough to get into his office right away. After I'd identified myself and explained what I wanted, I asked him, "How soon after the accident did you see Mr. Easter?"

"I believe I reached the plant not over twenty minutes after I was phoned. And the phone call, I was told, had been made immediately."

"Did you notice anything unusual about the condition of his eyes?"

"Nothing unusual considering the dilute acid that had been splashed into them. I'm not sure I understand your question."

I wasn't sure I understood it myself; I didn't know exactly what I was fishing for. I asked, "Was he in considerable pain?"

"Pain? Oh, no. Tetrianic acid causes temporary blindness, but without pain. It's no more painful that boric acid."

"Can you describe the effect for me, Doctor?"

"It dilates the pupils, as does belladonna. Ultimately it's as harmless. But in addition to dilation of the pupils, which is an immediate reaction, it causes temporary paralysis of the optic nerves and consequent temporary blindness. Normally the duration of blindness is from two to eight hours, depending on the strength of the solution."

"And the strength of the solution in this case?"

"Medium. Mr. Easter should have recovered his sight in not over six hours."

"But he didn't," I pointed out.

"He hasn't as yet. And that leads to one of two possible conclusions. One, that he is abnormal in his tolerance for the substance in question. In that case, it is merely a matter of time; his eyesight will return before much longer. The other possibility is, of course, hysterical blindness—blindness caused by self-delusion. I am almost certain this is not true in Mr. Easter's case. However, if his blindness persists more than a week, I shall recommend a psychiatrist."

I asked, "Isn't there a third possibility? Malingering?"

He smiled. "Don't forget, Mr. Hearn, that I am employed by the company and in the company's interests. He couldn't possibly pretend dilation of the pupils, which still persists. And he is *not* faking blindness. There are certain tests.

"And I am, as I said, reasonably sure it is not hysterical. I base that on the continued dilation of the pupils. Hysteria would be much more likely to continue the nerve paralysis alone."

"When did you examine him last?"

"Yesterday afternoon at four. I've been calling every day at that time."

I thanked him and left. For once, one of Marge's hunches had been wrong.

And I'd been stalling long enough on going to the Easters' house. I went there. I rang the doorbell.

A woman who turned out to be Mrs. Max Easter, Louise Easter, opened the door. I identified myself and she identified herself and she asked me in. She was a good-looking woman, even in a housedress. It would have been interesting to examine her to see if she had any bullet scrapes; but then her alibi was as good as any I've ever seen and besides there's Marge.

Her husband, Louise Easter told me, was still in bed in his room upstairs and did I want to go up? I said I did, but that first she might as well show me around downstairs because I wanted to learn the layout of the place.

She showed me around. The drawer from which Max's gun had been taken, the cabinet where the silverware had been, the shelf in the kitchen where the cotton gloves had lain.

"Those were the only things missing?" I asked.

"Yes. From downstairs, that is. He took Max's wallet and watch from the dresser upstairs. There was about twenty dollars in the wallet, and that's all the money there happened to be in the house. And the suitcase."

"How big a suitcase was it?"

She held her hands to show me; it had been about two feet by one foot by seven inches. Bigger than he'd have needed to carry what he took—but maybe he'd thought he'd find more.

I asked her to tell me just what had happened that evening, starting at the time she phoned Mrs. Armin Robinson to call off the movie date.

She said, "That would have been somewhere around half past six; I'd just given Max his dinner but hadn't washed the dishes yet. I decided I'd better not go and leave Max alone. But then Armin said he'd come around and talk to Max and that I should go. And by the time I nfished the dishes and got dressed, Armin was here. That would have been about half past seven, I guess.

"I didn't have to leave *right* away to get to the movie by eight—that's when our appointment was—so I stayed and talked with both of them, up in Max's room, for five or ten minutes, and then I left, and that must have been—oh, at least twenty minutes before eight, because I got to the show a minute or two ahead of time and Ianthe —Mrs. Robinson, that is—got there just at eight."

"Did you lock the front door when you left?"

"No. I wondered whether I should and decided not to because it isn't a spring lock. I'd have had to lock it from the outside and take the key and that would have seemed funny, to lock Armin and Max in. The back door was locked though."

"You think the killer got in after you left, between then and eight o'clock?"

"He must have, unless he was hiding in the basement. He couldn't have been upstairs; there are only the two bedrooms, the hall and the bath, and I was in all of them. And he couldn't have been downstairs, because when I came down, ready to leave, I couldn't find my purse right away and had to look for it. I found it in the kitchen, but I'd looked everywhere else first."

I asked, "How are your husband's eyes? Any improvement?"

She shook her head. "I'm afraid not—yet. And I'm getting really worried, in spite of what the doctor says. Up to this morning, anyway, there'd been no improvement at all."

"This morning?"

"When I changed the bandage and bathed them. I'll have to do it again in about an hour. You won't have to talk to him longer than that, will you?"

"Probably not that long," I told her. "But maybe I'd better start now, in that case."

We went up the stairs. The door of one of the bedrooms was ajar, just as it must have been Friday evening. And through it I could see Max Easter, his eyes bandaged, sitting up in bed. Just as the killer must have seen him when he'd walked up these stairs after Louise Easter had left.

I stood in the doorway where the killer must have stood first to fire the shot that killed Armin Robinson, before he'd stepped closer to the bed and tossed down the revolver on the mattress.

Louise Easter had preceded me into the room and said, "Max, this is Mr. Hearn from the Homicide Department," and I was acknowledging the introduction but without thinking about it because I was looking around the room, seeing the chair Armin Robinson must have been sitting on, the one next to the bed, and the hole in the plaster above and behind that chair where the bullet had been dug out of the wall. And I turned and saw the place where the other bullet had been dug out. It was about a foot and a half up from the floor and about five feet from the doorway.

The bullet that Max Easter had fired. The one that had showed minute traces of blood, silk and feathers. Not blood, sweat and tears —but blood, silk and feathers.

I visualized the line of fire—Max sitting up in bed aiming the gun at a sound, then lowering the muzzle as he heard the killer's knee hit the floor. I tried to visualize the killer standing somewhere in that line of fire, then crouching or kneeling to get under the muzzle of the gun.

But Max Easter had said something to me and I had to think back to the sound of the words to get that he had asked me to sit down.

I said "Thanks" and crossed over to sit in the chair that Robinson had sat in. I looked toward the door. No, from that angle, Robinson would not have been able to see the head of the stairs. No matter how far ajar the door had been, he couldn't have seen the killer until the man had actually stepped into the room.

I looked from Max Easter to Louise Easter and then around the room, and I realized that I hadn't said anything for some time and that Easter couldn't tell what I was doing.

I said, "I'm just looking around, Mr. Easter, trying to visualize how things must have happened."

He smiled a bit wanly. He said, "Take your time. I've got lots of it. Louise, I'm going to get up a little while; I'm tired of the bed. Will you get my bathrobe?"

"Of course, Max, but—" She didn't go on with the protest, whatever it had been going to be. She got his bathrobe from the closet and held it while he slipped it on over his pajamas. He sat back down on the edge of the bed.

He asked, "Would you like a bottle of beer, Mr. Hearn?"

I opened my mouth to say that I would like one but that I never drank on duty. Then I realized that he wouldn't be able to get the beer, that Louise would have to go downstairs for it, and that just possibly he had that in mind, that he might want to say something to me privately.

So I said, "Sure, thanks."

But when Louise had gone downstairs to the refrigerator, I found I'd been wrong. Apparently Max Easter had nothing to say.

He stood up and said, "I think I'm going to try my wings, Mr. Hearn. Please don't help me. Louise would have insisted if she'd stayed, but I want to learn to find my way alone. I'm just going to cross the room to that other chair."

He was feeling his way across the carpet toward the other side of the room—almost exactly toward the place where the plaster had been chipped out of the wall to extract the bullet he had fired. He said, "Might as well learn to do this. For all I know—" He didn't finish the sentence, but we both knew what he'd started to say.

His hand touched the wall, then groped for the chair. He wasn't going to touch it from where he stood so I said, "To your right, about two steps."

"Thanks." He moved that way and his hand found the back of the straight chair against the wall. He turned and sat down in it, and I noticed that he sat hard, as one does when the surface one sits on is lower than one had thought. As though a pillow might have been on the chair, but wasn't.

I'm not too bright, but I'm not too dumb. Pillow made me think of feathers. Blood, silk and feathers. A silk-covered chair pillow.

I had something, even if I didn't know what I had.

And just maybe, too, Max Easter's sense of direction, in walking for the chair, hadn't been as bad as it had seemed. He'd walked toward the place where the bullet had hit the wall. And if the chair was standing where he'd looked for it and if it had had a pillow on the seat the bullet would have gone through that pillow.

I didn't ask him if there'd been a silk pillow in that chair. I knew there had been.

I got a little scared.

Louise Easter was coming back up the stairs. Her heels clicked across the wood to the doorway and she came in with a tray that held three bottles and three glasses. She held the tray in front of me first and I took a glass and a bottle, but I wasn't thinking about beer.

I was thinking about blood. I knew now where the silk and feathers had come from.

I stood up and looked around me. I didn't see any blood, or anything that gave me an idea about blood, but I noticed something else unusual—the shade over the one window in the room. It was a double shade, very heavy, peculiarly constructed.

I got scareder. It must have shown in my voice when I asked about the shade.

Max answered it. He said, "Yes, I had that shade specially made, Mr. Hearn. I'm an amateur photographer; I use this room as my darkroom. Had the door fixed so it closes light-tight, too."

I counted back hours since—

I said, "Max"—without realizing that I was calling him by his first name—"will you take off that bandage?"

I'd put down the bottle and glass without having poured myself a drink. When something's about to break I want my hands free.

Max Easter reached up uncertainly for the bandage around his head. Louise Easter said, "Max, don't! The doctor—" and then her eyes met mine and she knew there wasn't any use saying any more.

Max stood up and took the bandage off. He blinked and rubbed his eyes with uncertain hands. He said, "*I can see!* It blurs, but I'm beginning to—"

Then his eyes must have blurred a little less, because his look fixed on his wife's face.

And he *did* begin to see.

And I made it as fast and as merciful—for Max Easter—as possible. I got her out of there, down to headquarters. And I took along the bottle that was labeled Boric Acid, but that contained the tetrianic acid that had been keeping him blind.

We brought Lloyd Eldred in. He wouldn't talk until two of the boys went out to his house with a search warrant. They found the suitcase buried in his backyard and brought it in with them. Then he talked.

V

Winding up something like that takes time; I didn't get home until almost eight. But I'd remembered to phone Marge to hold dinner.

I was still feeling shaky when I got there. But Marge thought talking it out would be good for me, so I talked; I told her about it:

"Lloyd Eldred and Louise Easter were planning to run away together. That was part of it. Another part of it is that Lloyd had embezzled some money from Springfield Chemical. He says about four thousand. He couldn't make it up; he'd lost it gambling. And they were due for an audit in two weeks—a routine annual audit—so he'd have had to lam anyway, even if it hadn't been for the Louise Easter part.

"But he wanted money to lam with, a stake to give them a start somewhere. He'd been putting through fake vouchers like mad and mailing checks to himself under other names. He had to have Max out of the way to do it; Max helped on the regular bookkeeping, besides his payroll work, and would have spotted it. And Wednesday of this week—day after tomorrow—is the semimonthly payroll. And they pay the workmen, but not the white-collar workers, in cash. With Max out of the way he could have got his hands on that money. It would have been plenty—if he could get away with it.

"So he rigged a little booby trap over the acid vat so that when Max pulled the pad of time slips, the jug would fall into the acid. That got rid of Max—but it wouldn't have kept him away long enough if Louise hadn't cooperated. And that was simple. He gave her some dilute tetrianic from the plant to substitute for the boric she cleaned his eyes with several times a day. She did it in a darkened room; I don't mean she pulled the shades down secretly, just that she told her husband it was supposed to be done that way. And she'd always do it an hour or two before the doctor came each day so when he'd take the bandage off to check Max's eyes, they'd be about the same as they were the first time he'd examined them."

Marge looked at me wide-eyed. "Then he *wasn't* really blind, George! But I just said that because—"

"Whyever you said it," I told her, "you were right. But wait; I haven't got near the payoff yet. The murder wasn't something that was planned; it just came up. You see, Armin Robinson had learned that Lloyd Eldred and Louise Easter were having a clandestine affair. He probably saw them somewhere—anyway, he learned it somehow. Of course he didn't know about the embezzlement or that they were planning to run away together. But he knew Max's wife was cheating on him—and Max was his best friend. That was what he'd been worrying about, whether to tell Max or not.

"And he'd made up his mind to tell Max that evening, when he was alone with him. Louise must have guessed it—from his attitude or the way he talked to her when he came she guessed that he knew something and was going to tell Max after she'd gone. She says she almost decided to stay home and break the date with Mrs. Robinson —and then realized that wouldn't stop things anyway, and that she might as well go and just hope Max wouldn't believe what Armin was going to tell him.

"Then, just as she was leaving, Lloyd Eldred came. He'd dropped around to pay a duty call on Max, and had brought him a present, something he knew Max would like and that would help him keep amused while he was blind. Something that he could play with in bed."

Marge saw it coming. The back of her hand went to her mouth. "You mean—"

"Yes," I said. "A kitten. Max is crazy about cats. They'd had one and it had been killed by a car only a week before. And Lloyd had to bring Max something he could enjoy without seeing—books and things like that were out, and you don't take flowers to a man. A kitten was the perfect answer."

"George, what *color* was it?"

I said, "Louise met him at the front door and told him Max was talking to Armin and what she thought Armin was going to say. And Lloyd told her to run along, that he'd take care of things. He didn't tell her how.

"So she left and Lloyd went on into the house. He was much more worried about it than Louise had been. He realized that if that much of the truth came out, there'd be a showdown and probably his embezzlements at the plant would come out too, and that his whole plans would be shot and that he'd have to lam without the payroll money he was waiting for and counting on.

"He put the kitten in his pocket and went to where he knew Max kept a gun and got it. And he saw the cotton gloves and put them on. He went up the stairs on tiptoe and stood outside the door listening. And when he heard Armin Robinson say 'Max, there's something that I hate to—' he stepped into the room. And shot Armin as Armin saw him and stood up. It's a good thing Armin didn't speak his name, or he'd have shot Max too."

"But why did he toss the gun on the bed?"

"He didn't want to take it away with him. And his first thought was simply to confuse things by leaving the gun. And leaving the kitten—it just happened that he'd got it in a way that it couldn't be traced to him—and walking out. You see, it wasn't a planned murder; he was ad libbing as he went along.

"He walked nearer to the bed and tossed the gun onto it and then took the kitten out of his pocket and was holding it by the scruff of the neck to toss it after the gun. And then he saw that Max had got the gun first grab, and was aiming it toward him, from only a couple of yards away. He dropped down on his knee to get under the shot as Max pulled the trigger. The muzzle of the gun went down as he dropped and Max shot. The bullet killed the cat—and buried itself in the wall after it'd gone through a silk pillow on the chair next to the wall.

"Then Max dropped the gun and it went onto the floor out of his reach—and the danger was over. Lloyd decided that his best bet was to make it look as nearly as possible like a burglary. He took the wallets and the watch, and a suitcase from the closet. To make it look like a burglary, he couldn't leave the kitten—burglars don't leave kittens. On his way to the closet he dropped the dead kitten on the chair, on the pillow that the bullet went through, to have his hands free. When he got the suitcase, he put kitten and pillow into it together because there was blood on the pillow.

"Meanwhile, Max hadn't moved—and he knew Max wouldn't dare to move until he heard the front door close. So he could take his time. He went through the downstairs and took the silverware and a few other little things. And left. Period."

Marge said, "George, *what color was that cat?*"

"Marge," I said, "I don't believe in intuition or clairvoyance. Or in coincidence—not *that* much coincidence. So I'm damned if I'm going to tell you, ever."

But I guess that was enough of an answer for her; she didn't ask again.

Shadows on the Road

Robert Colby

Scott Bender hustled the small gray sedan through the Mojave Desert, pushing seventy-five, with one hand on the wheel. He yawned and squinted into the declining sun, which finally relented with a last molten wink as it departed behind a distant mountain.

Scott was bored with the flat terrain, the furnace heat, the narrow, unbending highway; the rip of wind, the drone of motor. Drained by the hours of driving across the desert, he found it an effort even to speak to his companion, Doyle Lindsey, slouched beside him, smoking sullenly, with his stockinged feet propped up over the dashboard.

Both men were in their middle thirties. Scott Bender was the shorter—chunky solid, deceptively mild of manner, with round, pleasant features and a wavy crest of rich blond hair. Doyle Lindsey was tall and black-haired and perpetually thin. He had a long, hollow-cheeked face and sulking dark eyes. From the time they had left the outskirts of Phoenix, Doyle had been in high spirits and was now, like Scott, only a victim of the day's crushing heat and monotony.

"We shoulda traded this jalopy in for new wheels," Scott said after a while. "Something long and sleek with air conditioning," he added, lifting his voice against the wind and motor sounds.

Doyle puffed a cigarette and stared down the road. Apparently he didn't hear or was in no mood to answer; but in a moment he said de-

33

liberately, "No, you're wrong, Scott. We should not have traded this heap for a new one with air."

"Why not? We got enough loot to buy the best. Right?"

"That's not the point." Doyle tilted his head to glance at Scott. "A couple of guys who were barely making ten grand a year don't leave town in a rich man's automobile without raising eyebrows."

Scott nodded. "Yeah, that's true. But listen, we're going to pay through the nose for a new American car in Mexico—double, maybe."

"When the time comes," Doyle said, "we'll fly into San Diego and buy one there."

Scott and Doyle had casually informed friends and co-workers that they would enter Mexico for a leisurely tour of the country via Juarez, but in deference to sudden discovery and the resulting chase, they had secretly altered the plan and headed west through California in order to cross the border at Tijuana.

"We're in no hurry to spend the loot," Doyle continued. "We have it made any way you slice it."

"Slice it right down the middle, fifty-fifty," Scott answered, and grinned.

In the twilight the road unfurled to the horizon without a curve; the drab, arid landscape stretched in a fallow pancake of desert to the hulking, far-flung mountains; the bleak vista between was relieved by little more than such hardy survivors as yucca and cactus and weed.

"Got plenty of gas?" Doyle asked.

"Over half a tank," Scott reported.

"Good thing. I'll bet it's thirty miles of nothing to the nearest station."

"Maybe in the old days, but not now. Take a look at that." Scott pointed to a huge billboard dominating the right side of the highway beyond and read it aloud: " *'Stop! Three miles ahead!* DESERT MIRAGE MOTEL (too good to be true). Cool, luxurious rooms; fine food; your favorite mixed drink served in the cool, dusky Dream Lounge. Gas and repair service.' "

Doyle grunted. "How about that? In the middle of the damn desert."

Scott chuckled. "Anything, anywhere, for a buck."

"If it looks good, let's stop," Doyle said. "I'm beat and I like the sound of that favorite mixed-drink bit."

"I'm for jamming right on through across the border, even if we have to drive all night."

"We sweat it out in Phoenix for two weeks, business as usual while the cops comb the town for one decent clue, and now you're on edge, huh?"

"Okay, we'll take a look. But it couldn't be much, stuck out here in this sand-trap wilderness."

"You been to Vegas lately? That whole jazzy playground was built in this kind of sand-trap wilderness, Scotty-boy."

The Desert Mirage was a low, wandering structure of modernized oriental design with jade-green roof and splashes of vermilion. It sprang up incongruously from the barren face of the desert, as surprising and unreal as a great mansion adrift in mid-ocean.

"I don't believe it," Doyle said, "but I go for it. Sneak up on it before it gets away."

Scott slowed and swerved into the long curve of driveway which, flanked by royal palms, swept grandly to the entrance.

The lobby was vast, cool and artfully embellished by tiled mosaics of the Far East. Off it there was a restaurant and the Dream Lounge. They approached the bar and stood peering in from the entrance.

It seemed an exotic room, subdued, intimate, with a horseshoe bar and semicircular booths in red velvet. It was filled to near capacity with drink-happy travelers in assorted dress. Facing the entrance from a wing of the bar were two attractive brunettes with quick, darting glances. One of these offered a fragment of a smile when her probing gaze came to rest upon the two men in the doorway. Then she nudged her companion. Both women boldly stared.

"They're hooked," Scott said from a corner of his mouth. "Want to go ahead and reel them in?"

"You crazy?" Doyle murmured. "With half of Fort Knox in the car, we check in first, then we play games." He turned and steered Scott from the bar.

At the desk, a couple were being signed in by a clerk. Standing just behind him, consulting what appeared to be an index of rooms, was an elegant, fortyish man, fastidiously encased in a beige sharkskin suit, white shirt and charcoal tie. Spying Lindsey and Bender, he beckoned them to approach the counter.

"A room, gentlemen?" he said with an amiable smile which gleamed from a lean, strong-jawed face, topped by a disciplined overabundance of deep-red hair.

"Yes, we'd like a room," Doyle told him.

"Well, you're in luck, sir. I've got just two left. Would you like them both? Or would you prefer to share one?"

"One room, two beds," Doyle answered.

"Fine," said the red-haired man as he produced a pen and a registration card. Doyle filled in the card, writing both names and a single, previous address in Phoenix.

"Quite a spread you have here," Scott remarked. "Must be new, huh?"

"Yes, sir. I opened for business exactly eight months and six days ago."

"Are you the owner, then?"

"Yes indeed, I'm happy to say. Designed this place myself, helped to construct it."

Scott beamed. "Way out here in no-man's-land, too. I don't see how you operate so far from civilization."

"There were problems at first. But we're completely self-sustaining. We supply our own water, generate our own power."

"That so? Got to hand it to you, it's a real gem in the rough, Mr. . . ."

"Kittredge. Vern Kittredge. And now, you let me know if there's anything I can do for you gentlemen." He swung about, searched in the slots, rested a key on the counter.

Doyle, who had been listening in disapproving silence, consigned the key to his pocket. "How much we owe you, Mr. Kittredge?"

"Twenty-seven-fifty with the tax," Kittredge announced smoothly. Doyle counted the money from his wallet.

"You'll be in 248," said the owner. "That's the second level, midpoint on the right side of the building."

"See you around, Mr. Kittredge," said Scott, and they went off to the parking area.

Watching them retreat, Vern Kittredge shook his head and said to his clerk, "They all ask the same question: How did you get it together way out here? Think I'll write that up in a brochure, save myself about a million extra words a month." He paused. "Frank, I'm going up to the penthouse. Denise will be holding dinner. I won't be down again tonight unless you need me."

"With only one room to go, I certainly won't need much help," said Frank, and Kittredge departed for his "penthouse" apartment.

In 248, Doyle Lindsey was racking a couple of suits on the long pole of a spacious closet in a room of thick carpets, massively handsome furniture and tasteful décor. Chilled air drifted from the softly pulsing, reverse-cycle air conditioner.

"I think you'd better cool that sort of chitchat with people like Kittredge," Doyle said over his shoulder, making it sound like an order.

"Why?" Scott made an injured face.

Doyle crossed to a bulky suitcase and began to carry items from it to a dresser. "Because," he said, "we don't want to attract any special attention and we don't want to make any phony commercial friends, the shrewd ones who are used to reading people at a glance. For that kind, we're a couple of shadows—faceless, anonymous. Now you see us, now you don't, and you never remember anything about us."

"Yeah," said Scott, "guess you're right. I'm just too sociable by nature."

"Exactly." Doyle lit a cigarette. "You're too sociable and you're not very bright sometimes. But at least you listen."

"Well, thanks a lot!"

"For nothing."

"Don't push it, Doyle. I won't be needled."

Doyle ignored him and began to close the big suitcase, though it still contained some of his clothing and a sizable hardcover book.

"Empty the rest of it and we'll have a look at the goodies," said Scott.

"Don't be childish. Once you've seen it, you've seen it."

"The loot is half mine—okay?"

Doyle shrugged and brought a tiny screwdriver from his pocket. He dumped the remaining contents on his bed, found the hidden screws of the custom-made suitcase and removed the bottom lining. The turning of a final screw released one end of a leather strip which, when peeled back, exposed a zipper.

Zip—and they were staring at a tidy garden of U.S. green, neatly arranged and packaged, most of the bills in large, eye-opening denominations.

Scott plucked a banded wad of hundreds from the case and riffled them, lips drawn back in a toothy smile of joy. "That's a lot of cabbage," he mused. "One hundred and sixty thousand free rides on the old merry-go-round."

Doyle also smiled, though sparingly. "Not bad for a couple of amateur hoods," he said.

"Yeah." Scott nodded happily. "The one and only score and we clean that plant for the whole damn payroll. Got to hand it to you, Doyle, you're a brain and a half when it comes to planning a stickup."

"The holdup was pure mechanics," Doyle said. "The real genius was in the preparation and the timing. We didn't just quit good jobs and vanish. We had them brainwashed: a couple of devil-may-care types who saved for years to take a long look at the world, beginning with an economy tour of Mexico. They were ready for it, you see. Even then, after we pull the heist, we serve out our notice—business as usual to the last day. And now we fade. We get lost somewhere—and we're forgotten."

"Unless the cops come up with a clue," said Scott.

"They won't. We gave them two weeks, sitting ducks the whole time. And they didn't get close, not even a smell."

"Sure, we're in the clear," said Scott. He replaced the packet of bills, Doyle sealed the loot, restored his belongings and stowed the case in the closet.

"Now," said Doyle with a rubbing of palms together, "snap it up and get ready. Then we'll go down and warm up those two bright-eyed chicks languishing away in the bar."

In 254, the last available room at the Desert Mirage, a rollaway bed had been installed to accommodate the three middle-aged men who had just checked in. Ice and mix had also been delivered and now the threesome, seated in facing chairs about the room, were sipping highballs, darkly laced with bourbon.

The trio was composed of Charlie Sachs, the working owner of a small stable of racehorses; his trainer, Max Hardman; and a fast-buck lawyer, Sid Lerner, a personal friend of Charlie Sachs.

A paunchy, jolly-faced man, Charlie put down his drink and chuckled through his cigar. "So who's gonna sleep in the rollaway?" he said.

"You're built just right for it," Sid Lerner answered with a grin, while Max Hardman kept his usual poker face.

"Tell you what," Charlie said. "We'll toss for it."

Coins were produced and flipped, Sid lost good-naturedly; he was, after all, the slimmest of the three.

In a moment, the lawyer said, "I want to hear more about the fix, Charlie. What I know of horses you could put in your eye and never feel it. But what it boils down to, the race is fixed with Bold Blackie juiced up to win if he doesn't break a leg. Right?"

Charlie snorted, chewed his cigar, and sent his trainer an imploring glance.

"Sid, the days of fixed races, in the classic sense, are over," Max Hardman said. "Your typical boat race went out with spats. You can't dope a horse to win, because he's going to go through a chemical test for peppy juice after the race. No, it don't work that way at all. It's much more subtle, damn hard to prove, and practically legal."

"I'm listening," Sid declared.

"All right. There are three other horses in that race Friday that should beat Bold Blackie, no problem at all. The public will bet down on those three at odds from two-to-one or less, up to about four-to-one. Blackie will be eight-to-one on the morning line and he could rise as high as twelve-to-one before post time, especially since the favorite, Royal Front, will get a big play.

"But the owner of Royal Front knows his horse isn't *that* good; he could lose to one of the other top horses if he gets just one bad break. And he don't want to risk a bet at not much over even money. The other two owners will get better odds for their ponies, but not good enough to take the gamble.

"So Charlie gets together with those boys over a few drinks, and they decide to make Bold Blackie the winner at eight-to-one and up, all the owners but Charlie betting against his own horse."

"Crazy," said Lerner. "How does the horse know he's not supposed to win? You tell the jockeys to hold the top horses back so Blackie can win?"

"Not exactly," said Charlie, and smiled indulgently. "The stewards would frown on that and the jockeys can't afford to be set down or barred from the track. No, like Max says, it's more subtle. The other three owners tell their jockeys they're not trying, not betting Friday. They are waiting for a sharper spot in the meet to bring home the bacon.

"The jockeys don't need a blueprint, they know precisely what that means. They're paid to give the owner what he wants, long as it's legal and doesn't break any rules. So they let the horse run his own race. They don't maneuver for position. They let a horse run himself out before the homestretch; they don't try, they don't compete. And brother, that's another way of saying they're gonna lose for damn sure, because you gotta take aim of you're going to hit the target.

"On the other hand, I tell *my* boy I'm betting a bundle Friday, and I want the full treatment. I've picked my spot, I want a clever ride, and I expect him to cross that wire with Bold Blackie in front. Bold Blackie can do that with a good ride, because he's the best of the rest of the field.

"Then, with that sort of rig, all things being unequal for the top ponies, we should make a nice killing Friday, gentlemen."

Sid Lerner raised his glass. "I'll drink to that," he said.

They drank.

Doyle Lindsey and Scott Bender slept late and, wretchedly hung over from the night's partying, pushed on toward the Mexican border at a few minutes before noon.

Near 3 p.m., Mrs. Trisha Howland drove in from Los Angeles, arriving in her own splendid new automobile, a recent gift from her husband on their second anniversary. Trisha was twenty-eight, nineteen years younger than Gary Howland. Auburn-haired, trim and petite, her soft little features were haggard and taut as she inquired at the registration desk, then hurried off to join her husband, who had been sealed in room 116 for almost two days.

When he came to the door, opening it cautiously, she slipped inside and they embraced, clinging to each other in silence.

"You need a drink," Gary Howland said then. He iced a couple of glasses and poured Scotch liberally. She sagged into a chair and sipped as he leaned against a dresser and stared grimly down at his shoes, a graying, craggy-faced man, overweight but almost hand-some.

"I didn't even pack a suitcase," Trisha said. "I left minutes after I got your call."

"Thanks, baby," he mumbled, but did not look up at her.

"Why didn't you wait at home for me, Gary? We could have talked it out, figured something better for you than just to run blindly."

He glanced up fleetingly, was caught by the wide-eyed innocence and compassion on her pretty face. "I panicked," he said into his glass. "Just bolted away, no real destination in mind, just some re-mote hideout in which to think. I passed this incredible place, but I was exhausted so I turned back; didn't even think to register under a false name and address. Anyway, I thought you might very well be on the other side of the fence, so to speak."

"How very wrong, darling. The whole business is a simply incon-ceivable tragedy. I just can't imagine why, knowing me, you would jump to such a conclusion and then—"

"That's just it, Trisha. I didn't feel I knew you that well in a couple of years. Do we know anyone, really?"

"Obviously, I didn't know you, either, Gary." She paused, lighting a cigarette. "And you were so guarded on the phone, I never got a true picture of what happened. So why don't you start right from the beginning?"

"I could tell what happened in a minute. How I felt is much more complicated."

She nodded. "Why did you come looking for me in the middle of the day?"

"I had an appointment with Hamilton Burris. He was flying from Dallas to haggle over the terms for buying up his West Coast refin-ery. He came down with something or other and postponed the meeting. That left a big hole in the day, so I thought we'd make an afternoon of it, spend some time together for a change.

"I called you—no answer. I figured you'd be down on the beach, so I went home and changed. Then I drove to that spot near the burger stand where you hang out and I finally spied you a ways off to the right, down near the water. You were lying on the robe next to this young guy—muscle boy with the clean-cut all-American face and the woman-hungry eyes.

"You were just about three inches apart and he seemed to be mouthing off almost against your lips. It gave me a shock—a big jolt. I had never thought of you in that—that context, and my imagination began to spin. How many other times? How many other guys?"

"Yes, but didn't it once occur to you that—"

"Let me finish. Nothing occurred to me but the fact that I'm about twenty years older and maybe I had once seemed glamorous, running a big company, having wealth and power and so on. But then you got bored, had a craving for men your own age—the lean, athletic lover-boys—and decided to play both ends.

"Instant jealousy, born of hidden doubts about myself already planted. So I watched you from a distance, and when you got up and began to walk with him toward that shacky beach house, I followed. You disappeared inside with him, and then I was certain. I stood around about fifteen minutes, trying to get up nerve enough to go in and clobber him.

"But I knew that would be a farce—he'd beat me to my knees while you looked on in disgust or just giggled at my puny attempt. So I drove home wildly and raced back with the gun. I had no intention of killing him; I was just going to give him a scare.

"I knocked and he opened the door, and I shoved in behind the gun. I dashed through the rooms while he gaped and fumed, but you were gone. We had a few words and he got the drift, but he didn't seem in the least frightened of me. He was merely amused, in a mocking sort of way.

"'Where's Trisha!' I shouted. 'Is she coming back with a bottle for your little party? Wouldn't she be surprised if she found you dead, sonny-boy?'

"That produced only a sneer and a laugh. 'Why, you stupid old creep!' he said. 'She got dressed and went home. You just missed her.'

"I shot him then. He fell in a heap and I saw he was dead and I panicked."

"Oh, Gary," Trisha said, "it was *my* fault. And yet it wasn't. He was just a boy who spoke to me on the beach one day and I answered him to be polite. We talked a few minutes, I told him I was married, and he went off. But he lived so near and he came by where I was sunning myself several times again. I talked with him to pass time—

just talk. I thought of him as just a harmless, lonely guy who needed to confide in someone.

"That awful day, he asked me if I would like a cold beer, and I didn't see any harm in it. The sun was boiling and I was parched. So I went with him and he poured me a glass of beer and I drank it while we chatted for about twenty minutes. He appeared innocent enough and I felt almost maternal toward him. But then he began to get cute. Nothing crudely aggressive, just testing me, trying for a kiss, busy with the hands.

"I kidded him out of it and made a reasonably graceful exit. I stopped at Grace Fielding's on the way home, stayed an hour or so and went on. You didn't come at dinner time and I was frantic. Next morning it was in the papers: Bruce Kaufman shot dead in his beach shack, killer unknown; the single clue a spent bullet still intact, caliber thirty-eight. Even then I didn't guess, Gary. I just couldn't put it together with you as the outraged husband. Not until you phoned.

"But the why and how of it isn't important now. Simply tell me what you did with the gun, because apparently the only thing they've got is a bullet to match with it."

"I brought the gun with me," he said. "It's hidden in the case with my portable typewriter. I had considered typing a confession and one of those corny, dramatic, farewell notes before I used the gun on myself."

"Nonsense!" she said. "When we get home we'll take the boat out a mile or two, and then I personally am going to drop that gun over the side."

"I love you, baby," he said. "And I—I'm so very sorry."

She looked away. "We can't leave tonight," she murmured. "I'm too tired. I want a long, hot bath, then let's go down for cocktails and dinner. We'll take off at dawn and we'll go back with a nice little story about an impulsive second honeymoon. Is that okay, darling?"

Doyle Lindsey and Scott Bender paused for the night in the coastal town of Ensenada, having crossed the border at Tijuana without incident. They had gone out to dinner and had returned to their motel, a far less pretentious resting place than the cushy Desert Mirage. They had debated a good night's sleep against a tour of the night spots, but all that stolen loot argued for fun and games.

There was a small problem. They had nearly run out of ready cash in pocket, and it was necessary to raid the false bottom of the suitcase for a fresh supply. Consequently, Doyle set the case on a luggage rack, once again removed the lining and, yanking the zipper, opened the secret compartment.

Immediately, there was another problem, this one a disaster. The cash was missing—every last dollar.

"Gone!" said Scott with terrible astonishment. "I don't believe it!"

"No!" said Doyle, shaking his head vehemently. "No, no! Impossible! Not one person in this world knew the money was there but you and me. And since *I* didn't take it . . ." He groped in his pocket for the .32 automatic, which he then aimed carefully at Scott Bender. "So help me," he said with deadly sincerity, "you're going to tell me what you did with that dough or I'll kill you."

Late in the following afternoon, Gary Howland arrived with Trisha at their impressive home in the Palisades, unpacked and then opened the typewriter case to recover his .38 revolver. The weapon was not in evidence; instead, there was a note typed on his own machine and left in the roller:

> We have your .38 caliber, Smith & Wesson, snub-nosed revolver, serial #C247634, the gun with which you murdered Bruce Kaufman in a jealous rage.
>
> Please be advised that we are sending this weapon to the L.A. police with the appropriate details of your involvement in the crime, unless we have from you within three days the sum of twenty-five thousand dollars cash.
>
> The currency should be substantially wrapped and protected, and mailed to Box Holder, at the address below. Upon receipt of the money, the gun will be forwarded to you promptly.
>
> > Yours in all good faith, and with high hopes for your continued freedom from the dreary confines of San Quentin.

Below this there was given a postal box number in Las Vegas, Nevada.

On the next Saturday evening, Vern Kittredge, owner of the Desert Mirage Motel, was seated in the living room of his extravagant penthouse apartment, a separate structure reached by a private elevator and perched atop the roof of the main building. A corner of his mouth tugged by amusement, Kittredge was squinting at the sports page of a newspaper. His wife, Denise, a lovely young blonde of remarkable dimensions, entered just then from the kitchen, bearing a tray of appetizers and a couple of frigid, desert-dry martinis.

Vern scooped one of the martinis from the tray and tested it. "Ahhh," he sighed. "Made with loving care, a work of art. Shall I frame it, or drink it?"

"Well, I don't have a suitable frame," said Denise as she sank beside him with a merry expression, "so I think you'd better swallow this one before it dries up and blows away."

"Yes," he said, "it is delightfully dry. Would you like to glance at the sports page?"

"Darling, you know I detest sports."

"Including horse racing?"

"Well, just tell me about it. There was such a horse? Bold Blackie?"

"Yes, of course. I had to search diligently, but I found Blackie in the Friday *Racing Form*. Then I called DiVito in Vegas and had him place three thousand with a bookie, so the size of the bet wouldn't plunge the mutuel odds at the track."

"But of course it was all hot air," she teased, "and that miserable nag finished last."

"Oh, on the contrary, my dear. Bold Blackie skipped home two lengths in front and paid nineteen-eighty—just under nine to one."

"Mmm. Very nice. Close to twenty-seven thousand net, that figures."

"Right." He leaned back and lit a small, slender cigar. "This has been a week to end all others," he said proudly. "Far and away the biggest take since we opened. Twenty-seven grand from the racing coup; one hundred and sixty thousand from the bad boys in 248 with the trick suitcase; and twenty-five grand from the trigger-happy husband in 116."

"Howland, you mean, darling?"

"Yeah, Gary Howland."

"You got that money too?"

"DiVito had one of his boys pick it up at the box this morning, and he'll bring it along next trip."

"Are you going to send back the gun or milk him some more?"

He gave her a look. "Now, you know I always keep my word. The gun is on its way. Howland got off easy, but I was in a generous mood."

Denise was thoughtful. "Do you ever feel guilty about it, Vern?"

"Not a bit. I only take from the rich bad boys and the crooks, never the good guys."

"That's true, darling."

He put down his glass, sank a potato chip into the cheese dip, and munched. "Well," he said, "we've got close to a full house. Have you been checking for any live ones?"

"Yes, but so far, there's only a tax dodge down in 64. Some guy talking to his partner about a double set of books. I took notes."

"How much they holding out from Uncle?"

"Around half a million per. We'd get a nice cut out of that for informing—no risk."

"They still in?"

"Went to dinner, but they might be back now."

"Let's go see."

Kittredge left the room with his wife and they entered a study. He pressed a button beneath his desk and a section of wall slid back to expose a lighted cubicle. Inside, Kittredge poked another button and the wall closed. He sat then before a large console containing toggle switches labeled with room numbers. Above these switches were tiny globes which remained dark when a room had not yet been rented, red when occupied. Atop the console there was a speaker, and a monitor screen for the closed-circuit TV system with its hidden cameras.

Kittredge pushed the switch labeled 64 and there was only a faint hum from the speaker.

"Guess they're still out," said Denise.

"Let's make sure." Kittredge thumbed a button. On the TV screen an empty room was revealed, a bathrobe on one of the twin beds, a briefcase on the other.

"Nobody home," Kittredge said, cutting picture and sound.

"You want to try some of the other numbers?" Denise asked from her standing position behind him.

He nodded and for several minutes he fingered the banks of switches, listening to snatches of conversation without adding picture to sound.

He shook his head. "Bad night for larceny, it would seem. We'll try again later."

"You listen," she said, "but don't you ever *watch* the monitor screen, even when you're alone, darling? C'mon, 'fess up."

"No," he said firmly, "I don't. Only when I must, to gather what can't be understood from listening. Like watching the two gunmen to see where they had the money hidden so I could snatch it when they were out. Or to be sure a room is empty when I'm on the way to it. I think every honest citizen who comes to the Desert Mirage has a right to expect absolute privacy."

Tickled, Denise stared at him in wonder and grinned. "Absolute privacy, huh? Well, you *are* a man of honor, Vern dear."

He stood and put his arm around her and pressed the button to open the way. "What's for dinner, hon?" he said as they left the room.

Mr. Mappin Forecloses

Zena Collier

It had not been Mr. Mappin's experience that life was what you made it. He had found, on the contrary, that life made *you;* that the circumstances of life tightened around you, hemming you in and pinning you down relentlessly, so that Mr. Mappin, for instance, who had once seen himself as a diplomat of note, or a foreign correspondent, or even—and he was particularly fond of this idea—captain of one of those majestic floating palaces in which seem to be concentrated all the glamour, magic and romance in the world, was in fact just rounding out his twentieth year in the Mortgage Department of Trimble, Goshen & Webb, solicitors.

Twenty years earlier, he had come to Trimble, Goshen & Webb with high hopes, clear eyes and a blueprint for the future held always closely before him. It had been no small achievement to be accepted by a firm of such repute as Trimble & Co., and so he had had only faint regrets in laying aside those other dreams—"Mr. Mappin expressed tempered optimism today about his meeting with the Ambassador from Transylvania . . ." "George Mappin, in his latest communiqué from Hong Kong, says . . ." "Commodore Mappin requests the honour of the Countess' presence at his table tonight . . ."—in laying aside those dreams which perhaps more properly belonged to the realm of one's boyhood imaginings. For when all was said and done, "Mr. George Mappin, well-known city solicitor, quelled the angry shareholders' meeting with his customary eloquence" would not be such a bad second best.

And what had come of it? What had happened to those twenty

years? He had grown older, that was what had come of it. And he was in Mortgages. And while the first was a necessary evil, the second had not leavened the bread of bitterness that lately poisoned all his waking moments.

For the first two years he had been content to bide his time. He had had the chance to learn a little of everything—probate, litigation, insurance cases, estate conveyancing, even some tax and industrial property—before he had finally been assigned to the Mortgage Department under Mr. Carewe. And there he had done his best, dealing with local searches, abstracts, requisitions on title, indentures, leases, until he knew the work backward and forward and inside out. And in spite of the fact that this was not the practice of the law as he had imagined it—these abstract inquiries and recondite replies, the dry terms of an old art—he was fairly content, at first. Because, of course, it was only for the time being, until the Powers that Be remembered where they'd left George Mappin, and picked him up out of Mortgages and sent him on to bigger, more exciting fare.

But he had stayed there longer than he expected. It had been ten years, in fact, before finally the moment had come when he was summoned to Mr. Trimble's office. And his heart had beaten a quick tattoo of joy within his breast at the prospect of a change for him at last, at long last.

Mr. Trimble had waved largely at the client's chair beside the desk, and offered him a cigarette. "Now, let me see, you've been with us now for—how many years is it? Seven? Eight?"

"Ten, sir," Mr. Mappin said.

"Well, well, how the time does fly," said Mr. Trimble, shaking his white head regretfully. "You've been working under Mr. Carewe in Mortgages most of the time, haven't you?"

"That's right, sir."

This was it, this was finally *it*, Mr. Mappin exulted. What would it be? The company department, working in the field of high finance which was, thought Mr. Mappin, as exciting in its way as tiger shooting in Kenya, though a little less heady, perhaps. Or was it to be defamation—he'd heard that young Straus, who'd been doing all the defamation, was leaving Trimble's to start his own practice, so perhaps that was coming to him, to Mr. Mappin, now. Or insurance litigation —insurance was not quite so colorful but it was far preferable to

Mortgages. Anything in the world was better than Mortgages, and he waited anxiously for Mr. Trimble's edict.

"I'll come straight to the point," Mr. Trimble said. "How would you like to have Mortgages, Mr. Mappin?" Mr. Trimble beamed at him expectantly.

"Have Mortgages?" he had echoed, stupefied. "But—but Mr. Trimble, I *am* in Mortgages. Why, I've been in Mortgages practically ever since I came here—"

"I don't think you quite understand," Mr. Trimble said. "You see, at the firm meeting last week, when Mr. Carewe announced retirement plans, it was decided to offer you the Mortgage Department— to put you at the head of it, I mean. As you doubtless know and are aware"—Mr. Trimble sometimes found it difficult to speak without the redundancy of legal parlance—"this is a highly responsible position. It needs someone steady, like yourself. Someone with an eye for detail, for method, for caution."

"*Me?*" Mr. Mappin uttered the word incredulously.

"You," Mr. Trimble said firmly. "We feel you're just the man for the job, highly qualified on all those counts, and—"

"No," Mr. Mappin interrupted, a little wildly. "No, no, I'm not— those things you said. It isn't—I had thought—something with a little more challenge, more—" He groped for words.

Mr. Trimble leaned forward, resting his elbows on the desk, the palms of his hands touching. Not unkindly he said, "I understand, Mr. Mappin, I understand perfectly. But on the other hand, I do feel —that is, the firm feels—that both you and the firm will receive the greatest benefit if you do the type of job for which you're most suited."

But Mr. Mappin was desperate now, and he could not help bursting out, "Suited! Mortgages! Me?"

"A square peg, you know," Mr. Trimble said. "George"—and Mr. Mappin remembered later that for the first and only time, Mr. Trimble had called him George—"It's a wise man who knows his capabilities, and recognizes his limitations. Now we've been watching you lately, and it seems to me—to the firm, that is—that you do an excellent job where you are, and you can be of greatest service there."

With those words, Mr. Mappin knew that his battle was lost. Trimble, Goshen & Webb had not achieved their present standing through lack of good judgment. And as he sat there, slumping a little now in the client's chair, it was clear to him at last that his was not, after all, a brilliant mind, well stored and capable of daring strategy. Not his the gift of devilishly shrewd argument, the challenging cut and thrust of commercial negotiation. "George Mappin, well-known city solicitor, took center stage with some straight answers for angry shareholders" was after all only another dream.

Through the wreckage of his hopes, Mr. Trimble's voice came faintly to him. "You'll accept, then?" It was hardly a question.

His mind whirling, Mr. Mappin nodded slowly.

"Good," Mr. Trimble said briskly, and held out his hand. "Congratulations!"

Mr. Mappin's hand crept out. "Congratulations?" he echoed numbly.

"After all, it *is* a promotion," Mr. Trimble reminded him.

"Oh, yes. Yes, of course," Mr. Mappin said. "Thank you." And he turned and left.

He had returned to the Mortgage Department then, to a change of position, an increase in salary, a different desk—but still Mortgages. The dry rot of Mortgages. And for day after limitless day, Mr. Mappin handled with efficiency whatever came his way, giving satisfaction as always, getting precious little himself. And life went on. And Mr. Mappin knew that the only thing that would change would be himself, growing a little older every year, older and older, in Mortgages.

Bitterness began in him then. He sat at his desk and saw other men come into the firm, men younger than he, and his resentment grew with every year, with the advent of each new young man still wet behind the ears with the ink of examination papers, with each new man who was given a chance to show what he could do with defamation, patents and insurance litigation, and who progressed to more imposing offices upstairs (the greater your serniority at Trimble's, the higher the story), and some of whom even achieved partnerships in due course.

And that was another thing. The least they could do, after fifteen years, was offer him a partnership. Because, although he despised Mortgages, he *did* do the work well. But no, Mr. Mappin thought, nobody notices, nobody cares. Mr. Trimble, since that day in his office years before when he had offered, given, *forced* Mortgages on

Mr. Mappin, had never so much as uttered a word of praise. But a partnership would have been the way to show appreciation, Mr. Mappin reflected, it would have made up for a great deal.

Once Mr. Mappin had made an attempt to get out of Mortgages. He had gone to see Mr. Trimble and asked point-blank to be transferred.

"But—after all these years—aren't you *happy* in Mortgages?" Mr. Trimble had sounded amazed.

"I'd like a change," Mr. Mappin had said stiffly. "One gets tired of the same thing year in, year out."

"Tired? Tired of *Mortgages?"* Mr. Trimble looked at Mr. Mappin as though he had blasphemed. And finally he said, "Carry on for a while and we'll see. Because really, Mr. Mappin, you're so well suited to it—there isn't anyone we feel we can trust to do as well with Mortgages as you."

And Mr. Mappin had left Mr. Trimble's office knowing very well that nothing would come of it, that he would be left where he was.

Trapped, Mr. Mappin had thought.

And finally, out of the bitterness, the resentment, the disillusionment, had been born hatred. Hatred for the firm that had done this dreadful thing to him, that had shunted him off in a corner with Mortgages—he, George Mappin, who had dreamed of such a different kind of life. And the hatred built up, built up, built up until every breath he drew was tinged with the ugly taste of it.

It was some time before the end of his twentieth year with Mortgages that Mr. Mappin began to think with pleasure of murdering Mr. Trimble, who represented to him the firm that had treated him so badly. As soon as the idea occurred to him, Mr. Mappin felt better. It was something to think about at night as he lay awake, so that instead of working himself into a frenzy thinking of his wasted years, he could instead concentrate calmly and objectively on a subject that afforded him infinite enjoyment. Since there was, of course, no intention of actually putting his idea into effect, it was a pastime that did no one any harm, and it somehow gave him a sense of release.

So it became a regular habit, and every night as he prepared for bed, he looked forward to it with keen anticipation. He would undress quickly, turn off the light, remove his spectacles, and get into bed. Then he would turn on his back, stare into the darkness, and think. He would dwell with gusto on the pros and cons of various methods. He would pleasurably consider timing and alibis. Although Mr. Mappin was hardly a specialist in murder, he had read enough detective stories to be familiar with the axiom about the simplest plan being the best, and finally Mr. Mappin chose, hypothetically of course, a very simple plan. There was a period every afternoon when Mr. Trimble saw no clients, dictated no letters, accepted no telephone calls. From four until four-thirty every day he would simply relax—"My one resistance to the pressures of this workaday world," he called it—and woe betide anyone disturbing this rest period. His secretary, the switchboard operator and all the men had strict instructions to stay away from his office at that time. *Voilà*, thought Mr. Mappin, there it is, made to order. Just walk in there and—kill him.

There was the matter of a weapon. Guns were noisy, a knife too messy, and poison—poison was a science in itself and far too complicated. But on Mr. Trimble's desk, Mr. Mappin recalled, there stood a heavy brass paperweight in the shape of a Buddha. Ideal, thought Mr. Mappin.

And then what? Well, you simply killed him—Mr. Mappin always skipped quickly over the actual deed—and then, to give yourself a little time, you put the body in the cupboard that was in one corner of Mr. Trimble's office, closed the cupboard door, went back to your own office downstairs, and that was that.

The only flaw was that you might be seen leaving his office. But that would be the chance you would have to take, and actually it was only a slim chance because Mr. Trimble's office was all by itself on the sixth floor and at that time of day no one else would be going there.

And so, as other men count sheep, Mr. Mappin calculated the finer points of this detail or that, until at last he had it all worked out perfectly. It really seemed a pity that he would never have the chance to show what he could do in this new field. He could not help feeling that they would show him a great deal more respect at the office if they knew the sort of thing he was capable of.

Ah, respect—that was another thing. These new young men who came in. Two of them assigned to Mortgages right now. This very morning he'd intercepted a wink when he came in. Winking, indeed —over him! Had he been a member of the firm, they'd never have dared. Never. Well, it didn't matter, they wouldn't be in Mortgages for very long. No, not they. Because soon they'd be transferred to something else, something more spectacular, no doubt, the way *he'd* wanted to be transferred.

Again, the fires would flare up inside him.

Even Miss Ashley, it seemed to him, had been acting in a very odd manner toward him lately. Miss Ashley was the typist he shared with Mr. Lyons, because only firm members had their own secretaries. It would have been less of an insult if Miss Ashley had been even faintly pretty. (Mr. Trimble's secretary, Miss Burke, was a perfectly lovely creature, of course.) But Miss Ashley was a dumpy little woman with a receding chin and the unfortunate habit of giggling constantly over nothing at all. The other day, for instance, when he had happened, quite by chance, to recall the fact that next week would mark his twentieth year with the firm (speaking his thoughts aloud, talking more to himself than to her), she had emitted a sudden squeak of laughter, and then bitten it off suddenly when he looked at her, his disgust showing in his face.

Laugh, you foolish creature, Mr. Mappin had thought, churning inwardly. Is it so funny, then? Is it funny to you that I've wasted twenty years cooped up here? Is it really so very hilarious? And so overcome was he at that moment by the force of his feelings that he had to excuse himself and hurry out of the office on some imaginary errand, lest he should actually strike her.

The following week, Mr. Mappin caught a cold. On Monday he had a sore throat, on Tuesday he had a sore throat and a headache, and on Wednesday night he fell asleep the moment his head touched the pillow without once stopping to think about Mr. Trimble. On Thursday, he woke up with a fever. He took his temperature; it was a hundred and two.

He dressed himself wearily and dragged his aching bones from the house. He didn't know why he was going in today, it wouldn't be appreciated. But he would go anyway, because today marked twenty years of his association with Trimble & Co., and you never knew, somebody might, they just *might* remember the fact and mention it to him. He supposed that, to tell the truth, it was really in that hope that he was going in today. Because he felt very ill. His knees bent at the most unlikely moments, he felt hot and cold by turns, and his head felt as though it might explode at any second.

And after he arrived, he was sorry he had made the effort. Nobody said anything, and it was very obvious that nobody was *going* to say anything. And he had some pride, after all; if nobody was going to remember, he wasn't going to drop any hints. They might think he was asking for a pat on the back or something. And that, thought Mr. Mappin bitterly, would be utterly ridiculous, of course—the idea of George Mappin getting a pat on the back.

At two o'clock, he called Miss Ashley in, though he found it difficult to concentrate, feeling the way he did. But he would just stick this day out, he thought, and then he would go home and go to bed for a day or a week, or a month, if necessary, and hang the whole pack of them. *Let* the work pile up, who cared, who in blazes cared?

Just as he began to dictate, Mr. Trimble came in. "Pardon the interruption," he said, "but have you the Copeland settlement handy? Perhaps I could just glance at it—"

Mr. Mappin produced the deed and waited while Mr. Trimble ran an eye over it. "Hmmm," Mr. Trimble said, "I'd like to take this for a moment—"

"There's nothing wrong with it, is there?" Mr. Mappin asked. "There's no flaw on the title, the—"

"Gracious, no, nothing like that," Mr. Trimble said. "It's just that Mr. Copeland telephoned a few minutes ago and asked me to explain one or two points—"

"But I explained everything to them when they were here last week," Mr. Mappin said, surprised. "I thought I'd made everything clear—"

"Oh, I'm sure you did," Mr. Trimble said quickly. "But there's one small point that apparently just occurred to Mr. Copeland—something to do with those fishing rights—"

"But in that case, why didn't he ask *me* about it?" In spite of himself, Mr. Mappin's voice rose. "Since *I'm* handling the transfer—"

"Well, you know how these things are," Mr. Trimble said, already moving toward the door. "Reg Copeland and I run into each other a good deal at the club, so he probably feels that he can waste *my* time over trifling details with greater impunity than he can yours." He smiled rather carefully at Mr. Mappin and left. And Mr. Mappin, after a moment, got on with his dictation.

But he knew, smile or no smile, what Mr. Trimble had meant. Mr. Mappin sufficed when it came to mortgages for the Smiths and the

Joneses, run-of-the-mill stuff. But when it came to larger matters and really important clients, such as Mr. Trimble's friends the Reginald Copelands, George Mappin wouldn't do. Why, he'd been over every step of the transaction in detail with the Copelands the previous week, and Mr. Copeland had seemed perfectly satisfied at the time. And if there'd been a query, why had they gone over Mr. Mappin's head with it?

Sitting there, Mr. Mappin began to fume. Apart from everything else, how rude Mr. Trimble had been, speaking of "trifling details." But that's right, thought Mr. Mappin, first incarcerate me in Mortgages for twenty years, and then rob the work of any semblance of dignity, of importance, by calling it "trifling details." Was it in that light, then, that his twenty years of conscientious performance were now viewed by Mr. Trimble? Was it? *Was it?*

Mr. Mappin's heart was near to bursting with all he felt. His head ached, his nose streamed, and all at once further work was quite beyond him, and he dismissed Miss Ashley. Alone, he put his head in his hands and sat there while the years spun back in memory, years of emptiness, of pleasureless effort entirely unrewarded. And now, today, wouldn't you have thought Mr. Trimble would have said something, seeing him just now—even if it were only something trite, silly even, like "Many happy returns"?

Mr. Mappin sat there for a long time. He could not have told anyone exactly what he was thinking. He knew that he was feeling very odd, and that a sledgehammer was pounding inside his head, just over his eyes. He sneezed and groped wretchedly for his handkerchief. Time must be getting on, he thought, I wish I were home in bed.

He looked at his watch. The hands stood at five minutes past four.

Mr. Mappin did not know why, but now, looking at the time, watching idly as the second hand went slowly round, and round again, it seemed to him that there was something he must do. Something . . . Something. Something very important, if he were ever to have peace of mind again.

He got to his feet and the next thing he knew, he was walking slowly up the stairs, up, up, the fourth floor, the fifth, the sixth. At the sixth floor, he stopped and stood still for a moment, his hand pressed to his aching head. And he remembered, then, why he was there, and where he was going, and what he had to do.

The rest of the world seemed to have fallen away. It did not occur to him now to look out for other people, to wonder whether he would encounter anyone on the way, someone who might, perhaps, remember later. He simply concentrated on the main problem at the moment, which was that of putting one foot in front of the other and getting where he was going.

He walked straight down the corridor, came to the door marked "Emerson Trimble," opened it without knocking and went in. On the rug his feet made no sound, and Mr. Trimble did not look up from his desk, where he was concentrating on something he was writing.

Mr. Mappin approached. He stood right in front of the desk, and his hand rested lightly on the brass Buddha when Mr. Trimble finally looked up.

Mr. Trimble looked askance at him, glanced at his watch. "Four-ten," he murmured, and looked inquiringly at Mr. Mappin. "I assume you have something important to see me about, coming at this time."

"Yes," Mr. Mappin said. "Very important, Mr. Trimble." And without thinking twice about it, he raised the Buddha high and brought it down with all his strength on Mr. Trimble's head.

And so it was done, without a sound. Of course there was blood. Mr. Mappin had forgotten there would be blood, and averted his eyes from the sight he had created while the room swayed terribly about him.

And then he got on with what he had to do, first wiping his finger-prints carefully from the Buddha, then pulling Mr. Trimble's jacket up around—well, pulling up the jacket so that he would not be confronted with that sight again, and then, with a great deal of effort, getting the body, somehow, into the cupboard. It was all a nightmare, and for a while Mr. Mappin thought he would never manage it, but he did. Then he had a brilliant idea. Taking Mr. Trimble's overcoat and hat from the clothes tree, he put those too in the cupboard and locked the cupboard door. That way, anyone coming in to see Mr. Trimble after four-thirty would see the coat gone and assume that he had left early for an appointment or simply to go home. Of course, that wouldn't make a lot of difference, but it would give Mr. Mappin enough time for him to go back to his office and stick it out there till five o'clock, home time, without the crime being discovered. Because if, once the murder came out and people remembered that Mr. Mappin had left early, it might look suspicious.

He pressed a hand to his forehead, amazed that he could think of all these things now, when he felt so ill. As he took a last quick glance around the office to make sure that everything was in order, he noticed that there was some . . . mess on the blotter. The sheets on which Mr. Trimble had been writing were now bright crimson. Mr. Mappin took them, crumpled them as small as possible in his hand, and hid them carefully at the bottom of the wastepaper basket.

Then he left, walking back to his own office in a daze, still without encountering anyone. Really, it was amazing, he thought, Providence seemed to be with him in this. There seemed to be nobody about at all.

And then his fever increased, he felt as though he were on fire, and he ceased to think of anything whatever except the necessity of getting home and going to bed.

After a century it was five o'clock, and slowly, painfully, he put on his coat and hat and galoshes. He made his way to the lift, pressed the button, waited. At last it came and he got in, leaning weakly against the back, his eyes closed, while it moved slowly downward.

Surely—surely he must be very ill indeed. It felt almost as though they were going up instead of down. He opened his eyes. "Frank," he said to the attendant, "Frank, I'm on my way out—I want to go down."

What was this? *What ghastly thing?* For Frank ignored him, grinning, and they continued upward.

"Down, I said," Mr. Mappin repeated frantically. "Down! I want to go down, I'm ill, please take me down at once!"

The lift stopped, the door slid open and a dozen hands reached in for Mr. Mappin. There was laughter, a great deal of laughter, and a loud buzz of conversation. Who—? What—? Feeling blind suddenly, feeling as though he had lost his faculties, Mr. Mappin stumbled forward, pulled by the hands.

And then he saw where he was. This was the seventh floor, the Sanctum Sanctorum. But what was he doing here? And why were these people pulling him, urging him on his way?

He peered around and recognized faces that appeared as though through a mist—the telephone operator . . . Miss Ashley . . . Mr. Lyons and Mr. Hawkins . . . Miss Burke . . . some of the other girls

—and over there, coming out of that door—Mr. Webb, wasn't it? He rubbed his eyes. Yes, Mr. Webb, laughing, coming up to him now, patting him on the back.

And now they were taking him in through the door, all of them laughing, talking at the tops of their voices. He couldn't distinguish a word. But he recognized the room, in spite of what they had done to it. It was the room where the monthly firm meetings were held, where the members of the firm met together and discussed firm business. But now the room was arranged as if for a banquet, Mr. Mappin noted dizzily, with the tables set for dinner. And now they were leading him to the head table, seating him at the center of it, Mr. Goshen on his left, Mr. Webb second on his left, and at his right an empty seat, while all the others, the men, the girls, the whole staff, seated themselves.

He became aware dimly, through a terrible buzzing in his ears, that Mr. Webb was standing, speaking, saying something that Mr. Mappin felt instinctively must be of great importance, something to which he must pay careful attention. Parts of it he heard, but Mr. Webb's voice, eliding strangely, kept drifting off into nothingness and then returning all at once, like a transatlantic broadcast. Here and there, Mr. Mappin caught a phrase, ". . . and on this wonderful occasion . . . twenty years with Trimble . . . a tribute . . . pleasure to say . . . and as of today, a partner . . ."

Something rang a bell inside Mr. Mappin's head. For a moment the mists drew back and Mr. Mappin listened as Mr. Webb continued. "There only remains one thing to say," Mr. Webb went on. "And that is, George, we hope you'll forgive us for springing it on you in this fashion. But Mr. Trimble thought it would be nice to combine the two occasions and surprise you with a party. And oh, yes, by the way, Mr. Trimble's been busy most of the afternoon writing a speech"—general laughter—"writing a speech about it and forbidding anyone, on pain of death"—more laughter—"on pain of death, to set foot inside his office this afternoon!"

A lot more clapping, and Mr. Webb sat down.

Mr. Mappin sat there, trembling. Trembling and trembling.

Mr. Goshen bent his head and spoke softly. "Look here, George old man, you feeling all right?"

George old man, oh, George old man. How often and how often had Mr. Mappin longed for the sporty camaraderie of *George old man.*

Miss Burke leaned prettily across the table, smiling. "Mr. Trimble must be writing an epic," she said. "I'll go down and tell him we're waiting, shall I?"

"Yes, hurry him up, we can't start without him," said Mr. Webb, and then, turning to Mr. Mappin, he said, "I don't know about *you,* George old man, but I'm hungry!"

Mr. Mappin sat there. He watched the waiter approach and begin to fill the wine glasses. He gazed at the faces all around that swelled to the size of large balloons, then dwindled till they were tiny white blurs. He listened to the voices ringing cheerfully in the paneled chamber. And Mr. Mappin could not have eaten to save his life.

Granny

Ron Goulart

You could hear the old man screaming above the sound of the storm, the shrill cry emanating from a toothless mouth.

Roy McAlbin, medium-sized and slightly overweight, took a cigarette out of his trench-coat pocket and leaned against the veranda rail. The rain was falling heavily, just missing his back. "And what's that, Doctor Caswell?"

"I'm not a doctor, Mr. McAlbin," said the lean, middle-aged Caswell, standing straight on the doormat outside the entrance to the office building.

"Okay, Mr. Caswell, why is that old guy yelling in his cottage over there?"

Caswell, rubbing his left palm on the glass doorknob of his office door, frowned across the wooden veranda. "Mr. McAlbin, I can appreciate the fact that as a journalist, even a free-lance journalist unattached to any actual publication, you are curious. But I can't begin to answer every question which comes to mind."

"You're not a psychologist either, are you?"

"No, I myself am not, though we have both qualified doctors and accredited psychological personnel here at Paxville Woods."

"You've also got one of the best-known primitive painters in America." McAlbin puffed on his filtered cigarette, then rubbed his fingers over his damp, plump cheeks. "A lot of people are interested in Granny Goodwaller, Mr. Caswell."

"Yes, we know that, Mr. McAlbin," replied Caswell. "You keep putting an odd emphasis on the word *got*."

"Well, I'll tell you," he said. "I'm curious as to why Granny Goodwaller moved out of her apartment up the hill in your Paxville Village three months ago. I wonder why she's now here in your Paxville

63

Woods in a cottage nobody can get into. I'd like to interview her."

"Yes, I understood you when you first presented yourself and your case," said Caswell. He stopped rubbing at the glass knob and moved closer to McAlbin. "Paxville is a wonderful place for older people. Up there, beyond the woods, we have houses and apartments where our old-timers, singly or in couples, can live out their autumn years in well-ordered comfort. Down here in the hospital and cottage area we have, obviously, more medically oriented facilities. We have even put in an intensive-care cluster of private bungalows."

"Then Granny is ill?"

Caswell said, "Granny is ninety years old. She is, as you say, a major American artist. We were honored when she decided, nearly five years ago, to come and live in our then just starting Paxville complex. She is very old, Mr. McAlbin. She needs much looking after. She cannot be interviewed."

"But she's still painting?"

"Yes. Granny conserves her strength and continues to be quite productive. If you stop in either of the fine art galleries in Paxville Village or at the Gallery in Brimstone you'll see her latest work on display. The original oils may be a bit costly for someone in the free-lance writing game, but you'll also find many lovely greeting cards and prints."

"I've already seen the paintings in Paxville," said McAlbin. The old man in the brown shingle cottage down the hill had stopped crying. The rain still fell cold and hard. The afternoon was already growing dark. "The display of Granny's paintings at the Marcus Galleries in New York—those are recent, too?"

"Yes," said Caswell. "The Marcus Card Company helped to make Granny famous and she insists they get her best work. Well, I really can't give you much more time, Mr. McAlbin. Thank you for your interest in Granny. I'm going to tell her you called and I'm sure it will bring a sad, sweet smile to her face."

"Where does she work now? In this cottage of hers?" asked McAlbin. He dropped his cigarette butt over the veranda rail onto the short-cropped grass near the porch.

"She sometimes paints at the cottage, yes," said Caswell. "She has, in addition, a large workshop here in our main building."

"Could I see that?"

"It is merely a large room, full of stretched canvas, smelling of paint and turpentine."

"Seeing places where artists work helps me," said McAlbin. "I still intend to do a piece on Granny Goodwaller and her work. Since you won't allow me to visit with her, you can at least let me see where she creates her paintings."

Caswell said, after a sharp sniffing, "Very well. Come around this way." He went striding off along the porch, frowning back. "Don't strew any more cigarettes on the grounds, please."

Fifteen minutes later McAlbin left the place. Under his coat, wrapped in a paint rag, were a palette knife and a teacup he had grabbed in the chill studio while Caswell was lifting down an album of greeting-card proofs. McAlbin fisted his hands into his trench-coat pockets as he walked down the flagstone path toward the parking area. Some two dozen cottages were scattered around the ten acres of Paxville. The grass and shrubs were neat and trim, most of the flowers beginning to fade and brown. McAlbin had come here to Connecticut on a hunch. "I'm right," he said to himself. He got into his car and drove off toward town.

Dry leaves swooped and dipped, clattering against the small leaded windows of the Brimstone Art Gallery. McAlbin put one pale fist into the pocket of his coat and made a sound with his tongue that was a faint echo of the sound the wind and the dead leaves were making. "Nope, nope," he muttered. He was standing toward the back of the big one-room gallery and he'd been going carefully from one Granny Goodwaller painting to another. He was stopped now in front of a bright scene of little girls saddling a pony in a summer field: tiny figures and a stiff-legged dirt-brown pony. "Nope," repeated McAlbin.

"Not at all," said a gentle voice just behind him.

McAlbin turned and noticed a very pretty auburn-haired girl standing there, her face still slightly flushed from the morning wind outside. "Beg pardon?" he said.

"You were looking negative and I wanted to assure you little girls do have ponies that color." Freckles made two dim arcs beneath her bright eyes. "I did, for instance."

"You're reassuring," said McAlbin. "I never had a pony as a boy, but I did have a bicycle. My uncle painted it the same color as that ugly horse."

"You don't seem to care for Granny's work."

"Nope. If this area had to depend on people with my kind of taste, your whole Granny Goodwaller industry would collapse."

"It's not my industry exactly," said the girl. "I'm co-owner of a gift shop near Paxville Village."

"My name, by the way, is Roy McAlbin," he told her. "I'm a free-lance journalist. Who are you?"

"Nan Hendry." She smiled quietly. "You didn't come to this part of Connecticut to see our famous paintings, then?"

"Well, yes. But not exactly to admire them."

Nan touched her cheek with her left hand, tracing the arc the freckles made. "I don't quite understand."

"Look, Nan," he said, "would you be interested in dinner?"

"Yes, that might be nice. Tonight, did you mean?"

McAlbin refilled his glass, set the wine bottle near at hand on the checkered tablecloth. "I like this little inn," he said to Nan, "and this little inn restaurant. There's an almost European feeling about the place." The logs in the nearby fireplace crackled and shifted, and he paused. "Though they shouldn't be serving this New York wine. No, the only good domestic wines come from a few of the lesser-known California vintners."

"You've been to most places?" asked the pretty girl. "To Europe and all of the United States?"

"Sure. One of the great advantages of the free-lance life is travel. I need to pack only my camera and some underwear, plus my portable typewriter. Actually I don't even need that because I can write shorthand and just rent a typewriter someplace or cable in a story. Depends on whom I'm working for."

"Who is it this time?"

"Nobody yet. I'm keeping this one quiet until I get more material. Then I'll hit one of the news weeklies or some picture mag. Sell them the whole package for a flat fee."

"What, exactly, are you investigating? I mean, I don't want to pry into your methods. Still, I am interested."

McAlbin sipped his wine. "That's good, Nan. I'll tell you, you meet a lot of girls, here and overseas, who don't care for what a guy does at all. Any sort of shop talk bores them. Not that they're particularly domestic, either. No, they're just nitwits and not much else. By the time a man is thirty, which is what I just was three weeks ago, society thinks he should be settled down. I can't see any reason to settle down, though, especially with a nitwit."

"Obviously you aren't married."

"Nope. Most women wouldn't put up with the roving pattern of my life," he said. "I've been at this for six years now, almost seven, ever since I got out of the service. I have this, and I'm telling you because you seem to be an exceptional sort of girl and one who understands, this real drive toward finding the truth. Finding the truth, digging it out. Sometimes the truth will hurt people, sometimes even destroy them. You can't let that worry you. The truth is like a torch, sort of, and you have to keep it burning."

"Yes, I can understand that, Roy." Nan touched at her cheek, smiled. "A lot of men don't have the kind of courage you do. It reminds me of my father."

McAlbin laughed. "Really? Not of my father. Well, I can't really say. My parents never amounted to much. Now, I'm more or less an orphan anyhow."

"I'm sorry."

"It's just the truth. Nothing to be sorry over."

Nan said, "I really am interested in your work, Roy. If you want to talk about this current project of yours, I'd love to listen. Sometimes your kind of work can be pretty lonely, I imagine."

"Well," he said, "this is no marriage scandal or crime-syndicate stuff. It's not even political. I think, however, there is a nice little yarn here and I'm going to follow through. See, I was out in San Francisco a couple weeks back and I saw a show of new paintings by your Granny Goodwaller. I was only passing through Frisco, not even in the mood to look up the friends I have there. For all they know, I'm still over in the Pacific or some such place. Anyway, Nan, I got to looking at those paintings and something struck me. I don't know why nobody else has noticed. Probably because Granny Goodwaller occupies a rather peculiar place in American art; not a real artist and yet not merely a commercial painter. A primitive, yes, but a very successful one. Very rich."

"What," asked Nan, bending toward him, "did you notice?"

"The paintings are fake," said McAlbin.

Nan sat up and frowned. "You mean somebody out there is selling forged Granny Goodwaller paintings?"

"That was the first thing I thought," said McAlbin. "So I, carefully and quite subtly, asked the gallery people some questions. This was a very sedate art setup on Post Street and I found out they got their paintings from Paxville, Connecticut, from the gallery up in the retirement town that's been handling Granny's output for several years."

"But, Roy," said the lovely girl, "what would that mean?"

"If I'm right," he answered, "and I know enough about painting to be fairly sure I am, it means something odd is going on in Paxville. See, Nan, I've covered a couple of art-fraud cases before, though those involved fake old masters. I'm certain the dozen paintings I saw out in Frisco are fakes. So are most of them on display in Paxville and so are ten of the fifteen in the Brimstone Gallery where we met this morning."

Nan inhaled sharply. "What exactly do you think is going on, Roy?"

"It might just be Granny, being in her nineties, can't crank that stuff out as fast as she used to and has an assistant to help fill the orders." He leaned back, comfortable, and the firelight glowed on his plump face. "However, Nan, I came here because a nice counternotion occurred to me. I'm checking it out."

"Your theory is what?"

"The whole Paxville setup is private," said McAlbin. "I looked it up. I also found out Granny Goodwaller has no close relatives. Suppose the old girl had a stroke and couldn't paint anymore?" He rubbed his wine glass across his chin. "Or suppose, which is what really intrigues me, suppose the grand old lady of the American primitives had up and died. It might be to the advantage of the people around Paxville to keep her alive."

"That's dreadful," said the girl. "Why would anyone pretend Granny was alive if she was dead?"

"As long as Granny paintings keep coming off the assembly line a lot of money keeps coming into Paxville. Caswell and a couple of his buddies are partners in a company that handles the selling of Granny's work, as well as the merchandising of it. You know, they license the use of her paintings for greeting cards and calendars."

"Yes, I sell them in my gift shop." Nan let her slender hands rest on the tabletop. She shook her head. "I suppose what you suggest is remotely possible, Roy. Still, it seems like an awful thing for someone to do. What do the other people with whom you've discussed your theory say?"

"I'm not the confiding type," said McAlbin softly. "Not usually."

"Well, I appreciate your confiding in me. It's a pretty unsettling theory you have."

"Not only a theory," he said. "When I was out at Paxville a couple days ago I swiped a palette knife and a teacup that are supposed to belong to Granny. After I finish up here I'm going to have the prints checked out in Washington—and there are fingerprints."

"Well," said Nan. "And how much longer will you be here?"

"I still want to get a look at Granny's cottage on the Paxville grounds," said McAlbin. "And since I try to keep an open mind, I'll even try to get a look at Granny herself."

"Maybe I can help out."

"Oh, so?"

She frowned again. "I'll think about it and let you know," she said.

"I've been talking too much about myself anyway," said McAlbin. "Let's shift gears, Nan. Talk about you."

The girl looked down at her hands, biting her lip. Then she smiled across at him. "Very well, Roy . . ."

The next day was dry and clear. At ten in the morning Nan called him. McAlbin had been sitting on the edge of his bed in his room at the Brimstone Inn, making notes in one of the dime-store tablets he liked to use.

"I think I can help you," the girl said.

McAlbin doodled her name in the margin of the pad. "With what, Nan? I don't want you getting yourself tangled in this Paxville business."

"What you told me last night was very unsettling. I just don't like to see something like that going on here," she said. "Okay, you say you're not absolutely sure. I think you should make sure. I may be able to help you find out more."

"I appreciate that, Nan. Still, there are risks . . ."

"Don't let me foul up your plans, Roy. But I have an idea."

"Go ahead, tell me."

She said, "I know one of the attendants at Paxville Woods. No matter what you may think is going on out there, Ben is an honest man."

"Ben, okay. So?"

"You said you wanted to get inside, to get a look at the cottage where Granny lives."

"I sure do. You mean this friend of yours, honest Ben, can get me inside the place?"

"I can ask him. I wanted to make sure, first, it was okay with you." McAlbin nodded into the phone mouthpiece. "Sounds not bad."

"I'll get in touch with Ben and try to set up something for tonight or some night soon," the girl said in her soft, gentle voice. "If you don't mind, I'd like to drive you there."

"I'm not sure that'd be safe for you."

"Roy, I want to help. Please."

He nodded again. "Okay, Nan."

"I'll call you back soon as I know something."

"Thanks, Nan. I appreciate you."

She called him back in a little under two hours.

That evening, McAlbin stood in the thickening twilight and listened. There was a chill quiet all around. He reached out and touched the wire gate in the big hurricane fence. Then, very slowly, he turned the handle. The gate opened and no alarm sounded. He gave a coughing sigh. Nan's friend had done as promised. McAlbin eased through the gate and closed it after him. There was woodland here, stiff straight trees, crisp mounds of fallen leaves. He walked slowly downhill, moving as silently as he could.

After a few descending minutes he could see the lights of the cottages he wanted. Three of the six in this sector had lights on. McAlbin halted, still in the woods, and took a penciled drawing from his coat pocket. Granny's cottage was the third from the left. He lifted his glance from the tablet page to the view of the cottages. There were windows glowing in the cottage that was hers. He folded the paper away, slid out his miniature camera.

There were no attendants near the cottage. He stayed in the shadows of the trees and made sure. Then, while night began to drop slowly down around him, McAlbin advanced across the grounds. He bent low when he was near Granny's and approached parallel to the hedge around the cottage. He eased very carefully toward the lighted window.

A radio was playing old music inside. A rocking chair rocked. McAlbin adjusted his camera and walked to the window. He stretched to his full height and was able to see inside. There was an easel in the knotty-pine room. A half-finished painting of tiny people on a sleigh ride showed on the easel. McAlbin saw a gray head and a wool-shawled back. A hand was weakly brushing muddy brown paint onto the flanks of a tiny horse. He clicked a picture.

The hand placed the brush aside and then lifted off the gray wig. Caswell stood up, cast off the shawl and pointed a pistol straight at the window.

McAlbin spun, ran—in a new direction, not the same way he'd come.

The last of the daylight sank away, thin blue darkness filled the forest. The trees grew black. There was a quiet, ominous clarity all around him. McAlbin pressed his spread-fingered hands hard against his soft chest, chewed in the chill air through his mouth. He tried to breathe silently, but he had developed a dry wheeze while climbing slowly uphill through the wood.

He listened for pursuit and heard none. A thin, chill mist was moving through the sharp, bare trees. He continued to work his way upward. Leaves crackled at every careful step, noise of his progress went rippling down through the dry brush. McAlbin stopped again, listening hard. He heard no sounds but his own. Pain was growing up through his ribs, squeezing at his lungs. He sighed and resumed his climb.

McAlbin couldn't keep track of the trees. He got the impression they were changing their positions. Halting, he squinted into the cold darkness. He gave a quick, startled inhalation. There was someone standing, still and waiting, at the crest of the hill; someone waiting patiently, dark and straight as one of the dead trees. McAlbin was certain there was a man up there, to his left; one of the attendants probably, a big, wide man, anticipating him. McAlbin crouched, dropped to his hands and knees and began working slowly away from the waiting figure. He kept low, scuffing his palms and his soft knees on thorns, scraps of fallen tree limbs. He raised himself up long minutes later, scanning, then quickly dropped. There was someone else up there on the horizon waiting for him; another man, standing with arms folded and feet wide apart, blurred by the growing mist, but certainly there.

He began to crawl in a new direction, even more quietly, slowly. He tried to make no sound, to move and breathe without attracting any attention. The mist thickened and the chill of the deepening night increased. McAlbin looked at his watch. He found he'd been in the forest only thirteen minutes. He sighed again, moved ahead.

A long time later, about eleven minutes of actual time, he came to the edge of the wood and saw below him the small clearing off the roadway where Nan had parked the car. She was still there, her car shadowed by the low, spiky branches of an evergreen. Not caring about alarms now, McAlbin ran for the wire fence, leaped for a hold and climbed over. No bells rang.

He hit the outside ground and ran for the car. He grabbed the passenger door and jumped in. "Get away from here," he said, and then stopped.

Caswell was behind the wheel, the same small revolver in his right hand. With his left, he reached down and clicked off the car radio. "Trying to catch a weather report. Looks like we may have some snow tomorrow. Feels like it, too, don't you think?"

McAlbin got his breath, gasping. "Where's Nan?"

"One of my associates drove her home."

"You can't get by with all this, Caswell; tracking me like some kind of wild game and kidnapping Nan Hendry. This is suburban Connecticut, not some feudal kingdom."

"She isn't kidnapped, she's in fine shape," said Caswell. "Nan simply happens to be on our side, as are many people. You yourself, Mr. McAlbin, pointed out how many of the residents in our area are dependent on Granny for their living. With one thing and another, the old broad represented roughly a million and a half a year to us. When she died this spring we decided to ignore the fact. Her dreadfully simplistic style is quite easy to imitate. A young artist friend of Nan's paints the Granny pictures for us. No one but you has tumbled to our little operation."

"I made a mistake confiding in Nan, huh?"

"Never confide in anyone you don't have to," replied Caswell. "I wish nearly two dozen people in and around Paxville didn't have to be in on the Granny venture. However, a complex plan often means a large number of participants."

"Granny Goodwaller is already supposed to be ninety. How long can you pretend she's alive?"

"Five more years at least," said Caswell, "which will gross us well over five million dollars; perhaps even more if a couple of merchandising plans now in the works materialize. Then we can afford to let her die. Greed would enter in if we tried to keep this up forever, suspicion might grow. Fortunately Granny, much like yourself, has no immediate relatives, no one to cause us trouble. She, too, was an independent free-lance person."

"I'm not completely without connections. What are you thinking of doing?"

"I know you have a stubborn, often cruel, dedication to the truth," said Caswell. "Letting you go, no, that won't work. You can't be bribed, nor trusted to keep quiet. That teacup you got away with upset me, too. My prints may be on it and they are on file in certain places. No, you simply can't be let outside for the time being."

"What kind of arrogant talk is this? You think you can kill me because I found out your game? '

"We're not going to kill you, Mr. McAlbin," said Caswell. "Simply keep you here and out of trouble."

"How do you think you're going to keep me in an old folks' home?"

"Quite simple," said Caswell.

The door behind McAlbin opened and someone put a hand over his mouth and yanked him from the car.

Within a week they had pulled all his teeth, bleached his hair white, roughed his skin, put him in an intensive-care bungalow and fed him drugs. They told him he was a very sick old man—and, for quite a long time, he believed them.

The Landlady

Roald Dahl

Billy Weaver had traveled down from London on the slow afternoon train, with a change at Reading on the way, and by the time he got to Bath it was about nine o'clock in the evening and the moon was coming up out of a clear starry sky over the houses opposite the station entrance. But the air was deadly cold and the wind was like a flat blade of ice on his cheeks.

"Excuse me," he said, "but is there a fairly cheap hotel not too far away from here?"

"Try The Bell and Dragon," the porter answered, pointing down the road. "They might take you in. It's about a quarter of a mile along on the other side."

Billy thanked him and picked up his suitcase and set out to walk the quarter-mile to The Bell and Dragon. He had never been to Bath before. He didn't know anyone who lived there. But Mr. Greenslade at the Head Office in London had told him it was a splendid town. "Find your own lodgings," he had said, "and then go along and report to the branch manager as soon as you've got yourself settled."

Billy was seventeen years old. He was wearing a new navy-blue overcoat, a new brown trilby hat, and a new brown suit, and he was feeling fine. He walked briskly down the street. He was trying to do everything briskly these days. Briskness, he had decided, was *the* one common characteristic of all successful businessmen. The big shots up at Head Office were absolutely fantastically brisk all the time. They were amazing.

There were no shops on this wide street that he was walking along, only a line of tall houses on each side, all of them identical. They had porches and pillars and four or five steps going up to their front doors, and it was obvious that once upon a time they had been very swanky residences. But now, even in the darkness, he could see that the paint was peeling from the woodwork on their doors and windows, and that the handsome white façades were cracked and blotchy from neglect.

Suddenly, in a downstairs window that was brilliantly illuminated by a street lamp not six yards away, Billy caught sight of a printed notice propped up against the glass in one of the upper panes. It said BED AND BREAKFAST. There was a vase of yellow chrysanthemums, tall and beautiful, standing just underneath the notice.

He stopped walking. He moved a bit closer. Green curtains (some sort of velvety material) were hanging down on either side of the window. The chrysanthemums looked wonderful beside them. He went right up and peered through the glass into the room, and the first thing he saw was a bright fire burning in the hearth. On the carpet in front of the fire, a pretty little dachshund was curled up asleep with its nose tucked into its belly. The room itself, so far as he could see in the half-darkness, was filled with pleasant furniture. There was a baby-grand piano and a big sofa and several plump armchairs; and in one corner he spotted a large parrot in a cage. Animals were usually a good sign in a place like this, Billy told himself; and all in all, it looked to him as though it would be a pretty decent house to stay in. Certainly it would be more comfortable than The Bell and Dragon.

On the other hand, a pub would be more congenial than a boardinghouse. There would be beer and darts in the evenings, and lots of people to talk to, and it would probably be a good bit cheaper, too. He had stayed a couple of nights in a pub once before and he had liked it. He had never stayed in any boardinghouses, and, to be perfectly honest, he was a tiny bit frightened of them. The name itself conjured up images of watery cabbage, rapacious landladies, and a powerful smell of kippers in the living room.

After dithering about like this in the cold for two or three minutes, Billy decided that he would walk on and take a look at The Bell and Dragon before making up his mind. He turned to go.

And now a queer thing happened to him. He was in the act of stepping back and turning away from the window when all at once his eye was caught and held in the most peculiar manner by the small notice that was there. BED AND BREAKFAST, it said. BED AND BREAKFAST, BED AND BREAKFAST, BED AND BREAKFAST. Each word was like a large black eye staring at him through the glass, holding him, compelling him, forcing him to stay where he was and not to walk away from that house, and the next thing he knew, he was actually moving across from the window to the front door of the house, climbing the steps that led up to it, and reaching for the bell.

He pressed the bell. Far away in a back room he heard it ringing, and then *at once*—it must have been at once because he hadn't even had time to take his finger from the bell-button—the door swung open and a woman was standing there.

Normally you ring the bell and you have at least a half-minute's wait before the door opens. But this dame was like a jack-in-the-box. He pressed the bell—and out she popped! It made him jump.

She was about forty-five or fifty years old, and the moment she saw him, she gave him a warm welcoming smile.

"*Please* come in," she said pleasantly. She stepped aside, holding the door wide open, and Billy found himself automatically starting forward. The compulsion or, more accurately, the desire to follow after her into that house was extraordinarily strong.

"I saw the notice in the window," he said, holding himself back.

"Yes, I know."

"I was wondering about a room."

"It's *all* ready for you, my dear," she said. She had a round pink face and very gentle blue eyes.

"I was on my way to The Bell and Dragon," Billy told her. "But the notice in your window just happened to catch my eye."

"My dear boy," she said, "why don't you come in out of the cold?"

"How much do you charge?"

"Five and sixpence a night, including breakfast."

It was fantastically cheap. It was less than half of what he had been willing to pay.

"If that is too much," she added, "then perhaps I can reduce it just a tiny bit. Do you desire an egg for breakfast? Eggs are expensive at the moment. It would be sixpence less without the egg."

"Five and sixpence is fine," he answered. "I should like very much to stay here."

"I knew you would. Do come in."

She seemed terribly nice. She looked exactly like the mother of one's best school-friend welcoming one into the house to stay for the Christmas holidays. Billy took off his hat, and stepped over the threshold.

"Just hang it there," she said, "and let me help you with your coat."

There were no other hats or coats in the hall. There were no umbrellas, no walking-sticks—nothing.

"We have it *all* to ourselves," she said, smiling at him over her shoulder as she led the way upstairs. "You see, it isn't very often I have the pleasure of taking a visitor into my little nest."

The old girl is slightly dotty, Billy told himself. But at five and sixpence a night, who gives a damn about that? "I should've thought you'd be simply swamped with applicants," he said politely.

"Oh, I am, my dear, I am, of course I am. But the trouble is that I'm inclined to be just a teeny weeny bit choosy and particular—if you see what I mean."

"Ah, yes."

"But I'm always ready. Everything is always ready day and night in this house just on the off chance that an acceptable young gentleman will come along. And it is such a pleasure, my dear, such a very great pleasure when now and again I open the door and I see someone standing there who is just *exactly* right." She was halfway up the stairs, and she paused with one hand on the stair rail, turning her head and smiling down at him with pale lips. "Like you," she added, and her blue eyes traveled slowly all the way down the length of Billy's body, to his feet, and then up again.

On the second-floor landing she said to him, "This floor is mine."

They climbed up another flight. "And this one is *all* yours," she said. "Here's your room. I do hope you'll like it." She took him into a small but charming front bedroom, switching on the light as she went in.

"The morning sun comes right in the window, Mr. Perkins. It *is* Mr. Perkins, isn't it?"

"No," he said. "It's Weaver."

"Mr. Weaver. How nice. I've put a water bottle between the sheets to air them out, Mr. Weaver. It's such a comfort to have a hot-water bottle in a strange bed with clean sheets, don't you agree? And you may light the gas fire at any time if you feel chilly."

"Thank you," Billy said. "Thank you ever so much." He noticed that the bedspread had been taken off the bed, and that the bed-clothes had been neatly turned back on one side, all ready for someone to get in.

"I'm so glad you appeared," she said, looking earnestly into his face. "I was beginning to get worried."

"That's all right," Billy answered brightly. "You mustn't worry about me." He put his suitcase on the chair and started to open it.

"And what about supper, my dear? Did you manage to get anything to eat before you came here?"

"I'm not a bit hungry, thank you," he said. "I think I'll just go to bed as soon as possible because tomorrow I've got to get up rather early and report to the office."

"Very well, then. I'll leave you now so that you can unpack. But before you go to bed, would you be kind enough to pop into the sitting room on the ground floor and sign the book? Everyone has to do that because it's the law of the land, and we don't want to go breaking any laws at *this* stage in the proceedings, do we?" She gave him a little wave of the hand and went quickly out of the room and closed the door.

Now, the fact that his landlady appeared to be slightly off her rocker didn't worry Billy in the least. After all, she not only was harmless—there was no question about that—but she was also quite obviously a kind and generous soul. He guessed that she had probably lost a son in the war, or something like that, and had never gotten over it.

So a few minutes later, after unpacking his suitcase and washing his hands, he trotted downstairs to the ground floor and entered the living room. His landlady wasn't there, but the fire was glowing in the hearth, and the little dachshund was still sleeping soundly in front of it. The room was wonderfully warm and cozy. I'm a lucky fellow, he thought, rubbing his hands. This is a bit of all right.

He found the guest book lying open on the piano, so he took out his pen and wrote down his name and address. There were only two other entries above his on the page, and as one always does with guest books, he started to read them. One was a Christopher Mulholland from Cardiff. The other was Gregory W. Temple from Bristol.

That's funny, he thought suddenly. Christopher Mulholland. It rings a bell.

Now, where on earth had he heard that rather unusual name before?

Was it a boy at school? No. Was it one of his sister's numerous

young men, perhaps, or a friend of his father's? No, no, it wasn't any
of those. He glanced down again at the book.

Christopher Mulholland   231 Cathedral Road, Cardiff

Gregory W. Temple   27 Sycamore Drive, Bristol

As a matter of fact, now he came to think of it, he wasn't at all sure
that the second name didn't have almost as much of a familiar ring
about it as the first.

"Gregory Temple?" he said aloud, searching his memory. "Christopher Mulholland? . . ."

"Such charming boys," a voice behind him answered, and he
turned and saw his landlady sailing into the room with a large silver
tea tray in her hands. She was holding it well out in front of her, and
rather high up, as though the tray were a pair of reins on a frisky
horse.

"They sound somehow familiar," he said.

"They do? How interesting."

"I'm almost positive I've heard those names before somewhere.
Isn't that odd? Maybe it was in the newspapers. They weren't famous in any way, were they? I mean famous cricketers or footballers
or something like that?"

"Famous," she said, setting the tea tray down on the low table in
front of the sofa. "Oh no, I don't think they were famous. But they
were incredibly handsome, both of them, I can promise you that.
They were tall and young and handsome, my dear, just exactly like
you."

Once more, Billy glanced down at the book. "Look here," he said,
noticing the dates. "This last entry is over two years old."

"It is?"

"Yes, indeed. And Christopher Mulholland's is nearly a year before that—more than *three years* ago."

"Dear me," she said, shaking her head and heaving a dainty little
sigh. "I would never have thought it. How time does fly away from us
all, doesn't it, Mr. Wilkins?"

"It's Weaver," Billy said. "W-e-a-v-e-r."

"Oh, of course it is!" she cried, sitting down on the sofa. "How
silly of me. I do apologize. In one ear and out the other, that's me,
Mr. Weaver."

"You know something?" Billy said. "Something that's really quite extraordinary about all this?"

"No, dear, I don't."

"Well, you see, both of these names—Mulholland and Temple—I not only seem to remember each one of them separately, so to speak, but somehow or other, in some peculiar way, they both appear to be sort of connected together as well. As though they were both famous for the same sort of thing, if you see what I mean—like . . . well . . . like Dempsey and Tunney, for example, or Churchill and Roosevelt."

"How amusing," she said. "But come over here now, dear, and sit down beside me on the sofa and I'll give you a nice cup of tea and a ginger biscuit before you go to bed."

"You really shouldn't bother," Billy said. "I didn't mean you to do anything like that." He stood by the piano, watching her as she fussed about with the cups and saucers. He noticed that she had small, white, quickly moving hands, and red fingernails.

"I'm almost positive it was in the newspapers I saw them," Billy said. "I'll think of it in a second. I'm sure I will."

There is nothing more tantalizing than a thing like this that lingers just outside the borders of one's memory. He hated to give up.

"Now wait a minute," he said. "Wait just a minute. Mulholland . . . Christopher Mulholland . . . wasn't *that* the name of the Eton schoolboy who was on a walking tour through the West Country, and then all of a sudden . . ."

"Milk?" she said. "And sugar?"

"Yes, please. And then all of a sudden . . ."

"Eton schoolboy?" she said. "Oh no, my dear, that can't possibly be right because *my* Mr. Mulholland was certainly not an Eton schoolboy when he came to me. He was a Cambridge undergraduate. Come over here now and sit next to me and warm yourself in front of this lovely fire. Come on. Your tea's all ready for you." She patted the empty place beside her on the sofa, and she sat there smiling at Billy and waiting for him to come over.

He crossed the room slowly, and sat down on the edge of the sofa. She placed his teacup on the table in front of him.

"*There* we are," she said. "How nice and cozy this is, isn't it?"

Billy started sipping his tea. She did the same. For half a minute or so, neither of them spoke. But Billy knew that she was looking at him. Her body was half turned toward him, and he could feel her eyes resting on his face, watching him over the rim of her teacup. Now and again, he caught a whiff of a peculiar smell that seemed to emanate directly from her person. It was not in the least unpleasant, and it reminded him—well, he wasn't quite sure what it reminded him of. Pickled walnuts? New leather? Or was it the corridors of a hospital?

At length, she said, "Mr. Mulholland was a great one for his tea. Never in my life have I seen anyone drink as much tea as dear, sweet Mr. Mulholland."

"I suppose he left fairly recently," Billy said. He was still puzzling his head about the two names. He was positive now that he had seen them in the newspapers—in the headlines.

"Left?" she said, arching her brows. "But my dear boy, he never left. He's still here. Mr. Temple is also here. They're on the fourth floor, both of them together."

Billy set his cup down slowly on the table and stared at his landlady. She smiled back at him, and then she put out one of her white hands and patted him comfortingly on the knee. "How old are you, my dear?" she asked.

"Seventeen."

"Seventeen!" she cried. "Oh, it's the perfect age! Mr. Mulholland was also seventeen. But I think he was a trifle shorter than you are; in fact I'm sure he was, and his teeth weren't *quite* so white. You have the most beautiful teeth, Mr. Weaver, did you know that?"

"They're not as good as they look," Billy said. "They've got simply masses of fillings in them at the back."

"Mr. Temple, of course, was a little older," she said, ignoring his remark. "He was actually twenty-eight. And yet I never would have guessed it if he hadn't told me, never in my whole life. There wasn't a *blemish* on his body."

"A what?" Billy said.

"His skin was *just* like a baby's."

There was a pause. Billy picked up his teacup and took another sip of his tea, then he set it down again gently in its saucer. He waited for her to say something else, but she seemed to have lapsed into another of her silences. He sat there staring straight ahead of him into the far corner of the room, biting his lower lip.

"That parrot," he said at last. "You know something? It had me completely fooled when I first saw it through the window. I could have sworn it was alive."

"Alas, no longer."

"It's most terribly clever the way it's been done," he said. "It doesn't look in the least bit dead. Who did it?"

"I did."

"*You* did?"

"Of course," she said. "And have you met my little Basil as well?" She nodded toward the dachshund curled up so comfortably in front of the fire. Billy looked at it. And suddenly, he realized that this animal had all the time been just as silent and motionless as the parrot. He put out a hand and touched it gently on the top of its back. The back was hard and cold, and when he pushed the hair to one side with his fingers, he could see the skin underneath, grayish-black and dry and perfectly preserved.

"Good gracious me," he said. "How absolutely fascinating." He turned away from the dog and stared with deep admiration at the little woman beside him on the sofa. "It must be most awfully difficult to do a thing like that."

"Not in the least," she said. "I stuff *all* my little pets myself when they pass away. Will you have another cup of tea?"

"No, thank you," Billy said. The tea tasted faintly of bitter almonds, and he didn't much care for it.

"You did sign the book, didn't you?"

"Oh, yes."

"That's good. Because later on, if I happen to forget what you were called, then I could always come down here and look it up. I still do that almost every day with Mr. Mulholland and Mr. . . . Mr. . . ."

"Temple," Billy said. "Gregory Temple. Excuse my asking, but haven't there been *any* other guests here except them in the last two or three years?"

Holding her teacup high in one hand, inclining her head slightly to the left, she looked up at him out of the corners of her eyes and gave him another gentle little smile.

"No, my dear," she said. "Only you."

Three Ways to Rob a Bank

Harold R. Daniels

The manuscript was neatly typed. The cover letter could have been copied almost word for word from one of those "Be an Author" publications, complete with the *pro forma* "Submitted for publication at your usual rates." Miss Edwina Martin, assistant editor of *Tales of Crime and Detection*, read it first. Two things about it caught her attention. One was the title—"Three Ways to Rob a Bank. Method 1." The other was the author's name. Nathan Waite. Miss Martin, who knew nearly every professional writer of crime fiction in the United States and had had dealings with most of them, didn't recognize the name.

The letter lacked the usual verbosity of the fledgling writer, but a paragraph toward the middle caught her eye. "You may want to change the title because what Rawlings did wasn't really robbery. In fact, it's probably legal. I am now working on a story which I will call 'Three Ways to Rob a Bank. Method 2.' I will send this to you when I finish having it retyped. Method 2 is almost certainly legal. If you want to check Method 1, I suggest that you show this to your own banker."

Rawlings, it developed, was the protagonist in the story. The story itself was crude and redundant; it failed to develop its characters and served almost solely as a vehicle to outline Method 1. The method itself had to do with the extension of credit to holders of checking accounts—one of those deals where the bank urges holders of checking accounts to write checks without having funds to back them. The bank would extend credit. No papers. No notes. (The author's distrust of this form of merchandising emerged clearly in the story.)

Miss Martin's first impulse was to send the story back with a polite letter of rejection. (She never used the heartless printed rejection slip.) But something about the confident presentation of the method bothered her. She clipped a memorandum to the manuscript, scrawled a large question mark on it, and bucked it to the editor. It came back next day with additional scrawling: "This is an awful piece of trash but the plan sounds almost real. Why don't you check it with Frank Wordell?"

Frank Wordell was a vice-president of the bank that served Miss Martin's publisher. She made a luncheon date with him, handed him the letter and the manuscript, and started to proofread some galleys while he looked it over. She glanced up when she heard him suck in his breath. He had turned a delicate shade of greenish white.

"Would it work?" she asked.

"I'm not quite sure," the vice-president said, his voice shaking. "I'd have to get an opinion from some of the people in the Check Credit Department. But I think it would." He hesitated. "Good Lord, this could cost us millions. Listen—you weren't thinking of publishing this, were you? I mean, if it got into the hands of the public—"

Miss Martin, who had no great admiration for the banking mentality, was noncommittal. "It needs work," she said. "We haven't made a decision."

The banker pushed his plate away. "And he says he's got another one. His Method Two. If it's anything like this it could ruin the entire banking business." A thought came to him. "He calls this 'Three Ways to Rob a Bank.' That means there must be a Method Three. This is terrible! No, no, we can't let you publish this and we must see this man at once."

This was an unfortunate approach to use with Edwina Martin who reached out her hand for the letter and manuscript. "That is our decision to make," she told him coldly. It was only after he had pleaded the potential destruction of the country's economy that she let him take the papers back to the bank. He was so upset that he neglected to pay the luncheon check.

He called her several hours later. "We've held an emergency

meeting," he told her. "The Check Credit people think that Method One *would* work. It might also be legal but even if it isn't it would cost us millions in lawsuits. Listen, Miss Martin, we want you to buy the story and assign the copyright to us. Would that protect us against him selling the story to someone else?"

"In its present form," she told him. "But there would be nothing to prevent him from writing another story using the same method." Remembering his failure to pay the luncheon check, she was not inclined to be especially cooperative. "And we don't buy material that we don't intend to publish."

But after an emergency confrontation between a committee of the City Banking Association, called into extraordinary session, and the publisher, it was decided to buy Nathan Waite's story and to lock the manuscript in the deepest vault of the biggest bank. In the interest of the national economy.

"Economy," Miss Martin decided, was an appropriate word. During the confrontation a Saurian old capitalist with a personal worth in the tens of millions brought up the subject of payment to Nathan Waite. "I suppose we must buy it," he grumbled. "What do you pay for stories of this type?"

Miss Martin, knowing the author had never been published and hence had no "name" value, suggested a figure. "Of course," she said, "since it will never be published there is no chance of foreign income or anthology fees, let alone possible movie or TV rights." (The Saurian visibly shuddered.) "So I think it would be only fair to give the author a little more than the usual figure."

The Saurian protested. "No, no. Couldn't think of it. After all, we won't ever get our money back. And we'll have to buy Method Two and Method Three. Think of that. Besides, we've still got to figure out a way to keep him from writing other stories using the same methods. The usual figure will have to do. No extras."

Since there were thirty banks in the Association and since the assessment for each would be less than ten dollars per story, Miss Martin failed to generate any deep concern for the Saurian.

That same day Miss Martin forwarded a check and a letter to Nathan Waite. The letter explained that at this time no publication date could be scheduled but that the editor was very anxious to see the stories explaining the second and third ways to rob a bank. She signed the letter with distaste. To a virgin author, she knew, the check was insignificant compared with the glory of publication. Publication that was never to be.

A week later a letter and the manuscript for "Three Ways to Rob a Bank. Method 2" arrived. The story was a disaster but again the method sounded convincing. This time it involved magnetic ink and data processing. By prearrangement Miss Martin brought it to Frank Wordell's office. He read it rapidly and shivered. "The man's a genius," he muttered. "Of course, he's had a lot of background in the field—"

"What was that? How would you know about his background?" Edwina asked.

He said in an offhand manner, "Oh, we've had him thoroughly checked out, of course. Had one of the best detective agencies in the business investigate him—ever since you showed me that first letter. Couldn't get a thing on him."

Miss Martin's voice was ominously flat. "Do you mean to tell me that you had Mr. Waite *investigated*—a man you only learned of through his correspondence with us?"

"Of course." Wordell sounded faintly surprised. "A man that has dangerous knowledge like he has. Couldn't just trust to luck that he wouldn't do something with it besides write stories. Oh, no, couldn't let it drop. He worked in a bank for years and years, you know. Small town in Connecticut. They let him go a year ago. Had to make room for the president's nephew. Gave him a pension though. Ten percent of his salary."

"Years and years, you said. How many years?"

"Oh, I don't remember. Have to look at the report. Twenty-five, I think."

"Then naturally he wouldn't hold any resentment over being let go," she said dryly. She put out her hand. "Let me see his letter again."

The letter that had accompanied the second manuscript had cordially thanked the publisher for accepting the first story and for the check. One paragraph said, "I assume you checked Method 1 with your banker as I suggested. I hope you'll show him Method 2 also, just to be sure it would work. As I said in my first letter, it's almost certainly legal."

Miss Martin asked, "Is it legal?"

"Is what legal?"

"Method Two. The one you just read about."

"Put it this way. It isn't illegal. To make it illegal, every bank using data processing would have to make some major changes in its forms and procedures. It would take months and in the meantime it could cost us even more millions than Method One. This is a terrible thing, Miss Martin—a terrible thing."

Method 2 caused panic in the chambers of the City Banking Association. There was general agreement that the second story must also be bought immediately and sequestered forever. There was also general agreement that since Method 3 might be potentially even more catastrophic, there could be no more waiting for more stories from Mr. Waite. (Miss Martin, who was present, asked if the price of the second story could be raised in view of the fact that Mr. Waite was now, having received one check, a professional author. Saurian pointed out that Waite hadn't actually been published, so the extra expense was not justified.)

A plan was adopted. Miss Martin was to invite Mr. Waite to come up from Connecticut, ostensibly for an author-editor chat. Actually he would be brought before a committee chosen by the City Banking Association. "We'll have our lawyers there," Saurian said. "We'll put the fear of the Lord into him. Make him tell us about that Method Three. Pay him the price of another story if we have to. Then we'll work out some way to shut him up."

With this plan Miss Martin and her fellow editors and her publisher went along most reluctantly. She almost wished that she had simply rejected Nathan Waite's first submission. Most particularly she resented the attitude of the bankers. In their view, Nathan Waite was nothing more than a common criminal.

She called Nathan Waite at his Connecticut home and invited him to come in. The City Banking Association, she resolved to herself, would pay his expenses, whatever devious steps she might have to take to manage it.

His voice on the phone was surprisingly youthful and had only a suggestion of Yankee twang. "Guess I'm pretty lucky selling two stories one right after the other. I'm sure grateful, Miss Martin. And I'll be happy to come in and see you. I suppose you want to talk about the next one."

Her conscience nipped at her. "Well, yes, Mr. Waite. Methods One and Two were so clever that there's a lot of interest in Method Three."

"You just call me Nate, Miss. Now, one thing about Method Three: there's no question about it being legal. The fact is, it's downright honest. Compared with One and Two, that is. Speaking about One and Two, did you check them with your banker? I figured you must have shown him Method One before you bought the story. I was just wondering if he was impressed by Method Two."

She said faintly, "Oh, he was impressed all right."

"Then I guess he'll be really interested in Method Three."

They concluded arrangements for his visit in two days and hung up.

He showed up at Miss Martin's office precisely on time—a small man in his fifties with glistening white hair combed in an old-fashioned part on one side. His face was tanned and made an effective backdrop for his sharp blue eyes. He bowed with a charming courtliness that made Miss Martin feel even more of a Judas. She came from behind her desk. "Mr. Waite—" she began.

"Nate."

"All right. Nate. I'm disgusted with this whole arrangement and I don't know how we let ourselves be talked into it. Nate, we didn't buy your stories to publish them. To be honest—and it's about time —the stories are awful. We bought them because the bank—the banks, I should say—asked us to. They're afraid if the stories were published, people would start actually using your methods."

He frowned. "Awful, you say. I'm disappointed to hear that. I thought the one about Method Two wasn't that bad."

She put her hand on his arm in a gesture of sympathy and looked up to see that he was grinning. "Of course they were awful," he said. "I deliberately wrote them that way. I'll bet it was almost as hard as writing good stuff. So the banks felt the methods would work, eh? I'm not surprised. I put a lot of thought into them."

"They're even more interested in Method Three," she told him. "They want to meet you this afternoon and discuss buying your next story. Actually, they want to pay you *not* to write it. Or write anything else," she added.

"It won't be any great loss to the literary world. Who will we be meeting? The City Banking Association? An old fellow who looks like a crocodile?"

Miss Edwina Martin, with the feel for a plot developed after reading thousands of detective stories, stepped back and looked at him. "You know all about this," she accused him.

He shook his head. "Not all about it. But I sort of planned it. And I felt it was working out the way I planned when they put a detective agency to work investigating me."

"They had no business doing that," she said angrily. "I want you to know that we had nothing to do with it. We didn't even know about it until afterwards. And I'm not going to the meeting with you. I wash my hands of the whole business. Let them buy your next story themselves."

"I want you to come," he said. "You just might enjoy it."

She agreed on condition that he hold out for more money than her publisher had ostensibly been paying him. "I sort of planned on charging a bit more," he told her. "I mean, seeing they're that much interested in Method Three."

At lunch he told her something of his banking career and a great deal more about his life in a small Connecticut town. This plain-speaking, simple man, she learned, was an amateur mathematician of considerable reputation. He was an authority on cybernetics and a respected astronomer.

Over coffee some of his personal philosophy emerged. "I wasn't upset when the bank let me go," he said. "Nepotism is always with us. I could have been a tycoon in a big-city bank, I suppose. But I was content to make an adequate living and it gave me time to do the things I really liked to do. I'm basically lazy. My wife died some years after we were married and there wasn't anybody to push me along harder than I wanted to go.

"Besides, there's something special about a small bank in a small town. You know everyone's problems, money and otherwise, and you can break rules now and then to help people out. The banker, in his way, is almost as important as the town doctor." He paused. "It's not like that any more. It's all regimented and computerized and dehu-manized. You don't have a banker in the old sense of the word. You have a financial executive who's more and more just a part of a large corporation, answerable to a board of directors. He has to work by a strict set of rules that don't allow for any of the human factors."

Miss Martin, fascinated, signaled for more coffee.

"Like making out a deposit slip," he went on. "Used to be you walked into the bank and filled out the slip with your name and address and the amount you wanted to deposit. It made a man feel good and it was good for him. 'My name is John Doe and I earned this money and here is where I live and I want you to save this amount of money for me.' And you took it up to the cashier and passed the time of day for a minute."

Nate put sugar in his coffee. "Pretty soon there won't be any cashiers. Right now you can't fill out a deposit slip in most banks. They send you computer input cards with your name and number on them. All you fill in is the date and amount. The money they save on clerical work they spend on feeble-minded TV advertising. It was a TV ad for a bank that inspired me to write those stories."

Miss Martin smiled. "Nate, you used us." The smile faded. "But even if you hold them up for the Method Three story, it won't hurt anything but their feelings. The money won't come out of their pockets and even several thousands of dollars wouldn't mean anything to them."

He said softly, "The important thing is to make them realize that any mechanical system that man can devise, man can beat. If I can make them realize that the human element can't be discarded, I'll be satisfied. Now then, I suppose we should be getting along to the meeting."

Miss Martin, who had felt concern for Nathan Waite, felt suddenly confident. Nate could emerge as a match for a dozen Saurians.

A committee of twelve members of the City Banking Association, headed by the Saurian, and flanked by a dozen lawyers, awaited them. Nathan Waite nodded as he entered the committee room. The Saurian said, "You're Waite?"

Nate said quietly, "Mr. Waite."

A young lawyer in an impeccable gray suit spoke out. "Those stories that you wrote and that we paid for. You realize that your so-called methods are illegal?"

"Son, I helped write the banking laws for my state and I do an odd job now and then for the Federal Reserve Board. I'd be happy to talk banking law with you."

An older lawyer said sharply, "Shut up, Andy." He turned to Nate. "Mr. Waite, we don't know if your first two methods are criminal or not. We do know it could cost a great deal of money and trouble to conduct a test case and in the meantime, if either Method One or Two got into the hands of the public it would cause incalculable harm and loss. We'd like some assurance that this won't happen."

"You bought the stories describing the first two methods. I'm generally considered an honorable man. As Miss Martin here might put it, I won't use the same plots again."

Gray Suit said cynically, "Not this week, maybe. How about next week? You think you've got us over a barrel."

The older lawyers said furiously, "I told you to shut up, Andy," and turned to Nate again. "I'm Peter Hart," he said, "I apologize for my colleague. I accept the fact that you are an honorable man, Mr. Waite."

Saurian interrupted. "Never mind all that. What about Method Three—the third way to rob a bank. Is it as sneaky as the first two?"

Nate said mildly, "As I told Miss Martin, 'rob' is a misnomer. Methods One and Two are unethical, perhaps illegal, methods for getting money from a bank. Method Three is legal beyond the shadow of a doubt. You have my word for that."

Twelve bankers and twelve lawyers began talking simultaneously. Saurian quieted the furor with a lifted hand. "And you mean it will work just as well as the first two methods?"

"I'm positive of it."

"Then we'll buy it. Same price as the first two stories and you won't even have to write it. Just tell us what Method Three is. And we'll give you $500 for your promise never to write another story." Saurian sank back, overwhelmed by his own generosity. Peter Hart looked disgusted.

Nathan Waite shook his head. "I've got a piece of paper here," he said. "It was drawn up by the best contract lawyer in my state. Good friend of mine. I'll be glad to let Mr. Hart look it over. What it calls for is that your association pay me $25,000 a year for the rest of my life and that payments be made thereafter in perpetuity to various charitable organizations to be named in my will."

Bedlam broke loose. Miss Martin felt like cheering and she caught a smile of admiration on Peter Hart's face.

Nate waited patiently for the commotion to die down. When he could be heard he said, "That's too much money to pay for just a story. So, as the contract specifies, I'll serve as consultant to the City

Banking Association—call it Consultant in Human Relations. That's a nice-sounding title. Being a consultant, of course, I'll be too busy to write any more stories. That's in the contract too."

Gray Suit was on his feet, yelling for attention. "What about Method Three? Is that explained in the contract? We've got to know about Method Three!"

Nate nodded. "I'll tell you about it as soon as the contract is signed."

Peter Hart held up his hand for quiet. "If you'll wait in the anteroom, Mr. Waite, we'd like to discuss the contract among ourselves."

Nate waited with Miss Martin. "You were tremendous," she said. "Do you think they'll agree?"

"I'm sure they will. They might argue about Clause Seven—gives me the right to approve or disapprove of all TV bank commercials." His eyes twinkled. "But they're so scared of Method Three I think they'll agree to even that."

Five minutes later Peter Hart called them back to face a subdued group of committee members. "We have decided that the Association badly needs a Consultant in Human Relations," he said. "Mr. Graves"—he nodded toward a deflated Saurian—"and myself have signed in behalf of the City Banking Association. By the way, the contract is beautifully drafted—there's no possibility of a legal loophole. You have only to sign it yourself."

Gray Suit was on his feet again. "Wait a minute," he shouted. "He still hasn't told us about Method Three."

Nate reached for the contract. "Oh, yes," he murmured, after he had signed it. " 'Three Ways to Rob a Bank.' Method Three. Well, it's really quite simple. *This* is Method Three."

No Loose Ends

Miriam Allen deFord

The two men came into the big house silently, by the back door where neighbors could not see them. They had no key to the front door, and nobody would have opened it if they had rung the bell.

"All right," Ferguson said. "We stopped and had a drink or two. Is it any of your—"

Girdner looked at him coldly.

"It's very much my business. Do it once more and the deal's off. I'll find someone else. Go to your room, both of you."

She was due any minute.

She was late, as usual. Girdner grimaced. She'd be late for her own funeral.

As well as for her husband's.

It was almost 1 A.M. when he heard the car drive up. That was the one dangerous moment.

It was a dark moonless night; he had thought of everything, as he always did. He did not turn on the porch light, just opened the door softly to let her in. Then he himself drove her car to the side of the house, where the bushes were thick. To have directed her where to leave it would have meant an argument. He was soon back and shut the door behind him.

She was standing in the hall, waiting. He did not ask her into the living room.

"Is everything ready?" she asked in that arrogant tone of hers.

"Is everything ready with *you*?" he retorted. When it came to arrogance he could beat her hands down.

She smiled. "You mean the money? I brought it—half now and half—afterwards."

Girdner swallowed his anger.

95

"That was not the arrangement, madam. You are buying something, I am selling it. If you did not know I possessed what you want and could guarantee delivery, you would not have come to me in the first place. I must pay off my men tomorrow morning. Pay me what is due and that's the end of it."

She shook her head stubbornly. Girdner clenched his fists.

"What are you afraid of?" he said. "Blackmail? I am a tradesman. When my merchandise is sold I am no longer concerned with the customer."

"Not you—the men you've hired."

"That is the exact word—I hired them. I have hired them before and shall undoubtedly hire them again, or others like them. They are technicians—specialists. They have no interest except in doing their job and getting paid for it.

"Besides, please remember that in both my case and theirs, any future dissatisfaction would inevitably involve you. Neither of us could accuse the other without that. It protects us both—or all of us, if you prefer."

Reluctantly she opened her alligator-skin bag. He counted the currency carefully, inspecting the bills for number sequence and ratio of denominations. He laid the pile casually on the hall table, then reopened the door.

"Good night, madam, and goodbye. Don't turn on your car lights until you reach the highway." He smiled thinly. "After tomorrow your dreams will come true. Congratulations."

He closed and bolted the door after her, listened until he heard the car drive away, picked up the pile of notes, turned out the hall lamp, and climbed the stairs.

He went straight to bed and slept soundly for eight hours.

Dunlap, the deaf-mute whom Girdner had rescued from the slums years before, and who served him with slavish loyalty, gave Coates and Ferguson their breakfast in the kitchen. Girdner had his on a tray in his bedroom. When he had eaten, bathed, shaved, and dressed he came down to his study and rang for the two men to join him.

He looked them over with a critical eye: Coates, the larger one, was calm and taciturn as always, but Ferguson looked jittery and hung over. Girdner made a mental note to replace him on the next contract. He would do today, though; he was there only as an assistant to Coates, and Coates could be depended on to follow orders and handle things competently, as long as his pay was safely in his pocket.

There was plenty of time: James Wardle Blakeney never showed up in his office before 11:30 A.M.

"You know what to do," Girdner said crisply. "Any questions?"

Ferguson fidgeted. "Just the same as the Sanchez case, ain't it?"

"Utterly unlike the Sanchez case," Girdner snapped. "That was a straight snatch and the outcome was accidental. This time we're being paid to see that there *is* an accident." Ferguson had the bad taste to snicker. Yes, he must go, Girdner decided, and of course that meant he must be eliminated. How could a man of his experience deteriorate so? Coates, Girdner noticed, was frowning; he must be thinking the same thing.

"Besides," Girdner added, "you ought to have better sense than to mention old business."

"Oh, sure, sure," said Ferguson nervously. I wonder, Girdner thought, if this is because he let himself get married? Marriage ruined a good man in their line of work. Very deliberately he caught Coates's eye, and, out of Ferguson's sight-range, put several more bills on one of the two piles he had placed on the desk. Coates nodded imperceptibly.

"Here's your money," Girdner said. "Count it and then start out. You know the schedule and you've got your plane tickets. Everything okay?"

"Oh, sure, sure," Ferguson said again, stuffing his bills in a pocket without looking at them. Coates counted his carefully, nodded again, and put the money in his wallet. Goodbye, Ferguson, thought Girdner; he'd be joining James Wardle Blakeney before the day was over.

The two left by the back door. Girdner listened till he heard it close and heard Dunlap slip the bolt. Then, his worries over, he leaned back in his chair and lighted his first cigar of the day. Another good business deal taken care of. I think, he meditated, I'll give myself a rest—maybe make a trip somewhere before I take on another job. No sense in being greedy.

James Wardle Blakeney, if he had known it, had several traits in common with Augustus Girdner: he was aloof, proud, independent, stubborn, and punctual. He also had a number of traits quite unlike Girdner's, but they were of no importance at the moment.

For the sake of keeping in trim—a matter of vanity for a forty-four-year-old man with a twenty-six-year-old wife—whenever he was in town he made a point of walking the mile and a half from his townhouse to his office suite, no matter what the weather was, short of a hurricane or blizzard. He always took the same route, walking fast, paying no attention to his surroundings, his mind on the problems awaiting him.

The big problem today was the Metropolitan merger. Should he or should he not use that new gadget during the impending luncheon conference? Was it ethical? Could the beneficial results of its use outweigh its dubious propriety? Newnham, he reflected, was a slippery customer; he would undoubtedly have used it if he had been the one to acquire it. Yes, he decided, he would. He patted his breast pocket. Amazing, what technology could accomplish nowadays!

At which moment, to his annoyance, he was accosted by a man walking in the opposite direction. It annoyed him especially because he did not recognize the dapper, smiling little man who stood before him, his hand expectantly held out to be shaken.

"Mr. Blakeney!" the man said, his teeth gleaming. "How nice to see you again!"

Blakeney met too many people, in too many connections. No memory could fasten all their faces to their names. Moreover, he was noting uneasily, his memory no longer had the elasticity of twenty years ago. But politeness compelled him to take the proffered hand.

"Nice to see you, too, uh—" he began, hoping he was not being so abrupt as to offend someone who might feel he had a claim to be remembered.

But the little man, instead of speaking, grasped Blakeney's hand with a quite surprising strength, and to the financier's bewilderment and alarm pulled him like a reeled fish to a car that had stopped at the curb. Before Blakeney could collect his wits—he had been deep in what he was going to do about the Metropolitan merger—another man, this one big and burly, reached out for his other arm. Between the two of them he was dragged bodily into the car and in less than a minute he was sprawled on the floor of the back seat, gagged, blindfolded, with a rug over him and the big man's feet planted firmly on his spine. Blakeney squirmed and gurgled ineffectively as the car proceeded decorously down the street.

Blakeney ceased squirming very soon. It was obvious that he was being kidnaped for ransom; he thought that kind of thing had gone out before World War II. But he remembered very well the accounts he had read of similar occurrences, and it was the victims who had kept their heads and used their wits who not only had come out of it unhurt but had been able to lead the police to the criminals and in some cases had even recovered the ransom money. All his senses were blocked except for his ears, but he could use them.

He knew the routine by heart. He would be taken to an isolated hideaway and kept incommunicado, while the kidnapers either sent a ransom note to his wife or phoned her or contacted one of his business associates. It would probably be the latter, since Iris had no idea where or how to obtain the considerable sum which would of course be demanded. She or his associate would be warned not to notify the police; but they would do so, under cover, he feared. He would rather they didn't; unhappy things occurred to the kidnaped if their go-betweens didn't obey orders.

He heard when they turned onto the throughway, he heard when they left it and the paved highway changed to a dirt road, and other cars passing them became fewer and then nonexistent. Near every large city, within easy riding distance, there are still enclaves of undeveloped or abandoned land, where no one is likely to interfere. These men were professionals; they would have their hiding place prepared. He had a fairly good idea of the direction in which they had come from the city, and he could recall several such spots which at one time or another he had passed in his car and scarcely noted. There must be, he imagined, a rundown house on one of them.

Sure enough, the auto stopped—a ramshackle jalopy, from the feel of it, which again proved the expertise of these criminals: no doubt they had picked it up cheap in some used-car lot, and all that was required of the car was its ability to take them where they were going and back again, minus him and a keeper; after that the car would be dumped somewhere in a side street. No complications with stolen cars, that way. With his talent for administration Blakeney almost approved the arrangements: they were neat and businesslike.

"Out," said the big man in the rear, raising his feet from Blakeney's rug-covered body. It was the first word the big man had spoken. The rug was snatched off, and Blakeney wriggled stiffly to the open door and then to his feet on the rough ground.

He had a vague impression of trees around him; certainly there was one close by, against which he steadied himself until the pins and needles in his arms and legs subsided. Now they would hustle him into the house, which must be very near, and into a dark room which would be his prison cell until he was ransomed. He did not dream there was no house within a mile in any direction.

"Okay," said Ferguson. "Move away."

He was talking to Coates, who let go of Blakeney's arm. Ferguson stepped between two of the scrub pines in this cut-over tract and aimed carefully for the back of Blakeney's neck.

Blakeney fell prone, heavily, without a sound. There was a momentary twitch, and then he was still.

"Pretty good, eh?" Ferguson chortled. He laughed, a high whinnying laugh.

"Clean as a whistle," Coates agreed. "You always are, I've heard." Now for the changes in the original plan.

Ferguson was all keyed up. Coates looked at him in disgust. Girdner was right: Ferguson had been a useful man in his time, but his time was over. He had become expendable.

"Well, now," said Ferguson excitedly, "you roll him over—he's heavy. We'll leave his wallet on him—they have to find the identity cards—but a guy like that must carry plenty of cash, and there's no reason we shouldn't have it. Kind of a bonus," he tittered.

Plan change number one: *no* money must be taken from Blakeney or the police would know there had been a third person present. No time to waste.

Ferguson had his gun back in the holster and was lighting a cigarette. He kept on chattering and moving around.

"Then, as soon as we get that done, back in the car and off, eh? Get to the city, dump this heap where you said, and then we can separate and each beat it to the airport, and you go your way and I'll go mine. You ever do a job for Girdner before?"

"Twice," said Coates. "You?"

"More than that. But never one like this—just ordinary torpedo

jobs." He laughed. "This one sure is a dilly, isn't it? That guy Girdner—what a brain!"

"Zip your lip," said Coates. Loose talk was one thing he abomi-
nated.

Ferguson laughed again. He kept on chattering. "Who's to hear,
except you and our deceased friend here? Gosh, did you ever hear of
a setup like this one? How to become a wealthy widow in one swoop!
Wonder how she got on to Girdner in the first place?"

"Same way we did," said Coates. "Syndicate connections. She's
not a floozie but she's sure no ministering angel. Probably she had it
all worked out from the beginning. Now if you'll just—"

"Okay, okay, let me get my breath first. No hurry. Yeah, I guess
that was it. She's half his age and twice as pretty!" Ferguson giggled.
"He probably picked her up in a bar in the first place, and then she
trapped him. I kind of admire her. Of course Girdner must have
worked out the details with her; but the whole thing—to write the
ransom note to herself—at Girdner's dictation, I suppose, and he'd
see she had a safe typewriter that could be got rid of afterwards—
then to spill it to the fuzz, after she'd the same as paid the ransom already—and you can bet it was a big one—we got good pay but it's
only a small bit of the main amount—"

Coates had had enough. "Hey!" he said harshly. "Look there!"

Startled, Ferguson turned. Instantly Coates, twice Ferguson's
weight and strength, seized him, dragged Ferguson's gun out again—
both bullets must come from the same weapon—and before the
smaller man could collect his thoughts, Coates shot him through the
temple, the gun close enough to leave a powder burn.

Ferguson slumped in a heap. Deftly Coates fastened the dead
hand around the gun. No need to wipe for his own fingerprints—on
the car, either; he hadn't touched a thing that would show any, and
Ferguson's didn't matter any more.

Plan change number two: he couldn't take the car. That would be
another give-away that a third person had been concerned. Well, it
was early yet, and not more than four or five miles to the nearest bus
station in a small town. Anything left to do?

Yeah, Ferguson's share of the money; he, Coates, had earned it,
and besides, it would look suspicious if Ferguson had too much on
him. He took all but the reasonable sum Ferguson might be expected

to carry, and transferred the notes, with his own larger share, to the money belt he had brought along to keep his pockets from bulging. Ferguson's air-flight ticket? No, leave that; it would lead them to Ferguson even before they identified his prints. Coates hitched his trousers and looked around to make sure nothing had been forgotten.

All set. Ferguson had bought the car, Coates had never set eyes on the little man till they had met at Girdner's yesterday, so there was nothing to connect them. Just one question: should he hasten the discovery by an anonymous phone call? Girdner had made it plain that Blakeney's body must be found promptly; a dead husband had to be produced before the will could be probated. This place was isolated, but wouldn't hunters or kids or hikers taking a short cut be likely to stumble on it within the next day or so? Maybe not.

Well, before he took the bus he'd phone police headquarters in the city, give them the tip, and hang up. She was going to call the cops the minute she got the ransom letter she had mailed to herself, and by then it would be all over the newspapers and TV.

With a last glance at the satisfactory tableau Coates started confidently down the dirt road to the highway, alert to conceal himself at the sight of any wayfarer. Nothing living crossed his path except one lone jack rabbit. With his present luck, few cars would be on the highway at this time of day, and if he saw one coming he would start to jog. He didn't dress as square as Girdner, but he looked square enough to be taken for a devotee of the new fad of jogging; nobody would mistake him for a hitchhiker, anyway, and stop to pick him up.

He strode on, smiling at the memory of the sudden terror on Ferguson's face in the second before he died. Let them try to puzzle out why the kidnaper had killed his victim and then suddenly, for some inexplicable reason, killed himself with the same weapon.

A good job, well done, Coates gloated. A thoroughly professional job, no loose ends.

Everything went like clockwork. Iris Blakeney wasn't even nervous. You couldn't be nervous, not with an entrepreneur like Girdner in charge. All she had to do was follow his instructions precisely, and she did. Apparently one of his men had even phoned in a tip to insure the quick discovery of poor James, for his body had been found before dark that same evening.

She rehearsed herself in the shock and grief the news should bring her. Soon the phone would begin to ring, and then she would be besieged by reporters and by James's friends and relatives and business associates. Thank heaven she had none of her own. Only a week or so of fuss and bother, and then her new, her wonderful new life would start. Yes, a ring at the front door already; she tensed for the first encounter as she heard the maid go to the door.

Two men were ushered in. They were in civilian clothes but of course she recognized them as detectives. "Have you—have you any news?" she asked quaveringly, as if she hadn't heard on TV.

She listened in utter dismay as one of them began to recite the litany which precedes every arrest since the Miranda ruling. "What on earth—" she began, switching quickly from shock to outrage.

"Come off it, sister," said the other detective wearily. "Know what we found in the breast pocket of your husband's suit? One of those nice new little mini-tape-recorders. And when he fell it hit the ground and activated itself. And boy, has it been talking!"

Goodbye, Pops

Joe Gores

I got off the Greyhound and stopped to draw icy Minnesota air into
my lungs. A bus had brought me from Springfield, Illinois, to Chicago
the day before; a second bus had brought me here. I caught my passing reflection in the window of the old-fashioned depot—a tall hard
man with a white and savage face, wearing an ill-fitting overcoat. I
caught another reflection, too, one that froze my guts: a cop in uniform. Could they already know it was someone else in that burned-
out car?

Then the cop turned away, chafing his arms with gloved hands
through his blue stormcoat, and I started breathing again. I went
quickly over to the cab line. Only two hackies were waiting there;
the front one rolled down his window as I came up.

"You know the Miller place north of town?" I asked. He looked
me over. "I know it. Five bucks—now."

I paid him from the money I'd rolled a drunk for in Chicago and
eased back against the rear seat. As he nursed the cab out ice-rimed
Second Street, my fingers gradually relaxed from their rigid chopping
position. I deserved to go back inside if I let a clown like this get to
me.

"Old man Miller's pretty sick, I hear." He half turned to catch me
with a corner of an eye. "You got business with him?"

"Yeah. My own."

That ended that conversation. It bothered me that Pops was sick
enough for this clown to know about it; but maybe my brother Rod
being vice-president at the bank would explain that. There was a lot

of new construction and a freeway west of town with a tricky over-
pass to the old county road. A mile beyond a new subdivision were
the two hundred wooded hilly acres I knew so well.

After my break from the federal pen at Terre Haute, Indiana, two
days before, I'd gotten outside their cordon through woods like these.
I'd gone out in a prison truck, in a pail of swill meant for the prison
farm pigs, had headed straight west, across the Illinois line. I'm good
in open country, even when I'm in prison condition, so by dawn I
was in a hayloft near Paris, Illinois, some twenty miles from the pen.
You can do what you have to do.

The cabby stopped at the foot of the private road, looking dubious.
"Listen, buddy, I know that's been plowed, but it looks damned icy.
If I try it and go into the ditch—"

"I'll walk from here."

I waited beside the road until he'd driven away, then let the north
wind chase me up the hill and into the leafless hardwoods. The ce-
dars that Pops and I had put in as a windbreak were taller and fuller;
rabbit paths were pounded hard into the snow under the barbed-
wire tangles of wild raspberry bushes. Under the oaks at the top of
the hill was the old-fashioned, two-story house, but I detoured to the
kennels first. The snow was deep and undisturbed inside them. No
more foxhounds. No cracked corn in the bird feeder outside the
kitchen window, either. I rang the front doorbell.

My sister-in-law Edwina, Rod's wife, answered it. She was three
years younger than my thirty-five, and she'd started wearing a girdle.

"Good Lord! Chris!" Her mouth tightened. "We didn't—"

"Ma wrote that the old man was sick." She'd written, all right.
*Your father is very ill. Not that you have ever cared if any of us lives
or dies* . . . And then Edwina decided that my tone of voice had
given her something to get righteous about.

"I'm amazed you'd have the nerve to come here, even if they did
let you out on parole or something." So nobody had been around
asking yet. "If you plan to drag the family name through the mud
again—"

I pushed by her into the hallway. "What's wrong with the old
man?" I called him Pops only inside myself, where no one could
hear.

"He's dying, that's what's wrong with him."

She said it with a sort of baleful pleasure. It hit me, but I just grunted and went by into the living room. Then the old girl called down from the head of the stairs.

"Eddy? What—who is it?"

"Just—a salesman, Ma. He can wait until Doctor's gone."

Doctor. As if some damned croaker was generic physician all by himself. When he came downstairs Edwina tried to hustle him out before I could see him, but I caught his arm as he poked it into his overcoat sleeve.

"Like to see you a minute, Doc. About old man Miller."

He was nearly six feet, a couple of inches shorter than me, but out-weighing me forty pounds. He pulled his arm free.

"Now see here, fellow—"

I grabbed his lapels and shook him, just enough to pop a button off his coat and put his glasses awry on his nose. His face got red.

"Old family friend, Doc." I jerked a thumb at the stairs. "What's the story?"

It was dumb, dumb as hell, of course, asking him; at any second the cops would figure out that the farmer in the burned-out car wasn't me after all. I'd dumped enough gasoline before I struck the match so they couldn't lift prints off anything except the shoe I'd planted: but they'd make him through dental charts as soon as they found out he was missing. When they did they'd come here asking questions, and then the croaker would realize who I was. But I wanted to know whether Pops was as bad off as Edwina said he was, and I've never been a patient man.

The croaker straightened his suit coat, striving to regain lost dignity. "He—Judge Miller is very weak, too weak to move. He probably won't last out the week." His eyes searched my face for pain, but there's nothing like a federal pen to give you control. Disappointed, he said, "His lungs. I got to it much too late, of course. He's resting easily."

I jerked the thumb again. "You know your way out."

Edwina was at the head of the stairs, her face righteous again. It seems to run in the family, even with those who married in. Only Pops and I were short of it.

"Your father is very ill. I forbid you—"

"Save it for Rod; it might work on him."

In the room I could see the old man's arm hanging limply over the edge of the bed, with smoke from the cigarette between his fingers

running up to the ceiling in a thin unwavering blue line. The upper
arm, which once had measured an honest eighteen and had swung
his small tight fist against the side of my head a score of times, could
not even hold a cigarette up in the air. It gave me the same wrench
as finding a good foxhound that's gotten mixed up with a bobcat.

The old girl came out of her chair by the foot of the bed, her face
blanched. I put my arms around her. "Hi, Ma," I said. She was rigid
inside my embrace, but I knew she wouldn't pull away. Not there in
Pops's room.

He had turned his head at my voice. The light glinted from his
silky white hair. His eyes, translucent with imminent death, were the
pure, pale blue of birch shadows on fresh snow.

"Chris," he said in a weak voice. "Son of a biscuit, boy . . . I'm
glad to see you."

"You ought to be, you lazy devil," I said heartily. I pulled off my
suit jacket and hung it over the back of the chair, and tugged off my
tie. "Getting so lazy that you let the foxhounds go!"

"That's enough, Chris." She tried to put steel into it.

"I'll just sit here a little, Ma," I said easily. Pops wouldn't have
long, I knew, and any time I got with him would have to do me. She
stood in the doorway, a dark indecisive shape; then she turned and
went silently out, probably to phone Rod at the bank.

For the next couple of hours I did most of the talking; Pops just lay
there with his eyes shut, like he was asleep. But then he started in,
going way back, to the trapline he and I had run when I'd been a kid;
to the big white-tail buck that followed him through the woods one
rutting season until Pops whacked it on the nose with a tree branch.
It was only after his law practice had ripened into a judgeship that
we began to draw apart; I guess that in my twenties I was too wild,
too much what he'd been himself thirty years before. Only I kept
going in that direction.

About seven o'clock my brother Rod called from the doorway. I
went out, shutting the door behind me. Rod was taller than me,
broad and big-boned, with an athlete's frame—but with mush where
his guts should have been. He had close-set pale eyes and not quite
enough chin, and hadn't gone out for football in high school.

"My wife reported the vicious things you said to her." It was his
best give-the-teller-hell voice. "We've talked this over with Mother
and we want you out of here tonight. We want—"

"*You* want? Until he kicks off it's still the old man's house, isn't it?"

He swung at me then—being Rod, it was a right-hand lead—and I blocked it with an open palm. Then I back-handed him, hard, twice across the face each way, jerking his head from side to side with the slaps, and crowding him up against the wall. I could have fouled his groin to bend him over, then driven locked hands down on the back of his neck as I jerked a knee into his face; and I wanted to. The need to get away before they came after me was gnawing at my gut like a weasel in a trap gnawing off his own paw to get loose. But I merely stepped away from him.

"You—you murderous animal!" He had both hands up to his cheeks like a woman might have done. Then his eyes widened theatrically, as the realization struck him. I wondered why it had taken so long. "You've *broken out!*" he gasped. "*Escaped!* a fugitive from—from justice!"

"Yeah. And I'm staying that way. I know you, kid, all of you. The last thing any of you want is for the cops to take me here." I tried to put his tones into my voice. "*Oh! The scandal!*"

"But they'll be after you—"

"They think I'm dead," I said flatly. "I went off an icy road in a stolen car in down-state Illinois, and it rolled and burned with me inside."

His voice was hushed, almost horror-stricken. "You mean—that there *is* a body in the car?"

"Right."

I knew what he was thinking, but I didn't bother to tell him the truth—that the old farmer who was driving me to Springfield, because he thought my doubled-up fist in the overcoat pocket was a gun, hit a patch of ice and took the car right off the lonely country road. He was impaled on the steering post, so I took his shoes and put one of mine on his foot. The other I left, with my fingerprints on it, lying near enough so they'd find it but not so near that it'd burn along with the car. Rod wouldn't have believed the truth anyway. If they caught me, who would?

I said, "Bring me up a bottle of bourbon and a carton of cigarettes. And make sure Eddy and Ma keep their mouths shut if anyone asks about me." I opened the door so Pops could hear. "Well, thanks, Rod. It *is* nice to be home again."

Solitary in the pen makes you able to stay awake easily or snatch sleep easily, whichever is necessary. I stayed awake for the last thirty-seven hours that Pops had, leaving the chair by his bed only to go to the bathroom and to listen at the head of the stairs whenever I heard the phone or the doorbell ring. Each time I thought: *This is it.* But my luck held. If they'd just take long enough so I could stay until Pops went; the second that happened, I told myself, I'd be on my way.

Rod and Edwina and Ma were there at the end, with Doctor hovering in the background to make sure he got paid. Pops finally moved a pallid arm and Ma sat down quickly on the edge of the bed—a small, erect, rather indomitable woman with a face made for wearing a lorgnette. She wasn't crying yet; instead, she looked purely luminous in a way.

"Hold my hand, Eileen." Pops paused for the terrible strength to speak again. "Hold my hand. Then I won't be frightened."

She took his hand and he almost smiled, and shut his eyes. We waited, listening to his breathing get slower and slower and then just stop, like a grandfather clock running down. Nobody moved, nobody spoke. I looked around at them, so soft, so unused to death, and I felt like a marten in a brooding house. Then Ma began to sob.

It was a blustery day with snow flurries. I parked the jeep in front of the funeral chapel and went up the slippery walk with wind plucking at my coat, telling myself for the hundredth time just how nuts I was to stay for the service. By now they *had* to know that the dead farmer wasn't me; by now some smart prison censor *had* to remember Ma's letter about Pops being sick. He was two days dead, and I should have been in Mexico by this time. But it didn't seem complete yet, somehow. Or maybe I was kidding myself, maybe it was just the old need to put down authority that always ruins guys like me.

From a distance it looked like Pops but up close you could see the cosmetics and that his collar was three sizes too big. I felt his hand: it was a statue's hand, unfamiliar except for the thick, slightly downcurved fingernails.

Rod came up behind me and said, in a voice meant only for me, "After today I want you to leave us alone. I want you out of my house."

"Shame on you, brother," I grinned. "Before the will is even read, too."

We followed the hearse through snowy streets at the proper funeral pace, lights burning. Pallbearers wheeled the heavy casket out smoothly on oiled tracks, then set it on belts over the open grave. Snow whipped and swirled from a gray sky, melting on the metal and forming rivulets down the sides.

I left when the preacher started his scam, impelled by the need to get moving, get away, yet impelled by another urgency, too. I wanted something out of the house before all the mourners arrived to eat and guzzle. The guns and ammo already had been banished to the garage, since Rod never had fired a round in his life; but it was easy to dig out the beautiful little .22 target pistol with the long barrel. Pops and I had spent hundreds of hours with that gun, so the grip was worn smooth and the blueing was gone from the metal that had been out in every sort of weather.

Putting the jeep on four-wheel I ran down through the trees to a cut between the hills, then went along on foot through the darkening hardwoods. I moved slowly, evoking memories of Korea to neutralize the icy bite of the snow through my worn shoes. There was a flash of brown as a cottontail streaked from under a deadfall toward a rotting woodpile I'd stacked years before. My slug took him in the spine, paralyzing the back legs. He jerked and thrashed until I broke his neck with the edge of my hand.

I left him there and moved out again, down into the small marshy triangle between the hills. It was darkening fast as I kicked at the frozen tussocks. Finally a ringneck in full plumage burst out, long tail fluttering and stubby pheasant wings beating to raise his heavy body. He was quartering up and just a bit to my right, and I had all the time in the world. I squeezed off in mid-swing, knowing it was perfect even before he took that heart-stopping pinwheel tumble.

I carried them back to the jeep; there was a tiny ruby of blood on the pheasant's beak, and the rabbit was still hot under the front legs. I was using headlights when I parked on the curving cemetery drive. They hadn't put the casket down yet, so the snow had laid a soft blanket over it. I put the rabbit and pheasant on top and stood without moving for a minute or two. The wind must have been strong, because I found that tears were burning on my cheeks.

Goodbye, Pops. Goodbye to deer-shining out of season in the hardwood belt across the creek. Goodbye to jump-shooting mallards down in the river bottoms. Goodbye to woodsmoke and mellow bourbon by firelight and all the things that made a part of you mine. The part they could never get at.

I turned away, toward the jeep—and stopped dead. I hadn't even heard them come up. Four of them, waiting patiently as if to pay their respects to the dead. In one sense they were: to them that dead farmer in the burned-out car was Murder One. I tensed, my mind going to the .22 pistol that they didn't know about in my overcoat pocket. Yeah. Except that it had all the stopping power of a fox's bark. If only Pops had run to hand guns of a little heavier caliber. But he hadn't.

Very slowly, as if my arms suddenly had grown very heavy, I raised my hands above my head.

Pin Money

James Cross

"I think Howard has got hold of a very bold concept here, J.L.,"
Weatherby Fallstone III said enthusiastically. "Very strong."

He paused, smiling at Howard Grafton across the long table.

"Pioneering," he went on, "ground-breaking. Completely new. I
don't think we've ever done anything quite like it. I want to roll it
around in my mouth for a while and get the taste of it."

He watched the imperceptible shadowing of J. L. Girton's face.
Very neat, Fallstone, he thought. Like nothing we've done in the
past, like nothing J. L. Girton has approved or devised, like none of
the old stuff. Newer and better than J.L. Let's see Grafton weasel out
of that one.

"I think Weatherby is giving me too much credit," Grafton said
carefully. "Actually, it's a recombination of a few ideas J.L. sketched
out as early as 1958. If it seems fresh and new—why, that's a tribute
to the vitality of the concepts it was taken from."

Mousetrapped, Fallstone thought, that slick son of a bitch.

"I can see that," he said, "the basic fundamentals don't change.

"I think you have a winner, Howard," he went on generously.

"Sound creative thinking, Howard," J.L. said decisively. "How
does it strike you, Eldon?"

The white head of the vice-president in charge of client relations
bobbed sharply and he blinked once or twice. Eldon Smith had not
quite been asleep, but it would be hard to prove it to the men watching him, carefully and without charity.

"Perhaps," he said slowly, "perhaps we should sleep on it."

"I thought you had done that already, Eldon."

"Not at all, J.L. I find that closing my eyes helps me to visualize."

J.L. looked at him coldly. Then he smiled around the table.

113

"That about wraps it up. Thank you, gentlemen."

The executives of J. L. Girton and Associates began to file out quietly.

"Oh, Howard," J.L. said, "stay around for a minute. You, too, Weatherby."

"A good plan, Howard," J.L. said, when the three men were alone. "I like to see a man who can work creatively without getting himself out of touch with sound, tested concepts."

Grafton's round, bland, white face looked as though sincerity and gratitude had been applied to it like a face cream; he looked J.L. straight in the eye.

"Thank you, J.L.," he said modestly. "I only hope I can pull it off."

Then he looked at Fallstone out of the corner of his eye. This is a big one, he thought; I'll bet that skinny bastard's chewing nails.

"It'll be tough," J.L. said, "a real challenge. That's why I asked Weatherby to stay. He's going to beef up the old team, and between the two of you, I can look forward to a bang-up job."

"Grand, J.L.," Fallstone said enthusiastically. "Between us, we'll turn these ideas into something solid."

"Well, boys, get cracking on it. When you have a working plan of operation, let Frank Baker work out the housekeeping details."

The two men paused in the doorway for a moment in an elaborate charade of friendly courtesy. Then Fallstone, the larger man, put his hand on Grafton's shoulder in so affectionate a way that it was impossible to take offense, and started to propel him through the door.

"Oh, by the way," J.L. said. "I think you should know one thing—close the door a minute, Weatherby. Eldon Smith will be retiring at the end of the year. Past his prime, I'm afraid. All right, that's all I wanted to say."

Howard Grafton's office was closest and he got to it a few seconds before Weatherby Fallstone reached his identical cube—identical in square feet, in furnishings, in windows. But mine is closer to J.L.'s, Grafton thought for a moment before he realized that the choice of offices between the two men had been originally decided prosaically by the toss of a coin, with much good-natured joking and even, on the part of the winner, the offer to give first choice to the loser, "if it meant so much to him."

Grafton sat there quietly. A few feet down the hall, he knew, Fallstone was sitting in the same Mark II, executive-model swivel chair, with (imitation) leather upholstering, and thinking just about the same thoughts. It was about as clear as anything ever was at J. L. Girton and Associates. They were being told, as directly as they ever would, that sometime before the end of the year, when old Eldon Smith was retired, one of them would be the new vice-president in charge of client relations. And they were being told to get in there and compete, that J.L. had his eye on each of them. Short, chubby, genial Grafton versus tall, thin, enthusiastic Fallstone.

When Grafton got home that night, he told his wife about it. Lenore Grafton was small and curved and blond. Someday she would be too fat, but at the moment, she had reached a ripe perfection. She was quite a lot smarter than her husband, but some of her intelligence was wasted on the constant need to keep him unaware of this fact.

"I think we had better have J.L. and his wife out to dinner pretty soon," she said. "With that frightful woman, he must be dying for a decent meal."

"And a pretty face to look at," Grafton said with elaborate casualness. He was remembering the time he had stepped into the kitchen at the party and had seen J.L. and Lenore, still holding an ice tray in one hand, pressed back against the sink. They had been too busy to see him and he had drawn back and come in again a minute or so later with a good deal of preliminary noise.

Lenore looked at him levelly for a moment, as if she were receiving a message she was not sure she wanted to get. Then she went to the desk at the far end of the room and picked up her Florentine leather engagement pad.

"Any time after this week," she said. "I'll call her then; we don't want to push too fast."

For J. L. Girton and Lenore, at least, the dinner party was a great success. She was discreet enough, but she talked with him as much as with all the other guests combined. She sat girlishly on the floor at the foot of J.L.'s chair, laughing at his jokes or reacting to his autobiographical anecdotes with an open-eyed admiration and an interest that more than once caused her to lean forward so that he could get the maximum effect of her décolletage. Even when she was not with him, she was seated across the room from him at such an angle that her excellent legs in the short, swirling *discothèque* dress were never out of his sight.

Grafton, as a result, had to focus the bulk of his duties as a host on Mrs. Girton, a scrawny, faded, complaining shrew. It says a lot for his charm and geniality that he was able to bring her through the evening without her really noticing her husband's behavior.

Lenore did not like New York in the summer. The heat and crowds wilted her, she said. There was nothing new at the theaters; the city was full of tourists; the stores were doing nothing but remaindering their past mistakes. She liked to play golf or tennis, or lie in the sun at the beach and then cool off in the Sound, or even just stay in her air-conditioned house and read.

Thus, Grafton was a little surprised when she started coming into New York once or twice a week—for two months during one of the hottest summers the city had ever had. She came into town before noon, as she told him, window-shopped a little, lunched and spent the afternoon at a museum or, occasionally, a movie. Sometimes she took a train back just before his; at other times, she stayed in and they had dinner together. He did not want to know too much about what she was doing in town, so he did not ask many questions. He did not want to think about it any more than he wanted to think about the fact that J.L. seemed to be having more luncheons with clients than ever before and apparently had decided to improve his golf game by taking off several afternoons a week. Only once did he move obliquely toward the subject, and that was after several drinks before dinner one Friday evening.

"I'm a little worried about how I stand with J.L.," he said. "I don't seem to be seeing him as much as usual. He's always out of the office."

"I wouldn't worry too much about it, Howie. I think he appreciates you very much; and what's more, I think you're going to get the job."

That, however, was before the dinner party at the Fallstones'. Lenore was not at her best there. Her nose was red and swollen and runny with a summer cold, and her voice was hoarse. Grafton was alone with her a lot that evening; and even though they left early, he had plenty of time to watch Marcia Fallstone work on J.L. She was tall and slim and very darkly elegant, and J.L. was a rabbit to her cobra.

"That son of a bitch," he said to himself as they drove home.

During the next weeks, J.L. continued his leisurely pace of work, but Lenore was no longer coming into town. One afternoon in the corridor, Grafton passed Fallstone's open door and saw him chatting with Frank Baker.

"Well worth seeing," Fallstone said. "Marcia and I saw it last night. She's bored up in the country; but this way, when she comes in, we can have a night or two on the town each week."

"That son of a bitch," Grafton said to himself again, knowing that it was still a stalemate. When, a week or so later, J.L. abruptly reverted to his normal lengthy office hours, Grafton was sure of it.

It was still summer, but it was coming to an end, and sometimes the nights were chilly without the heat on. Grafton stared morosely into his fifth martini, not wanting to look at his wife in her backless red dress.

"I'm cold, Howie," she said. "Will you get me that stole—the Italian one. I don't want to catch a cold."

"Don't want to catch a cold," he mimicked her savagely, his voice thick with rage. "Why didn't you take care of yourself a month ago, for Chrissake! You can get pneumonia, for all I care."

She looked at him coolly and speculatively for a moment, as if she were examining a new form of life, but she said nothing. He could see the slight, almost imperceptible smile as she turned and left the room. And then Howard Grafton knew that the vice-presidency was not just something he wanted very badly, but something he would have to have because there was nothing else left to him.

The next day after work, he stopped off at the Biltmore bar and began drinking seriously. He did not go home that night, but stayed in a hotel. He was late to work the next morning and his head throbbed all day. It was something to him, but not enough, to observe that Weatherby Fallstone had an equally bad hangover.

That night at home, Grafton shut himself up in the library with a fifth of Scotch and tried to think. He would go to Fallstone and put it to him straight: They would toss a coin and the loser would resign from J. L. Girton and Associates. Like hell, he thought; no deal with that dishonest bastard! He would hire private detectives and get a dossier on Fallstone and give it to J.L. It took him thirty seconds to get rid of that idea—he didn't have the money; J.L. might react by getting rid of him; Fallstone's detectives, if he in turn hired some, could do just as good a job on Grafton. He toyed with the possibility of feeding the juiciest bits to a Broadway columnist, but who the hell would print them? Nobody had heard of either of them. He could not kill Fallstone himself, he didn't know how, and he was afraid. He didn't know how to hire someone to do it, and he was afraid of that, too. At the end of three quarters of the bottle, he knew that there was nothing he could do but sweat it out.

He was sweating even more after the Friday-morning think meeting. Fallstone had been praised by J.L. no less than three times, while one of Grafton's pet schemes had been dismissed as "not thought out yet." He had also been rebuked by J.L. for talking too long, for interrupting Fallstone and finally for inattention. When J.L.'s secretary buzzed him early in the afternoon, his hands began to shake and there was a gnawing at his stomach. He chewed three antacid tablets quickly and went into J.L.'s office.

"Oh, Howie," J.L. said, "you know that gadget you have, the one that makes soda water in the siphon. Bring it along when you come out tomorrow; the washer on mine is rotted and it takes a couple of days to get a replacement."

"Sure thing, J.L.," he said.

I can't stand much more of this, Grafton thought as he drove toward J.L.'s country place the next evening. Lenore was next to him, infinitely desirable in low-cut green satin that matched her eyes; but the soda-water machine was on the seat between them like a drawn sword. She looked straight ahead. When he spoke, she answered him briefly and politely; but she never spoke first.

I have an ulcer, Grafton thought; I am beginning to drink too much; my wife hates me; and I am going to lose my job, because I am going to have to quit when they choose Fallstone. I can't stand much more of this, I'll have to do something.

It did not help matters that they arrived simultaneously with the Fallstones. He clapped a hand sincerely to Fallstone's shoulder and it was then he saw the nervous tic, as Fallstone's left cheek jumped as if it had its own life. Behind him, the two women, having uttered little shrieks of delight, were depositing kisses a fraction of an inch away from each other's cheeks. Grafton embraced Marcia Fallstone, careful not to crush her dress. When he laid his cheek against hers, he was surprised at the flush of heat. As the Fallstones went on ahead of him, he noticed how polite they were to each other—almost as polite as Lenore and myself, he thought, with a surge of hope.

It was only after the cocktails and the buffet that Grafton, going up to the bar for his second after-dinner highball, noticed the genial, twinkling little man in the outrageous tartan jacket and the striped shirt and the clashing tie.

"Wonderful party," the little man said. "I should get out more often. Have you known Mr. Girton long, Mr.——?"

"Grafton, I'm in J.L.'s firm, Mr.——?"

"Dee, Dr. Dee. Doctor of letters, that is, sacred and profane."

The little man emitted a series of high-pitched whinnies.

"Sacred and profane," he repeated. "A little joke of mine—because of my business."

"What's that?" Grafton asked. Somehow, without his being aware of it, Dr. Dee had propelled him out a side door onto the large patio by the swimming pool.

"A little store for religious articles—books, pictures, icons, whatever you want."

"Where does the 'profane' come in?"

Dr. Dee lowered his voice.

"As you know, Mr. Grafton, there are many sorts of religions, and who are we to say which is the right one? If a customer wants a mandrake root, or a little bag to wear around his neck, well, who am I to say him nay? He can get it in the back room. Or perhaps he may believe that I can help him get the girl he wants, with a love potion; or possibly he may desire me to destroy an enemy. I do not tell him it will work—it is against the law for me to say that—but if he wishes to believe it will work, then I will sell it to him in the back room."

"Are they expensive?"

"The religious books? No, they are very reasonably priced."

"I mean the others."

"They are quite expensive. But then, I do not ask for payment at the time of sale. Only later, when the customer is satisfied."

"Don't you have trouble collecting?"

"Very little, Mr. Grafton. If the customer is satisfied, then he will believe in me. He would not want to make me wait for my money."

"Dr. Dee," Grafton said, "as you know, I am in advertising. I'm interested in some of your ideas, campaignwise, that is. Perhaps we could get together next week."

"My card, Mr. Grafton. I am open from nine to nine. But not Monday afternoon in the coming week, I fear. I have an appointment with my bootmaker.

"A nuisance," the little man went on, "but I have a slight pedal malformation, and my shoes must be made to order. Believe me, Mr. Grafton, you have no idea what the man charges. One would do better going barefoot."

Grafton glanced down at Dee's shoes. They were high, black and gleamingly polished, and small, almost tiny. There was something odd about their shape, and in a second, Grafton realized what was wrong with them: they were almost as wide as they were long; yet despite this, one got an idea that distorted as they were, they were still somehow padded out. Poor devil, he thought, it must be hell walking on those things, and yet he keeps smiling.

"Thank you, Dr. Dee," Grafton said, taking the card. "Perhaps I'll try you later in the week. It's been a pleasure meeting you."

"*Servus*, Mr. Grafton."

Later, when they went home, Grafton was not very sober. Lenore had to drive. All the way home, Grafton let his head rest on the back of the seat, feeling a faint spinning and dizziness and an odd air of detachment. Despite the amount he had drunk, he slept very badly, too fuzzy to sort out dreams from thoughts. One moment, Dr. Dee was handing him a large golden key, while Lenore and J. L. Girton applauded; the next moment, he was awake and sweating and running over his anemic checking account. To hell with it, he thought; nobody can do anything like that. But he said there was no charge unless it worked. Maybe he can; I've heard of some screwy things. Nothing to lose, I've tried everything else. If it failed, I wouldn't be out anything; and if it worked, it would be worth whatever he wanted to charge. Then he was asleep again, but in the split second in which he passed from wakefulness to sleep, he had made a decision.

Grafton was tied up with meetings all day Monday, but Tuesday morning he took the Lexington Avenue subway uptown and walked over to Third. Dr. Dee's shop was in the middle of the block, flanked by two large antique stores. The display window was full of Bibles, religious paintings, icons and crucifixes. At one corner was the inscription, in gilt Gothic, "Religious articles, Dr. John Dee," and below it, the street number.

The store was well patronized, but a clerk who looked like a spoiled priest came forward and greeted him unctuously.

"Is Dr. Dee in? He asked me to call."

"Please follow me, Mr. Grafton."

Grafton looked at him suspiciously.

"The name," the clerk said, "oh, that was quite easy. Very few customers ask to see Dr. Dee personally, and he had told us yesterday that a Mr. Grafton might be dropping in."

Dr. Dee's office was on the second floor, facing the street. Grafton did not quite know what he had been expecting—a stuffed crocodile on the wall, perhaps; skeletons dangling; a cone-shaped black hat with silver stars on it. But the office was actually similar to his own, though rather larger.

Dr. Dee bounced from his chair, with his eyes twinkling, and shook Grafton's hand vigorously.

"Dee-lighted," he said, giggling. "Dee-lighted, a little joke of mine, you get the play on words. But now, Mr. Grafton, to business. I know you are a busy man. Like an old friend of mine in New England. He used to have a sign over his desk, TIME IS MONEY: STATE YOUR BUSINESS. I, alas, am far too discursive, I fear. But sit down, Mr. Grafton, sit down."

Grafton lowered himself carefully into the Eames chair.

"Dr. Dee," he said, slowly and carefully, "suppose there were two men, each of them with a chance at a big job."

"What a shame," Dr. Dee said. "Heartbreak, jealousy, old friendships broken, insomnia, ulcers, bitter rivalry. What I would give to avoid such conflicts, Mr. Grafton, but I seem to see so many of them in my business."

"Could you fix it, do you have anything that would fix it so that one person wouldn't get the job?"

Dr. Dee reached into a drawer of his executive's desk and pulled out a tiny bottle full of a clear liquid. Instead of a cork, it had a medicine dropper attached.

Grafton stared at it in horror.

"I don't mean that," he said quickly. "It doesn't have to be that. I just want to knock him out of the running. Something that will make him look bad, say crazy things, make a fool of himself at staff meetings. Cut his own throat—figuratively, I mean," he added quickly.

"You wish for something that will guarantee that Weatherby Fallstone will not get the vice-presidency when Eldon Smith retires," Dr. Dee said. "Do not be surprised, Mr. Grafton. I always think it better to lay our cards on the table at once."

"How do you know it's Fallstone?" Grafton asked suspiciously.

"My dear Mr. Grafton, I circulate, I attend parties. If I may quote Scripture," Dr. Dee twinkled genially, " 'I go to and fro in the earth and walk up and down in it.' And you would be surprised how many things come to my attention."

Somehow, to Grafton the whole thing was still odd and disturbing, but he asked the inevitable next question, because there was really not much else for him to do now.

"Can you do it?"

"Why, yes, Mr. Grafton. It will be quite easy; I have just the thing."

Dr. Dee reached into the other side of his desk and brought out a small doll. He put it in Grafton's hand. It was made of some remarkably fleshlike plastic, and for a gruesome moment, Grafton thought he felt it move. He turned it over and looked at its face, and then he felt really sick. It was a perfect replica of Weatherby Fallstone, complete to button-down white oxford, black string tie and gray flannels.

"Do not be alarmed, Mr. Grafton. I rather thought that this was what you would be wanting, so I took the liberty of making it up in advance. This modern plastic is fascinating stuff."

"What do I do with it?"

"Just take an ordinary pin, the kind you get in a new shirt, and apply it as you think most effective. Stuck in the shoulder, it will produce sudden, agonizing bursitis that will guarantee a howl of pain. In the abdomen, a violent ulcer attack. Open the mouth, Mr. Grafton— it is easy; see, the lower jaw moves. Then tickle the throat and he will vomit suddenly in public—most disgusting. Scratch the tongue—can you see the little red tongue?—and he will babble, literally, ba-ba-ba-ba. It will not help him in making a presentation to a client. Or perhaps you would like to tickle his ribs with the pin. He will go off into uncontrollable giggling, like a teenage girl with hysterics. That will surely not recommend him for promotion."

"Is there any particular way to do it?"

"Lightly, lightly, Mr. Grafton. Softee, softee, catchee monkey. Continuous light pressure or stroking with the pinhead, and you can keep it up as long as you want. But do not stick the pin in him and leave it, or you will have a dead man. And I remember how sensitive you are on that point."

"I'll take it," Grafton said, wanting only to leave. "How much?"

"A thousand dollars when you are satisfied."

"You guarantee that this will put Fallstone out of the running?"

"I guarantee it, Mr. Grafton, though it is perhaps illegal to say so."

Grafton put the little doll in the velvet-lined wooden box (like a coffin, he thought) that Dr. Dee provided. Then he put it into his attaché case.

"My account will be payable upon satisfaction, Mr. Grafton."

"Don't worry," Grafton said, feeling the queasiness below his wishbone. "Don't worry, I'll pay it."

Friday was the day of the weekly think meeting. That morning, Grafton decided to have a bad cold. He got Lenore, who was still barely speaking to him, to call the office. Then he lay back in his bed and waited for eleven o'clock to come. At 10:30 Lenore came in quietly with some breakfast. For the first time in weeks her eyes were not veiled and hostile and her face was not set. She put the tray on the bedside table, then she leaned over and kissed him.

"Thanks, honey," he said. "Thanks for both."

"It's all right, Howie. Don't worry about it anymore. It's not worth it. Maybe it never was."

"I'm not going to worry anymore. Either I get it or I don't."

She kissed him again.

"I'm going shopping. Will you be all right?"

"Sure. I feel better. I may come down to the library and read."

When he heard her pull out of the driveway, he quickly called the office and asked for Weatherby Fallstone.

"Weatherby," he said, "I've got a bad cold."

"I'm sorry to hear that, old man. Take care of your health."

"Will you be at the think meeting?"

"Of course. Have one or two crackerjack ideas I want to try out."

"I expect I'll be back Monday. Will you take a few notes and give me a rundown?"

"Glad to, old man."

He hung up, gobbled his breakfast and went down to the study. He sat there with the little doll in one hand and a pin in the other. A few extra pins were on the desk. He called Fallstone again.

"Mr. Fallstone is in a meeting," the secretary told him.

"Never mind, I'll call back later."

He gave the think meeting 15 minutes to get under way. Then he began. He started with just a bad headache—not a screaming migraine, he thought, scratching the pin like a feather across the doll's forehead, just a bad hangover. He gave it about ten minutes before he opened the doll's lower jaw and began playing with the tiny tongue. After that he tickled its ribs for a while, and brought the performance to a crescendo by gently scratching its throat. He had a final idea of his own and put a folded handkerchief over the doll's eyes for five minutes. He put the doll back in its box and the box in his attaché case. When Lenore returned, he was reading *The New York Times*.

On Monday, he went in earlier than the usual executive hour, but his secretary was there to give him the news.

"It was awful, Mr. Grafton. Mr. Fallstone had a fit at the think meeting. He put his head in his hands and groaned, then he started babbling and talking nonsense. Then he started laughing and couldn't stop. And then"—she lowered her voice—"he was sick all over Mr. Girton's desk. They started to take him out and he was yelling he was blind, and they took him to the hospital."

"Terrible. How is he?"

"I heard he was OK, but they have him in some sort of a ward."

He was reading the *Times* slowly and with relish when the buzzer rang for him. He detoured for a moment en route to J.L.'s office and looked in on Fallstone's. There was no sign of life. Only piled-up personal belongings—pills, an umbrella, a few textbooks—stacked on the desk where the office boy had put them, gave evidence that anyone had occupied the room.

"I suppose you heard about it," J.L. said, waving him to a seat.

"Terrible."

"I can't understand it. He seemed so rational and calm. Drink, I suppose, poor devil. Well, we can't sit around weeping. Howard, I want you to start working very closely with Eldon. He'll be leaving in two months and there are a lot of loose strings you'll have to tie up."

"I really appreciate this, J.L. You know you can count on me."

He paused for a moment and spoke soberly.

"It's a shame it had to happen this way."

"Nonsense, Howard. Not your fault; now go out and start pitching."

The check he mailed to Dr. Dee that afternoon was more than his checking account held. To cover it, he had to cash a savings bond, quite a large one, and deposit the money. It was just about closing

time and the windows were shutting down, but Grafton kept them
open long enough to have his check certified. He had had checks
bounce before, but somehow he felt that this was not one he would
want to have returned marked "Insufficient funds." He sent it regis-
tered and special delivery.

In the next weeks, he learned by bits and pieces that Fallstone had
been released from the hospital, that he had been given a generous
severance check, that he was cruising the agencies with his scrap-
book, that he had been seen very drunk in a bar. After a while, it
didn't bother Grafton anymore. He was too busy.

He was alone in his office, working late on a prospectus that old
Eldon Smith had completely fouled up, when the pain came. It was
like a sword in his belly and he doubled up in agony, sliding from his
chair to the floor. There was a moment's respite and it came again. It
was then Grafton remembered that all the J. L. Girton and Associates executives had been at the party and it was then he knew that
Dr. Dee had talked to other people and not just to him. For an instant there was relief, while in a corner of his memory, a picture
flashed of Dr. Dee talking with Fallstone. Then the pain came again.

He was groaning, stretched out on the floor, when the night
watchman came by an hour later; but he was dead by the time they
got him to the hospital.

"I can't understand it," J. L. Girton said to Frank Baker. "He was
in perfect health. He had everything to live for. A terrible business.
Well, Frank, it's up to you now."

"I'll do my best, sir," Baker said with the boyish modesty that was
his particular stock in trade.

"Mr. Girton," he went on.

"J.L."

"J.L., I'd like to take an hour or so to tell Betty. It will mean a lot
to her. Just imagine. Vice-president."

"Of course, my boy, on your way! And don't forget to remember
me to your pretty wife."

Before he went to the apartment, young Frank Baker stopped off
at Dr. Dee's shop.

"I have the payment here," he said. "They just made me vice-president."

"Capital, my boy; I had a very strong feeling you would make good. I took a liking to you the first time we met."

"Can you tell me—are you allowed to, that is—how you managed it?"

"I did nothing much."

"You just made me vice-president, that's all. And just by mental power—just by wishing it for me."

Dr. Dee reached into the drawer and held up a little doll.

"You remember how these work, don't you?"

"Yes, you told me."

"Well, Grafton and Fallstone each had one—of each other. They eliminated each other."

"Dr. Dee, you mean you told both of them they'd get the job and then let me get it? Isn't that, well, kind of unethical?"

"Nothing of the sort, my boy. I told each of them I would see that the other *didn't* get the job. That's what they asked for, and I kept my word."

Dr. Dee returned the doll to the drawer. "You, on the other hand, asked for the job specifically." He smiled broadly. "And you got it."

Social Climber

Robert J. Higgins

His pad was in one of those old mansions they've carved up into apartments. When I got to the roof it was slantier than I expected, but it didn't give me any trouble.

From one of the chimneys I could get a good look at the window of the garret apartment. It was open and the screen was off. No sweat there. I edged along the roof with my crepe soles gripping the shingles.

When I got to the window I looked inside, then ducked so I couldn't be seen immediately.

The guy who lived there was home, but I'd known that. He was sitting there on an expensive-looking studio couch reading a magazine. There was a drink on the table next to him.

He jumped up when he heard me outside, and went to the window with a revolver in his hand.

He snapped, "Cool it right there!"

I came through the window then and I put my hands up. I was smiling and I said, "You don't need that hardware, Kurt. I'm on your side."

The stupid fuzz never could find Kurt, but once I decided to find him I didn't have any trouble.

I asked some of the fences and tracked him down okay. The cops were going crazy trying to catch the great Kurt Pieters—*The King of the Cat Burglars* the papers were calling him—and I had just jumped into his apartment.

The fences had warned me to take it easy with Kurt.

"He's a loner and he's an ugly one," they said. "He's staked out a claim to Park Hill. Don't let him catch you pulling jobs there, or you'll end up in the river."

So I was playing it cool.

"I don't know you," Kurt said with a voice of steel. Then he came over to me, holding his rod. He patted me all over with his free hand. He didn't find anything, but he still didn't trust me.

Kurt was blond, had a few pockmarks on his face, and was around twenty-seven, twenty-eight. He had a slim build like me, with plenty muscles for climbing. His slacks and shirt looked as if they came from the best shop in town.

"If you're a cop," he said, "I'm going to send you back out that window head first and it's four stories straight down."

"I know it's four stories down," I said. "Do you think any cop could climb a roof like yours, Kurt?"

"You're right about that and you're clean," Kurt said with the cutting edge going out of his voice. "Who are you?"

"May I sit down?"

"Sure," he said while he waved me to a chair. He went back to the couch and put his gun under the pillow.

"I'm Neil Winters. I'm in the same line you're in and I want to talk to you."

"Why'd you come in a fourth-floor window? Why didn't you come up the stairs?"

"To prove my point. There's only one other guy in town who could come in that window and that's you, Kurt."

"You're right. Only a real climber could do what you did. Do you want a drink, kid?"

"Just the soda," I told him. "I'm afraid booze'll ruin my coordination."

He handed over the soda and grinned.

"A little drink now and then never bothered me."

"But you're the greatest, Kurt," I said. "You're a natural climber. You could have been the top trapeze man in the country."

"You know about that, do you, kid?"

"Sure, Kurt. I'm a fan of yours," I said. "Look at this," and I pulled an envelope out of my pocket and handed it over.

"Hey, it's my clippings," he said when he pulled the newspaper stories out of the envelope. His face lit up when he read them.

I almost knew those clippings by heart. One said, *Cat burglar gets $40,000 in furs from executive's home.* Another one read, *Star's necklace taken from hotel penthouse.* And they went on like that and every one had a line like, *The police are seeking a former circus aerialist named Kurt Pieters as a prime suspect in the recent series of daring robberies.*

"Pretty good notices, huh, kid?" Kurt remarked when he finished reading. "I never thought to save 'em when they came out."

I hadn't thought about it at the start myself. I'd had to go through a lot of old papers to find some of the clippings, but I didn't tell Kurt.

"They're yours," I said.

"Thanks," he said, "But what about these?" He held up three of the newest clips. "I didn't do those jobs."

All three told about robberies that involved some really terrific climbing, but not too much loot.

"They were my jobs, Kurt," I said. "The cops and the papers blamed you for 'em."

"They should've known it wasn't me in that neighborhood," Kurt sneered. "There aren't any rich witches with their fancy jewels over there. If you want to work there, kid, it's fine with me. Just stay out of Park Hill. That's my territory."

"Sure it is, Kurt," I said. "You were there first."

"How did you get started in the business?" he asked, changing the subject. "You weren't flying in any show when I was around."

"I'm a steeplejack," I answered. "I do a lot of climbing in the daytime on high churches and flagpoles."

"Not very glamorous, huh?" he said.

"Nothing like the circus."

"Okay, kid," Kurt said. "Just why did you come? There must be more to it than the clips."

"I want to cut you into one of my jobs, Kurt."

"You're cutting me in! I don't go for that cheap stuff you've been getting."

"This is a big one, Kurt, and I can't do it without you. You think all the rich people live in Park Hill? I smelled out an old lady who keeps fifty or sixty grand in her apartment in cash!"

"In the Belmont neighborhood?"

"That's right. She's old Mrs. Wakefield, who lived there when Belmont was the fancy part of town. She never moved to Park Hill like the rest. She's in a big place like this one, Kurt. She had the building made into apartments. She lives on top, too."

He was hooked, but I knew he was testing me when he said, "Why doesn't she stay on the ground floor so she won't have to climb stairs?"

"Because she's eccentric and she only goes out once in a while. Everything's delivered. Anyway, the word is that she has a safe in her place and inside there's bundles of big bills!"

"Doesn't she like banks?"

"Oh, she has a lot more in the bank, but she wants to have some dough on hand so she handles it herself. Makes her feel secure."

"I've heard of dames like that. Sounds like a dream job. Why aren't you grabbing it all for yourself?"

"It's the safe, Kurt," I said. "I don't know enough about cracking 'em. You can open it and I can't. Anyway, there's plenty for both of us. Maybe thirty grand apiece and no splitting with fences. Besides, I figure if everything goes right maybe you'll give me a chance to team up with you later."

Kurt grabbed my hand.

"Shake, kid," he said. "It's a deal on this job. I'll let you know about teaming up after I see you work. Now, when's the old lady going out again?"

"That's the best part, Kurt," I answered. "Yesterday she fell and broke her leg and they took her to the hospital. Nothing's been touched in her apartment."

"We got ourselves a job," he said.

"How about right now?" I asked.

"Why not?" Kurt said. "I was just sitting here doing nothing. I might as well go out and pick up thirty grand."

I was in my working clothes already, all black for night climbing. It was close to midnight. I waited while Kurt changed and when he came out of his bedroom he was togged out like me. We both had jackets with good pockets for loot.

"My car's outside," I said. "But let's go out separately. I'll meet you at Fourth and Juneau."

I took the stairs going down and I got into the car and drove a couple of blocks. I was just putting my tools into my pockets when Kurt joined me. He came up so silently I was startled and a shoe polish can slipped out of my hand.

"Do you put black polish on your face?" he asked. "I never use it."

"Okay, Kurt. If you don't use it I won't either," I said.

We took off for Belmont and we were there in ten minutes. I parked the car on a dark street and we walked a block.

"There she is, Kurt," I said, pointing to a big, dark house. "Looks like everyone in the place has gone to bed."

"It's the one on top?" Kurt asked.

"That's it," I said. "Let's go."

The fire escape was on the back of the house, away from the street lights. We took it to the top and swung onto the roof. I could have made it faster only Kurt was ahead of me. The roof had slate shingles and we both sweated a little going across the top, but there were some chimneys to help us.

Kurt was breathing a little hard, probably more from thinking about the money than from the climb, by the time we reached a likely looking window. There wasn't much space between the sill and the eaves-trough and it was four stories down from there, but we were okay.

He jimmied the window and went in first. I swung around from the peak, but I didn't make it in as fast as Kurt.

"What are you doing out there? Do you want a cop to see you?" he whispered.

"I didn't have a good grip," I answered when I jumped in, and then the shoe polish can fell out of my pocket.

"Why did you bring that if you weren't going to use it?" Kurt snapped.

"I forgot I had it," I said as I picked up the can.

Kurt turned on his pencil flashlight and said, "Where's the safe? There's nothing in this room and I don't like all this dust. We'll leave tracks."

"She doesn't use this room, I guess," I said.

"Let's find it," he said and we searched the apartment. Nobody had lived there for months. There were a few pieces of old furniture and lots of dust and no safe.

Kurt was boiling when he said, "How come you picked the wrong apartment, kid?"

"It's worse than that, Kurt," I said. "I really blew it. I know Mrs. Wakefield lives in a garret apartment. We're in the wrong building!"

"And you want to work with Kurt Pieters!" he snarled. "Let's get out of here."

He went to the window and stepped right out, but something went wrong. He shot out of sight and I heard him scream once, but then he hit the ground and he was quiet.

I went out another window. When I got to the ground I took right off for the car. I stayed away from the front, where Kurt was lying.

The next day the papers had stories about the body of the great cat burglar, Kurt Pieters, being found outside an old house in the Belmont district.

According to the police he fell off the roof "under peculiar circumstances," but they couldn't understand why he broke into an unoccupied apartment in that neighborhood.

I thought about "Mrs. Wakefield" and I laughed.

I threw that shoe polish can down a sewer in a hurry. If the cops ever pick me up I don't want them trying to match the axle grease in the can with those greasy shingles Kurt slipped on!

Now it's my turn to work Park Hill!

I'd Know You Anywhere

Edward D. Hoch

16 November 1942

From the top of the dune there was nothing to be seen in any direction—nothing but the unchanging, ever-changing sameness of the African desert. Contrell wiped the sweat-caked sand from his face and signaled the others to advance. The tank, a sick sad monster wanting only to be left to die, ground slowly into life, throwing twin fountains of sand from the path of its tracks.

"See anything?" Grove asked, coming up behind him.

"Nothing. No Germans, no Italians, not even any Arabs."

Willy Grove unslung the carbine from his shoulder. "They should be here. Our planes spotted them heading this way."

Contrell grunted. "With old Bertha in the shape she is, we'd be better off not running into them. Six men and a battered old tank against the pride of Rommel's Afrika Korps."

"But they're retreating and we're not, remember. They just might be all set to surrender."

"Sure they might," Contrell agreed uncertainly. He'd known Willy Grove—his full name was an impossible Willoughby McSwing Grove—for only a month, since they'd been thrown together shortly before the North African invasion. His first impression had been of a man like himself, drafted in his early twenties into an impossible war that threatened to envelop them all in blood and flame. But as the weeks passed, another Willy Grove had gradually become evident, one that stood next to him now, peering down into the empty, sandswept valley before them.

133

"Damn! Where are they, anyway?"

"You sound like you're ready for a battle. Hell, if I saw them coming I think I'd run the other way." Contrell took out the remains of a battered and almost empty pack of cigarettes. "A sand dune on the Tunisia border is no place for a couple of corporals."

Grove squatted down on his haunches, resting the carbine lightly against his knee. "You're right there—about the corporal part, anyway. You know, I been thinking the last few weeks—if I get back to the states in one piece I'm going to go to OCS and become an officer."

"You found yourself a home."

"Go on, laugh. There's worse things a guy could do for a living."

"Sure. He could rob banks. What in hell do army officers do when there's no war around?"

Willy Grove thought about that. "Don't you worry. There's goin' to be a war around for a good long time, maybe the rest of our lives."

"Think Hitler will last that long?"

"Hitler, Stalin, the Japs. It'll be somebody, don't you worry."

Contrell took another drag on his cigarette, then suddenly came to sharp attention. There was something moving at the top of one of the dunes, something . . . "Look!"

Grove brought up his binoculars. "Damn! It's them, all right. The whole stinkin' German army."

Contrell dropped his cigarette and went sliding down the dune to tell the others. The officer in charge was a paste-colored captain who rode the dying tank as if it were his grave. He looked down as Contrell spoke and then spoke a sharp order. "We'll take Bertha up the dune and let them see us. They might think we've got lots more and call it quits."

"Sure. Sir." And then again, Contrell thought, they just might blast the hell out of you.

By the time the wounded steel monster had been moved into position, the first of the three German tanks was within firing range. Contrell watched the big guns coming to bear on each other—two useless giants able only to destroy. He wondered what the world would be like if guns had the power to rebuild too. But he had little time to think about that or anything else before the German gun recoiled in a flash of power, followed an instant later by the thud of the sound wave reaching them. A blossom of sand and smoke filled the air to their left as the shell went wide of its mark.

"Hit the ground!" Grove yelled. "They've got us zeroed in!"

Old Bertha returned the fire, scoring a lucky near miss on the nearest tank, but the odds and the firepower were all against her. The German's second shell hit the left tread, the third slammed into the turret, and Bertha was as good as dead. Someone screamed—Contrell thought it might have been the captain.

Grove was stretched out on the sand a dozen feet away. "Damn things are iron coffins," he said, gasping at the odor of burning flesh.

Contrell started to get up. "Did any of them get out?"

"Not a one. Stay down! They're coming this way."

"God!" It was a prayer on Contrell's lips. "What'll we do?"

"Just don't move. I'll get us out of this somehow."

Two of the enemy tanks remained in the distance, while the third one—basking in its kill—moved closer. Two German soldiers were riding on its rear, and they hopped down to run ahead. One carried a rifle, the other what looked like a machine pistol to Contrell. He tensed his body for the expected shots, his face nearly buried in the sand.

The German tank commander appeared in the turret and shouted ᴉething. The soldier with the machine pistol turned—and suddenly Willy Grove was on his feet. His carbine chattered like a machine gun, cutting down the German from behind. With his left hand he hurled a grenade in the direction of the tank, then threw himself at the second German before the man could bring up his rifle.

The grenade exploded near enough to knock the officer out of action, and Contrell moved. He ran in a crouch to the German vehicle, aware that Grove was right behind him. "I got 'em both," Willy shouted. "Stay down!" He pulled the dying officer from the top of the tank and fired a burst with his carbine into the interior. He clambered up, swinging the .50-caliber machine gun around.

"Hold it!" Contrell shouted. "They're surrendering!"

They were indeed. The crews of the other two tanks were leaving their vehicles, coming forward across the sand, arms held high.

"Guess they had enough war," Grove said, training the machine gun on them.

"Haven't we all?"

Grove waited until the eight men were within a hundred feet, then his finger tightened on the trigger and a burst of sudden bullets sprayed the area. The Germans looked startled, tried to turn and run, and died like that, on their feet.

"What the hell did you do that for?" Contrell shouted, climbing up to Grove's side. "They were surrendering!"

"Maybe. Maybe not. They might have had grenades hidden under their arms or something. Can't take chances."

"Are you nuts or something, Grove?"

"I'm alive, that's the important thing." Grove jumped down, hitting the sand with an easy, sure movement. "We tell the right kind of story, boy, and we'll both end up with medals."

"You killed them!"

"That's what you do in war," Grove said sadly. "You kill them and collect the medals."

30 November 1950

Korea was a land of hills and ridges, a country poor for farming and impossible for fighting. Captain Contrell had viewed it for the first time with a mixture of resignation and despair, picturing in his mind only the ease with which an entire company of his men could be obliterated without a chance by an army more familiar with the land.

Now, as November ended with the easy victories of autumn turning to the bitter ashes of winter, he had reason to remember those first impressions. The Chinese had entered the war, and every hour fresh reports came from all around the valley of the Chongchon, indicating that their numbers could be counted not in the thousands but in the hundreds of thousands. The word on everyone's mind, but on no one's lips, was "retreat."

"They'll drive us into the sea, Captain," one of his sergeants told Contrell.

"Enough of that talk. Get the men together in case we have to pull out fast. Check Hill 314."

The hills were so numerous and anonymous that they'd been numbered according to their height. They were only places to die, and one looked much like another to the men at the guns.

Some tanks, muddy and caked with frost, rolled through the morning mists, heading back. Contrell stepped in front of the leading vehicle and waved it down. He saw now that it was actually a Boffers twin 40-mm. self-propelled mount, an antiaircraft weapon that was being effectively used as infantry support. From a distance in the mist it had looked like a tank, and for all practical purposes it was one.

"What the hell's wrong, Captain?" a voice shouted down at him.

"Can you carry some men back with you?"

The officer jumped down, and something in the movement brought back to Contrell a sudden memory of a desert scene eight years earlier. "Willy Grove! I'll be damned!"

Grove blinked quickly, seeming to focus his eyes, and Contrell saw from the collar insignia that he was now a major. "Well. Contrell, wasn't it? Good to see you again."

"It's a long way from Africa, Willy."

"Damn sight colder, I know that. Thought you were getting out after the war."

"I was out for three weeks and couldn't stand it. I guess this army life gets to you after a while. How are things up ahead?"

Grove twisted his face into a grimace. "If they were any damned good, you think we'd be heading this way?"

"You're going back through the Pass?"

"It's the only route left. I hear the Chinese have got it just about cut off too."

"Can we ride on top your vehicles?"

Grove gave a short chuckle. "Sure. You can catch the grenades and toss them back." He patted the .45 on his side as if it were his wallet. "Climb aboard."

Contrell issued a sharp order to his sergeant and waited until most of his few scattered forces had found handholds on the vehicles. Then he climbed aboard Major Grove's "tank" himself. Already in the morning's distance they could hear the insane bugle calls that usually meant another Chinese advance. "The trap is closing," he said.

Grove nodded. "It's like I told you once before. The fighting never stops. Never figured back then that we'd be fighting the Chinese, though."

"You don't like fighting Chinese?"

The major shrugged. "Makes no difference. They die just like anyone else. Easier, when they're high on that stuff they smoke."

The column rolled into the Pass, the only route that remained open to the south. But almost at once they realized that the hills and wooded stretches on either side of the roads were filled with the waiting enemy. Contrell looked back and saw his sergeant topple over to the ground, cut through the middle by a burst from a hidden machine gun. Ahead of them, a truckload of troops was stalled across the road, afire. Grove lifted himself up for a better view.

"Can we get around them?" Contrell asked, breathing hard.

"Around them or through them."

"They're South Koreans."

Those still alive and able to run were scrambling off the burning truck, running toward Grove's vehicle. "Get off!" Grove shouted. "Keep back!" He reached down and shoved one of the South Koreans over backward, into the roadside dust. When another clambered aboard in his place, Grove carefully took out his .45 pistol and put a bullet through the man's head.

Contrell watched it all as if he were seeing an old movie unwinding after years of forgotten decay. I've been here before, he thought, thinking in the same breath of the medals they'd shared after the North African episode. Men like Grove never changed—at least, not for the better.

"They were South Koreans, Willy," he said quietly, his mouth close to the major's ear.

"What the hell do I care? They think I'm running a damned bus service?"

Nothing more was said about it until they'd rumbled south into the midst of the retreating American army. Contrell wondered where it would all stop, the retreat. At the sea, or Tokyo—or California?

They took time for a smoke, and Contrell said, "You didn't have to kill that Gook, Willy."

"No? What was I supposed to do, let them all climb aboard and get us all killed? Go on, report it if you want to. I know my military law and I know my moral law. It's like the overcrowded lifeboat."

"I think you just like to kill."

"What soldier doesn't?"

"Me."

"Hell! Then what'd you re-up for? Fun and games?"

"I thought I might do something to keep the world at peace."

"Only way to keep the world at peace is to kill all the trouble-makers."

"That Gook back there was a troublemaker?"

"To me he was. Just then."

"But you enjoyed it. I could almost see it in your face. It was like North Africa all over again."

Major Grove turned away, averting his face. "I got a medal for North Africa, buddy. It helped me become a major."

Contrell nodded sadly. "They do give medals for killing. And I guess sometimes they don't ask for too many details."

Someone called an order and Grove stubbed out the cigarette. "Come on, boy. Don't brood over it. We're moving on."

Contrell nodded and followed him. Once, just once, he looked back the way they'd come . . .

24 August 1961

Major Contrell had been in Berlin only three hours when he heard Willy Grove's name mentioned in a barside conversation at the Officers' Club. The speaker was a slightly drunk captain who liked to sound as if he'd been defending Berlin from the Russians single-handed since the war.

"Grove," he said with a little bit of awe in his voice. "Colonel Willoughby McSwing Grove. That's his name! They say he'll make general before the year is out. If you coulda seen the way he stood up to those Russians last week, if you coulda seen it!"

"I'd heard he was in Berlin," Contrell said noncommittally. "I know him from the old days."

"Korea?"

Contrell nodded. "And North Africa nearly twenty years ago. When we were all a lot younger."

"I didn't know he fought in World War II."

"That was before we were officers."

The captain snorted. "It's hard to imagine old Grove before he was an officer. You shoulda seen him last week—he stood there, watching them put up that damned wall, and pretty soon he walked right up to the line. This Russian officer was there too, and they stood like that, only inches apart, just like they were daring each other to make a move. Pretty soon the Russian turned his back and walked away, and damned if old Grove didn't take out his .45! We all thought for a minute he was going to blast that Commie down in his track, and I think we'd all have been with him if he did. You know, you go through this business long enough—this building up and relaxing of tensions—and after a while you just wish somebody like Colonel Grove would pull a trigger or push a button and get us down to the business once and for all."

"The business of killing?"

"What else is there, for a soldier?"

Contrell downed his drink without answering. Instead, he asked, "Where is Grove staying? Is he married now?"

"If he is, there's no sign of a wife. He lives in the BOQ over at the air base."

"Thanks." Contrell laid a wrinkled bill on the bar. "The drinks were on me. I enjoyed our conversation."

He found Colonel Grove after another hour's searching, not at his quarters but at the office overlooking the main thoroughfare of West Berlin. His hair was a bit whiter, his manner a bit more brisk, but it was still the same Willy Grove. A man in his forties. A soldier.

"Contrell! Welcome to Berlin! I heard you were being assigned here."

They shook hands like old friends, and Contrell said, "I understand you've got the situation pretty well in hand over here."

"I did have until they started building that damned wall last week. I almost shot a Russian officer."

"I heard. Why didn't you?"

Colonel Grove smiled. "You know me better than to expect lies, Major. We've been through some things together. You're the one who always said I had a weakness for killing."

" 'Weakness' isn't exactly the word for it."

"Well, whatever. Anyway, you probably know better than anyone else my feelings at that moment. But I kept them under control. There's talk of making me a general, boy, and I'm keeping my nose clean these days. No controversy."

"And I'm still a major. Guess I don't live right."

"You don't have the killer instinct, Contrell. Never did have it."

Major Contrell lit a cigarette, very carefully. "I don't think a soldier needs to have a killer instinct these days, Willy. But then, we've been debating this same question for nearly twenty years now, off and on."

"Haven't we, though." Willy Grove smiled. "I'm sorry I don't have somebody I can kill for you this time."

"What would you have ever done in civilian life, Willy?"

"I don't know. Never thought about it much."

"A hundred years ago you'd have been a Western gunman probably. Or forty years ago, a Chicago bootlegger with a Tommy gun. Now there's just the army left to you."

Grove's smile hardened, but he didn't lose it. Instead, he rose from behind the desk and walked over to the window. Looking down at the busy street, he said, "Maybe you're right, I really don't know. I do know that I've killed fifty-two men so far in my lifetime, which is a pretty good average. Most of them I looked right in the eye before I shot them. A few others got it in the back, like that Russian nearly did last week."

"You could have started a war."

"Yes. And some day perhaps I will. If I had the power to . . ." He let the sentence go unfinished.

"They're not all like you," Contrell said. "Thank God."

"But I have enough of them on my side. Enough of them who know that army means war and war means death. You can't escape it, no matter how hard you try."

He looked at the white-haired colonel and remembered the captain he'd spoken with in the bar earlier that afternoon. Perhaps they were right. Perhaps he was the one who was wrong. Had he wasted away his whole life pursuing an impossible dream of an army without war or killing?

"I'll still do it my way," he said.

"Good luck, Major."

A week later Contrell heard that a Russian guard had been killed at the wall in an exchange of gunfire with West Berlin police. One story had it that an American officer had fired the fatal shot personally, but Contrell was unable to verify this rumor.

5 April 1969

It was the day before Easter in Washington, a city expectant under a warm spring sun. The corridors of the Pentagon were more deserted than usual for a Saturday, and only in one office on the west side was there any activity. General Willoughby McSwing Grove, newly appointed Chairman of the Joint Chiefs of Staff, was moving into his suite of offices.

Colonel Contrell found him bent over a desk drawer, distributing the contents of a bulging brief case to their proper places. He looked up, a bit surprised, at his Saturday visitor. "Well . . . Contrell, isn't it? Haven't seen you in years. Colonel? You're coming along."

"Not as fast as you, General."

Grove smiled a bit, accepting the comment as a sort of congratulation. "I'm at the top now. Good place to be for a man of my age. The hair's all white, but I feel good. Do I look the same, Colonel?"

"I'd know you anywhere, General."

"There's a lot to be done, a damned lot. I've waited and worked all my life for this spot, and now I've got it. Our new President has promised me free rein in dealing with the international situation."

"I thought he would," Contrell said quietly. "Do you have any plans yet?"

"I've had plans all my life." He wheeled around in his swivel chair and stared hard out the window at the distant city. "I'm going to show them what an army is for."

Colonel Contrell cleared his throat. "You know, Willy, it took the better part of a lifetime, but you finally convinced me that killing can be necessary at times."

"Well, I'm pleased to know that you've come around to . . ." General Grove started to turn back in his chair and Contrell shot him once in the left temple.

For a time after he'd done it, Contrell stood staring at the body, hardly aware that the weight of the gun had slipped from his fingers. There was only one thought that crowded all the others from his mind. How would he ever explain it all at the court-martial?

The Pile of Sand

John Keefauver

The earlier arrivals at the beach saw the pile of sand and assumed it had been made by someone at dawn who had left it to go, perhaps, to have breakfast and would be coming back later in the morning to sculpt it into an entry for the sand-castle contest that day. That seemed like a good explanation, anyway (it was later agreed), for the existence of the gigantic pile of sand, at least twenty-five feet high, maybe thirty, with a proportionate base, sitting on the beach not far from the ocean's edge at 9 A.M. with not a soul near it. It appeared to have been thrown up hurriedly, or without design, anyway, as if it were the first step toward a giant sculpture, although it was puzzling that there was no dug-out area around the pile, from which the sand would have come for the mound. Not puzzling at first; later, when the whole town was talking about the sand hill.

At first no one had paid much attention to the mound (other than to wonder who had such a gigantic sculpture in mind, one which he must have had to start building at dawn) because everybody was intent upon building his own entry. But as the morning wore on and nobody came back to continue work on the mountain of sand, there was more talk about the strange pile, particularly after the judges arrived about noon and began to ask around if anybody knew whom the hill of sand belonged to. Was it an entry? Of course, no one knew anymore than the judges. So the thing just sat there, unattended and unworked on, as the hours passed, with parents telling their children not to climb on it or even touch it because it might be the beginning of a sculpture. Which was a difficult order for the kids to abide by,

143

for the great mountain of sand was a most tempting play hill. One boy, in fact, did scamper up the hill, to come tearing down, frightened when his father bawled at him. The father then tried to smooth out his son's footsteps on the pile, muttering all the time about the nut—most likely nuts, from the size of it—who made the thing and then went away and left it unguarded.

By 2 P.M. the judges began making their rounds through the more than a hundred sand creations up and down the beach for about a quarter of a mile: the castles, of course, of all sizes; the animals—the crocodiles and turtles and whales; the offbeat creations—the VW, the hamburger and piece of pie ("Lunch"), a bathtub with a woman in it, kelp used as plumbing, a mouse approaching a trap with a piece of cheese in it, the pyramids, sculptures connected with the space program. And the pile of sand. By three-thirty the judges had compared notes and awarded the first-prize ribbon to "Apollo 12." Second prize went to the VW, and the mouse and trap and cheese won third. The judges ignored the pile of sand; they considered it the work of kids who had tired of it.

Traditionally, after the ribbons had been awarded and people started to go home, children were allowed to destroy the sculptures. The incoming tide would cover them anyway, and the kids might as well have the pleasure. The children jumped savagely on the creations, screaming with delight, while the parents watched with almost equal pleasure. Occasionally an adult would join his child in smashing a sand design.

There wasn't much the kids could do about destroying the mountain of sand. They ran up and down it and kicked it, but they would have had to have a mechanical shovel to have knocked it down. Either that, or have worked hours with shovels to flatten it. Adults ignored the pile.

As the evening fog drifted in and the weather turned cool, there was a rapid departure from the beach, which now looked as if a battle had been fought over it. Only the great pile of sand remained unbroken. The evening high tide would take care of it, though. What nuts went to all that trouble and then never showed up to finish their job? What fools?

By dusk the tide was lapping at the base of the pile.

An early-rising beach-front resident noticed the police car parked in front of his house shortly after dawn, and when he went out to investigate, he saw the officer down on the beach looking at the pile of sand. When the officer came back to his car, he said to the resident, who had walked out to meet him, "That damn hill is still there. Looks like the tides didn't take an inch of sand off it." And sure enough, as the resident went out onto the beach himself, he saw that the high tides during the night and at dawn had flattened and smoothed the beach of all remains of the previous day's sculptures except for the giant pile of sand, which, if anything, appeared to be larger. The bottom three or so feet of the mountain were smooth where the tide had encircled it but, strangely, the water appeared to have washed away none of the base.

By midmorning a number of children were playing on the pile, but it was of such size that the only damage they did to it was to puncture it with footstep holes. Adults looked at it curiously, but none tried to keep the children from climbing on it now.

While the same beach-front resident was eating lunch he saw the car with the press sign park on the street in front. A photographer went down to the beach and took some pictures of the pile, and in that evening's local paper there was a photograph of the "Mysterious Mountain of Sand that Challenges the Sea." The story beneath the picture was written with much tongue in cheek.

That evening about a hundred people (the resident estimated) were around the pile waiting for high tide to reach it. Children played on it, including some older boys now. One man, though, yelled at his son to come down from the hill. "Why?" the boy wanted to know. "Don't argue with me! Come down from there!" As the tide gradually circled the pile, all the parents, though, made their children get off the mountain, leaving only the older youngsters, those whose parents were not with them. They whooped and laughed as the tide rose around the pile, until one boy, a younger one, became silent and finally jumped from the mound into the water and ran in to a dry part of the beach. Then the other boys followed him, one by one, until the scarred mountain of sand sat by itself in the onrushing water, which climbed inch by inch, foot by foot as darkness came on. Some onlookers had brought flashlights, but as they were forced back from the mound their lights gradually lost their effectiveness. When a patrol car on the road above the beach shone its spotlight on the pile of sand, though, they all could see that the mountain remained, as if while one wave was taking sand away, another was bringing it in.

The next day a larger crowd surrounded the pile of sand. The beach-front resident himself had seen the report of the "Sand Mountain" that "survived the night" on the early local television; the pictures clearly showed that the mountain was as big that morning as it had been the day before. And that afternoon another picture and story of the mound were in the local paper, this time on the front page. The story was still written with a light touch, and an oceanologist was quoted as saying that the mountain remained because of the "press's molehill," while the story quoted a geologist: "The sand of the sea speaketh in diverse ways—especially with the help of some local wags with many shovels and much true grit." During the evening the crowd was larger than the one of the previous evening, although more parents kept their children off the pile. There was some talk of digging into the mountain in order to flatten it or at least to see what the hell was inside it. None of the talk was serious, though. It would be a lot of work for nothing. Would be silly. Let the water wash it away.

As the tide rose around the pile, what talk there was quieted down, and as it became apparent that once again the mountain was going to withstand the evening high tide, the onlookers, including ones now along the road that rimmed the beach, became silent. A spotlight from a patrol car stayed on the mountain as the water rose, as if the mountain were a monument. Many spectators stayed even after the tide peaked, and just before dawn, when the tide peaked again, two old men stood beside the police car that had come up and stopped and turned its spotlight on the beach. The mountain still stood. As if, one of the men said, it were the only real sculpture that had even been there.

By the fourth day of the existence of the mountain of sand only a few parents would allow their children to play on it. Of course, there were older children, on the beach without parents, who climbed up and down the mound, but by the fifth day there was only a total of seven children who ascended the mountain, although it was a beautiful, sunny day and the beach was crowded. One man had brought a shovel and wandered up and down the beach, half-heartedly asking if there were any volunteers with shovels. There was none. So the man went to the hill by himself and jokingly started to plunge his shovel into the sand, then stopped as one of the younger boys on the mountain started to cry, then ran down the mound to the beach, still bawling, to be followed by the others, one by one, as if each were afraid to be left on the mountain alone. "What's the matter?" the crying child was asked. But all he did was blubber that he had become "scared." And the man with the shovel went back to his family on the beach and turned his back on the pile of sand.

On the seventh day of Sand Mountain, a Saturday, three carloads of men with cases of beer set up camp near the hill in midafternoon. Each had a shovel. Immediately a crowd gathered around them, to ask if they were going to flatten the mountain, to urge them to. "We sure as hell are!" said a man who apparently was their leader, a burly, hairy loudmouth in his early thirties. "Soon as we have a few beers."

The crowd waited impatiently as the men, bantering among themselves, lolling on their backs looking up at the mound, slowly drank their beer. To cries of "What you waiting for!" and "Come on!" and "Can't get anything done lying there!" they laughed and grinned and their leader said, "No hurry. That pile of sand ain't going no place. And if there's anything inside it, it ain't going no place either." Then seeing that a half a dozen or so men, men not in his group, had gone off and returned with their own shovels, he stood up and said, "Stay away. This is our baby." And then seeing that the six men with shovels weren't in any hurry to start digging on the mountain, he sat back down and opened another can of beer, the others with him then doing the same. As each drinker finished a beer, he carefully put his can on a stack which, crudely and in miniature, resembled the mountain of sand. None of the drinkers offered a beer to anyone outside his group, and none wore a bathing suit.

By early evening, with almost all the beer drunk and the tide beginning to lap around Sand Mountain, the leader got up and deliberately, dramatically, looking around first to see if he was being watched, destroyed the hill of cans with a kick. "Okay!" he bawled. "Let's go get that damned pile of sand!" And cheered on by some (most onlookers were silent), the men grabbed their shovels and charged up the mound.

They began to dig furiously, throwing the sand as far out from the mountain as they could. About twelve of them, they ringed the pile at various levels, led by their leader, chanting as they worked, "Mountain, mountain, dig it *down!* Mountain, mountain, tear it *down!* Mountain, mountain, get its *heart!* Mountain, mountain . . ."

Onlookers came as close as they could to the pile, to a point where the thrown sand landed just in front of them, while behind them, seeing the attack on the mountain, others streamed toward Sand Mountain from up and down the beach and from the road along the ocean. Cars were stopping now, the occupants getting out to watch. ". . . tear it *down!*" the onlookers now picking up the chant ". . . get its *heart!*" Until after only moments spectators with shovels were asking the beer drinkers if they could help, and receiving the go-ahead, climbed onto the mountain, too, and began to dig. ". . . dig it *down!*" Then men without shovels climbed the hill, to scoop into the mountain with their hands, and stand and throw, chanting. Then women were climbing the mountain, then teenagers and children. ". . . tear it *down!*" The pile of sand was covered finally with chanting, furiously digging, clawing, throwing, non-laughing people, becoming packed even tighter as the original beer-drinking diggers kept moving down the mountain as the top of it was flattened. ". . . get its *heart!*"

The water was rising now around the beheaded mountain, washing over the sand thrown down from the height of the remaining pile, flattening the thrown sand, drawing it back into the ocean. Rising inch by inch, foot by foot, as the sun dropped lower and lower, the water encroached until some men and women picked up their smaller children and waded from the base of the mountain to the dry beach. One woman fell and her child screamed in terror when she, hit from behind by a shovelful of sand, fell into the water. A policeman quickly grabbed them and pulled them out. His patrol car stood ready with its spotlight if it should get dark before the mountain had been destroyed. Its light was already on, aimed at the mound.

Gradually the mountain came down, until only the original shovelers were digging, slower now, panting, chanting less (although the onlookers were still chanting strongly, angrily). Then as the ocean began to lap over what was left of the mountain, the workers straggled off the slight rise and out of the water, until only their leader was left, sweating, panting hard, his chant now down to "dig, tear, heart!"

He waded out of the water the moment the ocean finally covered the mountain, disappointed, muttering, "Hell, there wasn't a *damn thing* in that pile of sand."

Out of habit, the beach-front resident was up at dawn. When he looked from his living-room picture window at the beach, he didn't know whether to feel disappointment or relief that the mountain was gone. Some of each, he guessed. But mostly relief.

From the distance he was not able to see the beginning of a new mountain not far from the one destroyed. Later in the day, though, he and others would see it as the morning high tide piled up more and more sand. And he would see the second baby mountain, too, near the first one, both growing at equal speed. By 9 A.M. both were larger than old Sand Mountain.

Payoff on Double Zero

Warner Law

Although she was typing from her shorthand notes, the middle-aged secretary kept sneaking glances at Sam Miller across the outer office. He was waiting to see her boss, Mr. Collins, who was the owner and manager of the casino in the Starlight Hotel. This is a relatively old establishment, not far out of town on the Las Vegas Strip.

To women in general, and to middle-aged secretaries in particular, Sam was almost surrealistically handsome, too all-American to believe in one look. He was in his early twenties, well over six feet tall, broad in the shoulders and lithe below. His blond hair was cut short, his face was tanned, his nose perfectly straight, his teeth white, his smile a gift of pleasure. His eyes were true blue and his gaze was of such clear and steady honesty that it made even a secretary with a pure conscience and a fine Methodist background feel somewhat shifty and sinful when she met it. She knew that Mr. Collins would be eager to hire Sam—though he'd pretend he wasn't and he'd give the boy a little hard time first. The Starlight needed dealers and rarely did they find one who was such a poster picture of integrity. More than that, Sam's looks would draw most of the women gamblers in Vegas, the younger ones with an urge to bed him and the older ones with an impulse to mother him. Then the intercom buzzed and Mr. Collins said that he was ready to see Mr. Miller.

Sam went in and carefully shut the door behind him. Mr. Collins posed behind his massive desk, right hand extended, a smile of limited cordiality on his face. Sam had heard that Mr. Collins was Balkan by birth, with a name of many jagged syllables that had been carefully naturalized and neutralized. He was a man in his sixties, olive in coloring, wearing a light-gray silk suit exactly shaded to match his hair.

Sam shook his hand and smiled and said, "How do you do, sir?"

"It's a pleasure to meet you, Sam Miller. Sit down. Tell me the story of your life." Mr. Collins had only a trace of a foreign accent.

Sam sat. "All of it?"

"Well, it can scarcely have been a very long life. How old are you?"

"Twenty-two, sir."

"Might I see your driver's license?"

"Sure." Sam took it from his wallet and handed it over the desk and Mr. Collins gave it a quick glance and passed it back.

"Have you ever been arrested?"

"No, sir."

"Be certain, now. The rules of the Nevada Gaming Commission require me to check."

"No, sir. I've never been arrested for anything."

"Why do you wish to be a dealer?"

"To make some money and save it, so I can go to college full time."

"Where do you come from originally?"

"I was born in Los Angeles and I went to Hollywood High, and then I enlisted in the Marine Corps, rather than be drafted."

"What did you do in the Marine Corps?"

"I got sent to Vietnam."

"Did anything happen to you?"

"Yes. I got shot three times."

"You have my profound sympathy. Were they serious wounds?"

"One was. It was in the stomach. The others were just flesh wounds. Anyway, I finally got discharged last summer."

"Do you happen to have your discharge papers on your person?"

Sam produced them and Mr. Collins looked them over and handed them back.

"And after your discharge?"

"My uncle had a liquor store in Hollywood and I went to work for him. But we were held up four times. Twice I got clobbered with revolver butts and once I was shot in the foot, and finally my uncle was pistol-whipped and he said the hell with it and sold the store and I was out of a job."

"You've crowded a good deal of action into your short life."

Sam smiled. "Not intentionally. And then somebody suggested I might get a job dealing up here in Las Vegas, and my math was always pretty good, and so I came up and took a course at Mr. Ferguson's Dealers' School and, as you've seen from the diploma your secretary brought in, I graduated yesterday."

Mr. Collins picked up the diploma and handed it to Sam. "Why did you come here—that is, instead of to some other casino?"

"Mr. Ferguson said he thought you might be hiring dealers and that you were a good man to work for. He also said that you were the smartest man in Vegas."

"Did he, now? It's the first I've heard of it. As it happens, however, I've just been talking to Ferguson on the phone about you. He says you were one of the best students he's had in a long time. How is your roulette?"

"Pretty fair, I think."

"We shall see. A little test. Thirty-two has come up," Mr. Collins began, and then rattled on with, "and a player has two chips straight up on it, one split, two chips on corners, four chips on three across and three chips on the first column. How many chips do you pay this player?"

It took Sam four seconds to answer, "A hundred and forty-seven."

"You forgot the column bet."

"No, sir, I didn't. You said the first column. Thirty-two is in the second column." Sam smiled a little. "Which you very well know."

Mr. Collins did not smile. "These are quarter chips. How much has the player won?"

"Seven stacks plus seven. Thirty-six seventy-five."

Now Mr. Collins smiled. "Can you start work this afternoon at four? That's the middle shift—four till midnight."

"Yes, sir."

"You'll get forty dollars per shift, plus your share of the dealers' tips. Like most casinos, we pool them and whack them up evenly. You'll average around two-fifty, two-seventy-five for a forty-hour week. Is that satisfactory?"

"Yes, sir." Sam rose as if to leave.

"Sit down. I have something to tell you. I and I alone own the gaming license here. I am not answerable to anyone. I have no connection with the Mafia nor any other bunch of criminals. We do not cheat our players, we do not cheat the Nevada Gaming Commission and we do not cheat the Internal Revenue Service. Furthermore, if any dealer tries to cheat the house in favor of himself or a player, he gets no mercy from me."

"Mr. Ferguson told me you ran an honest game."

"It is *more* than an honest game. A little test. Number seven has come up. Having made sure that the number is not covered, you clear the board of chips. But then a player says, 'Just a minute, here! I had a chip on seven, but you took it away!' You know for certain that this player is lying through his teeth. What do you do?"

"Well . . . I'd send for my pit boss."

"No. You apologize to the player and you pay him. Only if the player does this more than once do you call for your pit boss—who will have been at your side by that time, anyway. The point I am making is that as far as *you* are concerned, every player is honest and he is always right. You are not a policeman and you are not a detective. That is the job of your pit boss and it is also my job. *It is not yours.*"

"Yes, sir."

Mr. Collins rose and extended his hand. "Nice to have you with us. Keep your hands off our cocktail waitresses. There are plenty of other pretty girls in this town."

At three forty-five that afternoon, Sam walked again into the Starlight Hotel. Being one of the older Strip hotels, it was not a large one. The casino itself was a separate wing. People came to play there because it was neither noisy nor garish, like the newer and much larger Strip casinos. The slots were in a separate room, so their clatter did not disturb the serious gamblers. On the depressed oval that was the casino floor, there were two crap tables, three 21 tables and three roulette tables. There was no wheel of fortune and no bingo and no race-track betting. This was a casino for players who appreciated quiet. Even the stickmen at the crap tables kept their continuous chatter down.

Sam didn't know where to report for work, but he found a small bar through an archway on the upper level of the room and went in and inquired of the barman, whose name turned out to be Chuck. He told Sam how to find the dealers' room.

Sam followed a corridor to the rear of the building, where he found a room with some wall lockers and a few easy chairs and tables. Other dealers were there, hanging up their jackets and putting on their green aprons. A scrawny little man in a dark suit came up to Sam. He looked fifty and had a sour, sallow face.

"Sam Miller?"

"Yes, sir."

"I'm Pete and I'm your pit boss on this shift." He turned to the other dealers. "Boys, this is Sam Miller." They grunted friendly greetings. "You'll get to know 'em all," Pete told Sam. "But this is Harry." He took Sam over to meet a tall man of seventy with weary eyes. "You'll be working together. You can begin by stacking for Harry tonight."

"Pleased to meet you, sonny boy," Harry said and shook Sam's hand and looked at him and reacted. "My God—you look fifteen years old."

In the casino, Sam found that his roulette-table setup was almost identical with the one in Ferguson's school. There were six stools along the players' side of the table. By the wheel on the dealer's right were stacks of chips in different colors—white, red, green, blue, brown and yellow. They were all marked STARLIGHT but had no stated value. Since the minimum bet was a quarter, their value was so presumed.

Past the colors were stacks of dollar tokens. These were of base metal, minted for the casino. To the right of the tokens were stacks of house checks, with marked denominations of five dollars ranging upward to $50. The casino also had house checks worth $100 and $500 and $1000, but these were seldom seen in any quantity at a roulette table.

In front of the dealer was a slot in which rested a plastic shingle, and when players bought chips with currency, the bills were shoved down through the slot and into the locked cashbox under the table.

Since this was now the end of a shift, Mr. Collins came up with his keys and an empty cashbox. He exchanged one box for the other and walked off with the full one toward the cashier's office, followed by an armed and uniformed security guard.

For the first hour, Sam merely stacked the chips and the occasional checks that Harry shoved over to him. It was a quiet game, without plungers or cheaters or arguments. Then Harry went off for a break and Sam took over the dealing.

Not long after, a woman came up to Sam's table. She was in her fifties, tall and scrawny, and her mouth held more than her share of the world's teeth. She was wearing a gold-lamé blouse over orange slacks. She sounded rather drunk as she said, "Gimme a coupla stacksa quarters." She handed Sam a ten-dollar bill. He slotted the money and passed her two stacks of red chips. "I don' like red," she said. "It doesn't go with my slacks. You got another color?"

"How about green?" Sam asked her, smiling.

"Green is jus' fine," she said and soon picked up the two stacks Sam put in front of her.

Sam started the ball whirring.

"I been playin' this roulette for years and years," the woman announced to the table at large, "an' there's no such thing as a system. No such thing as a system! You just gotta let the chips fall where they may, as the fella said!"

She then turned her back to the table, with twenty chips in each hand, and tossed them all over her shoulders onto the board. They clattered down every which way and knocked other bets out of position, and a great many of the chips rolled off the table and onto the floor. The other players cried out in annoyance. Sam removed the ball from the wheel. Pete started over, pausing to push one of several buttons on a small table in the center of the enclosure.

"I'm sorry, ma'am," Sam told the woman, "but we can't bet that way."

She giggled. "I'm jus' lettin' the chips fall where they may!"

"Even so," Sam said with an engaging smile, "if your bets aren't in correct positions, I won't know how to pay you when you win."

The other players had been patiently bending over and retrieving green chips from the floor. Sam gathered them and stacked them for her and made sure they were all there.

"I'm real sorry to make all this trouble," the woman said, smiling at Sam. "Let's see, now. Most of 'em fell around twenny, so that's where I'll kinda put 'em. Around twenny." With drunken carefulness, she began to slather her chips around number 20.

In the distance, Sam saw Mr. Collins approaching from his office—

where he had just heard the warning buzz from Pete. He walked up and stood at the head of the table, but said nothing.

Sam put the ball in motion. The woman watched it spin. "It's just got to be twenny," she said. "Or else I am bankrupt!"

The ball fell into number 20. "Ooooooh!" She jumped up and down and clapped her hands. "I won! I won!"

Sam counted the green chips on the board. "Six straight up on twenty, nine splits, ten on corners. That's four hundred and forty-three chips, plus these twenty-five left on the board."

"How much is that in money?" the woman asked.

"One hundred and seventeen dollars," Sam said.

Mr. Collins had come up behind her. "My congratulations, Mrs. Burke," he said.

She turned. "Oh, dear Mr. Collins. How are you?"

"It's always such a pleasure to see you here," Mr. Collins said. "As a matter of fact, I've been meaning to call you. Before you break the bank, why don't you cash in and come and have a drink with me? I need your advice about a piece of real estate."

In moments, Mrs. Burke had been paid her winnings and was walking off happily on Mr. Collins' arm. Under the chatter of the players, Pete murmured to Sam, "Very nicely handled, son. What Howard Hughes and Kerkorian don't own in Vegas, Mrs. Burke does."

On Sam's second night of dealing, nothing whatever happened. But on his third night, there was trouble.

A fat-faced young man with a sullen mouth and pimples had been betting regularly on 14 and losing. He was playing with ten-dollar house checks, but he didn't look as if he could afford them, and he kept increasing his bets until he was up to fifty dollars a spin, straight up on 14. Despair came into his eyes.

This time, 15 came up. There was no bet on it. Sam cleared the board.

"Hold on, there!" the young man said. "What about my fifty on fifteen?"

Sam smiled politely. "I think it was on fourteen, sir."

Pete had already pushed a button and was at Sam's side.

"Not this time it wasn't!" the young man said. "I finally got tired of fourteen and bet on fifteen. You were just so used to seeing me bet on fourteen that you made a mistake, that's all."

Eighteen hundred dollars was involved. Sam glanced over at Pete, but before the pit boss could speak, a distinguished-looking white-haired man at the very end of the table called to Sam, "I'm afraid the young man up there is right." His manner was reluctant and apologetic. "I'm sorry to be difficult, but I did see him bet on fifteen. I wondered at the time if he'd made a mistake or was changing his number after all this time."

The smartest man in Vegas had by now come up behind the bettor. "Pay the bet, Sam," he said. "I want no arguments here."

"Yes, sir," Sam said and reached for some checks.

Pete stopped him with a hand and said, "We don't have that much here at the table, Mr. Collins."

This was not true.

"Oh?" said Mr. Collins. "Well, let's go to my office, then. If you and your friend would come with me, I'll see that—"

"My *friend?*" the young man asked. "I've never—"

The older man said from the foot of the table, "I've never seen that young fellow before in my life!"

"Oh?" Mr. Collins looked surprised. "I'm sorry. I'd presumed you two were friends."

"I never laid eyes on that gentleman before in my life!" the young man said.

"I understand," said Mr. Collins. "However, sir," he said to the older man, "I'll need a brief statement from you affirming that you saw the bet being placed. It's required by the Nevada Gaming Commission in these instances."

This was rubbish.

The older man sighed and picked up his chips and came round the table and offered his hand and a smile to the young man and said, "My name is John Wood."

"I'm George Wilkins and I'm real sorry to put you to all this trouble, but thank you for sticking up for me. What I mean"—he nodded toward Sam—"young fellows like this are obviously so new they make normal mistakes."

Sam wished he could knock this young man down and kick his teeth out. The two walked away with Mr. Collins. They did not return to the casino floor. When midnight came and Sam went off duty, he passed Mr. Collins on the upper level and asked him, "What happened to those two cheaters?"

Mr. Collins smiled. "Why do you so presume, Sam?"

"Because there was no bet on fifteen and anybody who said otherwise is a liar."

Laughing, Mr. Collins said, "Sam, you wouldn't believe how stupid some people can be. I asked to see their driver's licenses, as a matter of form. Without thinking, they showed them to me. What do you think I learned?"

"Don't tell me they have the same name?!"

"No, no. But their addresses showed that they live two houses apart. In Van Nuys, California."

"My God! What did you do to them?"

"Nothing. I left them alone in my office for a minute, and when I came back, they were gone. I presume they're well back in California by now." The smartest man in Vegas patted Sam on the shoulder and said, "Good night, Sam," and walked off.

It was around eleven on Sam's fourth night that things really began to happen. Sam was dealing and Harry was stacking for him. The table was crowded and all the colors were in use. Behind the seated players, others stood, betting with coins and house checks. As the ball began to slow, Sam said, "No more bets, please."

A man started shouting, "Let me through! Here, now—let me through! Get out of the way, damn it!"

He was a tall man in his seventies and he wore a white Stetson. He had a white mustache under a long red nose. He shouldered his way through the standers. He held two packages of bank-strapped currency above his head, and when he reached the table, he threw them both in the general area of number 23 and announced, "That's two thousand dollars right smack on twenty-three! Straight up!"

Sam quickly picked up the packs and tossed them off the betting area. "I'm sorry, sir." The ball fell into number 11.

The old man's reedy voice rose above the murmur at the table. "What's the matter, young fella? Something the matter with my money?" He was wearing a white-silk Western shirt and an apache tie with a gold tie slide in the shape of a nugget, and over all he had on a spotless white-buckskin with long fringes and with stitched patch pockets high and low. Sam had seen a similar suit in a Las Vegas store window for $295.

"This is perfectly good money!" the old man said, showing off the two packs. They contained $100 bills, which, as Sam knew, usually come from a bank strapped in units of ten. These looked to be fresh from the Bureau of Engraving and Printing.

Sam smiled at the old man. "Of course it is, sir. But, for one thing, you were too late for this roll; and for another, there's a two-hundred-dollar maximum bet on the numbers; and for still another, we don't use paper money on this table."

"Well, sell me some chips, damn it!"

"I will, sir, but we're out of colors and—"

Pete had come to the table and he now asked, "What denomination would you like to play with, sir?"

"Hundreds! Hundred-dollar chips, if you've got 'em." Everyone at the table was now listening and the old man turned and smiled and said, "My name's Premberton! Bert Premberton! From up Elko way! Pleased to make your acquaintance!" He shook hands with those whom he could reach.

"I'll have to get some hundred-dollar checks from the cashier, Mr. Premberton," Pete said. "How many would you like?"

"Well, now . . ." The old man pondered and brought out package after package of strapped hundreds from his various pockets and stacked them on the table in front of him. Twenty thousand dollars was visible. There was a stunned silence around the table. "Sold a ranch today," Premberton told everyone simply. "Or it finally got through escrow, I should say." To Pete, he said, "Oh, hell. Let's jest start with two thousand. But get plenty, while you're at it." He handed Sam two packages of hundreds and stuffed the others back into his pockets.

Sam handed them to Pete, who broke the paper straps and fanned the bills and nodded and said, "Two thousand. I'll be right back."

"Here, now!" the old man bellowed. "What if twenty-three comes up while you're gone, hey? I want two hundred on it, every time. Twenty-three is gonna be a hot one tonight, I can tell you for true!"

"You'll be covered on every roll, Mr. Premberton," Pete said, starting off.

"Take over for me," Sam told Harry and walked after Pete, catching up with him outside the roulette enclosure. "Pete?" The pit boss stopped and turned. "I don't like this old man," Sam said. "I've got a kind of feeling about him."

"Why?"

"Well, for one thing, he's been drinking, and I didn't like the way he butted his way to the table, and—well, I just don't trust him is all."

"It is not your job to trust people. As long as his money's good, I don't care if—"

"But maybe it isn't. Maybe it's—"

Mr. Collins had walked up to them. "Troubles?"

"Maybe it's counterfeit," Sam finished.

Pete smiled. "You have got to be kidding."

Mr. Collins took the bills from Pete and ruffled through them and handed them back and motioned the pit boss toward the cashier's window. Then he sighed.

"Sam, you still have a good deal to learn. For all practical purposes—as far as we are concerned—there is no such thing as a hundred-dollar bill that is counterfeit. Oh, they do exist, but they're extremely rare, for the reason that printers don't bother with them because they're so difficult to pass. We get fives and tens and twenties and now and then a fifty. But I don't think I've seen a funny hundred in twenty years. In any case, there are two places in which no one but an idiot would deliberately pass even *one* phony hundred-dollar bill, and one is a bank and the other is a casino. Both places have smart cashiers and men with guns."

"I'm sorry," Sam said. "I didn't know that. I was only trying to protect the house."

"It is not your job to protect the house. I thought I'd made that perfectly clear when we first met. Would you get back to your table now, please?"

"Yes, sir."

Pete came up to them, carrying a plastic rack nearly full of $100 house checks. "I got quite a few, just in case," he said. "And to make our boy detective here happy, I asked both Ruth and Hazel to check out those bills; they're both experts in the currency department, and they assure me that the twenty hundreds are the genuine article, with the serial numbers in sequence, just as they left the Bureau of Engraving and Printing."

"I'm sorry to be so stupid," Sam said and followed Pete back to the table, where he and the pit boss piled the checks neatly in stacks of twenty. Harry reached for one stack, knocked off four checks and handed the remaining sixteen to Premberton, saying, "Two thousand, sir, less four hundred for the last two rolls."

The old man grunted his understanding and placed two checks on 23. He then began looking around the casino as if for someone, finally saw her, put two fingers into his mouth and produced a shrill whistle. He waved a hand and shouted, "Over here, honey!"

A girl came toward the table and tried to get through the crowd. "Let her through, there!" the old man cried. "That's my little bride, there! Let her through, damn it!"

People gave way and the girl soon joined Premberton, who hugged and kissed her. The girl blushed and said, "Oh, Bert! Not here!"

The girl was spectacularly lovely. She was in her early twenties and had golden hair and large young breasts. Her mouth was full and sensuous, but her wide blue eyes gave her an expression of innocence.

"Folks! I want you to meet my sweet little honeybunch, Vikki!" He kissed her again and hugged her and then ran his hand up and around her buttocks. "We got hitched this very mornin'!" There was a silence around the table, partly of incredulity and partly of disapproval. "And the reason twenty-three is goin' to be a hot number tonight is that today is February the twenty-third and it's also my own little hot number here's birthday, and she's twenty-three this very day! What do you think of that?" Premberton turned to Harry and asked, "You're sure, now, that two hundred is all I can bet at a time?"

"Yes, sir," Harry said as the ball slowed. "That's our limit." The ball dropped once and bounced about and finally fell into 23 and remained there. "Twenty-three," Harry announced and smiled at Vikki. "Happy birthday, young lady."

"Hey, now!" the old man shouted and clapped everyone he could reach on the back. "What'd I tell you? Twenty-three's goin' to be a hot number tonight!"

Harry pushed three and a half stacks over to the old man. "Seventy checks, sir. Seven thousand dollars."

The other players started exclaiming in excitement and people who heard the commotion began to crowd around the table to watch. Premberton told Vikki to open her shoulder bag and he dumped the seventy checks into it. "You'll get that Rolls-Royce automobile for a weddin' present yet, honeybunch!" Then, to Harry, "Say, now! My little bride here can play, too, can't she?"

"Surely, sir," Harry said.

"Well, you jest do that, Vikki honey! You put two hundred on twenty-three along with me, you hear?"

After the old man had bet his two checks, Vikki added two more from her purse. Harry turned to Sam. "Take over for a couple of minutes, would you?" Harry walked off and Sam stepped into his place and Pete came up to stack for Sam. Other players began piling chips onto 23. Sam sent the ball spinning. It eventually fell into number 5.

"You got to do better 'n that, young fella!" the old man shouted.

Sam smiled at him. "I'm trying, sir. I really am."

"I sure wish we could bet more than four hundred," the old man said. "Twenty-three is sure goin' to be a hot one tonight!"

A man standing next to Premberton volunteered: "You can also play splits if you want to, sir, and corners and three across."

"How's that?"

Using his finger as a pointer, the man showed him what he meant.

"Well, I'm jest goin' to bet that way, then!" He started to cover the board all around 23 and then said, "I'm goin' to need some more chips, young fella." He brought out three more packs of hundreds and handed them to Sam, who broke the straps and counted the bills.

"Three thousand," Sam announced and slotted the money. Then he reached for the stack and a half Pete had ready for him and passed the checks to the old man, who finished covering 23 and its surrounding numbers. As the ball whirred, Sam figured that if 23 came up, the Prembertons would win $20,200. The number turned out to be 22, but the old man had $5000 coming to him because of his bets on splits and corners and three across. When Sam passed his winnings to him, the old man dumped them into Vikki's purse and bet again as before. The next three numbers were losers for Premberton, who was then almost out of visible checks.

"Better give me five thousand this time, young fella," he said, bringing five packages of money from his pocket. It was slotted and Sam gave him two and a half stacks. Harry returned and took over the stacking from Pete. The ball fell into 24. Sam paid the old man another fifty checks and these, too, went into Vikki's purse.

"Start thinkin' what color you want that Rolls-Royce automobile painted, honeybunch."

The next two numbers were zero and 36 and Premberton was down again in checks. "Five thousand more, young fella." The money came out and was counted and sent down into the cashbox and the old man got his two and a half stacks.

"Take over for me?" Sam asked Harry. To Pete as he passed, Sam said, "Got to take a leak." He crossed the casino floor and went up to the upper level, where Mr. Collins was standing, his eyes in constant motion as he surveyed and studied the activity below.

"How is it going, Sam?"

"Mr. Collins, I don't like what's going on at my table."

"Oh? Troubles?"

"Well, whenever that old man wins, he dumps his checks into his wife's bag, but when he loses, he cashes some more of his hundred-dollar bills."

"So?"

"She has close to seventeen thousand in there right now."

"So?" Mr. Collins shrugged. "Sam, some players feel luckier when they're playing with house money and others prefer to pocket our money and play with their own. It's their business. It is not yours."

"I know. But I keep getting the feeling there's something phony about the old man. I mean, as if he were Walter Brennan, playing a rich old rancher. Except that Walter Brennan would convince me and this Mr. Premberton doesn't. It's like he's overacting his part. And the way he fondles that pretty little girl who's young enough to be his granddaughter—well, it makes you kind of sick."

Mr. Collins smiled. "I see. It's not just a roulette dealer I've hired. I have in addition a drama critic and an arbiter of morals." His smile faded. "Has this old gentleman tried any funny business with his bets?"

"Well, no. Not yet, anyway."

"Nor will he. Sam, I'll tell you how to spot a potential cheater on sight. When an ordinary player comes into this casino, he will glance around casually and then decide where he wants to go and go there. But when a cheater comes in—and by this I mean someone who has cheated before elsewhere and may well do so here—he will stop and look carefully at the face of every dealer and pit boss on the floor, for fear he'll be recognized from the past. When I see this, I make sure that this player is watched every minute he's here."

"That's very interesting," Sam said. "I'd never thought of that."

"I saw this old man walk down from the bar. He looked around for the nearest roulette table and hurried to it. In addition, it happens that Chuck the bartender knows him. He's from up near Elko and he recently sold one of his ranches, which is why he has all this bank cash on him. Also, he got married this morning and he's celebrating."

"He told us, at the table."

"All right. Sam, I will tell you one more time and only one more time: The overall problems involved in running this casino are mine. They are not yours. Please don't make me lose my patience with you."

"No, sir. I'm sorry." Sam walked off and into the men's room and in a couple of minutes came out. As he passed the archway leading to the bar, he paused and then went in. There were few customers and Chuck was drying glasses.

"Hi, Sammy boy."

Sam said, "Chuck—this old man—this Mr. Premberton. Mr. Collins says you know him."

Chuck nodded. "He's a rancher from up near Elko. He got married this——"

Sam cut in with, "But do you know him? From before, I mean?"

"Well, no, but——"

"So how do you know so much about him?"

"He was in here earlier, talking to people, buying everybody drinks, showing off his new little wife—you know."

"Thanks, Chuck." Sam walked out of the bar and down to his table. Pete moved away so that Sam could take over the stacking. From the stacks of $100 checks, it was apparent that Premberton had lost a few thousand while Sam had been away. Now the old man handed Harry another five packages of hundreds, which went down the slot.

Sam passed two and a half stacks to Harry, who said, "You mind rolling? I'm really beat."

"Sure." As Sam took Harry's place, he glanced at his watch and saw that it was eleven forty-five. In fifteen minutes the shift would end.

Number 34 came up, and then 6. One of the players had given up his seat to Vikki, who now sat directly across from Sam. "Whatever happened to number twenty-three?" she asked with a smile. It began as a casual smile, but then she glanced up and saw that the old man was engrossed in betting and she looked at Sam and smiled, but directly now. With this smile, all innocence left her eyes.

Sam indicated 23. "I'm afraid it's hidden under all those chips."

"Well, see if you can find it for us."

Sam sent the ball spinning. "I'll do my very best, Mrs. Premberton." The number turned out to be 26. Sam gave the old man thirty-three checks, which Vikki dumped into her bag. There had to be over $20,000 in that bag by now, but then, almost as much had come out of Premberton's pockets.

The next two numbers were 2 and 12. The old man was out of checks again. "Gimme some of them chips, Vikki, honey."

"Oh, Bert. Don't you think we should stop? It's been a long day and it's almost midnight, and——"

"Jest one more roll. I got a hunch it'll be twenty-three."

Vikki passed a handful of checks to Premberton, who leaned over the table to bet and then silently collapsed and fell onto the table and lay still. When it was plain that he wasn't going to move, Vikki cried out and reached over and touched him.

Others at the table were saying, "Is he dead?" "He's had a heart attack!" "Get a doctor, somebody!"

Pete had already pushed buttons. Two security guards hurried up, herded people aside and got to the old man, who now groaned and opened his eyes and managed to push himself erect. The guards held him up.

"What happened?" Premberton asked.

Mr. Collins hurried up. "Help him to my office," he told the guards. "The hotel doctor is on his way."

"I'm all right," Premberton said. "Jest had a little dizzy spell."

"I insist," said Mr. Collins.

The guards started off with the old man. Vikki followed, but Sam called, "Don't forget your husband's checks, Mrs. Premberton." Sam hadn't started the ball rolling. He picked up the old man's bets and handed them to her.

"Thank you. You're very kind." She hurried off toward Mr. Collins' office.

The table quieted down as Sam started the ball rolling. "How did they do, all told?" Sam asked Harry.

He studied the stacks of checks by the wheel and said, "They're up a hundred. It's getting close to midnight, thank the saints. I'm really beat."

In a few minutes, after the graveyard shift had come onto the floor, Sam and Harry walked up to the higher level, where they met Mr. Collins coming out of his office.

"How's the old man?" Harry asked.

"All right, the doctor says. It was just a faint. His wife tells me he had no dinner and a lot of drinks, and I gathered that they'd spent the afternoon in bed."

"It kind of turns your stomach," Sam said. "That old man and that little girl."

"It may turn yours, sonny boy," Harry said sourly. "But I ain't quite dead yet and it don't turn mine." He walked off.

"They ended a hundred to the good," Sam told Mr. Collins.

"I'm just relieved it was nothing more serious than a faint."

"Do you suppose he can get back to their motel all right?" Sam asked.

"That's for *me* to worry about, Sam," Mr. Collins said in a warning tone.

"Sorry," Sam said and walked away.

In the dealers' room, Sam hung up his apron and chatted with some of the dealers and combed his hair and put on his jacket and then went into the bar and ordered a beer. He enjoyed it, and ordered another, and was starting on that when Mr. Collins came into the bar and up to him.

"Sam, the old man wants to see you."

"Me? Why? How is he?"

"All right. They're about to leave."

Sam followed Mr. Collins into his office, where Premberton was striding around, a highball in hand. Vikki was sitting, also with a drink.

"Hello there, young fella!" the old man said.

"How do you feel, sir?" Sam asked.

"Fit as a fiddle. I'm terrible sorry about causin' all that commotion at your table. And I meant to leave you a little tip. Gimme a hundred, Vikki." She did and the old man handed a check to Sam.

"Thanks very much, sir. And I hope that you and Mrs. Premberton will have a very happy marriage."

Mr. Collins said, "You'll have to excuse me. It's the end of a shift and I have to go and collect the cash from the tables."

"We're jest leavin' ourselves, sir," Premberton said. "Let's go cash in, Vikki honey, and see if we've won anything."

The four left the office together and Sam said good night to the Prembertons, who went off toward the cashier. Mr. Collins said to Sam, "The tip goes in the box."

Sam nodded and smiled and walked down to the floor and dropped the check into the dealers' tip box. Mr. Collins watched this and nodded approval and walked into the cashier's office.

Sam went back up to the bar to finish his beer. Through the archway he saw the Prembertons cashing in. Mr. Collins came out with some empty cashboxes and gave the couple a smile and started off for the tables. Soon Sam saw the old man and the girl walk out of the casino, arm in arm. In a few minutes, Sam finished his beer, left the casino and drove off up the Strip.

After about two miles, he came to the Slumbertime Motel and parked. He got out and walked along a ground-level porch to room 17. A light was on inside. Sam knocked. A man opened the door.

"Yes?" he asked.

Sam frowned. "I'm looking for Mr. Haskins."

"He must be in another room."

"No. He lives here, in seventeen. Or did."

"Well, I checked in here at ten tonight and he wasn't here then."

"I'm sorry to have bothered you," Sam said and hurried down the porch to the office, where he pinged the desk bell. In a moment, a man in a bathrobe came from a rear room. "I'm looking for Mr. Haskins and his granddaughter," Sam said. "They were in seventeen and sixteen."

"They checked out."

"They *did?*"

"About nine tonight."

"Oh. Did—did they leave anything for me? For Sam Miller?"

"Yes, they did." The manager found an envelope and looked at it. " 'For Sam Miller.' " Sam took the envelope, thanked him and hurried out to his car. Getting in, he tore open the envelope and found a sheet of paper with writing on it. In order to read it, he flicked on his overhead light. The note read:

> Dear Sammy darling honey. By the time you get this, Grandpa and I will be on our way to somewhere else. I mean, if everything goes OK at your casino tonight. I'm crossing my legs for good luck! Grandpa has decided not to leave you your share,

for two reasons. For one thing, he needs the $6000 more than you, because he's an old man and isn't young anymore, like you. Also, he thinks you're a wonderful person and should be straight, and he says he's afraid that if you get your first taste of what he calls ill-gotten gains, it will turn you into a crook like himself for the rest of your life and this he wouldn't like to see. Good-bye. I'll really miss you. You sure are good in bed, Sammy honey.

Love, Vikki.

Sam turned off the light and sat in the darkness for a moment. Then fury overcame him and he slammed both hands against his steering wheel again and again, and tears of frustration blurred his eyes.

And then the passenger door opened and the interior light went on and Sam turned to see Mr. Collins standing there.

"Troubles, Sam?" He slid onto the seat and shut the door.

Sam's eyes widened and his mouth fell open. "How? . . . How? . . ."

"I followed you here. I've been sitting in my car over there, and I saw you get turned away from that room, and I saw you get that letter from the manager, and I saw the look on your face when you read it." He brought out a cigarette. "So your friends ran out on you, did they—without giving you your cut?"

"I . . . I . . . don't know what you mean."

"Oh, knock it off, Sam." He lit his cigarette. "You're in serious trouble. Your only hope is to level with me. Where in the name of God did you three manage to *get* a hundred and eighty phony hundred-dollar bills? And what are the old man and his wife to you?"

Sam considered for a moment and then shrugged. "She's his granddaughter. Their name is Haskins." He turned on his overhead light. "Oh, hell." He handed Mr. Collins Vikki's note. "You might as well read this."

Mr. Collins did. "The old man may be selfish, but he's right, you know. That six thousand would have meant the end of you as an honest person." Sam turned off the light. "Where did you meet these two?"

"They were customers of my uncle's liquor store. I got to know Vikki and pretty soon we had a real thing going. Then, when my uncle sold the store, I was out of a job, and one day old Bert asked me how honest I was and I said that depended, and he told me about all these hundreds he had."

"Where did he get them?"

"He'd bought them a long time ago, very cheaply. But he'd never passed any. He had an idea about how they could all be changed in one place at one time—in a casino. He didn't care if he won, you see —he just wanted to change his counterfeits for good money. So he offered me a third if I'd help him and he paid my way through Mr. Ferguson's school. I had to get a job as a dealer up here, so I could find out exactly how things worked in a particular casino."

"Sam, you are a crook. You are a criminal."

"All I did tonight was to keep warning you about the old man and his money."

"You were just setting me up."

"I guess so." Sam sighed. "For all the good it did me."

"Was the old man's faint staged?"

"Yes. He knew he had to stop before midnight, when you'd open the cashboxes and spot his bills. But he figured that if he just stopped right then, you might be suspicious, so he faked a faint."

"And whose idea was it that you should try to *make* me suspicious of them?"

Sam smiled modestly. "Well, it was mostly mine—after I'd met you. I figured that if I questioned the first two thousand and you made sure they were genuine—then you wouldn't have any doubts about the next eighteen thousand. And also, I wanted to be sure you wouldn't connect me with it when it was all over."

Mr. Collins smiled a little. "It was a slick operation, Sam. And it almost worked. But your gamble paid off on the house number—which is double zero for you."

"Where did I go wrong?"

"Well, for one thing, you objected too much and I began to wonder why. And at the end, you wondered if the old man could get back to his *motel*. But meanwhile, the girl had told me they were staying at the Flamingo *Hotel*. I figured something was wrong somewhere. And when I opened your cashbox and found the funny money, it all fell into place."

"What . . . are you going to . . . do about me?"

Mr. Collins shrugged. "Nothing. I expect you back at work tomorrow." Sam looked at him in disbelief. "Sam, unless you're crazy, you'll never try anything funny on me again. And it's my solemn duty to the Nevada gaming industry to make sure you never work for anybody else."

"But . . . but what about the eighteen thousand in phony hundreds you're stuck with?"

"What makes you think so, Sam?"

"Because I saw Vikki cash in before you'd opened the cashboxes. That was good money she walked out with!"

"What makes you think so?"

"I . . . don't understand you."

"Because you'd finally made me suspicious, I'd opened *your* cashbox ten minutes earlier. It was while you were in the dealers' room and the bar. I saw to it that among the twenty thousand your friends walked out with were the same identical one hundred and eighty counterfeit hundreds they'd walked in with." Mr. Collins opened the car door and slid out. "Good night, Sam. See you tomorrow."

So saying, the smartest man in Vegas shut the car door and walked off into the darkness.

The Bitter Years

Dana Lyon

The woman finished cleaning up the sink from her solitary meal—the chicken breast cooked in wine, the crisp avocado salad, the beaten biscuits that she had made herself, with enough left over to heat for breakfast—and now the little house was in perfect order. The sun, in this rustic mountain village that she had selected for her permanent home, would sink quickly behind the wooded hills, so that there was never a long protracted period of dusk, and now there would be only a few moments left before everything was shrouded in darkness. So she must take her final look of the day at the ground made ready for her new lawn and garden.

Tomorrow, the man Samuel had said; tomorrow the soil will be ready for the seed and then, God willing, you may have a decent lawn for a change. He was proud of his preparations; no one yet had been able to grow a satisfactory lawn in this rocky section of the hills. Many had tried and had succeeded in growing a few scraggly blades. But she was determined to achieve a beautiful lushness out there in back, and then she would buy some awnings and outdoor furniture and perhaps put in a little fountain; and when she got back from her trip she could sit outdoors all summer long and just bask in the beauty and quiet brought to life through her own efforts. During the winters she would travel—Mexico, South America, the Mediterranean—but in the summers she would enjoy the home and lawn and garden for which she had waited so long.

Still glancing out the window she saw a whisk of white leaping onto the dark loam of the readied earth. She was instantly alert, flying out the back door, screaming "Nemo! Nemo!" to her little cat, which paid not the slightest attention because it had sunk to its belly in the soft damp soil. Unthinking, realizing only that the cat might sink all the way in, as in quicksand, she stepped into the dirt and found herself plunged into it almost to her knees, before her feet came to rest on the rocky hardness of the ground underneath.

"Damn!" she said to herself, and laughed. "Old fool that I am."

She pulled herself out of the foot-and-a-half depth of the loam, rescued the yowling cat, and plodded back into the house, there to strip and shower.

Oddly enough, she was pleased at the depth of the new soil. The man Samuel had done his work well—had obviously Rototilled the rocky ground as well as he could and had then hauled in great loads of top soil, weed-free and fertilized, now lying ready in the sun for tomorrow's fine grass seed. He hadn't cheated. He hadn't, as some garden workers might have done, merely put in a thin layer of dirt over the solid foundation, but had really prepared the grass for a lifetime of growth. (But he had still shaken his head, had still grumbled in the pessimistic manner of these mountainfolk who were too used to disappointment to tempt fate by hoping. "Grass seed just don't want to grow up here," he had muttered while he raked and smoothed, smoothed and raked. "Soil's empty. Air's too thin. Winter's too fierce." But he had kept on raking and smoothing, promising disaster but hoping in spite of himself.)

The woman smiled to herself, wiped herself dry from the shower, got into her night dress and lounging robe, washed the cat much to its enragement (for who, it seemed to be saying, can wash a cat better than itself?) and went to her easy chair in front of the television set.

She was alone. And safe. Safe at last. Happy and comfortable. Rested. Rested for the first time in her life and with that wonderful world cruise waiting for her, after her years of vacationless labor. Only a few weeks ahead now, but time for her to see the new young grass begin to come up and to know that it would be full-fledged on her return months from now. She had never been as content, excited as a young girl, as she was now. The bitter years behind, the exciting years ahead.

She grew weary and exasperated with the television, for in this mountain fastness there were only two stations available and on one there was a rock group, splitting the air with the modern sounds of yelling and shouting, and on the other an old Western, making loud noises too but those of the past, shooting and shouting and galloping hither and yon.

She turned off the set and went to her desk drawer, pushing aside the small revolver she kept there because she was living alone, and took out a pile of brightly colored brochures, to look through again, dreaming and visualizing, living in the future, ignoring the past: the magnificent ship where she would have an outside cabin all to herself and could have days and nights of quiet leisure; England with its magnificent history; the Continent—Paris, Venice, everywhere, even Crete—a cruise to last nearly a whole year. Above all, it was to be the first vacation of any kind in so many years that she couldn't even count them.

She gloated over the pictures, the colorful, impossible descriptions, and once again, as she had a dozen times before, took out the voluminous ticket, the directions, the receipt, the date of sailing, the pamphlets suggesting what kind of clothes to bring with her—all of it, everything, that had once been her impossible dream. Everything was now arranged for: Samuel to cut and water the new lawn, and care for Nemo; the post office to hold her mail (what mail?); Mr. Prescott, the one-man police department, to check her house periodically.

Everything in order, everything waiting. And finally—pure joy— there would be the trip down the mountain in the rickety old daily bus, the air flight to the city, the overnight stay in one of the big hotels, and then the taxi ride the next morning to the great white ship and all that it promised . . .

At first she did not hear the knock on the door. The house was quiet, the only sound that of Nemo purring at her feet; but she was lost in another world and the sound of the first knock did not penetrate.

It came again, and this time she heard it. Still lost, not even wondering who would be knocking after dusk had fallen, she went to the door and opened it, and saw a small man standing there.

"Yes?" she said, surprised but not yet apprehensive.

"Miss Kendrick?"

Prepared, yet not prepared, she held herself in the vise of total physical discipline. She did not flinch, nor did any expression appear on her face.

"No," she said quietly. "You must have the wrong place."

"I think not," said the man. He was wholly nondescript: five feet six or seven, thinning sandy hair, suit the same color, pale-blue eyes.

"My name is Stella Nordway," she said. "*Mrs.* Stella Nordway."

"Oh?" he said, smiling. "You've been married recently?"

"I have been a widow for ten years," she told him. "So you see, you are mistaken."

"May I come in?"

"No," and she started to close the door.

His face altered slightly. A flicker of fury, then almost instantly a mask of mediocrity that could totally obliterate him in a crowd. "I am an investigator," he said, "for the Halmut Bonding Company. They have employed me to find a woman named Norma Kendrick who embezzled more than a hundred thousand dollars from her employers over the last seven years. They want you, Miss Kendrick. *And* the money."

She said, "You may come in," and opened the door a little wider. He slipped through, instantly found the most uncomfortable chair in the room, short and straight-backed, and sat on the edge of it—as if taking his ease on the sofa might have lulled him into a lack of alertness.

"You are mistaken," she said again, almost helplessly. "I am not—"

"I am a trained investigator," he said. "For the last twenty-three years. This much I know: you worked for the Sharpe Wholesale Hardware Company, as its head bookkeeper. A large and prosperous establishment. You were competent and reliable. There was only one peculiarity about you: during the last seven years you refused to take the three weeks' vacation you were entitled to every year—"

"But I—" she broke in, then bit the words back. He had deployed her into a near admission. "But," she corrected herself quickly, "I have nothing to do with all this, so you see—"

"You are Norma Kendrick," he said. "I can't help admitting that I am rather curious as to what made you suddenly turn into an embezzler. For years you had been taking care of your invalid father and doing your daily stint at the office, coming home to the same routine every night. Then suddenly you decided to help yourself to the company's money. At the end of the first year you realized you couldn't leave your books—they would have been an open admission to the substitute bookkeeper they'd have to assign in your absence. I was appalled that Mr. Sharpe had not been more curious as to why you wouldn't take your vacation each year, but he said he had trusted you completely, since you were the daughter of an old friend and had shown your competence and reliability; and moreover, you had explained your lack of vacations by saying you couldn't leave your father in order to go anywhere, and that you were desperately in need of extra money for your father's medical bills, so if Mr. Sharpe would just pay you what he would have paid your substitute, in addition to your regular salary, you would appreciate it."

The woman sat frozen, afraid to speak, afraid not to. Instead she listened. There had to be a loophole somewhere. "So?" she prodded him, and he looked surprised, perhaps because he had expected another denial from her.

"So instead of a vacation you would frequently take a long weekend, say from Thursday to Monday, or Friday to Tuesday, and during these periods you managed to set up your second identity as Stella Nordway. You wore a blond wig, tinted glasses, more youthful clothes, and you bought this house. You also bought a single ticket for a world cruise. You did these things rather hurriedly, after seven years of dipping into the till, because not only had your father finally died, but the hardware company was about to be sold because the owner was ready to retire. This sale, of course, would entail a careful scrutiny of the books. Well, Miss Kendrick?"

Her mind fluttered.

"Are the police after me?" she said, in a final relinquishment to the inevitable.

He smiled. "Well, no. Not yet. As I said earlier, I work for the bonding company first, your employer second, and of course, as soon as you are located, then the law will step in. The police are also looking for you, but in a different direction. The bonding company will get their money—what's left of it—and the state will get its revenge. Your little house will go—"

He glanced around the neat attractive room and out the window at the dark sky, where the stars shone clearly and cleanly in the mountain air. He sighed with pleasure. It would be a lovely retreat for him after too much of a lifetime spent in the city. "Your trip around the world—and how I envied you that—will have to go—"

She was becoming confused. Why weren't the police here? Why hadn't he notified Mr. Prescott, the one-man police force, that this town was harboring a fugitive? Why was this person here, just telling her these things and doing nothing about it? She knew she had lost her gamble, but she had known it was a gamble from the beginning. The bitterness was gall.

The little man spoke again, half smiling.

"Mrs. Nordway—" he began.

"Mrs. *Nordway?*" she echoed. "But you—you insist that I am Norma Kendrick—"

"You can be either one you please," he told her quietly. "It's up to you."

She sank into the nearest chair, completely confused by now, her confusion greater than her terror. "What do you mean?" she stammered.

"Well, just this. You see, you have more courage than I have. More ingenuity. More gambling spirit. I have been tied to a sickly wife for too many years, just as you were tied to your father, and the more I looked after her, the worse her temper grew. She hated being dependent on me. There was no way I could earn enough money for escape. I am what I am. I have saved my company many thousands of dollars, perhaps millions, but my salary remains unimpressive . . . So what is your freedom worth, Mrs. Nordway?—or should I say Miss Kendrick? Whatever is left of the money you stole?"

She sat in an icy cocoon.

Not fear this time, but rage. She could understand the need for the law to make her pay—that was the consequence of losing her gamble; but to be robbed of everything she had hoped for and worked for and risked her freedom for by this oily inconsequential little opportunist sitting there so smugly—*that* was beyond acceptance.

She stood up. "There is not much money left," she said, careful to keep her voice noncommittal, "after buying the house and my cruise ticket. I would be left destitute."

"I'll take the house off your hands," he said lightly, now that he was winning, "and you can return your cruise ticket. Or, better still, let *me* have it—"

"I don't believe it's transferable," she said, almost absently. "Wait just a minute, I have it right here—" In moving toward her desk she paused for a moment in front of the window, looking out. "How did you get here?" she asked in the same absent voice. "I don't see your car outside."

"I left it down the street a ways," he said, "in front of the church. Under the circumstances it didn't seem like a good idea to let anyone know you'd had a visitor."

"I see," she said, and moved on to her desk where she rummaged around for a moment, picked up what she wanted, and held it close to the folds of her lounging robe. She remembered, for only an instant, that there were neighbors not too far away, so she moved quietly, unobtrusively, over to the television set.

"Do you like Westerns, Mr.—?"

"Jordan," he said automatically. "Why, I—" His voice sounded bewildered. Television? Now?

She turned on the volume control, high, and the crashing sound of cowboys still whooping it up with gun and horse filled the room. She lifted the small gun she was holding, and as he stared at her in his brief final moment of comprehension, she pointed it at him and shot him between the eyes.

There was no place to hide the body. The problem was as simple as that. No cellar in this tiny house; the ground too hard and rocky for digging; no car, for she had never learned to drive—no place at all to hide this neat little corpse with the small round hole in the center of its forehead.

She sat. She did not regret her action, knowing that even if she had realized ahead of time the complications in concealing her act, she would have shot him just the same. Rage had impelled her—not greed, not fear, not impulse—just an outraged need to kill this person, this thing, who was going to destroy her entire life and future for his own grasping ends.

She left him there on the living-room rug, where he had quietly toppled from his chair—there was little blood—and moved into the kitchen, staring out the back window at her cherished little garden, at the prepared soil for the new lawn in which she had such high hopes. She was numb with grief at the thought of all her bright plans for the future now seemingly destroyed. Disintegrated. Dead as the little man in the other room.

She stared out through the window at the black night, motionless. The lawn. The soil. Eighteen inches of black pulverized dirt above rocky hardness. A foot and a half. Deeper really than it actually needed to be. Deep enough? For a little man stretched out flat? With grass seed planted over him and growing into solid sod?

The dirt was very soft and slightly damp. She waited by the window in the dark, so that the neighbors would think she had gone to bed, watching the few scattered lights go out, one by one. This was a town for early sleep and early rising, and she must wait no longer than she had to . . .

At last the night was black and still. Still as death. She went into her backyard and dug up a space in the soft prepared soil the right size for the little man—though, of course, only eighteen inches deep— being very careful that the spade made no sound against the harder earth. Her eyes were accustomed by now to the gloom, whose only light was cast by the pale stars, and her movements were as silent as the night.

She brought the little man out to the backyard and laid him in his grave, arms decorously against his sides, and started to cover him with earth. She paused. He must lie flat, as flat as possible, for Samuel might want to rake and roll the dirt once more and there must be no chance of his tools going deep enough to strike something solid. It seemed to her that the little man's shoulders were bunched together, the way she had him placed; he must lie flatter, flatter.

The grave she had dug was wide but not deep, more space on either side of him than just above him. She tried again, stretching his arms out wide, at right angles to his body—ah, this was better, this was as flat as he would go. Now she could cover him and forget him. Soon, soon, the grass would flourish above him, entangle itself in its own roots, cover him forever, his identity, his total being now lost in other places. But not here.

Not here.

She went back into the house and slept. Her future was again safe . . .

It was not until some time later that she knew her plans were meaningless. Day by day she watched her rear lawn and waited with anticipation for the first green blades to rise, almost forgetting what lay beneath them. And the grass did come up. But not very well. It was as Samuel had said, she thought in despair; no lawn would grow decently in these mountains of rocks and barren soil and bitter winters. But the blades did come up, struggling to reach the sun, a patch here, a patch there, so that perhaps there might be some hope after all.

One morning, after a night of soft summer rain, she looked out at her lawn and saw that there was a change; for in the center of it now was a great stand of lush green grass, beautiful and thick and bright, and it was in the form of a cross, growing and flourishing amid the meager struggles of a few pale blades, growing and flourishing, burgeoning in the soft gentle breezes and the warm healing sun. Growing and flourishing.

So that is why the people of the little town wonder about the crazy old woman who mows her foolish struggling lawn twice a week, every week. Not since the first blades came up did she ever leave her house; not once was she ever away from home, even for a brief vacation; not once in the long years that followed did she ever miss the appointed time, rain or shine, spring or fall, when she must cut her lawn.

Man's
Best
Friend

Dee Stuart

The coroner said, "Accidental death." The only one who knew it was murder would never tell . . .

Emily squirmed uncomfortably between Fred and Cinnamon in the front seat. Cinnamon's coat brushing against Emily made her skin crawl even though the late August sun warmed the New England air.

Her husband, Fred, balding and affable, appeared not to notice.

Emily pinched Cinnamon's tail, hard. With a reproachful glance the dog moved over and stuck her nose out the window while Fred peered through horn-rimmed glasses at the road ahead.

"Here's our motel," he said, pointing the car into the driveway. "It's only four o'clock. We made good time."

In their room Fred ordered a beer and two ham-and-cheese sandwiches on rye.

"Don't order for me," Emily said. "Riding all day upsets my stomach."

"Okay," Fred said pleasantly.

When the beer and sandwiches came Fred set them on the table and sank down in a chair in front of the picture window. Taking a deep swallow of beer he held up the newspaper and gazed appreciatively over it at the bikini-clad swingers around the pool.

Just as Emily started to sit down, Cinnamon jumped onto the chair and sat staring expectantly at Fred. He broke off a chunk of sandwich.

"Speak!" he commanded.

Cinnamon gave a short, sharp bark. Fred gave her the chunk.

"Down!" commanded Emily. Cinnamon ignored her.

"I told you to leave that dog in the kennel," Emily said crossly. "Make her get down."

Fred looked hurt. "We always do this, Cin and I, when we're on the road. We watch the kids in the pool and have a sandwich." Fred, a manufacturer's representative, was on the road Monday through Friday.

"This week you're not on the road. We've rented a cabin in the mountains and it's *our* vacation, not that dog's! I put up with her riding in the *front seat, next to the window,* so she wouldn't get carsick. Now *I* want to sit down." She grabbed part of the newspaper and raised her arm threateningly in Cinnamon's direction.

"Down, Cinnamon, down," Fred said quickly.

Reluctantly the dog hopped down and stood at Fred's elbow, her eyes still begging for her sandwich.

Emily stared malevolently at Cinnamon. How was it possible that that *dog* could make *her* feel like a trespasser even in her own home. She tried to figure it out. It all began last fall when Fred made her stop teaching.

"Twenty-five years is long enough," he'd said. "I'm making a good living—house and car paid off. Stay home. Relax. Visit your friends."

But all Emily's friends were still teaching. She was lonely, leading an empty life in an empty house. And then he brought *that dog* home.

He walked in the kitchen door one Friday night, hands hidden behind his back. "I brought you a gift," he said proudly, and thrust the warm, wiggly, rust-colored puppy into her arms.

"Oh! He's cute." Emily smiled uncertainly.

"*She.* She'll keep you company," Fred said, pleased with himself. "And she'll protect you while I'm gone."

Then, of course, she'd no idea how that dog would disrupt her house—let alone her entire life.

Cinnamon stared at her, gray eyes shining with a peculiar light. Incredibly, Emily could swear that dog was smiling. Like a premonition the thought crossed her mind that no two women could live together peaceably in the same house. It made her feel uneasy. She set the dog down on the shining yellow linoleum floor, where it slid around on wobbly feet.

"What is he?" Emily asked, looking at the pointed ears with floppy tips and a bushy tail curling in a perfect circle.

"*She*. She's a crossbreed," Fred said defensively. "Part fox terrier, part Weimaraner, maybe a little husky at the tail." He stroked the short, smooth coat. "Her name's Cinnamon." The dog gazed at him with adoring eyes.

"It's a mongrel, is what it is. How big will it get?"

"Oh, foot-na-half, two feet." He scratched Cinnamon's ears. She nuzzled his hand.

"Well, you'll have to train it. I've got enough to do without cleaning up after any dog."

Fred trained Cinnamon. He taught her to beg, speak, fetch and roll over. He bathed and brushed her and took her for long walks. One day Emily said, "Seems to me you spend more time with that dog than you do with me!" The annoying thing was, he didn't deny it. Emily didn't tell him that while he was gone the dog slunk around listlessly and her tail drooped, even when Emily let her inside. She came to life only when she heard Fred's car pull in the driveway.

Gradually the dog's sad eyes and reproachful mien began to depress her. She was sick and tired of putting the dog out on the chain and of walking it besides. Once Emily found Cinnamon under her bed with her green satin slipper chewed almost beyond recognition.

"Bad dog!" she shrieked, striking at her. "You're going to have to go!"

Emily tried to think of a way to get rid of her. At last she hit upon what seemed to be the perfect solution.

"Fred, why not take that dog with you when you travel? She'll keep you company on the road."

At first he refused, but at last Emily convinced him she wouldn't mind. From then on, every Monday morning Fred would drive away with Cinnamon beside him, serene and haughty, eyes and ears alert, smiling as though she owned the car.

But I certainly had no intention of taking that dog on my vacation! Emily thought now.

"Time for dinner," said Fred, interrupting her reverie. Fred fed

Cinnamon, then he took Emily to the motel dining room. When they finished dinner it was almost dark, but lights flooded the pool, and swimmers, like shining fish, set the sparkling, transparent blue water in motion.

"Let's stay here for a while," Emily said, strolling across the grass and sitting in a chair on the cement apron by the pool.

"I have to walk Cinnamon."

"I'll wait for you here." Surely he wouldn't bring that dog near the pool.

He returned with Cinnamon tripping daintily at his side.

"You can't have that dog out here!" Emily flushed angrily.

"Nonsense. She knows how to behave. Sit, Cinnamon, sit."

The dog sat at his feet, ears cocked, nose in the air, surveying her world like an Egyptian sphinx. Fred gently turned Cinnamon's ears inside out and crossed one paw over the other. A boy belly-flopped into the pool spraying them with water and Fred quickly brushed the drops off Cinnamon's back, smoothing her fur.

Can't keep his hands off her, Emily thought. *Disgusting, lavishing all that affection on a dog. If he'd given me half that attention . . . maybe if we'd been able to have children . . . if Fred didn't travel so much . . .*

Cinnamon stood up and trotted toward the pool. "Stay!" Fred commanded. Cinnamon stopped, stared at the water and turned a pleading look on her master.

"No! Stay. Stay away from the water!"

Cinnamon stayed. Always obedient, well-behaved, Emily thought bitterly. And no wonder. Fred spent every free minute training her. More and more it seemed to Emily that Fred preferred to be with Cinnamon than with her. Was that the way it would be at the cabin? Fred and Cinnamon exploring, taking long walks alone together?

Now Cinnamon stretched out at Fred's feet. He scratched her stomach and she rolled over languidly, feet in the air, eyes closed in ecstasy. She stretched her black lips in a smile of pure bliss, the tip of her pink tongue lolling over her chin.

Embarrassed, Emily noticed that people were watching. Suddenly she heard the girl in the black fringed bathing suit exclaim, "Why, that dog's laughing! Look! She really is laughing!"

There, Emily thought triumphantly. She wasn't imagining it, that stupid dog was laughing—at her!

Now, watching the bathers, she wished desperately that she could swim but the water was always too cold to try to learn. *I wonder if that dog can swim,* Emily thought idly. *Probably.* She'd heard dogs swam instinctively when they were thrown in water. But for how long? And if one were held under . . .

When the pool closed and the lights went off they left, single file like ducks, Cinnamon prancing in the lead, Fred her proud escort and Emily tagging along behind.

No matter how hard she tried, Emily could not conquer the jealousy, anger and hurt now fused into a knot of hatred deep inside her. Lavishing all his love on a dog! It was indecent! She would not put up with it any longer.

There was no use asking him to give the dog away. He wouldn't. She would have to give him an ultimatum. Fred would have to choose between her and that dog . . . but he'd never forgive her . . . and there was the dreadful possibility, unthinkable, of course—still, he might choose that dog. But there was another way.

Emily waited until Fred was in bed watching TV. "I believe that dog has to go out again," she said.

"No she doesn't," Fred said, eyes on the screen.

"She seems terribly restless."

"No she isn't."

"*You* don't have to take her," Emily insisted. "I'll slip on my housecoat and . . ."

"No!" Fred said sternly. "Forget it!"

For a long time Emily lay awake wrestling with a sense of frustration and defeat. She would have to do it tomorrow.

From long years of practice Emily could set an alarm clock in her mind and wake up any time she wished. She awoke at five, just before dawn. Stealthily she took Cinnamon outside, leading her across the grass, wet with dew, toward the pool. It wasn't as dark as she'd hoped it would be.

Her heart hammered with fear that someone might see her. She'd have to risk it. If anyone questioned her she'd say the dog had fallen in the pool and she was trying to pull the wretched beast out. She started across the cement apron. Cinnamon sat down.

"Come. Come!" Emily said sharply.

The dog refused to move. Emily yanked on the leash. Surely that dog couldn't remember she wasn't allowed near the water! Exasperated, Emily dragged the dog toward the pool. The dog resisted, her nails scraping the cement.

"Em-i-ly!" From the balcony outside their room Fred shouted impatiently across the gray morning. "Don't try to walk her past the pool. She knows she's not allowed in there!"

Emily clamped her teeth together in a frozen smile, waved and started toward the parking lot, Cinnamon trotting obediently at her heels. She'd tell Fred the dog woke her up and wanted to go out. Furious, she vowed next time she would not fail.

Late that afternoon they drove along a winding sandy road deep into the woods. The scent of pine freshened the cool air and sunshine filtered through tall oak trees tinged with rust. They stopped before a rustic cabin perched atop a knoll.

"Look, Em, even though we're surrounded by mountains, you can see the lake right here from our porch."

With a secret smile Emily gazed at the lake glimmering in the sunshine. "And the trees are beginning to turn, red and ' . . ."

"There's a boat down there goes with the cabin. We'll have to do some fishing on that lake."

"Um-hm," Emily said thoughtfully. "But it's suppertime now."

Fred scooped the last spoonful of blueberries from his dish and drained his iced-tea glass. "Well, while you're cleaning up, Cin and I'll do a little exploring. Walk, Cin? Walk?

The dog cavorted delightedly, tail waving like a banner. Emily's lips thinned in a determined line.

An hour later when Emily was seething with anger they stamped onto the porch full of excitement.

"Guess what we found, Em! That path back of the cabin winds around and comes out on a lane. Down the lane almost hidden is a double track, all weeds now. We followed that awhile and then we saw it. An old stone farmhouse, all charred and gutted like there was a fire. We looked around inside—it was so dark I nearly fell in the cellar—there's a hole in the floor where the cellar steps were."

Emily began to listen attentively, her eyes gleaming.

"Outside's all overgrown. There's a grape arbor and wild roses and gentians. And guess what Cinnamon found?

Baffled, Emily shook her head.

"Cinnamon found a well! What *was* a well—a wide hole in the ground looks like it goes clear to China. I'd have fallen in if Cinnamon hadn't sniffed around and put on the brakes. She's so smart—know what she did? She sat right down. Wouldn't budge. Would you believe a dog could be so smart?"

"No," said Emily sourly.

Fred patted Cinnamon's head fondly. "You'll have to see the place, Em. Must be two hundred years old."

"Yes, I'd like to see it." *No dog's smarter than I am*, she thought. *I won't tolerate it!*

The next day after lunch Fred stretched out on the daybed. As soon as he began snoring Emily snapped the leash on Cinnamon's collar and stepped quietly out the back door. She hurried down the path to the lane and after two false starts found the double track leading to the old stone farmhouse. She climbed the sagging steps, crossed the porch to the front door and stepped gingerly inside. The floor that remained seemed solid. A few boards were rotting through, others were missing. Ahead yawned the black square where the cellar stairs had been.

Stepping lightly she walked on. When Cinnamon began to whine she stopped, picked up the dog and unsnapped the leash. She stood cold and shaking at the edge of the stairwell trying not to breathe the dank air of the charred wood and the earthen cellar. Cinnamon, squirming in her arms, whined louder.

All at once the truth struck Emily like a blow. The cellar was not deep enough. The fall would not do it. Cinnamon would bark and maybe no one would hear her. But her howls, echoing in the dark cellar could carry for miles.

Emily carried the dog outside, snapped her leash on and set her down. Cautiously she circled the house, watching Cinnamon carefully for signs of backing away as she sniffed. Fred would have warned Cinnamon away from the well as he had the pool. Emily started around the house again in a wider circle this time, plowing disgustedly through ankle-high grass and weeds that pricked her legs, Cinnamon nosing ahead of her.

Emily turned abruptly to avoid walking over some wide boards in her path. Floorboards from the house, Emily thought. Looks as though someone had set them there, side by side. But Cinnamon, nose searching out the earth's secrets, would not be sidetracked. Suddenly she jerked forward and the leash slipped from Emily's fingers.

"Drat you!" yelled Emily, enraged. "Go ahead. Get lost!" She could tell Fred that the dog had slipped out the cabin door and taken off. But if he found the dog wearing the leash, he'd know she was lying. Or she could tell him she'd taken Cinnamon out and the dog had gotten away. But if that stupid dog got hung up on a bush and strangled, he'd never forgive her.

She couldn't win. She'd have to get the leash off the collar or he'd know she'd taken the dog out. Her head throbbed. Her hands felt clammy.

Now Cinnamon stopped midway across the boards. The dog seemed to be smiling, beckoning her to follow. Emily ran toward Cinnamon, lunged for her collar and missed. Cinnamon skipped lightly across the boards. Angrily Emily tried to stamp on the end of the leash—and missed. Under Emily's weight the rotted boards spanning the old well parted and Emily plunged down, down through the damp-smelling darkness.

She tried to scream but her throat closed. It seemed as if she were falling forever, but she wasn't frightened, not really, not until she plunged deep into the freezing water.

Kicking her legs frantically, Emily managed to surface once. All she saw in the wide blue circle of sky above was Cinnamon peering over the edge, laughing.

Killer on the Turnpike

William P. McGivern

i.

The headlights rushed at him like long yellow lances. They swept by on his left in a formation of threes, each pair of lights following its own lane; but they might change direction at any instant, he thought, and plunge straight at his car. There was always the unknown enemy to fear . . .

He was traveling south on the Tri-State Turnpike. New York was a dozen miles behind him. Now he was safe, an innocent, anonymous unit in a vast complex of speeding cars and flashing lights. In the rear-vision mirror the lane behind him stretched emptily for several hundred yards. And ahead of him, less than a quarter of a mile away, was a Howard Johnson's restaurant and service station, gleaming like a necklace of diamonds in the darkness.

He pumped the brakes and swung off the pike, stopping on the graveled roadbed that flanked the highway. Now he was about two hundred yards from the restaurant.

The traffic rushed by him, the headlights splintering on his thick glasses. He blinked his large eyes. The noise and movement confused him—the spinning tires, the flashing lights and the exhaust fumes of roaring traffic. But one thing was untouched by the bewildering racket of the turnpike—the plans he had made. They were like a rock of purpose in tossing, uncertain seas.

191

He climbed from his car, removed his hat and bulky tweed overcoat and threw them into the back seat. Then he switched off the headlights, took the key from the ignition and hurled it with all his strength into the black fields bordering the pike. Let them figure that out, he thought, smiling with pleasure.

He was short and broad, heavily and powerfully built, with an iron-gray crew cut and strong, harshly drawn features. When he smiled, his teeth flashed in the darkness, white and pronounced. Everything about him projected a sense of purpose and determination. Everything, that is, but his eyes; they were mild and clear, and when he was excited, they glittered with a childish sort of anticipation and malice.

As he walked swiftly from his car, legs churning powerfully and shoulders hunched into the wind, he was conscious of only two needs. The first was for another car. That was terribly important. He must have a car. And secondly, and equally important, was the need for something hot and sweet to drink. After what he had done his whole body ached for the comfort and reassurance of steaming, heavily sugared coffee.

The time was seven-fifteen.

Trooper Dan O'Leary spotted the abandoned car five minutes later as he swept along with the northbound traffic. He speeded up to give himself room for a turn, then drove up onto the wide lane of grass which separated the north- and south-bound streams of traffic. When the highway was clear, he bumped down into the southbound lane and pulled up behind the apparently empty car, the headlights of his patrol car bathing it in yellow radiance. O'Leary picked up the phone that hung on the right side of the steering post and reported to the dispatcher at Turnpike Headquarters, sixteen miles south at the Riverhead Station.

"Patrol Two, O'Leary. I'm checking a stopped Buick, a '51 sedan. New York plates." He repeated the numbers twice, then glanced at a numbered milepost a dozen yards or so beyond the Buick. The turnpike was marked by such mileposts from the first exit to the last, and O'Leary had stopped at No. 14. He gave that information to the dispatcher and stepped from his car with a hand resting on the butt of his revolver.

This action was reflexive, a result of training which had been designed to make his responses almost instinctive under certain circumstances. There was seldom anything casual or whimsical about his work. He had stopped behind the parked car for good reasons: he could approach it under the cover of his own lights, and he was in no danger of being run down. His report to the dispatcher was equally a matter of training and good sense: if he was fired on or if the car raced away from him, its description would go out to a hundred patrols in a matter of seconds. And it was the same thing with his gun; the car looked empty, but O'Leary approached it ready for trouble. He flashed his light into the front and rear seats, noted the tweed overcoat and gray felt hat. There was no key in the ignition. He touched the hood and found it warm. Probably out of gas. He went around to take a look at the trunk.

While O'Leary made this preliminary investigation, Sergeant Tonelli, the dispatcher at the Riverhead Station; checked the license number O'Leary had given him against the current file of stolen cars. Tonelli, a tall, spare man with graying hair and thick white eyebrows, sat in the middle of a semicircular desk in the headquarters office. Strong overhead lights flooded the room with noonday brightness, pushing back the darkness beyond the wide, high windows. The glare of the turnpike swept past the three-storied headquarters buildings, six lanes of traffic flowing smoothly into the night. Directly behind Tonelli a door led to Captain Royce's office. The captain was at his desk checking certain arrangements and plans which he had submitted weeks earlier to the Secret Service. The plans had been approved, and Captain Royce was now giving them a last, careful inspection.

The current file of stolen cars was impaled on a spoke near Tonelli's big right hand, and he flipped through the lists with automatic efficiency while continuing to monitor the reports crackling from the speaker above his switchboard. Sergeant Tonelli was responsible for approximately one third of the hundred-mile length of the turnpike. This area was designated as Headquarters North. Two subsidiary stations, Substation Central and Substation South, divided the remaining sixty-odd miles between them; their responsibility was limited to traffic, and in all other matters they took orders from headquarters and Captain Royce.

Under Sergeant Tonelli's direct control were eighteen patrol cars, assorted ambulances, tow trucks, fire and riot equipment. In his mind was a faithful and imaginative picture of the turnpike at this exact moment; he knew to the mile the location of each patrol car and what it was doing; he knew of the speeding Mercedes-Benz being chased ten miles north; he knew of the accident that had plugged up the slow and middle lanes beyond Interchange 10, and he knew, of course, that Dan O'Leary, Car 21, was presently investigating a Buick parked at Milepost 14.

In addition to this routine activity, Sergeant Tonelli was considering certain areas of the problem that faced Captain Royce. The President of the United States would be riding on the turnpike tonight, entering in convoy at Interchange 5 and traveling south to the end of the pike, a distance of about forty miles. Sergeant Tonelli would dispatch certain of his patrol cars to that area in an hour or so, and he was turning over in his mind how best to take up the slack that would be caused by their departure.

But meanwhile he continued his check of the stolen-car file, a check which proved futile.

Trooper O'Leary returned to his patrol car and called headquarters. He said to Tonelli, "Car Twenty-one. O'Leary. Looks like the Buick's out of gas. The driver must have walked up to the Howard Johnson's. I'll check and see if he needs help."

"Proceed, Twenty-one."

O'Leary drove into the service area and pulled up to the gas pumps. A wiry, gray-haired attendant hurried to his car.

O'Leary rolled down his window. "Anyone been in for a can of gas, Tom?"

"Not a soul, Dan. Not since this morning, anyway."

"O.K., thanks," O'Leary said and drove back to the parking area that flanked the restaurant. The owner of the disabled car might have stopped for something to eat, he thought. O'Leary straightened his shoulders and dark-green jacket before walking into the warm foyer of the restaurant, but both of these corrective gestures were unnecessary; his back was straight as a board, and his uniform was trim and immaculate, from the shining black puttees to the wide-brimmed hat with the leather sling tight under his square jaw. O'Leary was twenty-eight, solidly and powerfully built, but his stride would have pleased a drill sergeant. There was almost a touch of arrogance in the set of his head and shoulders, and he handled his body as if it were a machine he understood and trusted completely. He had short black hair and eyes as cold and hard as marbles, but there was something boyish about the seriousness of his expression and the clean, wind-scrubbed look of his skin.

O'Leary had one fact that might help him find his missing motorist: he probably wasn't wearing a hat or overcoat. He had left them in the car.

But the hostess who escorted diners to tables remembered no such person. "Not in the last ten or fifteen minutes, Dan." She glanced around the restaurant, which was divided into two large wings, one on either side of a long soda fountain and take-out center. Both areas were crowded; the air was noisy with conversation and the clatter of cutlery and dishes. "Of course, he might have come in while I was seating someone."

"He couldn't have found a table for himself?"

"Not when it's crowded like this. But he might have gone to the take-out counter."

"Thanks. I'll check that."

O'Leary stood patiently at the take-out counter while the waitress took an order for hamburgers, French fries, milk and coffee from a thin young man who seemed vaguely embarrassed at putting her to so much trouble. He smiled nervously at O'Leary and said, "The kids are too little to bring in here. They'd play with the menus and water glasses instead of eating. My wife thinks it's easier to feed them in the car."

"She probably knows best," O'Leary said. "Anyway, eating in a car is pretty exciting for kids."

"Yes, they get a kick out of it." The young man seemed relieved by O'Leary's understanding air. When he went away with his sackful of food, O'Leary asked the waitress if she had served a man recently who wasn't wearing a hat or overcoat.

"Gee, I don't think so, Dan." She was a plain and plump young woman, with mild brown eyes. Her name was Millie. "How come he wasn't wearing an overcoat?"

"He left it in his car, which is out of gas about two hundred yards from here. I guess he figured he wouldn't freeze in that time."

At this point it was a routine investigation, a small departure from O'Leary's normal work of shepherding traffic along the pike, of running down speeders, of watching for drivers who seemed fatigued or erratic, of arresting hitch-hikers, or assisting motorists in any and all kinds of trouble. A car out of gas, the owner not in evidence at the moment; that's all it amounted to. He might be in a washroom, might have stopped in the service-station office to buy cigarettes or make a phone call. There was no law against his doing any of these things. But O'Leary wanted to find him and get his car back in operation. The safety of the pike depended on smoothly flowing traffic; any stalled car was dangerous.

"Do you want a cup of coffee?" the waitress asked him.

"No, thanks, Millie." There would be little time for coffee breaks tonight, he knew. A threat of rain was in the cold, damp air, and that meant the hazards of thickening traffic and difficult driving conditions. Also there was the convoy; every trooper on the pike had been alerted to that responsibility.

But at that moment there was an interruption which took O'Leary's mind off his missing motorist: a dark-haired girl came up beside Millie and said breathlessly, "Has Dan told you about the glamorous date he has tonight?"

"Now, Sheila," O'Leary said, and ran a finger under his collar.

"Tonight and every night," Sheila said with an envious sigh, which O'Leary knew was about as sincere as the average speeder's excuse and contrition. "You see, Millie," Sheila went on, "Dan and I had a date last Tuesday, and before we went home he took me up to Leonard's Hill. We could see the turnpike below us, the headlights blazing like long strings of diamonds in the darkness. And do you know what he told me?"

"Now, Sheila!" O'Leary said helplessly.

"He told me he loved the turnpike. Isn't that lucky for him? Night after night he's close to his one true love—a hundred miles of asphalt."

"It's concrete," O'Leary said miserably; he knew it was a token point, but he disliked inaccuracies about the turnpike, major or minor. The fact was, he *did* love that hundred-mile stretch of concrete. And sitting in the darkness with Sheila the other night, it had seemed natural to put the thought into words. Why was he such a fool? And why did she make him feel so helpless and vulnerable? The top of her head barely reached his shoulders, and he could swing her hundred-odd pounds into the air as easily as he would a child, but these things made no difference; he was clumsy and inept with her, driven to silly talk by something intangible and mysterious that radiated from her personality. It wasn't mere beauty, he knew that much; as an Irishman he was also a poet, and while he appreciated her green eyes and elegantly slim body, his heart and soul responded to more than these physical attractions. There was a quality of grace and strength about her, a thread of steel and music permeating her whole being, and because of this—*and because I'm a fool,* he thought—he had blurted out his feelings to her that night as they sat watching the traffic on the pike.

In his eyes the turnpike was a fascinating creation, a fabulous artery linking three mighty states, a brilliant complex of traffic rotaries, interchanges and expressways which carried almost a quarter of a million persons safely to their homes and offices each and every day of the year. Consider it, he had urged her, unaware that she was smiling at the clean, boyish line of his profile. This on their fourth date. She was not a regular waitress, but a part-timer filling in on evenings and weekends to help pay for her last year in college. Their fourth date and probably their last, he thought, for he had got on the subject of speeders.

As a logical corollary to O'Leary's affection for the turnpike was his dislike of those who abused its privileges; and speeders topped this list by a country mile. O'Leary always thought of them as small and shifty-eyed, although the last one he had caught was built like a professional wrestler. They regarded the turnpike as a challenge and troopers as natural enemies. They didn't have the brains to realize that the checks and safeguards, the radar and unmarked police cars were designed solely for their protection. Instead they acted like sullen, sneaky children, behaving only as long as the parental eye was on them. O'Leary knew their works very well; he had stood dozens of times at the scene of wrecks, with the moans of the dying in his ears, and seeing the wild patterns of ruptured steel and broken glass, and the nightmarish contortion human bodies could assume after striking a concrete abutment at seventy miles an hour.

He felt strongly about these matters and had tried to make Sheila understand his convictions; but after completing his lecture with an interesting recital of various statistics, he had turned to find her peacefully asleep, with shadows like violets under her eyes and still the faintest trace of a smile on her lips.

Millie had turned to wait on another customer. A woman with two children was trying to catch Sheila's eye. O'Leary adjusted his hat and the chin sling. Then he said quietly, formally, "I simply wanted you to understand—"

But she didn't let him finish. "I understand," she said, smiling up at him. "I couldn't resist teasing you a little. I'm sorry." She moved a sugar bowl, and the back of her fingers touched his hand. "It wasn't very nice of me, I'm afraid."

"Next Saturday?" he said, smiling with relief and pleasure. "Same time?"

"I'd love to."

The man who had abandoned the Buick twenty minutes earlier stood in the shadows of the parking lot watching O'Leary and the dark-haired waitress. It was like a movie, he realized with pleasure, the big plate-glass window and the people behind it outlined starkly by the restaurant's bright lighting. A silent movie, of course. He couldn't hear what they were saying, but he could see their shifting expressions and the smiles that came and went on their lips.

They weren't talking business, he thought, and took a deliberate luxurious sip from his container of hot, heavily sweetened coffee. But the big trooper had been very businesslike until the slim, dark-haired girl came along. Talking to the attendant at the gas pumps. Then going into the restaurant and quizzing the hostess and the stupid-looking little blonde at the take-out counter. Very serious and efficient. The man watching through the window had seen all that. But now the trooper's manner had changed. He and the girl were smiling at each other, trying to be impersonal, of course, masking their feelings; but it was nakedly apparent, disgustingly evident to the man sipping the sweet coffee in the dark parking lot. His name was Harry Bogan, and despite his irritation at their intimate, sugges-tive smiles, he was still grateful they weren't talking business. The trooper's business, that is. For it was from this slender, dark-haired girl that Bogan had bought his coffee and frankfurter. And the trooper hadn't asked her about it; that was obvious.

Without his overcoat Bogan was cold. But he stood motionless in the shadows until the trooper turned away from the counter after giving the girl a last quick smile and a soft salute. Then Bogan walked the length of the parking lot and moved silently into the opening between two cars. He ate his frankfurter in quick, greedy bites, savoring the tart bite of the mustard on his tongue, and dropped the empty, cradlelike container to the ground. Then he finished the coffee, tilting the cardboard cup high to let a little stream of liquefied sugar trickle into his mouth. He let the cup fall at his feet and drew a deep, satisfied breath. Sugar or honey usually made him feel grateful and at peace with himself.

He watched the doors of the restaurant as he pulled a pair of black-leather gloves over his thick, muscular hands. His eyes were bright with excitement. He shivered with pleasure as he found a crumb of sugar on his lip. His tongue moved dexterously, then flicked the tiny sweetness into his mouth.

Bogan did not have long to wait. Within a matter of seconds a plump, elderly man came hurrying along the line of parked cars, fumbling in his pockets for his keys. Bogan shifted his position slightly, moving into the deeper shadows until only his thick glasses glinted in the darkness, as steady and watchful as the eyes of a crouching cat.

O'Leary returned to his patrol car and reported to headquarters. Sergeant Tonelli said, "Captain Royce wants to talk to you, O'Leary. Hold on."

The captain's voice was hard and metallic, as arresting as a pistol shot. "O'Leary, did you get a lead on the man who abandoned that Buick?"

"No, sir. I drew blanks with the gas-pump attendants and the waitresses in the restaurant. He probably wasn't wearing a hat or overcoat—that's all I had to go on."

"Get back to that car. Don't let anyone near it. Lieutenant Trask and the lab men are on their way. That Buick was used in a double murder in New York not more than an hour ago. Get moving, O'Leary."

Lieutenant Andy Trask was short and muscular, with shoulders that bulged impressively against his black overcoat. At forty-five, the lieutenant was a study in somber tones—broad, tanned face, brown eyes and black hair that only in the past year had faded to silver along the temples. As the lab technicians went to work on the car, searching trunk and glove compartments, fingerprinting and photographing, Trask gave O'Leary an account of the information that headquarters had received in a three-state alarm from New York.

"We've got no description on the murderer, except that he's big, and was wearing a light-colored tweed overcoat and a gray hat. Here's what he did: around six-thirty this evening he walked into a little unpainted-furniture shop on Third Avenue in Manhattan and shot and killed the owners, a young married couple named Swanson. It wasn't a robbery; he just shot 'em and ran out. The Buick belongs to a druggist who'd parked it about a half block from the furniture shop, with the keys in the ignition. The killer was seen running from the shop by an old woman in an apartment across the street; but she's an invalid with no phone.

"It took her half an hour to get hold of her landlady. The landlady, like everybody else in the neighborhood, was down in the street talking about what had happened. So—half an hour later—the invalid tells her story. She described the clothes the guy was wearing and the license number of the Buick. But by that time the murderer had got through the Lincoln Tunnel and onto our pike." Trask turned and jerked his thumb at the Buick. "Now he's ditched this crate and more than likely is looking for another one. We've got to find him before somebody else gets hurt."

"With no description," O'Leary said slowly. "He's got rid of the tweed coat and gray hat. We've got nothing to go on. He could be off and running by now in another car." He glanced helplessly at the streams of traffic rolling smoothly past him. "Any car, lieutenant. With a gun he could force his way into a station wagon full of college kids. Or climb in with a nice little family group where he'd look like innocent old Uncle Fred. He could be in a truck, or in a trailer, holding a gun against some woman's head while her husband drives him off the pike. It's like chasing ghosts blindfolded."

The radio in Trask's black unmarked car cracked a signal sharply. Trask slipped into the front seat and picked up the receiver. He listened for a few seconds, a frown shading his somber features, and then said, "Check. We'll get at it." He dropped the receiver back on its hook and looked sharply at O'Leary. "You called it, Dan. He's off and running. There's a dead man up at Howard Johnson's, and an empty space where his car was parked. Come on."

The body of the dead man had been discovered by a young couple returning to their car after dinner. The woman almost fell over his legs. Her husband flicked his cigarette lighter to see what was wrong.

She began to scream then, both hands pressed to her mouth, and her husband ran back toward the bright lights of the restaurant, shouting for help.

Sergeant Tonelli received the report of the murder from the manager of the Howard Johnson's and relayed it immediately to Lieutenant Trask. He dispatched Trask and O'Leary to the restaurant and then flashed the information to the communications center at State Police Headquarters in Darmouth. This was the nerve center of a communications web which embraced every patrol car, station and substation within the state-police organization. In addition it was linked in a master net with the facilities of six nearby states; under emergency priorities Darmouth could alert the full resources of police departments from Maine to South Carolina, throw its signals across the entire North Atlantic seaboard.

Lieutenant Biersby was on duty in Communications when Sergeant Tonelli's message was brought to his desk. Biersby, short, plump and methodical, walked with no evidence of haste into an outer room where a dozen civilian clerks under the supervision of state troopers worked at batteries of teletypewriters and radio transmitters.

Lieutenant Biersby's special talent was judgment; each message flashed from his office required a priority, and it was his responsibility to establish the chronological order of precedence to be given the thousands of alerts and reports which clattered into the office on every eight-hour shift. A smooth flow, based on relative importance, was essential; lapses in judgment could jam the mechanical facilities and burden already overworked police departments with trivial details and reports.

As Lieutenant Biersby walked toward a teletypewriter operator, he considered the facts: a killer was loose on the pike, a sketchily identified man who had murdered two persons in New York City and another in the parking lot at Howard Johnson's No. 1 south. It was a reasonable inference that he had killed the third time to get possession of another car. But there was another possibility which didn't escape the lieutenant; the killer might have left the turnpike on foot. This would be difficult, since the pike was guarded by a nine-foot fence designed in part to keep hitch-hikers from getting onto the highway between interchanges. But a strong and agile man might manage it.

It was Biersby's decision—reached as he walked the twenty feet from his desk to the teletypewriter machine—to alert every police officer fifty miles from the spot the Buick had been abandoned; if the killer had left the pike on foot, he'd be within that circle. All hitch-hikers, prowlers and suspicious persons would be picked up for investigation. This was a routine and probably fruitless precaution, Biersby thought; because his judgment, which was blended of experience, instinct and vague promptings he had never succeeded in analyzing, told him that the killer was still on the pike. Speeding safely through the night, an anonymous man in an anonymous car, lost in the brilliant streams of traffic.

He said to the teletypewriter operator, "This is a Special. Get it moving."

The dead man was in his sixties, small, gray-haired, seemingly respectable; his clothes were of good quality, and a Masonic emblem gleamed in the lapel button of hs suit coat. He had been strangled; his face was hideous. He lay in a fetal position in an empty parking space that gaped like an empty tooth in the row of night-black cars. Near one outflung hand was an empty coffee container and one of the small cardboard cradles that were used for take-out orders of French fries or frankfurters. There was no identification in his clothes; his pockets had been stripped.

An ambulance had arrived, and the two interns were examining the body in the light from Lieutenant Trask's flashlight. Three white-and-blue patrol cars blocked off the immediate area, their red beacons swinging against the darkness, and troopers were posted about the parking lot to keep traffic moving. A crowd had gathered in front of the restaurant to watch the police activity.

Dan O'Leary stood behind Trask, frowning faintly at the empty parking space. When Trask turned away from the body, O'Leary touched his arm. "I've got an idea," he said. "The killer took the car that was parked here, that's obvious. Well, we might get a line on what kind of a car it was from the people who parked beside it. They arrived after he did probably, since their cars are still here. Maybe they can—"

"Yes," Trask said, cutting him off sharply. "Get those people out here. Fast."

O'Leary took down the license numbers from the cars on either side of the empty parking space and ran toward the restaurant.

The car on the left was a Plymouth sedan owned by a thin young man with horn-rimmed glasses and a nervous stammer. The owner of the car on the right was a middle-aged woman, a peaceful, padded sort of person, with the kind of composure that seemed to deepen under tension.

Lieutenant Trask, realizing that their memories might be short-circuited by haste or pressure, squandered a few seconds in lighting a cigarette. Then he said quietly, "We're trying to get a description of the car that was stolen from this space about fifteen minutes ago. It was here when you arrived. You parked alongside it. Now, take your time; do you remember anything about it? Any detail at all?"

"I wa—was in a hurry," the young man said shrilly. "I'm supposed to be in Cantonville by eight-thirty. I just ra-ran for a cup of coffee. I wa—wasn't thinking about anything else."

"Well, it was *big*," the woman said, nodding with impeccable assurance. "Its tail stuck out of the line. I had to make two tries before I could get in beside it."

Their recollections came slowly, haltingly. The young man recovered a remnant of poise and mentioned details of the bumper; the woman remembered something about the lights and fenders, they agreed it was a station wagon, and finally, after what seemed interminable indecision, settled on the color—either white or light yellow. Trask glanced at O'Leary. "Well?"

"If they're right, it's an Edsel station wagon," O'Leary said. "Can't be anything else."

"How far is the next interchange?"

"Twenty-eight miles," O'Leary said sharply. "And he's only been gone twenty minutes. He can't possibly make it. And he'll be easy to spot in a white Edsel station wagon. A Ford, Chevy or Plymouth would be another matter."

"Flash your dispatcher," Trask said, but O'Leary was already running to his car.

At headquarters Captain Royce, senior officer of the turnpike command, stood behind Sergeant Tonelli checking the reports coming in from interchanges and patrols. The tempo of the office had picked up a sharp, insistent beat in the last half hour; every available off-duty trooper had been ordered back to the pike, and riot squads had been dispatched to Substations Central and South. Royce was in his fifties, tall and sparsely built, and with a look of seasoned toughness about his sharply chiseled features. As a rule there was little suggestion of tension or impatience in his manner, but now, as he filled a pipe and struck a match, a tight, anxious frown was shadowing his hard gray eyes.

Trooper O'Leary's report had come in a half hour ago. Within thirty seconds the turnpike had been transformed into a hundred-mile trap; every patrol had been alerted, every interchange had been instructed to watch for the white Edsel station wagon. But so far there was no trace of the killer. Patrols had stopped three Edsels, but in each case the passengers were above suspicion—a carload of college girls, a Texan with a wife and four children, and four Carmelite nuns being transported at a stately speed by an elderly Negro chauffeur.

Royce looked at the big clock on the wall above the dispatcher's desk. It was eight-ten. The Presidential convoy would swing onto the pike at nine-forty. In just ninety minutes . . .

Sergeant Tonelli looked up at him and said, "Trooper O'Leary asks permission to speak to you, sir."

"Where is he?"

"At Interchange Twelve."

This was twenty-eight miles from Howard Johnson's No. 1. The killer might be miles beyond that now; he'd been gone from the Howard Johnson's more than forty-five minutes. "I'll take it in my office," Royce said, and went with long strides to his desk. As he lifted the receiver he saw that it had begun to rain; the turnpike flashed below his windows, and he could see the slick gleam of water on the concrete and the distorted glare from long columns of head-lights.

"This is Captain Royce. What is it, O'Leary?"

"Just this, sir. He's had time to make Exits Twelve or Eleven by now—if he's thinking about getting off the pike."

"What do you mean, *if?* What else could he be thinking about?"

"He made a mistake taking a white Edsel. Maybe he's realized it. Also he took it from the middle of a row of cars which gave us a lead on it. Maybe he's realized that, too. My guess is he won't try to get off the pike in that car. I think he'll try to ditch the Edsel before making a break."

"Hold on a minute." Royce glanced quickly at the turnpike map which covered one wall of his office. The interchanges were marked and numbered in red, the Howard Johnson's restaurants in green. Captain Royce saw instantly what O'Leary meant—before Exit 12 there was another Howard Johnson's restaurant and service area. This was designated Howard Johnson's No. 2; it was only twelve miles from No. 1. The killer might have driven only from No. 1 to No. 2; with the fifteen-minute head start he could have made it comfortably—and found another car.

"O'Leary, get back to Number Two on the double. Tonelli will dispatch."

Harry Bogan had gone as O'Leary had guessed—driven the white Edsel station wagon only as far as Howard Johnson's No. 2, then abandoned it in the parking lot. Now he stood in the shadows, watching the activity at the gas pumps, a stocky, powerful figure, with the light glinting on his thick glasses and the rainy wind brushing the wiry ends of his gray crew cut. He was smiling faintly, full lips softly curved, large mild eyes bright with excitement. The police would be sniffing around the exits now, he knew, the long blue-and-white patrol cars lined up like hungry cats at a mouse hole. Waiting to pounce.

Bogan knew he had made a mistake in taking the white Edsel station wagon, but he hadn't had time to be choosy. The important thing was to get away from the area where he had left the Buick. But now he could be more discriminating. He had special requirements, and he was prepared to wait until they were satisfied. Time wasn't important, and in that lay his safety. The police would think he was frantic, ready to bolt at the first whiff of danger. But that wasn't the case. The feeling of power and control sent a heady flash of warmth through his body.

He heard the thin cry of a siren on his right, the sound rising and falling like the howl of an animal. On the turnpike he saw the red beacon light of a police car sweeping with brilliant speed through the orderly lanes of traffic. And he heard other sirens approaching on his left. The first patrol car made a U-turn over the grass strip that divided the turnpike and swerved into the restaurant service area. An attendant coming from the gas-station office stopped within a few feet of Bogan to watch the patrol car flash past the pumps and pull to an expert stop at the parking area in front of the bright restaurant.

Bogan was amused. He said, "Seems to be in a hurry, doesn't he?"

The attendant glanced toward Bogan's voice, but saw only the suggestion of a bulky body in the shadow. "Looks like it," he said.

Bogan recognized the trooper; it was the one who had been simpering at the dark-haired waitress from whom he had bought his coffee and hot dog. Watching him stride along the row of parked cars gave Bogan a curious flick of pleasure. The attendant said, "Well, he's safer driving at a hundred than most guys are at fifty. That's Dan O'Leary, and he can really handle that heap."

The attendant returned to the gas pumps, and Bogan continued his patient examination of the cars lining up for service. He soon found what he wanted, an inconspicuous Ford sedan driven by a young man with horn-rimmed glasses. A college boy, Bogan guessed, noting a bow tie and crew-cut blond hair. This would do nicely. The car was like one of thousands rolling along the pike, and the boy looked intelligent. That was important. There was a lot to explain, and it would be tiresome explaining things to a fool.

By then two more patrol cars had arrived. The troopers had joined the one called O'Leary, Bogan saw. And O'Leary was standing beside the white Edsel, inspecting it with his flashlight. Bogan laughed softly. They thought they were so clever; strutting pompous fools with their uniforms and guns. They'd learn nothing from the big white station wagon. He had parked it off by itself; no one had seen him leave it. They could rip it to pieces, and it would tell them nothing. They had no way to identify him, no way to know what kind of car he would presently ride off in.

The young man was paying for his gas now, and Bogan moved slowly from the shadows. This would require nice timing, he realized. The attendant gave the young man his change and walked back to the next car in line. The young man rolled up his window and started the motor.

Bogan opened the door just as the car began to move. He slid onto the front seat and showed the young man his gun. "Now, let's go," he said quietly. "We've got a nice little ride ahead of us."

ii.

"I didn't really mean to kill them," Bogan said a few moments later as they were rolling smoothly along the pike. The young man's name was Alan Perkins, and Bogan had instructed him to drive in the slow, right-hand lane at about forty-five miles an hour. It was dark and windy outside, with rain spattering through the headlights, but the interior of the car was snug and warm. Bogan felt grateful and at peace with himself as he studied the reflection of his teeth and glasses in the windshield. The young man, Perkins, would be pleasant company. He had a clean, immature face, and was dressed neatly in a tweed jacket worn over a sweater. Very polite and obedient, Bogan thought, with his bow tie and glasses, and thin white hands grasping the steering wheel. He drove with care, hunched forward slightly, and never letting his eyes flick toward the gun gleaming in the dashboard light.

In a careful voice the young man said, "If you didn't mean to kill them, perhaps the best thing would be to tell the police about it."

Bogan smiled, admiring in the reflection the sudden emerging brightness of his big, white teeth. "No, that wouldn't be the best thing. There's no need to tell the police anything."

Bogan touched his forehead with his fingertips. This wasn't what he wanted to talk about: it was the other thing, the red heat of the summer, and watching them night after night from the humid darkness of his room. Yes, that had to be made crystal clear. "They hadn't been married long," he said, and was pleased at the low, judicial tone of his voice. "Naturally, they were selfish—it's something young people can't help, I know. But it's evil of them to shut out everyone else." He paused, aware that his breath was coming quickly. It was really so simple, so obvious, but when he tried to trap his thoughts with words, they skittered away like mice.

The young couple operated a small furniture shop on Third Avenue near Forty-eighth Street. That was accurate. Bogan knew; he had watched them from his room across the street. She was slim and blond; he was a tall redhead. They laughed a lot, but were serious about their business. They sold unpainted sections of tables and chairs and desks which could be fitted together with glue or a few nails. Frequently they worked at night, and the young man would bring in sandwiches and beer, and they would eat and drink, sitting on the counter, the girl in shorts, bare legs golden in the soft evening light and the young man grinning up at her.

Bogan felt his breath catch sharply in his throat; the memory of the couple he had killed reminded him of the trooper and the slim, dark-haired girl at the Howard Johnson's restaurant. He was rigid with pain. They were the same sort, selfish and greedy, driving everyone else away from the radiance of their love. They drew a magic circle about themselves that no one could pass through.

"Do you have a girl?" he said suddenly, and stared at Perkins' clean, young profile.

"No," Perkins said. He groped for something to ease the tension he could feel in the man beside him. "Girls can be a big waste of time. There's time for all that later, I guess."

Bogan nodded approvingly. If they would all just wait a while instead of rushing together to lock themselves in the charmed circle. That was the maddening thing about the couple in the furniture shop. Twice he had stopped to make a trifling purchase, and they had made him feel like an intruder, something gross and ugly profaning their happy isolation. They were polite enough on the surface, quick with a smile and a comment on the weather, but they gave him no warmth or affection. That was too precious to squander on anyone but themselves. He couldn't remember when he had decided to kill them; the thought must have been there always.

The planning had been a dreary business and strangely confusing —acquiring the gun from a disquietingly jocular pawnbroker, and then the tedious search for a car, which had been the most difficult problem of all. But eventually he found what he needed—the Buick used by the corner drugstore for deliveries. The young man who drove it obviously operated on a tight schedule, for he didn't remove the key when he went inside to pick up his parcels. When the car was parked at the curb, the key was always in the ignition; Bogan established this fact in a week of patient snooping. Thus the timing of his ultimate act was determined by the delivery schedule of the drugstore. And for some obscure reason this pleased Bogan; it lent a whimsical, unpremeditated tone to his plans.

Bogan felt in his pockets for a chocolate bar, then remembered that he had left his little stock of sweets in his overcoat. He felt his eyes sting with tears; he needed something sweet, but he had been so pressed and excited that he hadn't remembered to take the candy bars from his overcoat. It wasn't fair.

Bogan sat up straighter. Suddenly he thought of the dark-haired waitress at the restaurant—the one he had bought the coffee from. Why had he been such a fool? The need for something warm and sweet had been powerful, but he should have resisted it; she would tell the police what he looked like—and enjoy doing it, he thought sullenly and unhappily. She would like telling on him, getting him into trouble. He knew that from her face and eyes; there was no warmth there, only meaningless politeness.

"Don't get excited," he told himself, his soft lips silently forming the words. The trooper didn't ask her about me; there was still time.

He said quietly to Perkins, "We're going to have to make a U-turn."

"But that's not legal. We'll be stopped."

"We'll just make sure there are no patrol cars in front or behind us," Bogan said easily. "Anyone else will think we're an unmarked police car."

Bogan put the muzzle of his gun against Perkins' side. "You're a nice young boy. I don't want to hurt you. Turn into the left-hand lane, and we'll watch for one of those openings the police cars use."

Bogan felt a pleasant excitement running through him; he was almost glad of the way things were working out. It would be very satisfying to have that arrogant girl in his hands. And he realized that he had the bait to lure her to him—the name he had heard from the gas-station attendant: "Dan O'Leary."

Lieutenant Trask and O'Leary learned nothing from the white Edsel station wagon; it had been driven twelve miles, from Howard Johnson's No. 1 to No. 2, and then abandoned, the driver disappearing like a phantom. Lieutenant Trask had checked out the waitresses and countermen in the restaurant while O'Leary and a team of troopers searched the grounds and inspected the trucks that were lined up like huge animals in the truckers' area. They waked the drivers and examined the lashings and tailgates for any sign of forced entry.

After this O'Leary talked to the gas attendants. None of them remembered anything helpful. He did come on a bit of irrelevant information, however; one of the attendants mentioned that someone—a man standing in the shadows of the office—had made some comment about O'Leary's speed when O'Leary had driven into the area ten or fifteen minutes earlier. The attendant said he told the man Trooper O'Leary knew his business—or something to that effect. The attendant wasn't exactly sure of what he'd said, but it wasn't important in any case, O'Leary decided.

He rejoined Trask, who had returned to the Edsel station wagon. Trask had been in contact with Captain Royce. They now had an identification on the owner of the Edsel, the elderly man who had been killed at Howard Johnson's No. 1.

"He lived in Watertown," Trask said, flipping his cigarette into the darkness. "Name was Nelson, Adam Nelson, a widower, retired executive at the paint factory there. They got a line on him from the laundry marks in his shirt."

These markings—in this case a triangle with the digits 356 beneath it—had been relayed to state police headquarters by radio, where they had been checked against the master file of all laundry marks in the state. The sergeant in charge had established the location of the laundry from the triangle; a telephone call to the manager had established the identity of the customer from the digits 356.

Trask added, "He was on his way to spend a few days with a married daughter in Camden. None of which helps us a damn bit."

O'Leary was frowning faintly. He had been trying to fit together a picture of the murderer, and for some reason his guesses about the man bothered him; the portrait was flawed with inconsistency, and O'Leary had the tantalizing feeling that a significant fact was hidden somewhere in that blurred image.

What in heaven's name was it? O'Leary tried to analyze the inferences he had drawn from the man's behavior. The killer was both bold and deliberate. He had killed brutally and swiftly, with no signs of panic. He had made a mistake in taking a conspicuous car, but had corrected it cleverly—which meant he was thinking clearly under pressure. And he hadn't duplicated his first mistake; he had got away from the Edsel without being seen, and by now, it was safe to assume, was on his way in a less conspicuous car. Also, he seemed to be working according to a plan; time wasn't important to him, or he'd have taken a chance and tried to get through an exit in the Edsel. After all, he couldn't have known for sure that the police would identify the missing car. But he hadn't taken that chance; he was in no hurry. And he'd given the police credit for being as smart as he was.

It was a picture of a man who was ruthless and cunning. A man who thought clearly and measured his chances shrewdly. And that was where the inconsistency became apparent; the image was streaked with flaws, something was out of place, something incongruous. Because the killer had done something foolish. . . .

"What's the matter with you?" Trask said.

O'Leary put both hands over his ears; the traffic on the pike rushed by like a river of noise and light, and he tried to shut out the sound of it, tried furiously to find the truth that was hidden somewhere in this maze of facts and hunches, of inferences and intuitions. Then it was as if a clear and brilliant light had snapped on in his mind; then he had it.

He caught Trask's arm. "The dead man, Nelson; he'd had his dinner, right? He had left the restaurant and walked to his car. But there was a coffee container beside his body. And one of those little cardboard things they put hot dogs in. Remember?"

"Sure." Trask's dark face was impassive; but a flicker of understanding came to his eyes. "Go on."

"Those containers belonged to the killer," O'Leary said. "He ate and drank there beside Nelson's car. Then he dropped them on the ground."

"Which means he went into the restaurant after all," Trask said, his voice sharpening. "But you told me you checked out the waitresses. They should have remembered a guy without a hat or coat on a night like this."

"I didn't check all of them," O'Leary said. He suddenly felt sick with guilt and apprehension. "I talked to the hostess. She'd have spotted anybody who wanted a table. Then I went to the take-out counter. But I only questioned one of the girls on duty. I—I forgot about the other one."

"You forgot?" Trask said sharply. "What do you mean by that?"

"She's a friend of mine, Sheila Leslie." O'Leary drew a deep breath. "I was more interested in her than my job, that's all, lieutenant. But I wasn't after a murderer then. I was after the owner of a stalled car. Which is no excuse."

"I guess it's not," Trask said. "But you've put us back on the right track. We'll find the girl who sold him that coffee. When we know what he looks like, we'll seal off this pike till it's damn near water-tight. I'll call Captain Royce on the way. Let's go."

O'Leary ran toward his car. The killer must have bought his coffee from Sheila, he realized; if he hadn't done that one compulsive, dangerous thing, they might never have got a line on him. He could have drifted through their nets like a wisp of smoke. And then O'Leary remembered something that caused a strange coldness to settle in his stomach; the killer had corrected one mistake. He had got rid of the Edsel. Would he try to correct his other mistake—by getting rid of the only witness who could identify him?

O'Leary snapped on his red beacon and jammed his foot hard on the accelerator.

Harry Bogan sat in the rear seat of Alan Perkins' sedan, which was now parked close to the entrance of Howard Johnson's No. 1. He was smiling softly; they had made two U-turns in doubling back to the restaurant, and for all the attention they received they might have been lazily circling about a sleepy village on a Sunday evening. He held his gun so that it pointed at Perkins' head. "We'll have to wait until a car pulls in alongside us," he said. "You remember what you're to tell the driver?"

"Yes, I remember," Perkins said.

"You're a good boy. I don't want to hurt you."

They were close enough to the restaurant for Bogan to see the dark-haired girl at work behind the take-out counter. She was slim and cool and swift in her white uniform, her skin smooth and glowing under the bright light, her teeth flashing now and then in quick smiles. They meant nothing, he knew, and felt his heart speeding with anger. A bone thrown to a hungry dog, nothing more. The smile that told of her real feelings wouldn't be squandered on the lonely and miserable persons lined up at her counter. She would save that for the trooper, inviting him with her eyes and lips into the warm, selfish circle of her love.

They did not have long to wait. A small, middle-aged man in a leather jacket pulled in beside them and climbed from his car.

"All right," Bogan said quietly, and touched the young man's neck with the muzzle of his gun.

Perkins rolled the window down and called to the man in the leather jacket. "Pardon me, sir, but would you do me a favor?"

The man turned, peering into the darkness toward Perkins' voice. The shadows blurred Perkins' face and obscured Bogan completely. The man came a step closer, craning his head forward slightly. "Well, if I can, I don't mind," he said in a soft Southern accent.

"There's a waitress inside I want to send a message to," Perkins said. "You can see her from here—she's the dark-haired one at the take-out counter."

The man glanced toward the restaurant, nodding slowly. "I see her all right. Just what kind of a message is it?"

"Just tell her Trooper O'Leary wants to see her outside for a second."

Bogan smiled in the darkness; the trooper's name had been a gift, a priceless bit of luck, and he accepted it as a talisman of success. He was filled with confidence by the mysterious confluence of events working in his favor.

"Trooper O'Leary, is that it?" the man said. "Well, I'll tell her for you." He laughed softly. "Man taking messages to pretty girls can get in a fix of trouble sometimes. But this is kind of different."

"Listen to me, for heaven's sake," Perkins said to Bogan, as the stranger walked with a leisurely, shuffling gait toward the restaurant. "It won't work. She'll be frightened; she's liable to scream or something." He turned his head slowly, cautiously, until he could see the shine of Bogan's glasses. "Please, there's no need—to hurt anybody. I'll take you anywhere you want to go. You can ride in the trunk. I give you my word of honor."

"I don't need your help to get off the turnpike," Bogan said, laughing softly. "Now you just do as I told you. When she gets that message, you drive up and stop in front of the entrance. Keep the motor running. That's all you've got to worry about." He prodded the boy's cheek with his gun, sharply, cruelly. "Do you understand?"

"Yes, all right." Perkins barely whispered the words.

They watched the man in the leather jacket make his way through the crowded restaurant to the take-out counter. He removed his hat and raised a hand to get the dark-haired girl's attention.

The girl smiled at him, and when he spoke she leaned forward slightly, her head tilted slightly to one side. She glanced toward the windows; the man had gestured in that direction, obviously telling her where he had received the message. The girl gave him a quick, warm grin then and came swiftly around the counter and walked to-

ward the revolving doors of the restaurant, one hand pushing at a
stray curl on her forehead. She stopped briefly to speak to the hostess, who was standing at the cashier's counter. Asking permission to
step outside for a moment or so, Bogan thought, smiling faintly. A
very proper little girl, obedient and responsible. She was moving
again, walking toward the entrance.

"All right," he said quietly.

Perkins backed his Ford out of line, then cut the wheels and drove
toward the entrance, which was marked as a no-parking area. The revolving doors glittered as they spun around, and the girl came out
onto the broad sidewalk. An awning protected her from the rain, but
the cold wind whipped the skirts of her white uniform about her slim
legs.

Perkins stopped, and Bogan reached forward and opened the front
door. The girl came toward the car, bending to look into the dark interior. "Dan, is that you?" she said, in a clear, unworried voice.

Bogan glanced quickly out the rear window. A family was hurrying
toward the restaurant, a mother, father and four small children, but
the parents were involved in shepherding their charges and paid no
attention to the stopped car and the girl standing beside it.

"I have a message from Dan," Bogan said.

"What is it?" She put her head in the car, bracing herself with a
knee against the front seat. The family with the four children had
filed out of sight, and when she said, "What is it?" the second time, a
bit sharply now, Bogan caught her arm and pulled her into the front
seat. "Go!" Bogan said to Perkins, and before she could scream, he
had the gun in her face, and the car was leaping forward, the door
swinging shut with a bang.

She would have screamed, regardless of the gun, but Perkins' voice
cut through her terror. "Don't!" he cried. "Please do what he says.
He'll shoot."

"That's true," Bogan said, pleased with the young man. "Now
drive over to where the trucks park." He still held the girl's arm and
could feel the tremors shaking her body.

"Now, what do you want with me?" she said in a dry, careful
voice.

"That will have to wait a bit. We'll have time to talk later." The
fear in her eyes and face satisfied something deep inside him; and he
remembered how the girl in the furniture shop had looked when he

raised the gun, her face blank with panic, eyes wild and frantic. Once as a child he had seen a horse trapped in a burning barn; and the girl's eyes were like those of the poor horse, crazed and helpless. The sight of her fear had been almost unendurably exciting.

The area reserved for the big trucks was a hundred yards beyond the gas station, an unlighted expanse of concrete the size of a football field, with parking spaces indicated by lines of white paint. Bogan directed Perkins to the far end of the lot. The slowly moving car merged with the darkness, an inconspicuous shadow against the marshy fields that stretched off in the distance.

In the silence that settled when Perkins cut the motor, Bogan heard the girl's shallow, uneven breathing. The sound was satisfying; no longer laughing and confident, he thought, no longer warmed by the admiring eyes lingering on her slim body. Now she would pay attention to him. In a quiet, deliberate voice Bogan explained what he wanted them to do, and they obeyed carefully and quickly, like children trying to appease a fearsome, unpredictable adult. It wasn't the gun they responded to, but the tension coiling beneath his surface calm. They knew with a primitive instinct that he was hoping they might disobey him, that he would relish the excuse to lose his self-control.

They got out of the car on the girl's side and stood motionless until he joined them. Then the girl, on order, climbed into the rear-seat section and lay face down on the floor. Bogan had already removed his tie and belt. He gave them to Perkins, who knotted the tie about the girl's wrists and looped the belt about her ankles, buckling it with trembling fingers. When he straightened up, Bogan inspected his work, then closed the rear door. "Now climb into the front seat," he told Perkins, but when Perkins turned to obey, Bogan struck him heavily with the barrel of his gun, the blow landing just above his right ear. Perkins pitched forward, moaning in pain, but Bogan caught him before he struck the ground and carried him into the field adjoining the parking lot. He rolled the limp body into a muddy ditch and returned to the car, whistling softly between his teeth.

Safety lay on him like a balm, filling him with a warm complacence. Perkins wouldn't recover consciousness for hours, if at all; and the only other witness who might identify him was trussed up helplessly in the back of his car. Now there was nothing left but to get off the turnpike. And he knew how to solve that problem.

He started his car and drove along the wide, curving lane that led to the turnpike, laughing as he merged smoothly with the swift, southbound traffic. The rain was coming down harder, bouncing on the shining concrete, and the Ford was swiftly lost in the dark streams of cars, with no more identity than a leaf in a storm or a chip swirling down a stream. The beams of oncoming headlights broke on his thick glasses and glittered against the excitement in his eyes.

"Are you all right?" he said in a high, pleased voice. "Are you comfortable?"

The girl lay with her wrists bound at the small of her back, her cheek flat against the rough carpeting on the floor of the car. She was trembling with cold and with fear, but she said evenly, "Where are you taking me?"

"Well, I'm not sure," Bogan said. In truth, he didn't know; but when they left the turnpike he would make up his mind. He would find a place that was dark and quiet. A field, he thought, or the bank of a stream, where he could rest, where they might talk for a while.

He glanced quickly over his shoulder; she lay with her knees bent, her feet raised in the air, and he saw the soles of her small white shoes, and the shine of his belt looped about her ankles. For the time being everything was all right. "Just don't worry about anything," he said, smiling.

In the manager's office of Howard Johnson's No. 1, Trask and O'Leary questioned the man in the leather jacket who had delivered the message to Sheila Leslie. "Let's try it once more," Trask said evenly, after the man told his story for the third time. They had checked his identification and knew he was a family man, steadily employed by a construction company in Philadelphia. He had a gasoline credit card in his wallet, snapshots of his wife and children, and seemed to be a responsible citizen. But Trask said, "Let's go over it again from the start—every detail, everything you saw and heard and said."

The man sat in a straight-backed chair under clear, soft overhead lights. He was about fifty, with thinning hair, work-roughened hands, and he wore jeans and a woolen shirt under his leather jacket. "Well, like I told you," he said, blinking his eyes nervously. "First the man called to me, speaking nice and polite, and asked me to do him a favor. The car he was setting in was one of the popular makes, but I

can't rightly say which one. It wasn't new. Maybe a '50 or '51. It was
a dark color, like I already told you. So he asked me to tell this girl
that's missing that Trooper O'Leary wanted to talk to her."

O'Leary closed his eyes and ran a hand over his face. She was
gone, helpless in a killer's hands, and it was his fault. He hadn't done
his job; instead of questioning her swiftly and impersonally, he had
blushed and simpered like a fool, letting his feelings for her come between him and his work.

"Well, I went into the restaurant and told her," the man in the
leather jacket said. "And she smiled real nice and thanked me and
went outside. I sat down to my dinner, where I was when you got
here and began asking for who gave her the message." One of the
waitresses had remembered that someone had spoken to Sheila just
before she went outside; and Trask and O'Leary had shouted for silence in the restaurant, and when they explained what they wanted,
the man in the leather jacket had got uneasily to his feet. "I didn't
think I'd done nothing wrong," he said now, eyes swinging quickly
from Trask to O'Leary. "I was just doing a man a favor."

"You're sure he used my name?" O'Leary asked him sharply.
"You're sure he said O'Leary?"

"Yes, I'm positive about that."

"Let's go back to the start," Trask said. "It was a young man who
gave you the message?"

"Nearly as I could make out, yes."

"And he was alone in the car?"

"Well, there seemed a kind of shadow in the back, but I didn't see
anybody." The man hesitated, then said, "The young guy sounded
kind of funny, he talked fast, I mean, like he was speaking words he'd
memorized."

O'Leary forced himself to think; his emotions were roiling inside
him, blunting his memory and judgment. While Trask went over the
man's story again, O'Leary paced the small office, the overhead lights
shining on his pale, set features. He got himself in hand with a conscious effort. It occurred to him once again that the killer's pattern of
action suggested a generous time schedule; twice he might have got
off the pike, once in the white Edsel, again in the car he had commandeered to pick up Sheila. But he hadn't made a break for it. This
might mean he had some special plan for getting off the turnpike,
that he had found a loophole in the pike's defenses. But how to ac-

count for the fact that he had used the name O'Leary to lure Sheila outside? How had he known the name? And that Sheila would respond to it? Then O'Leary recalled the irrelevant bit of information he had gleaned from the gas-station attendant at Howard Johnson's No. 2. Someone had mentioned O'Leary's driving, and the attendant had told him that O'Leary was safer at a hundred than most people were at fifty. Or something to that effect. But had the attendant actually used his name?

Trask completed his questioning of the man in the leather jacket, thanked him and excused him. When the man had gone, O'Leary told Trask of the conversation with the attendant at Howard Johnson's No. 2.

"You get back there," Trask said. He swore softly. "Weve got to get a lead, and fast."

"He's got the girl in his car," O'Leary said desperately. "That's a lead, isn't it? We can search every damn car on the pike."

Trask looked away from O'Leary, pained by what he saw in the big trooper's face. He gestured impatiently at the flash of the turn-pike traffic which they could see through the windows of the manager's office.

"There's twenty-five or thirty thousand cars rolling out there to-night. Doctors on emergency calls, pregnant women, businessmen making plane and train connections, parents hurrying to sick kids. How can we tie up that traffic? And where would we get the men to search the cars? The pike would be stalled bumper to bumper in a matter of minutes. We'd block the highways coming in from three states. Maybe we could stop all cars of a certain kind—like we stopped those Edsels. Or pick up men answering to a fairly general description. But we can't bring that traffic to a halt without some-thing to go on, Dan. Now you get back to Number Two. Maybe that attendant can give us the lead we need."

O'Leary covered the twelve miles in eight minutes, with his alarm beacon flashing and siren screaming. The attendant he had talked with earlier was a young man with short red hair and a pink, weather-raw complexion. He recalled the incident. "I was just com-ing out of the office, and a man standing there said something about it looking like you were in a hurry. Well, I told him you knew how to handle your car, that's all."

"Think hard," O'Leary said. "Did you use my name?"

"Well, sure. I thought I told you. I said Trooper O'Leary or maybe Dan O'Leary, but I know I mentioned your name."

"What did this man look like?"

"He was standing kind of in the shadows. I just glanced over my shoulder at him; you know, the way you do when something doesn't mean much. He was pretty big, I'd say. And he was wearing glasses. I saw 'em flash when he turned his head."

A big man with glasses, O'Leary thought with despair; a description that might fit half the men driving the pike tonight. He questioned the other attendants then, hoping someone might have seen the man leaving the shadows of the office. But he drew blanks; none of them had seen him or noticed any unusual activity around the pumps.

O'Leary returned to his patrol car and flashed Sergeant Tonelli at headquarters. He told him what he had learned, but his heart sank as he repeated the meager description—a big man with glasses. Might as well say he had two arms and legs.

"Check," Tonelli said in his hard, impersonal voice. "You'll proceed south now, O'Leary. Report to Sergeant Brannon at Interchange Five and take further orders from him. You're going to be working the Presidential convoy."

O'Leary was filled with bitter guilt and despair; the plans being made to find the killer obviously didn't include him. He wouldn't have even the meager solace of trying to save Sheila. His hands tightened on the steering wheel. "Look, sergeant, just one thing. The killer isn't in any hurry to get off the pike. Have you noticed that?"

O'Leary's question was considerably out of line, but Sergeant Tonelli was a man who understood a number of things that weren't spelled out in the department's training manual and training directives. He said quietly, "We've noticed it, Dan. But we don't know yet what's behind it. You get moving now."

"Check," O'Leary said and turned his car into the curving approach to the dark turnpike. He felt helpless and miserable, consumed with a leaden fear.

Sheila had fought down her first panic, which had been like the fear of smothering she had known as a child. Once when she was very small her brother and his friends had locked her in a trunk during some game or other and had gone off and forgotten about her.

For a long time afterward she couldn't bear anything that threatened her breathing—swimming under water, a dentist's wad of cotton in her mouth, even the slight pressure of a locket at the base of her throat was enough to make her heart pound with terror. But she had finally conquered that dread; she had faced the issue with common sense, refusing to pity herself, refusing to let herself be shackled by morbid fears.

Now, lying helpless in the rear of Bogan's car, she tried to apply the same therapy to her straining nerves. So far nothing had happened to her; her body was cold and cramped, and dust from the carpeting had made her eyes water but that was all. She knew she was safe as long as they were on the turnpike. After that she would be completely helpless. He could take her anywhere, do anything he wanted with her. She faced that fact clearly. It meant she must get away from him before he drove off the pike. Somehow she must make him stop. Dan had told her any stopped car would be quickly checked by the police, with the trooper concealed by his own headlights and emerging from their brightness with a hand on his gun.

It seemed a hideous irony that she had been amused by his earnest discussion of the various methods used in policing the turnpike—and just a tiny bit bored by his enthusiasm for his work—when that skill and energy might be the only thing that could save her life. She tried to stop thinking about Dan O'Leary. It would make her cry, she knew, and there was no time now for that kind of self-pity. She could think of him later; of his tall, alert way of walking, and the fine, dark hair on the backs of his big clean hands, and the way he got a joke a split second after she did and grinned a bit sheepishly at her swifter understanding.

Now she must make this madman bring the car to a stop. "Please," she said in a weak voice. "I'm going to be sick. I feel dizzy."

"Well, that's too bad. But it's not much longer." Bogan glanced at his watch and then at a numbered milepost that gleamed ahead of him in the darkness. He was a bit behind schedule, but not seriously so. The rain had made him lose time. He smiled, studying the shifting reflection of his face in the windshield. Even though his car was dark, there was enough light flashing from oncoming cars to project the square image of his face on the streaming windshield. The rain water blurred his features at rhythmic intervals, then the windshield wiper smoothed them out: it was interesting, this alternate fading and sharpening of his reflection.

"Please," she said again. "I'm freezing. There's no circulation in my arms and legs. Please stop and untie my ankles."

"You're Trooper O'Leary's girl, I know," he said. "I saw the way you smiled at each other. Are you going to marry him?" He was still smiling at the way his face went in and out of focus with the snap of the windshield wiper. "Answer me. Are you going to marry him?" he said coldly.

She was silent; the changed tone of his voice sent a chill through her cramped body. She tried to guess at his thoughts, to form some picture of his needs and compulsions; but it was as hopeless as attempting a jigsaw puzzle blindfolded. "I'm not sure," she said at last.

"You're not sure," he said, mocking her in a high, petulant voice. The lying little beggar. They would get married all right and buy a little house and pull all the blinds down so no one could see them. And keep everyone outside their little circle of pleasure.

He remembered how it had been in his own home, the long nights that belonged only to his father and mother, and finally his guilty relief and happiness after his father's death. There was just his mother and brother then, and it was very nice. She baked sweet cookies and told them stories. It went on for such a long and pleasant time. Until his brother brought home a girl. They had fought about that; Bogan had warned him of the terrible thing he was doing, but his brother had got married anyway, and then there was just his mother and himself, and that was the best time of all. He worked as a night watchman because the sunshine hurt his weak eyes. She kept their apartment shaded in the daytime, and they watched television together, and she made his meals and took care of his clothes. When she died he asked his brother if he could live with him, but there were children now and no room for him. That was when he had got the tiny place on Third Avenue and begun to watch the couple in the furniture shop.

Bogan shook his head sharply; his thoughts were distracting him, flickering brightly and erratically against the quiet darkness of his mind.

"Please!" the girl cried again. "Fumes are coming up through the floorboards. I can't breathe."

"I'll roll down the window," he said, smiling. "I'm not going to stop, so you might as well forget your little tricks."

The cold, damp wind swept over her chilled body. She was suddenly close to panic; this was what excited him, to toy with her in a cat-and-mouse fashion, relishing her helplessness. If she couldn't get him to stop, there was no hope—unless a patrol car flagged him down. But the police obviously had no way of identifying him. Otherwise he wouldn't be driving along so confidently. How could she attract the attention of the police? To herself or to the car, it made no difference.

But she could do nothing at all while she was helpless. She began to strain at the bands about her wrists, twisting her hands until the skin was raw, exerting all her wiry strength against the silken fabric. The young man hadn't done too efficient a job, and she blessed him for it. Perhaps he'd given her this chance deliberately. The knots were loose, and her struggles produced a precious half inch of slack. That was almost enough, for her hands were quite small. She tried again, twisting her wrists silently and desperately until the knots slipped again. This was enough. She freed her hands and put them over her mouth to silence the sounds of her rapid, shallow breathing.

But there was still not much she could do. She could unlatch the rear door, but to push it open against the windstream would be almost impossible in her cramped position. And it wouldn't serve any purpose unless she intended to throw herself from the car. That thought instantly led to another—if not herself, what else was there to throw from the car? Specifically, through the opened window beside the driver's seat? The crumpled silk tie that had bound her wrists probably wouldn't attract anyone's attention. She felt cautiously about the floor of the car, but found only a folded newspaper and what seemed to be an empty cigarette package. No good. It had to be something that would point to her.

She thought of removing a shoe, but after a painful effort realized that it wasn't possible. She could arch her back and grasp her ankles in her hands, but she couldn't unbuckle the belt or untie the shoelaces in that position. And she couldn't risk turning over and sitting up. He would be sure to see the top of her head in the rear-view mirror. But the thought of shoes prompted her to take a personal inventory. Ring, small comb, hair ribbon, a pencil clipped in the pocket of her uniform. That was all; and none of these had any special significance. They would mean nothing to whoever found them.

"That's enough air," Bogan said, and began to roll up the window.

"No, please!" Her heart was beating wildly; she had just remembered the apron she was wearing, the short, starched apron with the name of Howard Johnson's stitched in red above the single pocket. "Please don't close the window. I'm suffocating." The terror in her voice was genuine; if he closed the window now her only chance would be gone.

"Well, we don't want that," he said, and rolled the window down again. "We want you nice and healthy for your handsome trooper. You wouldn't be pretty if you smothered to death."

iii.

She worked quickly to untie the knot that secured the apron about her waist. When it came free she raised herself cautiously on one elbow and looked up at the window, careful to keep her head below the top of the front seat. It wasn't possible, she realized with despair; his big shoulder and arm completely sealed off the area between the back seat and open window. If she tried to push the apron past him, he would feel the pressure of her hand and sense that she was moving behind his back.

Bogan said, "We're running a bit late. I'll have to step on it. But don't you worry. I won't be caught speeding."

The car swerved into the left, or passing, lane, body rocking on its springs, and she saw his head and shoulders move forward out of sight at the same time. He had hunched closer to the windshield to see more clearly while passing. Now the sway of the car told her they had cut back into the middle lane, and at the same time she saw his head and shoulders loom above her, returning to their customary position.

She breathed a soft prayer. When he moved forward, the open window had been clear and unobstructed by his bulk. And if he passed another car he would be likely to push himself forward again.

She made a ball of the apron in her right hand and raised her arm cautiously. When he passed another car she wouldn't be able to look up to see if he had moved forward; he would be close to the rear-

view mirror then and apt to notice any movement behind him. She
would have to gamble, shoving the apron up and out the window
without looking, and praying that her hand didn't strike his shoulder.

They drove for several minutes in the middle lane.

"That's enough air," he said with a vicious snap to his voice.
"When I get around this truck, the window goes up and stays up.
Why should I care whether you're comfortable? Do you have any
sympathy for me? Do you care about me at all?"

The car swerved to the left and gained speed, with the tires whin-
ing on the wet pavement. She counted to three slowly, trying to control the paralyzing fear that gripped her body. Now, she thought, but
couldn't force her hand to move. The car was swerving back into the
middle lane, and she bit down viciously on her trembling lip and said
"Now!" in a desperate little whisper.

She thrust her hand toward the window, dreading a contact with
his body, but she felt nothing but the wet wind like ice against her
knuckles. A fold of the cloth made a tearing noise in the windstream.
She held the apron between thumb and forefinger, felt it tug and
belly against her grip, then released it; and as she snaked her hand
away from the window, Bogan settled back in the seat, and her
fingers made a tiny whispering sound on the fabric of his coat.

But he didn't seem to notice. He said, "If you want to smother, go
ahead," and rolled the window up tightly. "Why should I care?"
There was a dangerous, vengeful tone in his voice. "I don't care if
your face turns black and your lungs burst." Bogan flipped on the
car's radio.

She lay completely still, exhausted by fear and tension. The back
of one hand was tight to her lips to hold back a sob.

The salesman whose name was Harry Mills swore angrily and
fluently as he swung his car onto the graveled roadway that flanked
the turnpike. His wife, Muriel, was in tears; her voice shook as she
said, "We could have been killed, Harry. You almost lost control."

"Of course I did," Harry Mills said furiously. "I couldn't see the
road for a full five seconds. The damn thing was plastered right over
the windshield wipers. I'm going to report this." He climbed from his
car, redfaced and pugnacious, and walked around to his wife's side.
"Some cop'll stop pretty soon," he said, and turned his overcoat col-

lar up against the rain. "We're alive and kicking, hon. I guess we're lucky at that."

"What was it?" she asked in the same high, frightened voice. "What did those fools throw from the window?"

"Well, it's still tangled in the wiper," he said, and he began to extricate the soggy piece of cloth which had blown from the car ahead of him to plaster itself across his windshield. He spread it out on the hood. "Well, how about that?" he said, and pushed his hat up on his forehead.

The flaring red light of a patrol was already bearing down on him, swerving expertly through the lanes of heavy traffic. The time was nine-thirty-five.

At headquarters Captain Royce stood with Sergeant Tonelli and Lieutenant Trask studying the large map of the turnpike on the wall of his office. There had been no trace of the killer in the last forty-five minutes. Captain Royce knew that he had left Howard Johnson's No. 1 with the girl at approximately eight-fifty. Forty-five minutes meant forty-five miles; and in forty-five miles the killer had had opportunities of leaving the pike anywhere between Exit 12 and Exit 5. All those interchanges were under surveillance, of course; a car-to-car search wasn't possible, but Ford, Plymouth and Chevrolet sedans were being given close attention, particularly those that were driven by large men wearing glasses. The killer might have slipped by, but Royce was reasonably certain he was still on the pike.

He glanced at the big clock on the opposite wall, and Sergeant Tonelli checked his wrist watch.

In two more minutes the Presidential convoy was scheduled to enter the turnpike at Interchange 5.

Tonelli cleared his throat. "Those reporters are still outside, Captain," he said.

"Good place for 'em," Royce said.

Newspapermen and TV and radio reporters had been streaming into headquarters in the last hour. They might give Royce and the turnpike a bad time if he didn't brief them on what was going on and what plans had been put into effect to trap the killer; but Royce was prepared to accept this. All off-duty troopers were now back on the pike; it was a hundred-mile trap, guarded by every marked and unmarked patrol car that was certified for service. Three special riot squads were cruising at twenty-mile intervals, ready to converge on any alarm with tear gas and shotguns. And Lieutenant Biersby at Communications had alerted all police within a hundred miles of the pike, and this net was being widened with every passing minute. The toll collectors, who were not police officers but unarmed civil servants, had been replaced by special details of state police who had been transferred to Royce's command.

If this information was phoned in by a reporter to a radio or TV station, it would be on the air in a matter of minutes. And it would sound very good, Royce thought. People listening in would nod approvingly, no doubt, and decide the cops were doing a job after all. It might even allay a bit of their indignation the next time they got a ticket for speeding. But against the advantages of a good press, Royce placed one all-important fact—the killer might have a radio in his car, and he would certainly be interested in the details of the plans being made to trap him.

A bell rang at the dispatcher's desk, and they heard the crackle of the radio with a distant voice reporting. The dispatcher turned quickly and glanced at Captain Royce, who had walked to the doorway of his office.

"Interchange Five reporting, sir," he said. "The President is on the pike. An eight-car convoy, with our patrols at the front and back. Traveling in the right lane at about fifty-five."

"All other patrols reported in position?" Royce said.

"Yes, sir."

Royce nodded and rubbed a hand over his damp forehead. Then he walked back to the map. He could visualize the progress of the convoy, and he knew the density of the surrounding traffic and the weather conditions on that stretch of the pike. None of it was favorable; the highway was slick with rain, and the traffic was both sluggish and heavy.

"Captain Royce!" the dispatcher in the outer office called in a rising voice. "Would you come here, sir?"

Royce, with Tonelli and Trask at his heels, reached the dispatcher's desk in long strides.

"Car Sixteen just reported, sir," the dispatcher said quickly. "He's just checked a stopped car. The driver pulled off the pike because a

Howard Johnson's apron was thrown from the car ahead of him and hit his windshield. The apron came from the driver's window of a fifty-two Ford with New York tags. The wife got the last three license numbers: six four two."

"Where was this?"

"Patrol Sixteen stopped at Milepost Fifty-four at—" The dispatcher checked his pad. "I got his request to pull off the pike two minutes ago."

Royce made a swift calculation; the '52 Ford had those two minutes, plus the time it had taken the stopped motorist to hail a patrol. A total of five minutes, say; which would take him down to Milepost 50, at Interchange 5.

"Who's closest to fifty?" he asked sharply.

"O'Leary, Patrol Twenty-one. He's tailing the President by a couple of hundred yards." He added unnecessarily, "Keeping the traffic behind the convoy slow."

When O'Leary received his orders from the dispatcher at headquarters, he was traveling in the middle column of southbound traffic at Milepost 48. The Presidential convoy a few hundred yards ahead of him rolled smoothly in the right lane; he could see the red beacon of the tail patrol car flashing in the darkness.

O'Leary sat up straighter, big hands tightening on the steering wheel. He repeated the three digits the dispatcher had given him, then said "Check!" and replaced his receiver. His heart was pounding with hope and excitement. He had been slowly closing the distance between himself and the convoy in the last five minutes, and he was fairly certain he hadn't passed any '52 Ford sedan. Which meant the killer was ahead of him, somewhere in the lines of traffic between himself and the convoy. Checking his rear-view mirror, O'Leary swung into the left lane, controlling the smoothly powerful car as if it were an extension of his body. He flashed by three slower cars, and after checking their license plates, swung back into the middle lane. He remained there long enough to inspect the plates ahead of him, and to his right, then swerved back to the high-speed lane and passed the cars he had eliminated. The rain made his work difficult, but he made his moves with deliberate precision, sweeping in and out of the traffic with effortless skill.

It was at Milepost 43 that he made contact; the Ford was traveling in the middle lane, fifty yards behind the Presidential convoy, but gaining slowly on it.

O'Leary dropped back discreetly and grabbed the receiver from beside the post of the steering wheel. "O'Leary, twenty-one," he snapped to Sergeant Tonelli. "I've got him. Milepost Forty-three south, middle lane."

"Hang on, here's the captain."

Captain Royce said sharply, "O'Leary, did you get a look at the driver?"

"No, sir. I'm three or four car lengths behind him."

"Any sign of the girl?"

"No, sir."

"Pull on past him. We'll cover with unmarked cars from now on."

"Check!" O'Leary was ready to turn into the left lane when he saw the Ford suddenly pick up speed and pull abreast of the Presidential convoy. The eight-car convoy was proceeding at fifty-five, with intervals of perhaps one hundred and fifty feet between each sedan.

"Good Lord!" O'Leary muttered softly. The Ford was moving to the extreme right of the middle lane, angling slowly toward one of the intervals that separated the cars in the convoy. He picked up his receiver and cried harshly, "Tonelli, he's trying to get into the convoy. That's what he's been waiting for!" It was a wild, desperate plan, but there was a spark of brilliance to it; if the Ford sliced into the convoy ahead of a carful of Secret Service agents, it would be detected instantly. But if it moved into an interval between newspapermen or Presidential aides, it might not be noticed. And once in the convoy the killer was assured of a safe exit from the pike; the President wouldn't be stopped at a toll gate—the entire convoy would be waved on with deferential salutes.

Captain Royce was already issuing commands that cracked like pistol shots from O'Leary's speaker. To unmarked Patrols 30 and 40 he gave the location and license number of the Ford and ordered them to intercept it, slow it down, keep it out of the convoy. To O'Leary he said, "Pull up beside him. He won't try anything with you there. When Patrols Thirty and Forty get into position, pull on ahead a few hundred yards. And for heaven's sake, be careful. We can't have a wreck, and we can't have any shooting."

"Check!" said O'Leary and swung out into the left lane. As he pulled up beside the Ford, he saw the driver hunched forward over the wheel, but the streaming rain made it impossible to single out the details of his features; he had an impression of bulk, the flash of eyeglasses, nothing else. O'Leary slowed down to pace the Ford, which was still edging toward the right side of the middle lane. In the right lane the Presidential convoy rolled smoothly down the pike, stately and decorous, with patrol cars at the head and rear of the column. O'Leary noticed that the Ford was swinging back gradually to the center of its lane; the driver had obviously spotted him and was postponing his move. In his rear-vision mirror O'Leary saw a pair of headlights rushing up on him through the rain that slashed vividly through the darkness.

This would be the first of the unmarked patrols. O'Leary moved a car length ahead of the Ford, then another, giving the trooper speeding up behind him room to cut into the middle lane and position his car in front of the killer's.

Sheila must be lying on the floor of the Ford, O'Leary realized, and the thought was a maddening one; he hated to leave now, but there was no place for impulsive heroics in the business of policing the turnpike. And his years of training and discipline were strong enough to counterbalance any temptation toward individual action. If she was in the car, her best chances of safety lay in police teamwork. If she was in the car—the thought made him feel sick. But he knew the killer might have knocked her unconscious, or killed her and thrown her body into the fields alongside the pike. To stop and get rid of her body would have taken only a few seconds; and in that brief time he would run little risk of being spotted by a patrol.

O'Leary stepped on his accelerator and moved ahead of the convoy; in his rear-vision mirror he saw a black station wagon cut smoothly in front of the Ford.

Harry Bogan cursed at his luck, cursed at the rain driving in thin, silver columns through his headlights. He hunched himself forward and wiped steam from the windshield with the palm of his hand.

A few minutes before, he had been laughing with boisterous good humor. The plan was going to work; he had been convinced of it. The intervals between the cars in the convoy were long, and the rain was a fine, steaming cover for the move he had planned to make. He had read in the newspapers of the President's trip, that he was attending a floodlighted ground-breaking ceremony at a veterans' hospital in Plankton, near Exit 5, and that he was traveling back to Washington that night.

And then, as Bogan approached Exit 5, he had picked up a broadcast from the local station in Plankton which assured him that his plans to intercept the President's convoy were timed exactly right. The mayor was being interviewed; he spoke of the honor done the village by the President's visit, of the inspiring message the President had delivered not only to Plankton but to the nation, to free men everywhere. Bogan had listened intently, irritated by the big words, the round, oratorical voice booming in the car. And then the mayor had said, "Although he has been gone from us only a few short moments, we nevertheless miss him deeply, and our hearts wish him Godspeed on his journey."

That was what Bogan had needed to know—the time of the President's departure from Plankton. Until then he had been guessing; now he was certain.

But suddenly, as he was preparing to execute the final step, a police car had come up alongside him and had hung there with maddening persistence. And when it had finally driven on, a fool in a black station wagon was hogging the road in front of him, slowing him down to forty miles an hour and arrogantly ignoring the furious blast of his horn.

The convoy had pulled away from him, the red lights of the patrol cars fading into the darkness, and the black station wagon had then swung sedately into the right lane to let Bogan pass. But now another fool was in the way, a man in a small pickup truck who seemed either drunk or suicidal; he weaved erratically in front of him, frustrating all his attempts to get by.

Bogan no longer felt inflated by the proud sense of accomplishment. Everything had become confusing and pointless; as with the breach with his brother and the long years of bitter and meaningless disappointments, there was no rhyme or reason to what was now happening to him, only the feeling of having been wronged somehow and the need to strike back at his tormentors. But his trail of splintered thoughts had come to a sustaining end. Every hand was raised to destroy him. But they wouldn't find it so easy.

He called sharply to the girl in the back seat. "You think you're going to marry your big handsome trooper, don't you? You think I'll turn you over to him safe and sound, eh? Pretty and sweet, so he can paw you. Is that what you're hoping?"

Sheila was lying on her side. In that position she was able to work at the buckle that secured the belt about her ankles. "Where are you taking me?" she said. There was no purpose to her question: she hoped only to distract him from his ugly preoccupation with herself and Dan. She couldn't bear the thread of obscene excitement in his voice, the frenzy of his insinuations.

"You'll know where I'm taking you when we get there," he said.

She had given up hope that her apron would be found. She imagined it wet and crumpled on the highway with thousands of tires grinding it into a soggy, unrecognizable mass. The only chance now was when he stopped to pay his toll at an exit; if it were possible, if he didn't discover that her hands were free before then, she would claw open the door and throw herself from the car. He would shoot her, of course; she knew from what he had been saying and the sound of his voice that he intended to kill her one way or another. But she could choose the way; and she knew that a bullet would be infinitely preferable to being alone with him in the anonymous darkness that stretched beyond the turnpike.

Bogan laughed suddenly. The pickup truck had moved out of his way. He hadn't lost more than a few minutes. The President's convoy was traveling under the legal limit, probably only a mile or two ahead of him. There was still time to catch up with it. He pushed down on the accelerator.

At headquarters battle plans were laid. Sergeant Tonelli had marked the turnpike map with a red thumbtack at the killer's position and a dozen green ones to indicate the patrol cars surrounding him. Captain Royce sucked on his cold pipe and considered the problem to be solved; they would get the killer, of course, but the job was to get him without hurting anyone else. The Presidential convoy was now well out of danger. After pulling ahead of the killer's blocked-off car, the convoy moved to the left lane and increased its speed to seventy miles an hour, with a patrol car clearing the way with sirens. The convoy was streaking toward the last exit now, and the killer couldn't possibly catch it; and even if his car were fast enough, there were patrols available to cut him off.

"We might take him right on the pike," Tonelli suggested. "Box him in, and knock him off the road. There'd be guns in his face before he knew what hit him."

Royce frowned at the map, considering the traffic and weather conditions in the killer's area. He didn't like Tonelli's idea; blocking a car at high speed was never an easy mission, but tonight it would be especially hazardous. He trusted his men and had a fierce pride in their skill and judgment, but he didn't intend to expose them to the caprices of a madman under these circumstances. Also, there were the civilian motorists to consider; if there was shooting or if the killer attempted to evade the patrols, it could cause a panic that might result in a bloody wreck.

"We'll let him get off the pike," Royce said. "He's got just three more chances, at Exits Three, Two and One. We'll take him when there's no chance of involving anybody else."

"And what about the girl?"

Royce turned from the map and stared at the windows; outside the weather had worsened, and the rain rolled in waves down the wide panes. He could see the flash of the turnpike traffic moving sluggishly through the storm.

"We'll try to keep him so busy he won't have time to worry about her," he said slowly. "It's all we can do. And it isn't much. Right now he's dangerous. He lost the convoy, and if he's not a complete madman he'll know he can't catch it. His plans have gone wrong, and he'll be expecting trouble." He rubbed his forehead. "If we could just calm him down a bit, make him feel confident. Then we could . . ." Royce paused, still staring at the windows. A grim smile touched his hard, seasoned features. "He's looking for a convoy, isn't he, sergeant? Supposing we arrange one for him?"

"What do you mean?"

"Listen, then get hustling. Flash Interchange Two, and Sergeant Brannon at Substation South. We're going to put a convoy on the pike ahead of the killer. Our convoy. With escort patrols at the front and rear. We'll get him into it. Then we'll spring the trap."

The eight black sedans were commandeered from the municipal administrations of townships at the southern end of the pike. They were assembled in convoy column fifteen minutes after Royce's order was transmitted to Sergeant Brannon, and at one minute after ten o'clock they rolled smoothly through Interchange 2 and merged with the southbound traffic on the pike. The convoy moved into the right-hand lane, with the escorting patrols clearing a path with their sirens. At the head of the column was Trooper Frank Sulkowski, a seasoned veteran who kept the convoy speed down to fifty miles an hour. At the rear was Dan O'Leary. He was watching his rear-vision mirror for any glimpse of the killer's Ford. The eight sedans herded between them were manned by troopers and detectives in civilian clothes, and the drivers were purposely allowing an inviting interval between each car. The convoy was a moving trap, with seven holes baited to tempt the killer.

O'Leary lifted his receiver and spoke to Sulkowski. "I think we're too fast, Frank. Let's drop it a bit."

"Check."

Their exchange was monitored by the dispatcher at headquarters, who relayed it to Captain Royce. "Convoy's in lane three, Milepost Eighteen. Reducing speed below fifty."

Royce nodded and checked the position of the killer's car on the map. Standing beside him was Major Townsend, the state-police commandant's chief of staff. He had arrived a few minutes before, a wiry man in his late fifties, for a personal report from Royce on the situation.

"Milepost Eighteen," Townsend said. "And where's the Ford?"

"A quarter of a mile behind. We've got it under surveillance. He's coming up steadily."

"And if he bites? What then?"

"The convoy will close up its intervals and swing over into the middle lane. Unmarked cars in lanes one and three will come up on each side of him. He'll be in a four-car box."

"And supposing he doesn't bite? Is there anything about the look of our convoy that might make him suspicious?"

"I don't think so, Major. Not unless he's a mind reader. There's nothing about our convoy to distinguish it from the President's. Particularly on a dark, rainy night like this one. Its rate of speed is consistent, and it's moving along right where the killer will expect it to be—in the right-hand lane, same number and type of cars as the President's, with patrols at the front and rear, beacon lights flashing."

"All right," the major said. "Assume he sticks his head into the noose. Where do you intend to take him into custody?"

Royce moved closer to the map and pointed to Exit 1, the last interchange on the pike. "Right here, sir."

O'Leary didn't identify the Ford until it pulled up alongside him in the middle lane; until that instant it had been nothing but a blur of approaching brightness in his rear-vision mirror. Now he saw the driver's bulky silhouette and, as the sedan crept past him, the license number. He picked up his receiver and spoke to Sulkowski. "He's just passing me, Frank."

Other voices cracked from O'Leary's radio phone—the dispatcher at headquarters, and then the troopers in the unmarked cars tailing the Ford.

O'Leary watched the killer's car pull slowly abreast of the convoy, red taillights winking in the rainy darkness. Then the car picked up speed suddenly and swerved right, taillights disappearing abruptly. The killer had slipped in between the third and fourth sedans in the convoy.

O'Leary said sharply, "He's in, Frank!"

"Check!" Sulkowski said. "Close up the intervals now and hang on."

The drivers of the third and fourth sedans in the convoy skillfully shortened the intervals between themselves and the Ford, and then the column of cars curved gracefully as Sulkowski swung into the middle lane. Unmarked patrols came up swiftly in lanes one and three to position themselves alongside the killer's car. The carefully timed mission was complete; the killer was boxed in on all sides, caught in a moving trap that rushed him along toward the last exit on the pike.

Captain Royce's plans to capture the killer were based on the fundamentals of simplicity and surprise; the police convoy would be escorted to the toll gate at the extreme right side of the interchange and kept well clear of normal turnpike traffic. The highway beyond the exit stretched a half mile to the Washington Bay Bridge, and this area was blocked off; all other traffic was being diverted to secondary roads.

At headquarters Royce explained the final details to Major Townsend. "We'll stop the convoy right here," he said, turning to the map and pointing to the right-hand toll booth at Exit 1. "About fifty yards this side of the toll booth we've placed a traffic standard of red blinker lights. When the convoy stops, a trooper will salute the first car and point to these lights, indicating that he wants the driver to stay on the right of them. Then he'll salute again and wave the car on past the toll station. He'll repeat this performance at the next two cars. The killer's car comes next. The killer will be watching, naturally, but all he'll see is a respectful trooper waving the President's convoy into its proper lane, expediting its departure from the pike." Royce prodded the surface of the map with his finger. "Meanwhile, troopers will be coming up behind the killer with their guns drawn. Dan O'Leary, who's the tail escort on the convoy, will leave his car and move up on the right. Troopers and detectives from the convoy cars will join him, covering the killer on both sides. They'll take him from behind, and they'll kill him if he makes a fight of it." Royce glanced at Major Townsend. "See any bugs in it?"

"No, it looks all right. I don't like exposing the trooper in front of the killer. And I don't like the fact that the girl's in the car. But if things were as simple as I'd like them to be, we could go fishing and let a pack of Girl Scouts make the arrest."

"I know," Royce said and rubbed his forehead; the strain of the last three hours was evident in the lines about his mouth and eyes. "We'll need a break."

The dispatcher left his station and strode into Royce's office. "Captain, a trucker discovered the body of a young man at Howard Johnson's Number One. In a ditch near the truckers' parking lot. He's not conscious, but they seem to think he's in fair shape. His papers show he's the owner of the Ford the killer's driving."

"Ambulance on the way?"

"Yes, sir."

"And the boy's got a chance?"

"Seems like it, sir. He's lost some blood and has a nasty lump on his head, but he's breathing pretty well."

"That's one bit of good news," Royce said. "Maybe we'll get another break now." He turned and frowned at the map. "We'll know in a few minutes."

In the speeding convoy Bogan was laughing softly with relief and excitement. He felt snug and confident in the smoothly rolling column of official cars: in front and back of him, reassuringly close, were the privileged black sedans of the President's convoy, and on either side of him, coincidentally and luckily were cars that happened to be traveling at exactly his rate of speed. No one could get at him now; he was safe from everyone in this speeding steel cage, rushing to freedom behind an invincible shield of power and authority.

He felt cunning and triumphant once more, all of his emotions raised to a thrilling pitch of excitement. He called to the girl, "We'll be leaving the turnpike soon. Courtesy of the police." He laughed softly, savoring the warm confidence running through him. "We're very important people, did you realize that? We're riding right along with the President. The police will salute and bow as we go by. It's a pity you can't sit up here with me and enjoy it."

Sheila had managed to unbuckle the belt about her ankles, but Bogan's words destroyed her hopes; if they didn't stop at the toll booth, what had she accomplished by freeing her legs?

"You're making a mistake taking me with you," she said desperately. "The police will be searching for me. If you let me go, I promise I won't—" She stopped, knowing the hopelessness of her appeal and despising the sound of animal fear and entreaty in her voice.

"You won't tell on me, is that what you were going to say? I'm sure you wouldn't," he said with heavy sarcasm. "But the police won't find us. Don't worry about that. Not before we have our little talk. We'll go somewhere nice and quiet. And I'll get some coffee and sweet rolls. I know just the kind you'll like. They're covered all over with sugar, and inside there's a thick filling of jelly. I'll untie you and you'll be comfortable." Bogan frowned and touched his forehead; there was a strange, confusing pain there. What was it he wanted to explain to her? It had something to do with the big trooper she wanted to marry. Yes. He had to tell her that wasn't right. And there was the thing about his family, his father and brother, and the young couple in New York, the girl with the slim, bare legs she displayed so cruelly. They hadn't been nice to him, he remembered, and he thought it would be interesting to talk to them too. But he couldn't do that. Somehow they got away from him.

With saving instinct, Bogan knew he shouldn't be thinking about these things; they would confuse and anger him, and he needed all his cunning and strength to fight the forces ranged against him.

"You shut up," he said petulantly, sullenly. "You got me into this trouble. That's what I'm going to talk to you about later. You wait."

"Please," she said, and for the first time her voice broke; she knew then he wanted to kill her. "Please don't—"

"Shut up!" he cried in a low, harsh voice, and hunched forward, eyes narrowing with tension.

The convoy was slowing down. Ahead he saw the arched lights of Interchange 1 glowing brilliantly in the darkness. The streams of turnpike traffic were fanning out as they entered the broad approach to the last exit. The convoy swung past a line of troopers standing at attention and turned toward the blinker lights and the toll booth at the far right side of the interchange. They were coming to a stop, and Bogan felt his heart pounding with fear; this was all wrong, no one could stop the President's convoy—unless they were looking for something. The thought was a lightning flash of terror in his mind. He pulled the gun from his pocket and rolled his window down halfway. A spray of cold rain struck his face. Beads of moisture collected on his glasses, and the traffic lights and police beacons splintered against them like threatening lances. In the silence he could hear the girl's rapid breathing.

"Don't you move or make any noise," he told her quietly. "If you do, you'll be responsible for the men I'll have to kill."

Bogan wiped his glasses with the tip of his index finger, clearing a small tunnel of visibility through the rain and lights and shadows. When he saw a trooper approaching the first car in the convoy, Bogan raised his gun and rested it on the edge of the rolled-down window. But the trooper stopped a good six feet from the first car, came to attention and saluted smartly. He pointed toward the standard of blinker lights, obviously directing the driver to the right of them, then saluted again as the car moved ahead slowly. The performance was repeated with the second car, and Bogan realized that this was simple routine, a respectful policeman directing the convoy into its appointed, privileged lane. He withdrew his gun from the window and let out his breath slowly. Everything was all right; the feeling of relief was so intense that he almost laughed aloud. Now the car immediately ahead of him was moving out, and the trooper was walking toward him with long, swinging strides, a tall black figure in the slashing rain.

Bogan heard the girl stirring behind him and heard the metallic click as the lock of the rear door was released; then a thin edge of cold air touched the back of his neck. He twisted about desperately, fear leaping through him in sudden, shocking waves. The girl was free, he saw; the belt was gone from her ankles, her hands were clawing at the partially open door. He felt nothing then but a despairing ache of betrayal; she was worse than all the rest, tricking him in silence, cunningly plotting to frustrate all his plans.

And then, through the rear window, Bogan saw the figure of a uniformed man running at a crouch toward his car. He cursed furiously and released the clutch; and at the same instant he turned and fired at the trooper approaching his car from the front. The thrust of the car under full power caused the rear door to close with a crash, and Bogan heard the girl scream in pain. *Her fingers,* he thought, as he swung the car to run down the trooper who had hurled himself to the roadway at Bogan's shot. *Slim white fingers, soft as velvet in a caress.* Bogan twisted the wheel savagely, swerving clear of the trooper and rushing at the toll booth. Escape was important, not the fool lying there in the rain. *Take care of him later, take care of them all later.*

O'Leary was six feet from the rear of the Ford when Bogan fired at the trooper. He leaped forward, closing the distance in one stride, but the car was already lunging away from him, swerving off sharply to the left; but then it swung back crazily to the right, heading for the toll booth, and O'Leary hurled himself at the rear door, catching the handle in both hands. The speed of the car jerked him off his feet, swinging his body in a bruising arc along the turnpike, but he kept his grip for a precious second, and managed to release the catch and open the door.

The Ford bucked spasmodically as Bogan shifted gears, and in that momentary halt O'Leary flung the upper part of his body into the back seat of the car. He wrapped his arms around Sheila's knees and let his weight go limp; and when the car surged forward again, his legs dragged along the ground, and then he was free, slamming painfully against the wet concrete with Sheila's light weight held desperately in his arms.

O'Leary came to his knees and held her tightly against him for an instant, isolating her from the roar of cars, the flash of gunfire. She was crying hysterically, saying his name over and over, but there was no recognition in her eyes or face. The terror would not leave her for a long time, but she was clinging to someone who would be with her until it did.

O'Leary left her with detectives who had poured from the convoy sedans and ran back to his own patrol car. The Ford had crashed past the toll booth and was racing down the half-mile stretch of highway that led to the bay bridge. But there was no escape now; three blue-and-white patrol cars were speeding after it, maneuvering for position with merciless precision. There were no other cars on the road; Bogan roared down a deserted tunnel, with patrol cars closing in on three sides.

O'Leary shot past the toll booth after the pursuing police cars, holding his microphone to his lips. "He's all alone," he said. "The girl's out of the car, she's safe." His report sounded in the patrols ahead of him and at headquarters in Riverhead.

Captain Royce said, "Don't get careless now; don't take any chances. He's not going anywhere." And he issued an order to the bridge police to open their span.

The bridge barriers slid automatically into place, and the powerful cables at the four corners of the bridge began to turn on their drums, lifting the span slowly into the air. "Take him when he stops," Royce said.

Bogan saw water sparkling ahead of him, spreading away like a broad, calm meadow at dusk, with a soft wind stirring the leaves of grass, so that they flashed with the last glancing rays of evening light. It was very lovely; quiet and peaceful. But he couldn't stop crying. The tears streamed from his mild eyes and ran coldly down his cheeks. He needed someone to comfort him; someone he wasn't afraid of.

The patrol cars were racing up behind him, he saw—stalking him like great dangerous animals.

Brilliant red lights flashed in his eyes, and he saw a barrier, and beyond that a heavy chain swinging across the highway. And beyond that, nothing but the wide, peaceful meadow that looked like water in the curious confusion of nighttime lights and shadows. He heard the crash of his car against the barrier and then the wrenching, snapping sound of the chain giving, and then he was free at last, soaring toward the dark, mild meadow, as effortlessly as a bird, or a child's paper airplane.

Dan O'Leary swung his car about and snapped off his siren and beacon lights. He sat for half a moment with his arms crossed on the steering wheel, his forehead resting on the backs of his hands. It was all over; the Ford had plunged into Washington Bay, and after the noise of the crash and a plume of white spray, there was nothing left but the spreading ripples on the surface of the black, silent water.

O'Leary said a prayer that Sheila was safe. Then he started back to Interchange 1, where she was waiting for him. He drove at less than the legal maximum speed, steadily and precisely, his big hands firm on the wheel, his eyes alert on the road ahead of him. There was no need to hurry this last half mile to Interchange 1, he thought gratefully; the important part of him was already there.

Payment Received

Robert L. McGrath

Chulie Ross was a strange one, and that was a fact. For a nine-year-old kid, he had more queer ways than a pup hound dog. Not dumb, just different. Tetched. A book-readin' kid. So nobody in Sunrise paid him much mind, and when he showed up luggin' this black kitten the mornin' they was fixin' for a necktie party with Tanner Higgins the honor guest, nobody bothered to shoo him off. They just paid him no mind a-tall.

"Let's get it over with!" someone hollered.

"Got to let 'im have his last say," came another voice. "String a man 'thout his last say, an' his spirit'll dog you seven times seventy years!"

They were all there, all the men from Sunrise: white-maned Rim Cutler—for lack of judge, preacher, marshal, and a few other assorted officials, he filled whatever shoes was most needed at the time; tattooed Seth Anders—he'd sailed the seas to India, where a lot of odd Hindu notions rubbed off on him; God-scared Tanner Higgins—sometime schoolmaster, a quiet, still-water-runs-deep man, convicted of the murder of his best friend; and a baker's dozen other citizens, all het with the fever of gettin' it done before sunrise, in the town tradition.

"All right, men!" old Rim Cutler bellowed. "Reckon any man's got a right to his last say. Start sayin', Tanner, but make it fast. We ain't got all day."

"What's the use?" Tanner Higgins said, sittin' sorry on the horse, hands tied behind his back. "We've been through it all before."

241

"That all you got to say?" Rim Cutler asked.

"I didn't kill him!" Tanner Higgins yelled. "I didn't have anything to do with it!"

Rim Cutler juiced the dust with amber. "Then who did?"

"I've told you—I don't know!" Tanner shook his head, hopeless.

"Your ax, warn't it?" Rim Cutler said.

"Yes, it was my ax—but I didn't do it!"

"Your girl he was chasin', warn't it?"

"Yes, she was my girl! But I wouldn't kill a man over a woman!"

"Maybe money, then," Rim Cutler suggested. "Some says Jack Bronson had money. Maybe that was it."

"Look, for the last time, I didn't kill Jack! He was a good man— my best friend! I couldn't have killed him! I couldn't kill anybody!"

"We're wastin' time, Rim," Seth Anders cut in. "Sun's comin' up. Let's get this thing over with!"

"All right, boys," Rim Cutler said. "Get that horse over here."

"Mr. Cutler, sir," a small high-pitched voice broke in, insistent.

"What—oh. Go on home, Chulie. This ain't no place fer kids."

"Mr. Cutler, you—fixin' to horsewhip Tanner Higgins?"

"Well"—Rim Cutler looked around, uncomfortable—"I reckon you might call it that. Now git on home, where you belong."

"He didn't do anything, Mr. Cutler. He didn't."

"Say, will somebody take this blabbin' kid out of here?"

"He didn't kill Jack Bronson, Mr. Cutler. He didn't."

"Go on, git! This ain't no place fer a kid!"

Seth Anders' arm swooped down to pull the boy up to the saddle, but the black kitten spooked and the tiny claws found home. "Ouch, you little son of a—"

"I know who did it," Chulie Ross said then, smoothin' the black kitten's fur. "I know who killed Jack Bronson."

For a moment, no sound. "What was that again, son?" Rim Cutler could speak soft when he wanted.

"I—I said I know who killed Jack Bronson. And it wasn't Mister Higgins."

"Huh!" Seth Anders snorted. "I s'pose you did it."

Chulie looked at him, strokin' the kitten, sayin' not a word.

"All right, son," Rim Cutler said. "You know who did it. You tell us about it."

"Do I have to?" Chulie looked around at them.

"Reckon you do, Chulie," Rim Cutler said. "We got to see justice done this day."

"It was—it was—" Chulie looked from man to man, and there was some squirmin' done.

"Come on, son. Speak up!"

"It was—him!"

A small finger pointed. Seventeen pairs of eyes, includin' the black kitten's, went to one man.

"Like hell it was!" Seth Anders exploded, face clouded red. "You gonna take that dummy kid's word?"

"Ain't said we would," Rim Cutler drawled. "But we ain't stringin' nobody this day. Sun's up."

The red ball in the east had cleared the rim. The eyes left Seth Anders, checked the dawn of day, then settled uneasy on each other, on Tanner Higgins, on Rim Cutler, on Chulie Ross and the black kitten.

"What makes you think Seth Anders killed Jack Bronson, Chulie?" Rim Cutler asked, gentle.

"I—I saw him do it," the boy squeezed out the words. "I—I was hiding."

"He's a damn liar!" Seth Anders put in, louder than need be.

"Chulie," old Rim Cutler spoke low, "you sure you know what you're sayin'? You sure you didn't"—he looked around at the rest, sober—"didn't read all this in a book?"

"I saw him do it," Chulie insisted. "Me—and Jack."

"Jack? You mean Jack Bronson?"

"No, Jack—my little cat," Chulie said. "We saw him do it."

"Now, why," asked Rim Cutler, patient, "would Seth here want to hurt anybody? Why would Seth want to kill Jack Bronson?"

The boy looked at Seth Anders, but he held steady. "Money," he said then. "It was money."

Seth Anders got down from his horse fast, reachin' for the boy. The black kitten spooked again, spit, and barely missed hookin' the other hand.

"Jack—my cat—doesn't like—him."

Everybody eyed Seth Anders now, and no mistake—his once red face was white as the inside of a store-bought flour barrel.

"It—it's him!" A whisper rasped out of the throat of Seth Anders.

"What's the matter, man? You gone daft?"

"It—it's him—come back. Him! Him!" A cry, a sob, in the early mornin'.

"Chulie," Rim Cutler said, "you take that kitten of yours and mosey over yonder a piece."

Dust squirted as the boy dragged himself away.

"Now," Rim Cutler bellowed, "you got somethin' you want to say, Seth?"

"I—I did it," the voice broke. "I did it! I didn't know he'd come back. I didn't know! I didn't expect that!"

"You use Tanner's ax?" Rim Cutler asked.

"I—I borrowed it. Didn't intend to kill 'im. Wouldn't give me the money." Whinin' now. "I didn't know—he'd come back!"

"Boys, I reckon we almost made a mistake," Rim Cutler said. "I reckon we owe Tanner Higgins here quite a debt. Reckon it'll take a passel of time to pay it off."

The man with hands tied behind his back was limp, his shirt dark with sweat. "I reckon I owe a debt to Chulie Ross," Tanner Higgins said, quiet. "And maybe someone else, too." He looked up at the sky; the others turned away and looked at the ground.

"Reckon you better come with us, Seth." Rim Cutler motioned to the rest. "Might as well head back." With a swipe of his knife, he cut the bonds on Tanner Higgins' hands. Then he slapped the man on the leg, hesitated a moment, and walked away.

Tanner Higgins waited, and when they were gone, got off the horse and walked slow toward the boy. "I want to thank you, Chulie," he said. "That was a brave thing you did." He held out his hand, and the boy grasped it, shy. "But you should have told them sooner, several days ago, when they had the trial. Why didn't you tell them sooner?"

"I—I didn't know what they were going to do," the boy said. "Mr. Higgins . . ."

"Yes, Chulie?"

"Mr. Higgins, what did Seth Anders mean when he said, 'It's him!' What was he talking about?"

"Well, Chulie, I think he figured that black kitten of yours was really Jack Bronson, come back to haunt him. It's a thing they call reincarnation—sort of a superstition."

"Like black cats bring bad luck?"

"That's right, Chulie. Since your kitten is named Jack, and all, Anders thought Jack Bronson's spirit was right there in the cat, and was after him."

"Mr. Higgins, I'd like to tell you something."

"Yes, Chulie?"

"Jack Bronson couldn't be in this here kitten of mine. It's a she—her real name is Jackie—only I was afraid they'd laugh at me, so I called her Jack."

Tanner Higgins wiped his forehead with the back of his hand, again looked reverent at the sky.

"Mr. Higgins . . ."

"Something else, Chulie?"

"Yes, sir. I—I didn't really see Seth Anders kill Jack Bronson. I—I just thought maybe he did it."

"You—what?"

"I thought maybe it was him. He always poked fun at me—for reading."

"Oh." Tanner Higgins shook his head.

"Way I figure, maybe now you and I are even, Mr. Higgins."

"Even, Chulie? How do you mean?"

"I did you a favor," Chulie Ross said. "I paid you back."

"For what, Chulie? You didn't owe me anything."

The boy stroked the black kitten nestled in his arms. "Sure I owed you, Mr. Higgins. Don't you remember? You're the one who taught me how to read!"

Agony Column

Barry N. Malzberg

Gentlemen:

I enclose my short story, THREE FOR THE UNIVERSE, and know you will find it right for your magazine, ASTOUNDING SPIRITS.

> Yours very truly,
> Martin Miller

Dear Contributor:

Thank you for your recent submission. Unfortunately, although we have read it with great interest, we are unable to use it in *Astounding Spirits*. Due to the great volume of submissions we receive, we cannot grant all contributors a personal letter, but you may be sure that the manuscript has been reviewed carefully and its rejection is no comment upon its literary merit but may be dependent upon one of many other factors.

> Faithfully,
> The Editors

Dear Editors:

The Vietnam disgrace must be brought to an end! We have lost on that stained soil not only our national honor but our very future. The troops must be brought home and we must remember that there is more honor in dissent than in unquestioningly silent agreement.

> Sincerely,
> Martin Miller

Dear Sir:

Thank you for your recent letter to the Editors. Due to the great volume of worthy submissions we are unable to print every good letter we receive and therefore regretfully inform you that while we will not be publishing it, this is no comment upon the value of your opinion.

Very truly yours,
The Editors

Dear Congressman Forthwaite:

I wish to bring your attention to a serious situation which is developing on the West Side. A resident of this neighborhood for five years now, I have recently observed that a large number of streetwalkers, dope addicts and criminal types are loitering at the intersection of Columbus Avenue and 124th Street at almost all hours of the day, offending passers-by with their appearance and creating a severe blight on the area. In addition, passers-by are often threateningly asked for "handouts" and even "solicited." I know that you with me share a concern for a Better West Side and look forward to your comments on this situation as well as some kind of concrete action.

Sincerely,
Martin Miller

Dear Mr. Millow:

Thank you for your letter. Your concern for our West Side is appreciated and it is only through the efforts and diligence of constituents such as yourself that a better New York can be conceived. I have forwarded your letter to the appropriate precinct office in Manhattan and you may expect to hear from them soon.

Gratefully yours,
Alwyn D. Forthwaite

Dear Gentlemen:

In May of this year I wrote Congressman Alwyn D. Forthwaite a letter of complaint, concerning conditions on the Columbus Avenue–West 124th Street intersection in Manhattan and was informed by him that this letter was passed onto your precinct office. Since four months have now elapsed and since I have neither heard from you nor observed any change in the conditions pointed out in my letter, I now write to ask whether or not that letter was forwarded to you and what you have to say about it.

> Sincerely,
> Martin Miller

Dear Mr. Milner:
  Our files hold no record of your letter.

> N. B. Karsh
> Captain, #33462

Dear Sirs:
  I have read Sheldon Novack's article in the current issue of CRY with great interest but feel that I must take issue with his basic point, which is that sex is the consuming biological drive from which all other activities stem and which said other activities become only metaphorical for. This strikes me as a bit more of a projection of Mr. Novack's own functioning than that reality which he so shrewdly contends he apperceives.

> Sincerely,
> Martin Miller

Dear Mr. Milton:
  Due to the great number of responses to Sheldon A. Novack's "Sex and Sexuality: Are We Missing Anything?" in the August issue of CRY, we will be unable to publish your own contribution in our Cry from the City column, but we do thank you for your interest.

> Yours,
> The Editors

Dear Mr. President:
  I was shocked by the remarks apparently attributed to you in to-day's newspaper on the public assistance situation. Surely, you must be aware of the fact that social welfare legislation emerged from the compassionate attempt of 1930 politics to deal with human torment

in the systematized fashion and although many of the cruelties you note are inherent to the very system, they do not cast doubt upon its very legitimacy. Our whole national history has been one of coming to terms with collective consciousness as opposed to the law of the jungle, and I cannot understand how you could have such a position as yours.

Sincerely,
Martin Miller

Dear Mr. Meller:

Thank you very much for your letter of October 18th to the President. We appreciate your interest and assure you that without the concern of citizens like yourself the country would not be what it has become. Thank you very much and we do look forward to hearing from you in the future on matters of national interest.

Mary L. McGinnity
Presidential Assistant

Gentlemen:

I enclose herewith my article, WELFARE: ARE WE MISSING ANYTHING? which I hope you may find suitable for publication in INSIGHT MAGAZINE.

Very truly yours,
Martin Miller

Dear Contributor:

The enclosed has been carefully reviewed and our reluctant decision is that it does not quite meet our needs at the present time. Thank you for your interest in *Insight*.

The Editors

Dear Senator Partch:

Your vote on the Armament Legislation was shameful.

Sincerely,
Martin Miller

Dear Dr. Mallow:

Thank you for your recent letter to Senator O. Stuart Partch and for your approval of the Senator's vote.

> L. T. Walters
> Congressional Aide

Dear Susan Saltis:

I think your recent decision to pose nude in that "art-photography" series in MEN'S COMPANION was disgraceful, filled once again with those timeless, empty rationalizations of the licentious which have so little intrinsic capacity for damage except when they are subsumed, as they are in your case, with abstract and vague "connections" to platitudes so enormous as to risk the very demolition of the collective personality.

> Yours very truly,
> Martin Miller

Dear Sir:

With pleasure and in answer to your request, we are enclosing a photograph of Miss Susan Saltis as she appears in her new movie, "Chariots to the Holy Roman Empire."

> Very truly yours,
> Henry T. Wyatt
> Publicity Director

Gentlemen:

I wonder if CRY would be interested in the enclosed article which is not so much an article as a true documentary of the results which have been obtained from my efforts over recent months to correspond with various public figures, entertainment stars, etc., etc. It is frightening to contemplate the obliteration of self which the very devices of the 20th Century compel, and perhaps your readers might share my (not so retrospective) horror.

> Sincerely,
> Martin Miller

Dear Sir:

As a potential contributor to *Cry* I am happy to offer you our "Writer's Subscription Discount" meaning that for only $5.50 you will receive not only a full year's subscription (28% below newsstand rates, 14% below customary subscriptions) but in addition our year-end special issue, *Cry in the Void* at no extra charge.

Subscription Dept.

Dear Contributor:

Thank you very much for your article, "Agony Column." It has been considered here with great interest and it is the consensus of the Editorial Board that while it has unusual merit it is not quite right for us. We thank you for your interest in *Cry* and look forward to seeing more of your work in the future.

Sincerely,
The Editors

Dear Congressman Forthwaite:

Nothing has been done about the conditions I mentioned in my letter of about a year ago. Not one single thing!

Bitterly,
Martin Miller

Dear Mr. Mills:

Please accept our apologies for the delay in answering your good letter. Congressman Forthwaite has been involved, as you know, through the winter in the Food Panel and has of necessity allowed some of his important correspondence to await close attention.

Now that he has the time he thanks you for your kind words of support.

Yours truly,
Ann Ananauris

Dear Sir:

The Adams multiple-murders are indeed interesting not only for their violence but because of the confession of the accused that he "did it so that someone would finally notice me." Any citizen can understand this—the desperate need to be recognized as an individual, to break past bureaucracy into some clear apprehension of one's self-worth, is one of the most basic of human drives, but I am becoming increasingly frustrated today by a technocracy which allows less and less latitude for the individual to articulate his own identity and vision and be heard. Murder is easy: it is easy in the sense that the murderer does not need to embark upon an arduous course of training in order to accomplish his feat; his excess can come from the simple extension of sheer human drives . . . aided by basic weaponry. The murderer does not have to cultivate "contacts" or "fame" but can simply, by being *there*, vault past nihilism and into some clear, cold connection with the self. More and more the capacity for murder lurks within us; we are narrow and driven, we are almost obliterated from any sense of existence, we need to make that singing leap past accomplishment and into acknowledgement and *recognition*. Perhaps you would print this letter?

> Hopefully,
> Martin Miller

Dear Sir:
　Thank you for your recent letter. We regret being unable to use it due to many letters of similar nature being received, but we look forward to your expression of interest.

> Sincerely,
> John Smith, for the Editors

Dear Mr. President:
　I intend to assassinate you. I swear that you will not live out the year. It will come by rifle or knife, horn or fire, dread or terror but it will come and there is no way that you can AVOID THAT JUDGEMENT TO BE RENDERED UPON YOU.

> Fuck You,
> Martin Miller

Dear Reverend Mellbow:
　As you know, the President is abroad at the time of the writing but

you may rest assured that upon his return your letter, along with thousands of other and similar expressions of hope, will be turned over to him and I am sure that he will appreciate your having written.

Very truly yours,
Mary L. McGinnity
Presidential Assistant

Guessing Game

Rose Million Healey

The little boy with the round, innocent face and fair hair sat swinging his legs and watching Martha work.

"Don't you want to know what I've got in here?" he asked her.

Martha didn't turn from her dusting, nor did she bother to answer him. It was the first time they'd been alone together, Martha and Mrs. B.'s grandson. Martha didn't care for him much. If she'd known about him, she thought, maybe she wouldn't have taken the job. Sighing, Martha bent her knees and applied her dust rag to the piano legs. It wasn't that she didn't like children; she'd had two of her own, hadn't she, and might be a grandmother herself if it hadn't been for the war taking John Joseph and the Lord not blessing Young Martha with the looks to get a husband. No, it wasn't a coldness toward children in general, she told herself, slowly rising and flicking the keyboard daintily with her duster. But there was something about little Jeffrey that upset her and made her ill at ease. He wasn't like other boys, and that was a fact. He was quiet, but that wasn't it. Boys don't necessarily have to be rowdy. It wasn't that he was impudent, either. I could handle a scamp easily, she thought. Something for which there was no name, or at least not one that Martha knew, was wrong with Jeffrey Belton III. He had a way of regarding you with a narrow-eyed stare when he thought you weren't noticing. There would be a faint smile on his lips that somehow wasn't the sweet thing a smile on a child's face should be.

Martha whirled around to see if she could surprise that look on his face now. He wasn't looking at her at all but at a small cardboard box he held in his lap.

Feeling her gaze, he glanced up. "Bet you'll never guess," he said, "what I've got in here."

255

He held the box up and shook it invitingly. Something rattled back and forth inside.

Martha tried to answer pleasantly. After all, he was only a baby. "What do I win, if I guess right?" she asked.

The little boy regarded her solemnly.

"You never will. Never in a million, trillion years," he told her.

"But if I do?"

"I'll give you my allowance for next week," Jeffrey promised, after a moment's hesitation.

Martha flushed. "No, no, I don't want your money," she said. "I tell you what"—she pushed a vase aside on the mantelpiece and dusted carefully—"if I guess, you help me dry the dishes tomorrow morning. If I don't guess, I'll give you something nice."

"What?" the little boy asked.

"Oh, I don't know. Something nice."

"Will you give me what I ask for?"

"That depends," Martha told him, running her cloth over the gilt-framed mirror.

"On what? What does it depend on?"

"Whether I have what you ask for or not."

"Oh, you have it," Jeffrey assured her. "Is it a deal?"

Martha smiled. He was like other children, really, just harder to know. Playing the game, she hedged: "Well, hold on now. Not so fast. What is this something I have that you might win?"

"I can't tell you," the little boy said, as she had been sure he would.

"Is it something I won't mind giving up?"

"You shouldn't mind," he said. "You have plenty of others."

One of the toy automobiles her son had collected when he was young, Martha thought. She had shown them to Jeffrey during her first week in the house in an attempt to win his affection. They hadn't seemed to impress him at the time, but she should have realized he was shy. Well, one car out of so many wouldn't matter. And, besides, what had she kept them for but to make other little boys happy?

"Is it a deal?" Jeffrey demanded again.

"Yes, yes," Martha replied. "A deal."

"You promise?"

"Certainly."

"Say it."

"I promise," Martha said. She caught the little boy's reflection in the mirror. His eyes were slits of pale blue, and a suggestion of a smile played about his mouth.

With an effort, Martha forced herself to say heartily, "Now, then, what can it be? What *can* it be?" She faced the little boy and looked down at the box he clutched with both hands.

"Is it a—"

"Wait!" Jeffrey commanded. He scrambled off the chair. "How many guesses do you get?"

"That's right," Martha said. "There should be a limit. How many do you think I should have?"

"Three. Like in the storybooks."

Martha patted the blond head.

He drew away instantly, then came back. "You can pat my hair if you want to, Martha," he murmured in a purring tone.

Suddenly, Martha didn't want to. She pretended not to hear him. Looking around the room, she said, "Looks as if I'm finished in here. Better get busy on the bedrooms."

"Why don't you do the kitchen?" the little boy suggested. "I can drink my milk while you're guessing," he added slyly.

It wasn't easy to make him drink milk, she knew; Martha obediently led the way to the kitchen.

He perched himself on the table in the middle of the room. From there he had a good view of Martha wherever she might go. Uneasy under his gaze, Martha poured the milk and handed it to him. As she turned from him, she stumbled slightly, and the boy laughed.

"Clumsy Martha. Clumsy Martha," he sang out in a clear, happy treble.

He liked to see people uncomfortable or hurt. She had noticed that before. It made her shudder.

At the sink she started the breakfast dishes. Hoping to end the game as quickly as possible, so Jeffrey would leave her to play in the living room with his jigsaw puzzle or outside on his swing, she said:

"Is it a toy?"

"No, no, no!" the boy yelled triumphantly.

"Am I warm?" she asked.

"You're not a bit warm. You're icy, icy cold. Brrr. I'm shivering, you're so cold! Guess again."

Martha shook the soap flakes into a pan.

"Is it—" She tried to think of any articles she'd seen him carrying around. For some reason, she really did want to win the game. It wasn't the car; she'd give him that anyway. But somehow she felt she should try hard to win. To refresh her mind on the size of the box, she glanced over her shoulder at the boy. He was staring at her again and with such an expression of cruel anticipation, she almost dropped the saucer she held.

"Go on. Guess," the boy urged.

The box was about two inches wide and four inches long. It was probably six inches deep. A number of things ran through Martha's mind and were rejected: a deck of cards, a scarf, stamps from his stamp collection? But it rattled. Whatever was inside rattled. Martha bit her lips.

"Well?" the boy said.

"I'm thinking," Martha snapped. She could sense his satisfaction at having upset her, and with difficulty she calmed herself.

"Let me hold the box," she suggested.

"Why?" the little boy asked. He scooted back on the table away from her.

"I want to see how heavy it is," Martha explained.

The boy seemed to weigh his decision carefully.

"No," he answered at last.

"Why not?"

"Your hands are all wet," he pointed out. "And besides, when we started to play, that wasn't in the rules."

Martha felt a keen pang of disappointment.

"It's not fair," she said, returning to her dishes. "How can I possibly guess if I haven't any hint?"

"Oh, I'll give you a hint."

"You will?" Martha knew her eagerness was silly. She knew she was being much too serious about a guessing game with a child, but she couldn't help it.

"I'll give you three questions," Jeffrey announced magnanimously, and Martha felt a surge of hope.

"How big is it?" she asked.

"As big as—" The boy lolled his head back and rolled his eyes at the ceiling. "As big as your finger," he said and grinned at some private joke.

Martha thought: A matchbox, a stick of candy, a pencil?

"What color is it?"

The boy considered the question, frowning. Then he smiled. "It *was* pink," he told Martha.

Absently Martha scrubbed the oatmeal pan. Beads, a lipstick, oh, why couldn't she get it?

Stalling for time, she asked, "You weren't fibbing, were you? It definitely isn't a toy?"

Jeffrey looked shocked. "I don't tell fibs," he said. Impatiently, he demanded, "Why don't you guess?"

"It's a—a penny," Martha blurted desperately, and the boy danced with joy.

"Wrong!" he screamed. "Wrong! Wrong! Wrong!"

He jumped to the floor and ran up and down wagging his head from side to side and saying, "Wrong, wrong, wrong," until Martha told him sharply to stop it.

Obediently he stood still beside her at the sink. He leaned against the sideboard panting, and she could look down at the clean little scalp and the fine hair and the downy little neck. She almost regained her perspective. Almost.

Then he spoke in a breathy whisper: "You just have one guess left, Martha."

The warning sounded vaguely sinister.

The pit of Martha's stomach turned cold.

"It's a foolish game. I don't want to play anymore. Run along outside."

Instead of the protest Martha had expected, the little boy remained silent. He pulled a drying towel from the rack near the stove, and shifting his box under his arm, began drying the silverware.

Finally Martha couldn't stand the quiet any longer.

"Have I ever seen one?" Martha asked.

Without looking at her, his eyes riveted on the knife he held, Jeffrey commented, "That's your last question."

Martha had the sensation of seeing the final lifeboat lowered while she stood on a sinking ship.

"You've seen one," he said. "In fact, you have some. In fact, it's what I want from you, if I win."

"But you said it's *not* a toy!" Martha exclaimed.

"It isn't," the little boy said, still twisting and turning the knife in his hand. He had abandoned all pretense of drying it. The sunlight glinted on it, and Martha stood, mesmerized, staring at it as it glistened and grew dark, then gleamed again.

The little boy started talking in a low monotone: "It's got a nail, the thing that I have in the box, but the nail's not to keep it together. And it used to be pink, but now it's all gray and purplish. I got it from Lilian. She worked here before you."

Martha swallowed. "What is it?"

"You have to guess."

"I can't. I don't know."

"Don't you really know?" He looked directly at her. "Martha, you have such nice hands. You shouldn't get them all red with dishwashing. You ought to wear gloves."

The little boy moved as if to touch her hand, and Martha stepped away from him, hiding her wet hands in her apron.

"What's in the box?" she asked.

Jeffrey's gaze traveled to her hidden hands. "You know," he said.

"I don't believe you," Martha managed at last.

"Lilian didn't either. And she said I'd never do it. She said I couldn't. But one day, when she was asleep in her room, and Grandmother was away—"

"What do you have in that box?" Martha demanded.

"That's for me to know and you to find out," the little boy teased softly.

Martha lunged at the box. The knife in Jeffrey's hand slipped. There was blood on Martha's hand, and she screamed at the sight. Grasping the boy's shoulders, she said, "What's in there? What do you have in there?"

The knife clattered to the floor, and the box crumpled beneath the weight of the boy's arm as he clamped it tightly to his side.

"Show me what you have in there. Open that box. Open it!"

"Martha!"

Mrs. Belton stood in the doorway. She looked trim and smart in her tailored suit. Her silver hair was newly washed and set. She carried two small parcels. Her expression was changing from puzzlement to anger when Martha looked up at her.

"What *are* you doing, Martha?" Mrs. Belton asked.

Martha sat back on her heels and looked dazedly around. She

found she was kneeling in front of the little boy, clutching his shoulders and peering into his face like a crazy woman.

As if on cue, the little boy began to cry. Two huge tears crawled down his cheeks, and he shook free of Martha. Running to his grandmother, he wailed, "Oh, *Maman*, she's so mean. So scary. So mean."

Mrs. Belton stooped to the child who grabbed her skirt and whimpered pitifully.

"What is this all about, Martha?" Mrs. Belton asked in the tone of someone trying hard to be reasonable and fair-minded.

"I—he—oh, Mrs. Belton," Martha gasped.

"I come home and find you mistreating Jeffrey. Have you a reason? Was he naughty?"

"I wasn't naughty. I didn't do anything to her," the little boy protested, snuggling his nose close to his grandmother's thigh.

Mrs. Belton stroked his hair.

"Well, Martha?" she questioned with a lift of her arched eyebrows.

"Ask him what he has in that box," Martha said. "Make him show you."

"What earthly difference can it make—"

"Just make him show you, that's all," Martha said, rising laboriously. "Make him open it up."

Holding her grandson away from her slightly, Mrs. Belton asked, "Jeffrey?"

The little boy looked up innocently at his grandmother. "Yes, *Maman*?" he said.

"What have you in there?"

"Nothing, *Maman*."

"He's not telling the truth," Martha said. "Make him open it."

Her frown deepening, Mrs. Belton looked first at the child and then at Martha. She put out her hand, and Jeffrey slowly, oh, so very slowly, gave her his box.

As the older woman removed the crushed lid, Martha held her breath. She waited for the exclamation of disgust and horror. It didn't come. Surprised, Martha looked at Mrs. Belton, whose eyes rose to meet her own.

"The box is empty," Mrs. Belton said.

"It can't be!" Martha rushed across the room and took the box into her own hands. A cardboard box. Empty. "But it rattled," she said. "It rattled."

She looked up to see Mrs. Belton regarding her strangely.

"I'm afraid I'll have to let you go, Martha."

Martha drew in her breath sharply at the injustice. "But I'm not to blame," she protested. "The box—"

"You can see for yourself, there is nothing in it."

"Then he—he emptied it while we weren't watching him. Look in his pockets," Martha said.

The little boy moved back involuntarily, and Martha saw the movement.

"Search him!" she demanded loudly. "Search him!"

Mrs. Belton stiffened. She placed herself between Martha and the little boy.

"Control yourself," she told Martha. "I must ask that you leave at once."

"I—"

"That's enough," Mrs. Belton said. Her voice was gentle but firm.

An hour later, Martha's bags were packed, and she was standing beside Mrs. Belton's desk receiving her final check.

"I'm sorry about this," Mrs. Belton said.

"So am I."

"I can't understand what could have possessed you. It's not as if Jeffrey's a worrisome boy. He's a model. Never gives me a moment's trouble."

"No, ma'am," Martha said. She had made up her mind to say no more about the matter. What was the use? Besides, there was the possibility that she had been wrong. Perhaps she was getting old and fanciful. Perhaps children did make her nervous.

"Such a dear, sweet boy," Mrs. Belton was saying. "He's given me all the love he had for both his parents before they died in that terrible auto accident. Sometimes I'm afraid he loves me too much. He just wants to be alone with me all the time. He said to me only last night, 'Maman,' he said, 'I wish I could be with you alone forever and ever. You're the only one in the whole world who loves me.' Does that sound like a bad boy?"

"I guess he's going to get his wish," Martha said, ignoring the question. She folded the check and put it into her purse.

Mrs. Belton's jaw tightened at the obvious rebuff. She had wanted Martha to admit her error. A vague uneasiness flickered in her eyes. She glanced out the window at her grandson as he swung back and forth in the garden swing. The sun shining on his yellow hair reassured her.

At the door, Martha paused. "Why did the woman before me leave?" she asked on impulse.

"Lilian?" Mrs. Belton mused. "She had an accident."

"What kind of accident?" Martha asked, knowing what the answer would be.

"The hara-kiri sword Mr. Belton brought home from Japan fell off the wall in her room and cut her finger. Severed it completely, in fact. It was a very regrettable accident. I was so sorry to lose her."

"Yes," Martha said and stepped out into the sunlight.

The little boy glided to and fro in the garden swing. To and fro.

The $2,000,000 Defense

Harold Q. Masur

The trial had gone well for the prosecution. Strand by strand, a web of guilt had been woven around the defendant, Lloyd Ashley. Now, late in the afternoon of the fifth day, District Attorney Herrick was tying up the last loose ends with his final witness.

Understandably, the case had made headlines. An avid public kept clamoring for more and more details, and the newspapers obligingly supplied whatever revelations they could find. For all the elements of a *cause célèbre* were present—a beautiful wife, allegedly unfaithful; a dashing Casanova, now dead; and a millionaire husband, charged with murder.

Beside Ashley at the counsel table sat his lawyer, Mark Robison, seemingly unconcerned by the drama unfolding before him. His lean face was relaxed, chin resting on the palm of his hand. To a casual observer he seemed preoccupied, almost uninterested; yet nothing would be further from the truth. Robison's mind was keenly attuned, ready to pounce on any error the district attorney might commit.

Defense counsel was a formidable opponent, as the district attorney well knew—they had both trained in the same school, Robison having served as an assistant prosecutor through two administrations. In this capacity he had been tough and relentless, doing more than his share to keep the state prison at Ossining well populated.

As a muskrat takes to water, so Robison found his natural habitat in the courtroom. He had a commanding presence, the ego and voice of a born actor, and the quick, searching brain so essential to a skilled cross-examiner. He had, too, an instinct with jurors. Unerringly he would spot the most impressionable members of a panel, playing on their emotions and prejudices. And so, where his defenses were inadequate, he would often wind up with a hung jury.

But the Ashley case was more serious. Robison's defense was more than inadequate, it was virtually nonexistent.

Robison sat motionless, studying the prosecution's final witness. James Keller, police-department specialist in ballistics, was a pale, heavy-set man, stolid and slow-spoken. District Attorney Herrick had taken him through the preliminaries, qualifying him as an expert, and was now extracting the final bit of testimony that should send Lloyd Ashley to eternity, the whine of a high-voltage electric current pounding in his ears.

The district attorney picked up a squat black pistol whose ownership by the accused had already been established. "And now, Mr. Keller," Herrick said, "I show you State's Exhibit B. Can you tell us what kind of gun this is?"

"Yes, sir. That is a .32 caliber Colt automatic, commonly known as a pocket model."

"Have you ever seen this gun before?"

"Yes, sir, I have."

"Under what circumstances?"

"It was handed to me in the performance of my duties as a ballistics expert to determine whether or not it had fired the fatal bullet."

"And did you make the tests?"

"I did."

"Will you tell the jury what you found."

Keller faced the twelve talesmen, who were now leaning forward in their chairs. There were no women in the jury box—Robison had used every available challenge to keep them from being empaneled. It was his theory that men would be more sympathetic to acts of violence by a betrayed husband.

Keller spoke in a dry, somewhat pedantic voice. "I fired a test bullet to compare with the one recovered from the deceased. Both bullets had overall dimensions of three-tenths of an inch and a weight of seventy-four grams, placing them in a .32 caliber class. They both bore the imprint of six spiral grooves with a leftward twist which is characteristic of Colt firearms. In addition, every gun develops with usage certain personality traits of its own, and all these are impressed on the shell casing as it passes through the barrel. By checking the two bullets with a comparison microscope—"

Robison broke into Keller's monologue with a casual gesture.

"Your Honor, I think we can dispense with a long technical dissertation on the subject of ballistics. The defense concedes that Mr. Ashley's gun fired the fatal bullet."

The judge glanced at Herrick. "Is the prosecution agreeable?"

Grudgingly, Herrick said, "The state has no desire to protract this trial longer than necessary."

Secretly, however, he was not pleased. Herrick preferred to build his case carefully and methodically, laying first the foundation, then each plank in turn, until the lid was finally clamped down, with no loophole for escape and no error that could be reversed on appeal. There were times, of course, when he might welcome a concession by the defense, but with Robison—well, you never knew; the man had to be watched.

When Robison resumed his seat, Lloyd Ashley turned to him, his eyes troubled. "Was that wise, Mark?" With his life at stake, Ashley felt that every point should be hotly contested.

"It was never in dispute," Robison said, managing a smile of assurance.

But the smile had no effect, and seeing Ashley's face now, Robison felt a twist of compassion. How radically changed the man was! Ashley's usual arrogance had crumbled, his sarcastic tongue was now humble and beseeching. Not even his money, those vast sums solidly invested, could give him any sense of security.

Robison could not deny a certain feeling of responsibility for Ashley's plight. He had known Ashley for years, in a business way and socially. He could recall that day only two months ago when Ashley had come to him for advice, grim with repressed anger, suspecting his wife of infidelity.

"Have you any proof?" Robison had asked.

"I don't need any proof. This is something a man knows. She's been cold and untouchable."

"Do you want a divorce?"

"Never." The word had been charged with feeling. "I love Eve."

"Just what do you want me to do, Lloyd?"

"I want you to give me the name of a private detective. I'm sure you know someone I can trust. I'd like him to follow Eve, keep track of her movements. If he can identify the man for me, I'll know what to do."

Yes, Robison knew a reliable private detective—a lawyer sometimes needs the services of a trained investigator, to check the background of hostile witnesses whose testimony he might later want to impeach.

So Ashley retained the man and within a week had his report. The detective had trailed Eve Ashley to a rendezvous with Tom Ward, an investment counselor in charge of Ashley's securities. He had watched them in obviously intimate conversations in an obscure cocktail lounge in the Village.

The one thing he had never anticipated, Robison told himself, was violence. Not that Ashley was a coward. But Ashley's principal weapon in the past had been words—sharp, barbed, insulting. When the call came through from Police Headquarters that Ashley was being held for murder, Robison had been genuinely shocked, and he had felt a momentary pang of guilt. But Robison was not the kind of man who would long condemn himself for lack of omniscience. And Ashley, allowed one telephone call, demanded that Robison appear for him.

At the preliminary hearing in Felony Court, Robison had made a quick stab at getting the charge dismissed, presenting Ashley's version with shrewdness and skill. The whole affair had been an accident, Robison had maintained. No premeditation, no malice, no intent to kill. Ashley had gone to Ward's office and drawn his gun, brandishing it, trying to frighten the man, to extract a promise that Ward would stay away from Ashley's wife. He had been especially careful to check the safety catch, not to release it before entering Ward's office.

But instead of suffering paralysis or pleading for mercy, Ward had panicked, thrown himself at Ashley, and grappled for the gun. It had fallen to the desk, Ashley swore, and been accidentally discharged. He had been standing over the body when Ward's secretary found them.

Hearing this version, the district attorney had scoffed, promptly labeling it a bald fiction. The state, Herrick contended, could prove motive, means, and opportunity. So the magistrate had no choice.

Lloyd Ashley was bound over for action by the grand jury which quickly returned an indictment for murder in the first degree.

And now, in General Sessions, Judge Felix Cobb presiding, on the fifth day of testimony, Herrick was engaged in destroying Ashley's last hope. He held up the gun so that Keller and the jury could see it—a small weapon which had erased a man's life in the twinkling of an eye.

He said, "You are acquainted with the operation of this gun, Mr. Keller, are you not?"

"I am."

"In your opinion as a ballistics expert, could a gun of this type be accidentally discharged—with the safety catch on?"

"No, sir."

"You're certain of that?"

"Absolutely."

"Could it be discharged—with the safety on—if it were dropped from a height of several feet?"

"It could not."

"If it were slammed down on a hard surface?"

"No, sir."

"In all your experience—twenty years of testing and handling firearms—have you ever heard of any such incident?"

"Not one, sir."

Herrick headed back to the prosecution table. "The defense may cross-examine."

"It is now five minutes to four," the judge said. "I think we can recess at this point." He turned to the jury. "You will remember my instructions, gentlemen. You are admonished not to discuss this case among yourselves, and not to permit anyone to discuss it in your presence. Do not form or express any opinions until all the evidence is before you. Court stands adjourned until ten o'clock tomorrow morning."

He straightened his black robes and strode off. Everyone else remained seated until a tipstaff had led the jurors through a side door. A court officer moved up and touched Ashley's shoulder.

Ashley turned to Robison, his face drawn and tired. He had lost considerable weight during these last few weeks and the flaccid skin hung loose under his chin. His sunken eyes were veined and red, and a vagrant muscle kept twitching at the corner of his right temple.

"Tomorrow's the last day, isn't it, Mark?"

"Almost." Robison doubted if the whole defense would require more than a single session. "Except for the summation and the judge's charge."

The guard said, "Let's go, Mr. Ashley."

"Listen, Mark." There was sudden intensity in Ashley's voice. "I've got to talk to you. It—it's absolutely vital."

Robison studied his client. "All right, Lloyd. I'll be up in about fifteen minutes."

Ashley left with the guard and disappeared through a door behind the judge's bench. A few spectators still lingered in the courtroom. Robison gathered his papers and notes, slid them into his brief case. He sat back, fingertips stroking his closed eyelids, still seeing Ashley's face. The man was terrified, and with considerable justification, Robison thought. Despite the judge's admonition to the jurors, advising them not to reach any decision, Robison's experience told him they had done just that.

He could read the signs. He could tell from the way they filed out, the way they averted their eyes, not looking at the defendant. Nobody really enjoys sending another human being to the electric chair. Ashley must have felt it too, this sense of doom.

When Robison reached the corridor, he saw Eve Ashley waiting at the south bank of elevators. She seemed small and lost, the very bones of her body cringing against themselves. Robison started forward, but she was swallowed up in the descending throng before he could reach her.

Eve's reaction had surprised him. She was taking it hard, ill with self-condemnation and remorse. He remembered her visit to his office directly after the murder. "I knew he was jealous," she said, her eyes full of pain, "but I never expected anything like this. Never." She kept clasping and unclasping her hands. "Oh, Mark, they'll send him to the chair! I know they will and it's all my fault."

He had spoken to her sharply. "Listen to me. You had no way of knowing. I want you to get hold of yourself. If you go to pieces, you won't be any good to yourself—or to Lloyd. It's not your fault."

"It *is* my fault." Her lips were trembling. "I should have known. Just look what I've done. Two men. Tom is already dead, and Lloyd soon will—"

"Now stop that!" He had gripped her shoulders.

"You must get him off," she cried fiercely. "Please, Mark. If you don't I'll never forgive myself."

"I'll do my best."

But he knew the odds. The state had a solid case. Motive, means, and opportunity . . .

The elevator took him down and he went around to the detention cells at the White Street entrance. After the usual routine he gained admittance to the counsel room, and a moment later Lloyd Ashley was brought in. They sat on opposite sides of the table, the board between them.

"All right, Mark." Ashley's clenched hands rested on the table. "I want the truth. How does it look?"

Robison shrugged. "The case isn't over. Nobody can tell what a jury will do."

"Stop kidding, Mark. I saw those men—I saw their faces."

Robison shrugged again.

"Look, Mark, you've been my lawyer for a long time. We've been through a lot of deals together. I've seen you operate. I know how your mind works. You're smart. You're resourceful. I have the utmost respect for your ability, but I—well, I . . ." He groped for words.

"Aren't you satisfied with the way I'm handling your defense?"

"I didn't say that, Mark."

"Don't you think I'm exploiting every possible angle?"

"Within legal limitations, yes. But I've seen you try cases before. I've watched you handle juries. And I've seen you pull some rabbits out of a hat. Now, all of a sudden, you're so damn scrupulous I hardly recognize the same man. Why, Mark? What's happened?"

"I can't find a single loophole, Lloyd, that's why. Not one crack in the state's case. My hands are tied."

"Untie them."

"How?" Robison asked quietly.

"Listen, Mark"—Ashley's fingers were gripping the edge of the table—"you know almost as much about my financial affairs as I do. You know how much money I inherited, how much I've made. As of now, I'm worth about four million dollars." He compressed his lips. "Maybe that's why Eve married me; I don't know. Anyway, it's a lot of loot and I'd like a chance to spend some of it. But I won't have that chance, not if they convict me."

Ashley moistened his lips, then went on: "Dead, the money will do me no good. Alive, I can do all I want to do on a lot less. If anybody can get me off the hook, even at this stage of the game, it's you. I don't know how, but I have a feeling—hunch, intuition, call it what you will. You can think of *something*. You've got the imagination. I know you can pull it off."

Robison felt a stir of excitement.

Ashley leaned forward. "Down the middle," he said, his voice hoarse. "An even split, Mark, of everything I own. Half for you, half for me. A two-million-dollar fee, Mark. You'll be financially independent for life. Just figure out an angle! I want an acquittal."

Robison said promptly, "Will you put that in writing, Lloyd?"

"Of course!"

Robison took a blank sheet of paper from his brief case. He wrote swiftly, in clear unmistakable language. He passed the paper to Ashley, who scanned it briefly, reached for the pen, and scratched his signature. Robison, his fingers a trifle unsteady, folded the document and put it away.

"Have you any ideas, Mark?"

The lawyer sat motionless, his flat-cheeked face devoid of expression. He did have an idea, one that was not entirely new to him. He remembered, three nights ago, sitting bolt upright in bed when the brainstorm suddenly struck him. He had considered the idea for a moment, weighed its possibilities, then putting his head back he had laughed aloud in the darkness.

It was ingenious, even amusing in a macabre way, but nothing he would actually use. Now, abruptly, his thinking had changed, all scruples gone. There was considerable persuasive power in a fee of two million dollars. Men had committed serious crimes—including murder—for much less.

Now the possibilities of his idea stood out, sharp and clear and daring. There was no guarantee of success. He would have to cope with certain imponderables—most of them in the minds of twelve men, the twelve men in the jury box.

"Leave it to me," Robison said, standing abruptly. "Relax, Lloyd. Try to get some sleep tonight." He swung toward the door with a peremptory wave at the guard.

The declining sun had cooled the air, and Robison walked briskly, details of the plan churning in his mind. Ethical? He would hardly call it that. But then Robison was not often troubled by delicate moral considerations. As a trial lawyer he'd been consistently successful. His voice was a great asset: it could be gentle and sympathetic or blistering and contemptuous. Neophytes around the Criminal Courts Building still talked about Robison's last case as an assistant district attorney, remembering his savage cross-examination of the defendant, a man accused of armed robbery. He had won a conviction, and upon pronouncement of a maximum sentence, the enraged defendant had turned on him, swearing revenge. Later he had received venomous, threatening letters from the man's relatives.

So Mark Robison had acquired a pistol permit. And each year he had had it renewed. He always carried the permit in his wallet.

His first stop was on Centre Street, not far from Police Headquarters—at a small shop that specialized in firearms. He examined the stock, carefully selected a Colt automatic, pocket model, caliber .32, and a box of shells. The proprietor checked his permit and wrapped the package.

Robison then took a cab to his office. His secretary, Miss Graham, paused in her typing to hand him a list of calls. Seeing the abstracted look on his face, she did not bother to ask him about the trial. He went on through to the inner room.

It had recently been refurnished and Robison was pleased with the effect. Hanging on the far wall, facing the desk, was a picture of the nine Justices of the United States Supreme Court. The extraordinary occurrence that now took place before these venerable gentlemen was probably unparalleled in all their collective histories.

Mark Robison unwrapped his package and balanced the gun for a moment in his hand. Then, without further hesitation, he inserted three bullets into the clip and rammed the clip into the butt. His jaw was set as he lifted the gun, aimed it at his left arm, slightly above the elbow, and pulled the trigger.

The echoing explosion left his ears ringing. Robison was no stoic. He felt the stab of pain, like a branding iron, and cried out. The next instant he gritted his teeth while his thumb reached for the safety catch and locked it into position.

A moment later the door burst open and Miss Graham's apprehensive face poked through. With sudden dismay she saw Robison's pallor and the widening stain on his sleeve. She stifled a scream.

"All right," Robison told her harshly. "It was an accident. Don't stand there gaping. Call a doctor. There's one down the hall."

Miss Graham fled. Her urgent story stopped whatever the doctor was doing and brought him on the double with his rumpled black bag.

"Well," he said, sparing the gun a brief look of distaste, "what have we here, another one of those didn't-know-it-was-loaded accidents?"

"Not quite," Robison said dryly.

"Here, let's get the coat off." The doctor helped him, then ripped the lawyer's shirt sleeve from cuff to shoulder, exposing the wound, and probed the inflamed area. The bullet had scooped out a shallow trench of flesh.

"Hmm," said the doctor. "Looks worse than it is. You're a lucky man, counselor. No muscles or arteries severed. Loss of tissue, yes, and some impairment of articulation—"

He reached into his bag and brought out some antiseptic. It burned Robison's arm like a flame. Then having dressed and bandaged the wound, the doctor stepped back to appraise his handiwork.

He looked faintly apologetic. "You know the law, counselor. Whenever a doctor is called in for the treatment of a gunshot wound, he is required to notify the police. I really have no choice."

Robison repressed a smile. Had the doctor been ignorant of the law, Robison would have immediately enlightened him. Most assuredly he *wanted* the police here. They were an essential part of his plan.

He could already picture the headlines: *Robison Accidentally Wounded. Defense Counsel Shot Making Test*—and the stories telling how he had tried to simulate the conditions that had existed in Tom Ward's office—by deliberately dropping a gun on his desk . . .

Promptly at ten o'clock the following morning a court officer arose in Part III and intoned the ritual. "All rise, the Honorable Judge of the Court of General Sessions in and for the County of New York."

A door behind the bench opened and Justice Cobb emerged briskly, his black robe billowing behind him.

"Be seated, please," the attendant said, tapping his gavel. "This court is now in session."

The judge looked curiously at Robison, eyeing the wounded arm supported by a black-silk sling knotted around the lawyer's neck. "Call the witness," he said. James Keller was duly sworn and resumed his seat on the stand.

The twelve jurors bent forward, stirred by excitement and anticipation. District Attorney Herrick sat at the prosecution table, vigilant, wary. Robison smiled to himself, remembering the district attorney's tight-lipped greeting. Did Herrick suspect? Possibly.

"The defense may cross-examine," Judge Cobb said.

There was a murmur from the spectators as Robison pushed erect. He half turned, letting everyone have a look at his wounded arm in its silken cradle. He saw Eve Ashley in the first row, her eyes eloquent with appeal.

Robison walked to the clerk's table and picked up Ashley's gun. Holding it, he advanced toward Keller and addressed the witness. "Now, Mr. Keller, if I remember correctly, you testified yesterday that you fired a test bullet from this gun, did you not?"

"Yes, sir, I did." Keller's tone was guarded.

"You wanted to prove that this gun and no other fired the fatal bullet."

"That is correct."

"I assume that you released the safety catch before making the test?"

"Naturally. Otherwise I would still be standing there in my laboratory pulling the trigger."

Someone in the courtroom tittered, and one of Herrick's assistants grinned. Keller's self-confidence mounted visibly.

Robison regarded him sternly. "This is hardly a moment for humor, Mr. Keller. You realize that your testimony may send an innocent man to the chair?"

Herrick's hand shot up. "I move that last remark be stricken."

"Yes," said the judge. "It will be stricken and the jury will disregard it."

"Then you're absolutely sure," Robison said, "that the safety catch must be released before the gun can be fired?"

"Positive."

"Are you equally positive that the safety catch on a gun of this type cannot be joggled loose under certain circumstances?"

Keller hesitated. "Well, yes, to the best of my knowledge."

"Have you ever made any such test?"

"What do you mean?"

"Did you ever load this gun—State's Exhibit B—and try dropping it on a hard surface?"

"I—I'm afraid not, sir."

"Even though you knew what the basis of our defense would be?"

Keller shifted uncomfortably and glanced at Herrick, but he found no help in the district attorney's expressionless face.

"Please answer the question." Robison's voice was no longer friendly.

"No, sir. I did not."

"Why, Mr. Keller? Why didn't you make such a test? Wouldn't it seem the obvious thing to do? Were you afraid it might confirm the defendant's story?"

"No, sir, not at all."

"Then why?"

Keller said lamely, "It just never occurred to me."

"It never occurred to you. I see. A man is accused of first-degree murder; he is being tried for his life, facing the electric chair, and it never occurred to you to make that one simple test to find out if he might be telling the truth."

A flush rose from Keller's neck up to his cheeks. He sat silent, squirming in the witness chair.

"Let the record note that the witness did not answer," Robison said. "Now, sir, you testified yesterday that a gun of this type could never be discharged by dropping it on a hard surface, did you not?"

"With the safety catch on."

"Of course."

"I—yes, I believe I did."

"There is no doubt in your mind?"

Keller swallowed uncomfortably, glancing at Robison's arm. "Well . . . no."

"Let us see." Robison transferred the gun to his left hand, jutting out of the sling, its fingers slightly swollen. His right hand produced a .32 caliber shell from the pocket of his coat. His movements were awkward as he loaded the gun and jacked a shell into firing position. He stepped closer to the witness and started to offer the gun with his left hand, but he stopped short with a sudden grimace of pain. The expression was telling and dramatic. Then ruefully he shifted the gun to his right hand and extended it to the witness.

In distinct, deliberate tones he said, "Now, Mr. Keller, will you please look at the safety device on State's Exhibit B and tell us if it is in the proper position to prevent firing?"

"It is."

"Then will you kindly rise, sir? I would like you to prove to his Honor, and to these twelve jurors, and to the spectators in this courtroom, that the gun in question *cannot possibly be discharged by dropping it on the judge's dais.* Just lift it, if you please, or slap it down."

A murmur rustled through the courtroom as Herrick landed on both feet in front of the bench. The muscles around his jaw were contracted with anger. "I object, your Honor. This is highly irregular, a cheap grandstand play, inherently dangerous to every—" He caught himself, swallowing the rest of his sentence. His own words, uttered impulsively, had implied a possibility, however remote, that the gun might go off.

In contrast, Robison sounded calm and reasonable. "If it please the court, this witness made a statement under oath as a qualified expert. I am merely asking him to prove his own expert statement."

Judge Cobb spoke without pleasure. "Objection overruled."

"Go ahead, if you please, Mr. Keller," Robison said. "Demonstrate to the court and to the jury that State's Exhibit B could not *possibly* have been fired in the manner claimed by the defendant."

A hush fell over the courtroom as Keller rose. He lifted the gun slowly, and held it suspended over the bench, his face a mixture of anxiety and misgiving.

Robison held his breath as Keller's arm twitched. The judge, trying to look inconspicuous, started to slide down his chair, as if to minimize himself as a target.

"We're waiting," Robison said softly, clearly.

Beads of moisture formed along Keller's temples. Had he flexed his muscles? Had he lifted the gun a little higher? No one in the courtroom could be sure.

"Please proceed, Mr. Keller," Robison said, sharply now. "The court hasn't got all day."

Their eyes met and locked. Deliberately Robison rearranged his sling. Keller took a long breath, then without warning he dropped back into his seat. The gun hung loose between his knees.

A sigh of relief swelled in the courtroom.

The verdict, everyone conceded, was a foregone conclusion. Robison's closing speech was a model of forensic law, and the judge, charging the jury to be satisfied beyond a reasonable doubt, left them little choice. They were out for less than an hour before returning a verdict of Not Guilty.

Lloyd Ashley showed no jubilation—the strain had left him on the edge of nervous exhaustion. Robison touched his shoulder.

"All right, Lloyd. It's over. You're free now. Let's go back to my office. I believe we have some business to transact."

Ashley roused himself. "Yes, of course," he said with a stiff smile.

They got through the crowd, and hailed a cab. The closing speeches and the judge's charge had taken all afternoon, so it was growing dark when they reached Robison's office. He ushered the way into his private room and snapped on the light.

By way of celebration the lawyer produced a bottle and poured two drinks. Both men emptied their glasses in single gulps. Robison passed the humidor and snapped a lighter for his client. Ashley settled back, inhaling the rich smoke of a long, thin cigar.

"Well, Mark," he said, "I knew you could do it. You performed your share of the bargain. I suppose now you'd like me to fulfill mine."

Robison made a deprecating gesture.

"Have you a blank check?"

There was a pad of blank checks somewhere in the outer office, Robison knew. He kept it handy for clients who needed legal representation but who came to him with insufficient funds. He went out to the reception room, rummaged through a storage cabinet, and finally located the pad.

Lloyd Ashley had shifted chairs and was now seated behind Robison's desk. He accepted the blank check and Robison's pen. Without flicking an eyelash, he wrote out a check for two million dollars.

"I said fifty-fifty, Mark. There may even be more coming to you. We'll know after my accountant goes over the books."

Robison held the check, his eyes transfixed by the string of figures. There was a faint throbbing in his wounded arm, but he didn't mind. Ashley's voice came back to him, sounding soft and strange.

"Oh, yes, Mark, there's more coming to you. Perhaps I can arrange to let you have it now."

Robison looked up and saw the .32 caliber automatic in Ashley's hand, his thumb on the safety catch.

"I found this in your desk," Ashley said. "It must be the gun you used last night. Ironic, isn't it, Mark? You now have the one thing that means more to you than anything else in this world—money—and you'll never be able to spend a penny of it."

Robison did not like the look in Ashley's eyes. "What are you talking about?"

"Remember that private detective you recommended? Funny thing, after that trouble with Ward I never had a chance to take him off the case. So he kept watching Eve all the time I was in jail. As a matter of fact, he brought me a report only two days ago. I don't suppose I have to tell you about it—who she's been seeing, who the other man really is."

Robison had gone white.

The gun in Ashley's hand was very steady. "You know, Mark, I feel you're almost as responsible for Ward's death as I am. After all, who persuaded Eve to use him as a decoy, so that you and she could be safe? It must have been you. Eve never had that much imagination."

Perspiration now bathed Robison's face and his voice went down to a whisper. "Wait, Lloyd, listen to me—"

"No, I'd rather not. You're too good at winning people over. I saw a demonstration of your powers in court today, remember? I've been planning on this for two days. Finding your gun merely accelerated the timetable. There's a kind of justice in this, I think. You forced me into killing the wrong man. Now I see no reason why I shouldn't kill the right one."

Of the two shots that rang out, Mark Robison heard only the first.

The Man
in the
Well

Berkely Mather

There were six of them in the waiting room when Sefton arrived, so he ran a cursory eye over them and went out again and hung about in the doorway of a haberdasher on the other side of the Strand.

He had not been frightened by what he saw, but let there be a dignity about all things—even applying for a job. There were two young men in duffel coats, one of them with a beard, a hard-bitten elderly character who might have been an ex-bosun from the Irrawaddy Flotilla, two one-time sahibs who looked absurdly alike in their yellowing bloodlessness and a woman who looked as if she had just crossed the Gobi on a camel. If this was the short list he was willing to bet on his chances.

He had lit his sixth cigarette by the time the last of them emerged, so he nipped it economically and crossed through the midmorning traffic and went up the narrow stairs again. A clerk took his name in and after a brief wait led him through to an inner office. A lanky, elderly man rose from behind a littered desk and held out his hand.

"Mr. Sefton?" he inquired. "Sorry if I've kept you waiting. Please sit down. You must excuse this mess—my agent has lent me his office for these interviews."

Sefton bowed, sat, balanced his hat on his knees and waited. The other man gazed at a spot on the wall over Sefton's head, screwed up his eyes and pursed his lips.

As phony as the papers say he is, Sefton thought, and added savagely, Silly old goat.

Minutes ticked by, traffic rumbled outside and from nearby Charing Cross an engine whistled shrilly. At last the old man broke the silence.

"There have been many other applicants, Mr. Sefton," he said softly.

"Which you short-listed down to seven—none of whom so far have suited," Sefton answered. "I hope I will. I am very keen on joining you."

The other looked slightly nettled.

"May I ask where you gathered that information?"

"Counted heads in the waiting room when I arrived and then timed their exits from across the street. None of them stayed long." His grin robbed the statement of offense. "I think I'm your man, Professor Neave."

"That remains to be seen," Neave answered stiffly. He shuffled through a file of letters in front of him and selected one that Sefton recognized as his own. "Would you care to elaborate on this a little?"

"Sure," answered Sefton promptly. "Eight years as assistant engineer with the Sontal Gem Mining Corporation in Mogok, Upper Burma. I speak good Burmese and can get along in most of the dialects—Shan, Chin and Karen. I know the country well and was an M.T. officer in the Royal Indian Army Service Corps during the war. I get along with people, can take and carry out orders"—he paused very slightly—"and I can keep my mouth shut."

"Why did you leave the Sontal Corporation, Mr. Sefton?" the professor asked.

"For the same reason as the rest of the staff," Sefton told him. "The Japs were ten miles up the track and traveling fast. We sent the married men and their families to Rangoon before the railroad from Mandalay was cut off, and we ourselves set fire to the whole shebang and got out in the last vehicle to leave. We only got to Yeu—that's just north of Bhame—when our petrol gave out. We walked the rest of the way to the Chindwin, right through the dry belt. I say 'we'— but only I made it. Dysentery, malaria and starvation did for the rest. It was a bad year and the monsoon was late."

"How long did the journey take you?"

"Just over three months. Our speed was that of the sickest man."

"And then?"

Sefton shrugged. "Nothing much more to it. I crossed into Assam by the Tiddim Track and fell in with our forces in Imphal. I was a long time in the hospital and then I joined up. I fought my war with the Fourteenth Army and finished as a major."

"What have you been doing since?"

"I put my gratuity and savings into a small engineering shop in Lancashire in the first place—and lost the lot. Since then I've had a variety of jobs in my own line of country—deep drilling in Brazil, and I've been up the Gulf with an oil concern among other things—"

"Are you married?"

"No—and I haven't a soul in the world dependent upon me."

"What remuneration would you expect?"

"I don't want anything—except to go with you."

The professor brightened visibly for a moment and then covered up. "I don't understand, Mr. Sefton," he said.

Sefton leaned forward.

"I told you I'd had a series of jobs, Professor," he said earnestly. "All of them have been reasonably well paid and I left each one of them of my own accord—often in the face of strong persuasion to stay on. Restlessness—inability to find a niche in this postwar world —call it what you like, but I know I'll never be able to settle down until I get it out of my system."

"Get what out of your system?"

Sefton paused and gazed out of the window for a full minute before answering. "It's hard to say," he said at length. "Put it this way. I was a reasonably settled young man with a career ahead of me with Sontal. The war finished all that. The corporation never started up again. I had seen my friends die on that trek and I'd been unable to help them. I'm not neurotic, but—but—" he spread his hands. "Oh, hell, I don't know—I've just got a yen to go out there again, to see the places we walked through—to feel the sun beating down on me and to get the stink of the jungle back into my nostrils. I want to face up to something I've been running away from all these years and to realize how little it all means in retrospect." He stopped suddenly. He had rehearsed this speech carefully but now he wondered if he had not overdramatized it. *Hell, that wouldn't have deceived a kid,* he thought ruefully, and added aloud, "This must all sound very silly, Professor."

But the professor smiled sympathetically, "Not at all. I think I understand. I was part of a lost generation myself in 1918. All right, Mr. Sefton—you've been very frank with me. Let me tell you something about myself and *my* reason for going out there." He pushed a box of cigarettes across the table and Sefton, noting the virgin ash tray, realized that he was the first who had been thus favored and felt his confidence rise accordingly. "I take it that you know a little about me— my one-man expeditions—my modest reputation as an author and popular lecturer—?"

Sefton looked suitably shocked. "Who doesn't, Professor?"

"None of the previous applicants, apparently," answered the professor with more than a touch of sourness. "One young man had heard, without particular interest, a fifteen-minute talk of mine on television. The woman confused me with Professor Lever, the ornithologist, while most of the others were far more interested in what I could pay them than in the journey and its objects. Still, be that as it may—I want a man who knows Upper Burma, who is prepared to rough it, who can drive one jeep and maintain two and who, in short, is prepared to accompany me on a trip over the old Burma Road from Calcutta to as far as we can get toward the China border. A man who can relieve me of the chores of the trip while I collect material and take pictures for my next lecture tour, but who at the same time can be rather more—er—intellectually congenial than the average paid employee." He rose and held out his hand. "I think you might well be that man, Mr. Sefton."

In Sefton's heart was a paean of joy and relief.

He halted the jeep at the top of the last rise before Kohima. Down the winding road that led back toward Manipur he could see the second jeep snaking round the hairpin bends that multiplied the crow-flight distance tenfold. The road had all but gone back to the jungle since he had last seen it in the closing days of the war. Then it had been a tarmac miracle of engineering that had carried four lines of heavy military traffic round the clock. The teak-built culverts and Irish bridges had now for the most part rotted through, and Sefton, breaking trail, had had to stop many times since they had crossed the Brahmaputra at Gauhati to allow the professor to catch up.

He lit a cigarette and tried for the fiftieth time to fight down the feverish impatience that bedeviled him. Left to himself he could have pressed on through to the dry belt in a week, but with this old fool's insistence on stopping to take photographs, plus his maddening refusal to travel in the heat of the afternoon, it looked as if the time might well be quadrupled. And now it seemed more than probable that they would be held up in Imphal. The Indian government was engaged in sporadic jungle fighting with the Naga tribes who, promised their autonomy when the British left, were demanding it in terms that bordered on small-scale warfare. Politics! Politics had stopped his getting into Upper Burma twice before. What the hell had it to do with him? All he wanted was a couple of hours in a pagoda near Yeu . . .

The professor had arrived now. He pulled up triumphantly in just the very spot he should have avoided, and Sefton bellowed wrathfully.

"For God's sake—how many times have I told you not to stop in mud?" He strode over and pushed the old man roughly out of the driver's seat and jabbed furiously at the starter. The engine roared but the wheels spun impotently. He cursed and got the towrope out of his own jeep and for the twentieth time yanked the professor onto firm ground.

"There are certain fundamental rules for good manners, too," answered the professor tartly. "Things are getting a little out of hand, Sefton. I would remind you that although you are not drawing a salary, *I* am in charge of this expedition."

"You want to get across Upper Burma to the Chinese border, don't you?" snarled Sefton. "OK then, suppose you leave it to someone who knows, and do as you're damned well told."

"I'm not a child and this is not my first experience of the jungle." Neave was thoroughly angry now. "If things are to go on like this I would much prefer to take a paid driver on from Imphal and to pay your passage back to Calcutta by lorry."

Sefton recognized danger signs and temporized.

"I'm sorry, Professor," he said and drew his hand wearily over his brow. "All this rather brings things back—and I think I have a touch of fever coming on." He smiled bravely. "You were quite right to slap me down. I'll behave from now on."

The professor accepted his apology with a slight inclination of his head and turned stiffly back to his jeep.

Once over the Chindwin, you old bum, thought Sefton as they

started off again, and you can go to blazes. I'll have to watch my step till then, though—I don't want to be left stranded when I'm this close.

The old man's Delhi-endorsed papers took them through the checkpoint at Imphal without question and even with an offer, which Sefton politely declined, of an escort as far as the border. They camped that night at the top of the Tiddim Track where rusting Japanese tanks made green hillocks under the creeping undergrowth which still, after twelve years, could not altogether cover the scars of that last fierce battle.

Sefton lay under his mosquito net and watched the pre-monsoon clouds gathering over the pass and blotting out the stars. They had been gathering that night he crossed. He stretched out on his camp bed and listened to the jungle night sounds and the professor's gentle snores the other side of the fire. His thoughts went back over the years.

There had been six of them at first in that crazy truck. Findlay, the Scotch manager—tall, grim, ascetic—who was a Sanskrit scholar and who some said was a secret convert to Buddhism; Muirson the Eurasian clerk; the two Karen coolies; and Ngu Pah, the pretty little Burmese nurse who had insisted on standing by her tiny hospital until the last moment; and himself. The Karens had deserted early and Muirson, opium-besotted and malarial, had died at the end of the third week. That left the three of them. Three oddly assorted people on foot in the middle of the freakish dry belt after the truck had finally petered out. There was a well in the pagoda to which they had struggled before Findlay collapsed, and Ngu Pah, the lightest of them, had climbed down the rotten rope to see if any dribble remained in the sand at the bottom. But it had been bone dry. The rope had broken as she struggled back and had left her clinging to the masonry a few feet from the top and they had been hard put to it to rescue her.

It was that night that he made his decision. Findlay could obviously go no farther and Ngu Pah was showing signs of failing too. Her tiny frame had borne the brunt of that hellish journey as she had carried her full share of the water and rations and finally the heavy wash-leather bag that Findlay would entrust to nobody but her.

He knew what that bag contained because he had seen Findlay making his selection from the trays of pigeon-blood rubies before

they had dynamited the strong room and set fire to the rest. They
had been unable to send their usual shipments out to Rangoon for
some months, so there had been a lot of stuff to choose from. That
bag must have weighed seven pounds if it weighed an ounce. My
God—seven pounds of uncut rubies. She had not let the bag out of
her possession for an instant after Findlay had handed it to her. She
had even slung it round her neck when she climbed into the well.
Sefton wondered when she had first begun to suspect his intentions.
He had tried for years to justify to himself that final act of treachery.
He no longer bothered now. In Sefton's world it was every man for
himself. He had stolen the bag that night while she slept and Findlay
raved in his delirium—and with it he had also stolen their last half-
gallon of water and the pitiful remains of their rations, and he had set
out on the last desperate stage to the Chindwin and safety.

She had cheated him though—the little devil. He made the discovery the night before he crossed the border. He had opened the bag to
make a careful selection of just what he could carry on his person
with safety, meaning to cache the rest where, if the war went the
right way, he could come back and collect it later. He remembered
the feel of the rough sand and gravel that poured over his hands as he
untied the thong. He had screamed and groveled in his rage out there
in the jungle, and then, when sanity returned, he thought about
going back—but the Japs were closing in fast and he could see the
smoke from burning villages a scant five miles behind him. That's
where the stuff had gone—down the bloody well—and that's where
it was now. Obviously they couldn't have survived long. Findlay was
almost a goner when he left them, and Ngu Pah couldn't have gone
down the well again to recover the stones because the rope had
snapped. He had often tortured himself with the possibility of the
girl surviving the war and going back for them, but he had brushed
that aside. Without food and water she could not have lasted another
week. No—the rubies were still there, at the bottom of the well—of
that he was convinced.

Twice he had raised the necessary money and gone out to Rangoon on the pretext of starting up in engineering, but try as he would
he had been unable to get permission to go through to Upper Burma.
There had been constant internecine warfare along the line of the Irrawaddy since the British had left, and both sides regarded visitors
with suspicion. He had tried it without permission and had narrowly

missed being shot for his pains. The third time he had attempted to go out they had refused him a visa, as had the India government when he applied for a mining license in the Shan hills. The professor's advertisement had been a heaven-sent final chance. He would *get* there this time—by God he would.

His plan of action was made. Their road lay through Yeu—there was no other way in. He would come down with a simulated attack of malaria there. The way to Mandalay was easy, so he would persuade the professor to go on alone, promising to catch up with him in a few days. They weren't on such friendly terms that the old man would boggle much at that. He *would* catch up too—but then he'd quit. He had enough ready cash to pay his way back to England—and more than enough wit to get the stones in with him.

He grunted, flicked his cigarette out into the damp undergrowth, swatted a mosquito and dropped quietly to sleep.

They reached Yeu four days later without incident except for a few further bog-downs on the professor's part. Sefton had suffered from malaria often enough to be able to simulate the symptoms with a degree of realism that frightened the other man. He had even had the forethought to break the thermometer in the medicine chest so that his temperature would not give the lie to his agonized shaking each evening.

He had no difficulty in recognizing the turnoff to the pagoda as they drove past it that last afternoon. It was a few miles east of a tiny village that had been deserted in those panic-stricken days, but which was now repopulated. There was a well there which might have saved the other two had they known about it. A yellow-robed priest sat under a spreading peepul tree at the junction of road and track with a brass begging bowl before him for the offerings of the faithful. He was the first they had seen since crossing the Chindwin and the professor was delighted in spite of his preoccupation with Sefton's fever. He leaped out of his jeep, camera ready, but the priest dropped his eyes to the ground and covered his shaven head with a fold of his robe.

"The camera is a form of evil eye," Sefton explained. "These poonghies don't like 'em. Come on—plenty more of the idle devils where we are going. There's a whole monastery full of them in Yeu. By God, I'll be glad to get there—I'm feeling lousy."

They put up at the monastery rest house, and the professor wandered happily about with his camera for a couple of days while Sefton realistically recuperated. The old man was mildly indignant at Sefton's suggestion that he should go on alone but the latter worked on him skillfully. The Buddhist Feast of the Tooth would just about be starting in Meikhtila—the faithful came from all parts of Asia for this—opportunities for photography that it would be a crime to miss. Just catch the first rafts of teak coming down the Irrawaddy with the break of the monsoon. He'd be all right here—the monks were pretty decent to travelers. Catch him up in Mandalay in a week—as fit as a flea again. The old man at last capitulated, and with many a guilty backward glance, went on up the road.

Sefton gave him half a day for safety, and then set off back along the road they had come. He had no fear of the pagoda being occupied. They built these things on the top of practically every hill in Upper Burma, put a statue of the Buddha inside, a couple of dragons outside to guard him against evil spirits, dug a well for his refreshment and thereafter avoided the place like the plague.

It was just as he had last seen it. Perhaps the purple bougainvillaea over the archway that spanned the entrance to the small courtyard was a little more luxuriant, and the monsoon rains, short-lived but fierce in these parts, had washed some more of the white plaster from the pinnacled roof, but the Buddha was unaged, sitting, feet crossed beneath him, soles upward, forefinger and thumb of the right hand grasping the little finger of the other, jeweled lotus on his brow, as serenely as he had sat and watched fifteen years before.

He drove on a hundred yards or so and hid the jeep in a bamboo thicket. It was not necessary—nobody had seen him come this way, and anyhow no Burmese would dream of walking a mile or so uphill to investigate. It was the secretiveness of his nature that made him do it—just as the beasts of the jungle are at pains to conceal their tracks even when no danger threatens. He took a coil of rope and an electric torch from the toolbox and hurried back. He was sweating now in spite of the evening cool. His heart was hammering and his breath was coming in short, sharp gasps that almost choked him.

There was a carpet of dead leaves inside the pagoda that rustled and crackled under his feet as he skirted the image and hurried round to the well at the back. The shaft dropped sheer and black and the beam of his torch hardly reached the bottom of it. He dropped a stone over the edge and heard with satisfaction a slight thud as it landed on dry sand. There probably never had been water in the damned thing at all. There were some, Findlay among them, who said that these shafts had never been intended as wells at all but were relics of some older and darker religion in which they had figured in other and more sinister roles—human sacrifices or something.

He knotted the rope round a projecting stone cornice and paid it out into the darkness until its slackness told him it had reached the bottom; then he swung his legs over and commenced his descent. It was easy at first, as the masonry was rough and offered some purchase to his feet. It had only been that which had saved Ngu Pah. Lower down, however, the sides became marble smooth and he was glad that he had the forethought to wear rope-soled *espadrilles*.

The ease with which he found the rubies came as an anticlimax that was almost a disappointment. He felt like a child who had been set too simple a task in a party game. He saw them in the first beam of his torch even as his feet touched the sand. They lay on a ledge in the masonry, wrapped in the rotting remains of a once-bright-blue silk scarf—a heap of dull pebbles which even in their uncut and unpolished state threw back the light of the torch in a reddish effulgence.

He wanted to shout and to sing—to throw them in fistfuls over his head like confetti. Instead, he sat down in the sand and lit a cigarette with trembling hands and then trained the beam of the torch on the rubies and just gazed.

It was a good ten minutes before he was steady enough to remove his sweat-soaked shirt and scoop the rubies into it—and a further agonizing ten before he was satisfied with the security of the bag he made of it. He finally fastened it under his belt; then, belaying the rope twice round his waist, he commenced the hard climb up.

He had gone a good fifteen feet before it happened—his body bowed stiffly outward from the side of the well—feet pressed firmly against the stones. He was not aware of falling. The first realization came to him as he lay flat on his back in the sand with the rope coiled loosely about him and the chunk of masonry which had missed his head by inches beside him. He started to scream then—shrilly and horribly—and he was still screaming and tearing at the sides of the well when the moonlight at the top of the shaft was blotted out by the head and shoulders of a man—a man with a shaven poll and a swathe of yellow cotton across his chest. He could not make out his face but he knew it was the priest from the track junction and he stopped screaming and started to babble in Burmese.

The priest answered in English with a strong Edinburgh accent. "I knew you'd be back for them, Sefton, in the fullness of time."

Sefton tried to speak but his throat muscles refused to function. The voice went on. "Aye, vultures always return to their carrion— and that is what those stones are. I intended to steal them from my employers in the first place. I had already broken faith by intent. It was that knowledge that brought me to the samadhi of the Middle Way. These robes are not a disguise, Sefton—they are my atonement."

Mad, thought Sefton and fought down another wave of hysteria. "Findlay!" he called shakily. "Findlay—I came back to see if I could find any trace of you. I haven't rested, Findlay, in all these years—"

"That I can well believe," answered Findlay. "A man cannot escape his karma. Well, you have the chance to make your peace now —as I have."

"Findlay—you can't do this to me—you can't—don't murder me—" He was babbling now.

"I have done nothing. In your greed you tied your rope to an unsafe stone. Do you not see the symbolism of it?"

"Findlay—Findlay—listen to me—I know what you must have thought at the time, but I went off to find food, water, for all of us. I couldn't return, Findlay—before God I couldn't—I got lost and then I fell ill myself—I wandered for weeks before I was picked up and then I'd lost my memory. You've got to believe me, Findlay—you've *got* to—"

Findlay appeared not to hear him. His voice droned on dreamily, "Aye—the divine symbolism of it all—the sacrifice of little Ngu Pah —three times she made that five-mile journey for water and food for me after you had stolen our reserve. She died on her return from the last one and I made shift to bury her under the bougainvillaea at the gate. Did ye no sense something as you entered, or had your greed blinded you to everything except those scraps of crystallized alumina?"

"I don't want your damned rubies—"

"They're not mine—nor yours," Findlay answered. "They've returned to the earth that formed them. Down there they can do no more harm."

"All right then—let them stay here," Sefton sank to his knees in the sand, "but you've got to help me out, Findlay—"

"I can neither help you nor hinder you, Sefton. That is your karma—as *this* is mine." And Findlay held his hands over the opening to the shaft. Against the patch of light Sefton saw with a turning of his stomach that the fingers had degenerated into formless stubs. "Leprosy, Sefton—a curse turned blessing because it was only that which held me back from taking the jewels out myself—and thereby gave me my chance of atonement and peace."

"You can't leave me here—that's murder. You're a Buddhist, you say—Buddhists can't kill—not even animals. Get another rope, Findlay—get another rope!" His voice had dropped to a pleading whisper.

"I shall not kill you, Sefton," said Findlay, "not even by negation. You must make your own choice, though. If I get another rope I cannot tie it securely myself with these fingers. I must therefore get help from the village. You will have to come up empty-handed in that case—I should insist on that and ask the villagers' assistance if you broke faith."

"The—the other choice—?" Sefton croaked.

"I shall drop food and water to you for as long as you need it."

Sefton screamed again. "Listen, Findlay! There's money down here—millions! Be sensible. They've got cures for leprosy in Europe now—and you can get a pair of artificial hands that'll do everything your own could. There's enough here and to spare for both of us. Get a rope long enough to loop round the statue and drop both ends to me—you needn't try to tie it. Just let me come up so we can talk it over. If you don't agree to anything I say I'll go away peacefully and never come back—I swear it—"

"If you came up and I were alone, Sefton, you'd kill me," Findlay said. "You know that is in your heart already. I couldn't prevent you —nor would I try—but if that happened I would be robbing you of any chance you may still have of finding peace. That would be against the course of the Middle Way. We are all involved in the destiny of others and a man may not stand by and watch another destroy himself."

Sefton broke then. He fell forward on his face and pounded on the sand with his fists and howled like an animal in torment.

The villagers hauled him up at midnight and the monks at Yeu tended him carefully until the professor, worried at his non-arrival in Mandalay, came back to look for him. Then they shipped him home to a large house set behind high walls in the quietness of the English countryside, where he has found peace—except when the moon is full and he struggles in his canvas jacket and screams about rubies and ropes and a priest who is fed by the faithful at the roadside.

Crawfish

Ardath F. Mayhar

It's chill, down there in the river, I reckon. She don't know, though.
Can't know. Them big innocent brown eyes are starin' away down
there, unless the crawfish . . . God, I wish I didn't know nothin'
about crawfish.

She's got this soft white skin, like to a baby rabbit or some baby
animal, sort of. It shined, like, even through the muddy old river
water. I could see her, shinin' and shinin', as she sank. Her hair
moved all out loose on the water, dark and curling in the moonlight.
It kept moving in the water, all the way down . . . them
crawfish . . .

She was a tramp, I tell you. Everybody knowed it, I reckon. Smiling and smiling at everybody went by. I moved way down in the bot-
tom-lands, 'count of that. No fancy traveling salesmen comes down
here. No Avon women selling damnation. No men in cars and men in
trucks that'd look at her when she worked out in the yard. Bending
over, showing her legs! Tramp, just tramp!

Must of been born that way. She was just fourteen when I hitched
up with her, and hadn't had time to learn nothing about men, then.
Just naturally bad, flirting when we went into town, smiling at them
tellers in the bank, in their white shirts and city suits. Looking with
eyes of lust and fornication at them. First time, when I got her home,
I beaten the living daylights outen her.

Way she cried and took on, you'd of reckoned she was crazy. Her
Pa never had no gumption with his womenfolks. Let 'em have their
own way clear to ruination, seems like. His woman even had money
to spend, when she felt like it. So I guess Mattie wasn't all the way to
blame for her sinful ways.

Still, beating didn't do no good—not to last. She'd go round with her head down and her eyes on the ground, like is fitten, for a while, then she'd see something, maybe just a flower or a bird or some such sinful uselessness. All that decency would be gone in a minute, and she'd be laughin' to herself. And when she laughed, any man inside a mile would be starin' at her like they knowed her already.

I come home, one evenin' and she was full of talk. Met me at the door, jabbering fit to make me deaf. I slapped her a couple of times and quieted her down, like as my Pa used to my Ma, iffen she said more than is fitten for a woman. She didn't say nothin' else, just slapped the supper on the table and went off in the back to the garden and started pullin' weeds. I looked round to make sure she wasn't meetin' nobody, afore I set down to eat.

Next day, Miz Rogers, down the road, met me at the end of the row and asked me, real sly like, who'd been visitin' Mattie yesterday. Seemed like I got hot all over—it just seemed to rise up from my feet clean to my head, and I was so mad I could of busted. Miz Rogers, she looked at me kind of scared-like and took off afore I could answer.

It was away before noon, but I took the mules in and unhitched. When I got to the house, she was gigglin' in the kitchen. I crept up, real sly like, and peeped in. They wasn't no one there. She was crazy. Clean crazy and a whore, too.

I slammed the screen open till the spring busted. My head was like to bust, too, with the blood poundin' and poundin'. She looked round and turned white and funny-lookin'. After she picked herself up from where I knocked her, I started tellin' her what she was. The Whore of Babylon was nice to what I called her.

I slapped all her lies back into her teeth. She was gabblin' about flat tires and women with thirsty children, but she quit that, soon enough. She wasn't so all-fired pretty, after I got through with her. Her nose was all lop-sided and her eyes was so swole you couldn't see what color they was. I figgered, Hell, I might as well of married a homely woman, iffen I was goin' to have to keep mine all bunged up to keep the men away from her.

Next day, I went down to see Pa. Didn't let on what was goin' on, but Pa, he's read the Bible and helled around some, so he guessed pretty close. He told me he knowed of some land that was for rent, down close to the river. Said iffen I wanted, he could find somebody to take over my place and finish my crop. It was still early in the spring, so's I had time to make a crop down there in the wet land.

So we moved. There was a fair cabin on the place. Not fancy . . . she started sayin' something about havin' to carry water so fur, but I just had to look at her mean by then, and she shut right up. I broke a garden patch, and she put in a nice garden, but seemed like she didn't care iffen it growed or not. She didn't put no more flowers round the front, neither, so's I knowed she'd done it, t'other place, just to bend over and show her legs to the men on the road. She didn't fix up the cabin none, neither. Just went around like she was listenin' to somethin' inside her head. Her Maw come, a time or two, but I didn't care about havin' her come round givin' Mattie fancy notions, so I got rid of her quick as I could.

Got so I hated to come in, after finishin' work. I'd stay out till dark, near, or go night-fishin' with the niggers down the river. She kind of looked at me like I was somethin' scary. Give me funny feelings, the way she looked at me.

No sir, when I took her where she couldn't go smilin' at the men and flirtin' all over town on Saturday no more, she kind of dried up. Never even tried to talk to me no more. I might even of let her, so's to liven up the quiet some, but she kept her lips tight shut over her broke tooth and let the mosquitoes buzz.

Her eyes got queerer and queerer. They was big to start with, but it got so that they was deep as the pool down at the river, and just as full of strange things. I'd go in at night and she'd watch me, starin' and starin' like I was a bug or a snake. She was crazy, I tell you.

Anyways, one evening, I come in dead tired. Crop was laid by and I'd been fishin' all day, but it was so hot it like to of took your breath. They wasn't no air, down there, 'count of the woods just closed in all round like walls and kept it out.

While I was eatin' supper, she was standin' by the wash-pan, waitin' for the dishes. All of a sudden, she turned round with the meat knife in her hand and started for me. Iffen I hadn't of looked up, she'd of killed me where I set. Seems like, when she done that, everything just come together, like. I took her round the neck and shut my hands tight and when I opened 'em up, she was dead.

My folks has always been mighty proud and upstandin' people, round here. And Pa, why it'd kill Pa iffen they hung me over a woman. So I took her through the woods, down to the river.

I could hear the snakes slidin' off in front of me, while I carried her

down the path. The 'gators was bellowin', and the moon was comin'
up full. It was right hard, gettin' her down the bank to the deep
water. She was right smart tall, if she was so slim. I got her down,
though, and tied on some weights offen the nets we'd been settin'
that day. They wasn't too heavy, but nobody never come there
noway. So I put her down in the water. And she sunk, slow, and the
moon made her go down shinin' and shinin', real soft, like a dream.

Wasn't till the next day I started thinkin' about them crawfish.
Iffen you never seen a body that's been et by crawfish, you don't
want to. It's a sight to turn a goat's stomach, let alone a man's. I kept
thinkin' about her, down there, with them things eatin' out her eyes,
nibblin' on that soft skin. Seems like I couldn't rightly stand it. For
two days I held myself down. I took out and went with the niggers
down the river and never come back till the morning of the third
day. This morning . . . seems like forever.

Something drug me down there to the big pool. It's like I couldn't
help myself at all. And when I got there, I couldn't see nothin'. I
would of thought she'd of riz some by then. Seems like I had to see
what they'd done to her, though. Thinkin' was a lot worse than
knowin'. I took a sweet-gum sapling and started dredgin' around in
the deep water, wadin' out fur as I could. I didn't want to, couldn't
hardly stand it, but something made me keep pokin' and feelin'
around with that pole, till it caught her.

Must've been caught on a snag or something, cause when the pole
hooked her, up she come, slow and easy, just like she gone down.
And I throwed up in the water until my insides like to of come out
my mouth. Then I had to go and git rocks and rope and sink her
good, so's I couldn't never see what they'd done to her, never no
more.

I guess I must've went off my head, like. I come to wanderin'
round in the woods, all black and blue from bumpin' into things. I
went back to the house, but it stared at me outen its windows till I
couldn't even go nigh it. Then I went up to Pa's. Course, I didn't tell
him nothin' about what had happened, but I could see him won-
derin'. He loaned me a clean pair of khakis and five dollars, and I
come on into town. Seems like I had to see people, be away from the
woods.

First thing you know, Will Pollard come up and winked. "Got a
jug hid out in the back of the hardware store," he says.

So I went with him. Guess he didn't get much of that jug. I must've drunk most of it. Next thing I remember, Will was lookin' at me with his eyes bugged out and his face fish-belly white.

And now you've got me locked up in here, and they're all down there, right now, fixin' to drag her out. And you're lookin' at me like I was the one that was crazy and sinful. And they're goin' to see what I seen when she come up.

Damn them crawfish!

The Strange Case of Mr. Pruyn

William F. Nolan

Before she could scream, his hand had closed over her mouth. Grinning, he drove a knee into her stomach and stepped quickly back, letting her spill writhing to the floor at his feet. He watched her gasp for breath.

Like a fish out of water, he thought, like a damn fish out of water.

He took off his blue service cap and wiped sweat from the leather band. Hot. Damned hot. He looked down at the girl. She was rolling, bumping the furniture, fighting to breathe. She wouldn't be able to scream until she got her breath back, and by then . . .

He moved across the small living room to a chair and opened a black leather toolbag he had placed there. He hesitated, looked back at her.

"For you," he said, smiling over his shoulder. "Just for you."

He slowly withdrew a long-bladed hunting knife from the bag and held it up for her to see.

She emitted small gasping sounds; her eyes bugged and her mouth opened and closed, chopping at air.

You're not beautiful anyway, he thought, moving toward her with the knife. Pretty, but not beautiful. Beautiful women shouldn't die. Too rare. Sad to see beauty die. But you . . .

He stood above her, looking down. Face all red and puffy. No lipstick. Not even pretty now. No prize package when she'd opened the door. If she'd been beautiful he would have gone on, told her he'd

301

made a mistake, and gone on to the next apartment. But she was
nothing. Hair in pin curls. Apron. Nothing.

He knelt, caught her arm and pulled her to him. "Don't worry," he
told her. "This will be quick."

He did not stop smiling.

A Mr. Pruyn out front, sir. Says he's here about the Sloane case."

"Send him on in," said Lieutenant Norman Bendix. He sighed and
leaned back wearily in his swivel chair.

Hell, he thought, another one. My four-year-old kid could come in
here and give me better stories. Stabbed her to death with my fountain pen, Daddy. Nuts!

Fifteen years with the force and he'd talked to dozens of Dopey
Joes who "confessed" to unsolved murders they'd read about in the
papers with Ben Franklin's kisser on it. Oh, once he'd struck oil. Guy
turned out to be telling the truth. All the facts checked out. Freak.
Murderers are not likely to come in and tell the police all about how
they did it. Usually it's a guy with a souped-up imagination and a few
drinks too many under his belt. This Sloane case was a prime example. Five "confessions" already. Five duds.

Marcia Sloane. Twenty-seven. Housewife. Dead in her apartment.
Broad daylight. Her throat cut. No motives. No clues. Husband at
work. Nobody saw anybody. Score to date: 0.

Bendix swore. Damn the papers! Rags. Splash gore all over the
front page. All the gory details. *Except*, thought Bendix, the little
ones, the ones that count. At least they didn't get those. Like the fact
that the Sloane girl had exactly twenty-one cuts on her body below
the throat; like the fact that her stomach bore a large bruise. She'd
been kicked, and kicked hard, before her death. Little details—that
only the killer would know. So, what happens? So a half-dozen
addled pinheads rush in to "confess" and I'm the boy that has to listen. Mr. Ears. Well, Norm kid, somebody's got to listen. Part of the
daily grind.

Lieutenant Norman Bendix shook out a cigarette, lit it, and
watched the office door open.

"Here he is, Lieutenant."

Bendix leaned forward across the desk, folding his hands. The cigarette jerked with his words. "Come in, Mr. Pruyn, come in."

A small man stood uneasily before the desk, bald, smiling nervously, twisting a gray felt hat.

About thirty-one or so, guessed Bendix. Probably a recluse. Lives alone in a small apartment. No hobbies. Broods a lot. They don't have to say a word. I can spot one a mile away.

"Are you the gentleman I'm to see about my murder?" asked the small man. His voice was high and uncertain. He blinked rapidly behind thick-rimmed glasses.

"I'm your man, Mr. Pruyn. Bendix is the name. Lieutenant Bendix. Won't you sit down?"

Bendix indicated a leather chair.

"Pruyn. Like in sign," said the bald little man. "Everyone mispronounces it, you know. An easy name to get wrong. But it's Pruyn. Emery T. Pruyn." He sat down.

"Well, Mr. Pruyn." Bendix was careful to get the name right. "Want to go ahead?"

"Uh—I *do* hope you are the correct gentleman. I should hate to repeat it all to someone else. I abhor repetition, you know." He blinked at Bendix.

"Believe me, I'm your man. Now, go ahead with your story."

Sure, Bendix thought, rave away. This office lacks one damned important item: a leather couch. He offered the small man a cigarette.

"Oh, no. No thank you, Lieutenant. I don't smoke."

Or *murder*, either, Bendix added in his mind. All you do, Blinky, is read the papers.

"Is it true, Lieutenant, that the police have absolutely no clues to work on?"

"That's what it said in the papers. They get the facts, Mr. Pruyn."

"Yes. Well—I was naturally curious as to the job I had done." He paused to adjust his glasses. "May I assure you, from the outset, that I am indeed the guilty party. The crime of murder is on my hands."

Bendix nodded. Okay, Blinky, I'm impressed.

"I—uh—suppose you'll want to take my story down on tape or wire or however you—"

Bendix smiled. "Officer Barnhart will take down what you say. Learned shorthand in Junior High, didn't you, Pete?"

Barnhart grinned from the back of the room.

Emery Pruyn glanced nervously over his shoulder at the uniformed policeman seated near the door. "Oh," he said, "I didn't realize that the officer had remained. I thought that he—left."

"He's *very* quiet," said Bendix, exhaling a cloud of pale-blue cigarette smoke. "Go on with your story, Mr. Pruyn."

"Of course. Yes. Well—I know I don't *look* like a murderer, Lieutenant Bendix, but then"—he chuckled softly—"we seldom look like what we really are. Murderers, after all, can look like anybody."

Bendix fought back a yawn. Why do these jokers pick late afternoon to unload? God, he was hungry. If I let this character ramble on, I'll be here all night. Helen will blow her stack if I'm late for dinner again. Better pep things up. Ask him some leading questions.

"How did you get into Mrs. Sloane's apartment?"

"Disguise," said Pruyn with a shy smile. He sat forward in the leather chair. "I posed as a television man."

"You mean a television repairman?"

"Oh, no. Then I should never have gained entry, since I had no way of knowing whether Mrs. Sloane had *called* a repairman. No, I took the role of a television representative. I told Mrs. Sloane that her name had been chosen at random, along with four others in that vicinity, for a free converter."

"Converter?"

"To convert black-and-white television to color television. I read about them."

"I see. She let you in?"

"Oh, yes. She was utterly convinced, grateful that her name had been chosen, all excited and talking fast. You know, like women do."

Bendix nodded.

"Told me to come right in, that her husband would be delighted when he got home and found out what she'd won. Said it would be a wonderful surprise for him." Mr. Pruyn smiled. "I walked right in carrying my bag and wearing some blue coveralls and a cap I'd bought the day before. Oh—do you want the name and address of the clothing store in order to verify—"

"That won't be necessary at the moment," Bendix cut in. "Just tell us about the crime first. We'll have time to pick up the details later."

"Oh, well, fine. I just thought—well, I put down my bag and—"

"Bag?"

"Yes. I carry a wrench and things in the bag."

"What for?"

"To use as murder weapons," smiled Pruyn, blinking. "I like to take them all along each time and use the one that fits."

"How do you mean?"

"Fits the personality. I simply choose the weapon which is, in my opinion, best suited. Each person has a distinctive personality."

"Then"—Bendix watched the little man's eyes behind the heavy lenses—"you've killed before?"

"Of course, Lieutenant. Five times prior to Mrs. Sloane. Five ladies."

"And why have you waited to come to the police? Why haven't you confessed before now?"

"Because I chose not to. Because my goal has not been reached."

"Which was?"

"An even six. In the beginning I determined to kill exactly six women and then give myself up. Which I have done. Every man should have a goal in life. Mine was six murders."

"I see. Well—to get back to Mrs. Sloane. What happened after she let you in?"

"I put down my bag and walked back to her."

"Where was she?"

"In the middle of the room, watching me. Smiling. Very friendly. Asking me questions about how the converter worked. Not suspecting a thing. Not until . . ."

"Until what, Mr. Pruyn?"

"Until I wouldn't answer her. I just stood there, in front of her, smiling, not saying a word."

"What did she do?"

"Got nervous. Quit smiling. Asked me why I wasn't working on the set. But, I didn't say anything. I just watched the fear grow deep in her eyes." The little man paused; he was sweating, breathing hard now. "Fear is a really wonderful thing to watch in the eyes of a woman, Lieutenant, a *lovely* thing to watch."

"Go on."

"When she reached a certain point, I knew she'd scream. So, before she did, I clapped one hand over her mouth and kicked her."

Bendix drew in his breath sharply. "What did you say?"

"I said I kicked her—in the stomach—to knock the wind out of her. Then she couldn't scream."

Quickly Bendix stubbed out his cigarette. Maybe, he thought, maybe . . . "Then what, Mr. Pruyn?"

"Then I walked to the bag and selected the knife. Long blade. Good steel. Then I walked back to Mrs. Sloane and cut her throat. It was very satisfying. A goal reached and conquered."

"Is that all?" Bendix asked.

Because if he tells me about twenty-one cuts, then he's our boy, thought Bendix. The kick in the stomach could be, just *could* be, something he'd figured out for himself. But, if he tells me about the cuts . . .

"Oh, there's more. I rolled her over and left my trademark."

"What kind of trademark?"

The small man grinned shyly behind the thick glasses. "Like the Sign of the Saint—or the Mark of Zorro," he said. "My initials. On her back. E.T.P. Emery T. Pruyn."

Bendix eased back in his chair, sighed, and lit a new cigarette.

"Then I removed the ears." He looked proud. "For my collection. I have six nice pairs now."

"Wouldn't have them *with* you, I don't suppose?"

"Oh, no, Lieutenant. I keep them at home—in a box, a metal box in my antique rosewood dresser."

"That's it, eh?"

"Yes, yes, it is. After I removed the ears, I left and went home. That was three days ago. I arranged my affairs, put things in order, and came here to you. I'm ready for my cell."

"No cell, Mr. Pruyn."

"What do you mean, Lieutenant?" Emery Pruyn's lower lip began to tremble. He stood up. "I—I don't understand."

"I mean you can go home now. Come back in the morning. Around eight. We'll get the details then—the name of the clothing store and all. Then, we'll see."

"But, I—I—"

"Goodnight, Mr. Pruyn. Officer Barnhart will show you out."

From the door of his office, Norman Bendix watched the two figures recede down the narrow hall.

An odd one, he thought, a *real* odd one.

He pulled the Ford out of the police parking lot and eased the car into the evening traffic.

So easy! So wonderfully satisfying and easy. Oh, the excitement of it—his sojourn into the Lion's Den. Almost like the excitement with the knife. That bit about the kick in the stomach. Dangerous, but wonderful! He remembered the lieutenant's look when he'd mentioned the kick. Delicious!

Emery Pruyn smiled as he drove on. Much more excitement was ahead. Much more . . .

Ludmila

David Montross

Usually Grandmother screeched at her the minute the door opened, asking why Ludmila had loitered in the woods, or if she'd been bad in school and made to stay for punishment. Sometimes the old woman didn't even say that much before flinging her pillow at Ludmila, who was always ready to jump to one side or the other. But today was different. No pillow slung at her this late afternoon. No screeching either.

"Babushka?" Risking a glance at Grandmother, she saw the old woman's thin white braids spreading from under the pillow, and the blankets pulled up high as she'd arranged them hours ago. She wanted to say, "Forgive me for this morning, Babushka. I didn't mean to be a bad girl. Do please forgive me and say something. Please."

Because if Grandmother didn't speak now, then she wouldn't say anything for days and days. Not one word. Maybe not until after it was time for snow to fly, and the hut to be crowded with Ludmila's Papa and her brothers, after they returned from harvest.

Quietly so as not to awaken Grandmother, she set a string bag of beets and cabbage and a precious sliver of salt pork on the table, and hurried to throw faggots on the fire. Babushka complained of being cold even in the hottest weather, and now finding fallen wood was harder, and Ludmila had to wander in greater circles through the forest each day. Next spring she'd ask Papa and her brothers to leave a larger wood pile for her before they went off for the summer to cut the grain. If Babushka wanted the hut kept hotter this summer than last, she'd want more heat than ever next year.

But then Ludmila would be thirteen, and surely she'd be able to cut her own wood. At least the lower branches of fir and birch which

309

grew right up to the clearing. If she could do that, the men would be free to dig the well that someday would bring water right inside the hut, or build a shelter of some kind around the vegetables so rabbits and deer couldn't rob the garden as they had recently. Why, there was almost no food at all for this coming winter. The thought made her hungrier than usual. There were hardly any rubles left either, until Papa got home.

Careful not to look at Grandmother, who hated to be caught sleeping, Ludmila fried the pork and peeled the beets and chopped the cabbage and put them all to boil on the hearth, using the last water in the pail. Very quietly she put her shawl on again and went out across the clearing to the stream which chubbled over the rocks, sounding almost like Shura's balalaika.

If she stayed outside awhile, Babushka might sleep on, and there'd be less time for her to complain before they went to bed. Anyway, it was nicer out here alone, thinking and looking around at the shrubs and trees. It smelled better too; inside the hut it was awful.

She'd pretend when she did go in that she'd just come from school and the food store, and Grandmother could screech or throw her pillow as usual. Then they'd eat soup and go to bed, and in a day or two or a week Papa and the boys would be home. Babushka was quieter when they were around.

But as Papa said last spring, "If you were held in bed by useless legs, dear little Ludmila, you'd fret and whine and be mean too."

Since Papa said it, it must be so. Wasn't he the best father in the world? Helping with her lessons and always appearing at school on dark winter days just as she started the long lonely walk home through the woods. Comrade Varvara, the schoolteacher, said people must produce according to their ability, and reap according to their need. But Grandmother ate without producing any food. Papa said at her age that was natural; in her time she'd produced plenty.

This summer when birds and animals ate the vegetables and there was no grain or any feed for the cattle or sheep or pigs or chickens, old Nikolai at the food store said the coming winter would bring out the wolves for sure. Nobody in the village had seen one for at least three years, but everyone knew that when people died of hunger, the wolves always came.

Ludmila had never seen one either, but she'd heard them howling

often enough. And Babushka was always saying that bad little girls
were only good for feeding wild animals.

Ah, it would be nice when Papa and the seven brothers returned.
This week probably, old Nikolai had said, shaking his bald head
sadly, because early return meant bad harvest, and less food for everyone. Still Papa would keep the wolves away from the hut; he always had before.

Once they were all at home, there'd be no more dark and lonely
mornings when Ludmila had to get up from beside Babushka, break
ice on the pail of water left by the banked fire, and cook kasha after
she pushed the pan under Grandmother.

Sometimes the old woman sat so long and fussed so about the way
Ludmila fixed her blankets and fluffed her pillow afterward, she had
to run all the way through the golden birches and green firs to the
road and past the village houses to the collective hall where the
schoolroom was. Then Comrade Varvara gave her extra homework to
do by candlelight. If only Grandmother could produce candles even,
or not be such a long time on the pan.

Oh, there was the first star. And others beyond it, getting brighter
in spite of the rising moon, which tonight was as yellow as the
birches by day. A lovely night filled with whisperings from the forest.

Last year Papa and the boys had been a month later than this,
roaring with song as they tramped through the trees from where the
lorries let them off in the village. Racing when they saw her waving,
to see which of them reached her first. Whoever did would lift her off
her feet and smother her squeals with kisses, taking his time before
letting her go to the next in line. But none of them ever raced to kiss
Grandmother.

How lovely to have them back early this year, if Nikolai was right.
But sad about the people who'd starve this winter, maybe some from
their own collective.

Which of the family might die?

Not Papa because he was healthy and strong. Nor the boys because they were young and strong. Not Babushka because if neither
healthy nor young, she was the strongest of them all. Papa said so
often. Every time Babushka asked him.

"Who's the strongest of us all?"

"You are, dearest little Mother."

Babushka would nod and grin, showing her shrunken gums, and the seven boys and Ludmila would laugh and cheer. Because Papa always stood where Grandmother couldn't see him, and winked as he answered to show what he truly thought.

But with all of them so strong that left only one who was weak. A bad little girl who couldn't cut her own wood, and begrudged the time Babushka spent on the pan each morning, and hated bringing her water to wash, and arranging the blankets and the pillow under the thin white braids.

Poor old woman. It was easy to hate her, hard to remember she was old and crippled. But who could love her when she smelled so and screeched so? This morning when Ludmila was already late for school, Babushka threw her pillow because it was hard and lumpy she said, and Ludmila began to cry. She'd thrown the pillow back at Grandmother, watching it fall on the old face. Minutes later she'd run as fast as she ever had to school, crying all the way.

More stars. And in the moonlight, shadows running short and long ahead of her as she left the stream and crossed the clearing to the door of the hut. She set the pail down, not wanting to go inside.

A screech or a pillow in her face? A complaint or a demand? What would happen if she screeched back? Or threw the pillow again? What if she didn't go inside, but stayed out here waiting for Papa and the boys?

When they came, she'd want to go inside. Then the hut would ring with talk and laughter, and Oleg's violin at night with Shura's balalaika and Papa's rhythmic clapping. Rodion and Vukuly and Kyril would dance a gopak, and afterward she'd waltz with all of them, counting to make sure they didn't fight over who was her next partner. They didn't have music and dancing every night because once a week the men would go to the village and drink beer and talk to their friends.

If she starved to death this winter who would they dance with? She snuffled and wiped her nose on a corner of the shawl. Dying might not be so bad. In heaven she'd know for herself what her mother looked like, although Comrade Varvara said there was no heaven. When she told Papa, he said, "That may be, but your mother was an angel." Only he couldn't remember if she'd been big or little, plain or pretty, only that she was just right for him, and he'd never find another like her.

Babushka said no woman, and certainly not her son's second wife, deserved such devotion. Anyway, he hadn't needed a second wife, not with seven fine sons already. What had the second wife ever done for anybody but produce a useless afterthought? A good thing Ludmila was the last baby, she was always so hungry. Sometimes when Babushka talked about weak little girls, bad little girls, hungry little girls, Ludmila wanted to hurt her.

Two years ago when Babushka started to get up one morning, she fell out of the bed she shared with Ludmila. Papa came running around the curtain that divided the hut, and Ludmila was so frightened she put her thumb in her mouth, something she hadn't done for a long time. Babushka lay with her eyes closed and her breathing was as loud as her snoring. When Papa knelt beside her and began to cry, Ludmila cried too.

But Grandmother finally opened her eyes and rolled them around in her head. And still later she grunted and said, "Ludmila . . . Ludmila . . . she pushed me . . ."

A doctor who came to examine her for admission to a state hospital said she'd had a stroke and would never walk again. And he said there were few enough beds for the living let alone for the dying, so there was no reason to move her. She could go any time, from a sudden shock or just because her heart stopped, or she might linger for years. But that was their problem; his concern was for those who would recover and produce again.

Ludmila had wanted to ask, What about me? because the summers were bad enough as it was, and if Grandmother had to stay in bed, next summer would be longer and harder than ever with the men away.

Two years ago. An endless time, and never a "thank you" or "please" from Babushka. Only screeching and thrown pillows except when Papa was home last winter and got angry. "Enough, old woman. You're too harsh with Ludmila. She's doing more work than you'll ever do again."

Babushka had hardly spoken all winter, she was so offended. And she took to pinching in the night, her cruel fingers finding Ludmila's arm or leg or an ear. She'd pinch and pinch until Ludmila couldn't stand it, and then she'd push Grandmother away. But the old woman never fell out of bed again.

Ludmila sighed and reached for the bucket at her feet. Opening the door, she hesitated, waiting for the pillow to come flying at her. But Grandmother lay exactly as she'd lain earlier. And the pillow was still pressed over her face from this morning.

Very carefully, Ludmila set the pail down, took the pot off the hearth, and ladled soup into her bowl. Then she took a spoon and enjoyed every mouthful. Without a glance at the bed, she got up and ladled out the rest of the soup and ate that as well.

The One Who Got Away

Al Nussbaum

It was Saturday evening and I was standing beside the line of traffic coming from Tijuana. As each car stopped beside me, I asked the occupants the usual questions: "Where were you born?" and "Are you bringing anything back with you?"

Once in a while I'd check a truck or tell a driver to pull over for a closer examination, but I didn't do it often. I only did it when we'd had a tip from an informer, or the people seemed exceptionally gay and friendly, or I had one of my hunches. I didn't have many hunches, but they'd proven correct in almost every case, so I always paid attention to them.

When I saw Jack Wilner I had a hunch he was up to something. He was in one of the opposite lanes, heading into Mexico behind the wheel of a shiny yellow convertible. The top was down and the blaring radio was tuned to a San Diego rock station. The whole thing seemed too showy—like a magician's antics when misdirecting his audience.

It was the beginning of my shift—I was working the 8 P.M. to 4 A.M. tour—so I made a note of his license number with the intention of giving him a good going-over when he came back.

I watched carefully for the car, but it didn't return before I went off duty. I gave the other customs officers copies of the license number and a description of the car, and went home.

By the next night I had almost forgotten about the yellow convertible, but the following Saturday evening I saw it again. The top was down, the radio was blasting, and it was on its way to Tijuana as before. I had the same feeling as I'd had the first time. I ran to the telephone and called the *aduana*, the Mexican customhouse, and asked them to check out the convertible.

When I got back to the traffic lane, I saw in the distance that the convertible had already been pulled over. Khaki-uniformed men swarmed around it, and a couple of them were busy removing door panels, while others checked the trunk and beneath the hood. Jack Wilner—of course, I didn't know his name then—stood to one side, nonchalantly smoking a cigarette. He was tall and thin, and even from far away I could see that he dressed with a youthful disregard for color.

I got busy with the cars coming into the country and didn't look over that way again for almost an hour. When I did, I was just in time to see the convertible as it pulled away from the *aduana*. Wilner turned to wave good-bye to the Mexican officers lined up watching him, then picked up speed.

So, they had found nothing. In that case, I reasoned, he must be smuggling something *into* the United States, so I watched for him to return. I stayed around a little after my shift was over and gave out the car's description and license number again. I asked everyone to be sure to pass the description and number to the next shift, if one of them didn't stop him.

Monday and Tuesday were my days off, but I called the customhouse both nights to see if the convertible had been checked out yet. It hadn't—and that's the way it went the rest of the week. The convertible didn't pass our border station.

But on Saturday evening I looked across into the far lanes, and there it was, heading into Mexico again.

I watched it with my mouth hanging open and then mentally kicked myself for being so stupid. Just because he'd left the country at this point didn't mean he had to return at this point. Mexico and California shared over a hundred miles of border, and there were many places where he could cross back into the United States.

Up until now, my inquiry into the activities of the driver of the yellow convertible had been just that—*my* inquiry. That wasn't good enough anymore. I went to my supervisor and told him about my hunch, and he sent out notices to all the other checkpoints along the

California-Mexico border. A customs officer has to rely on informers and instinct. Informers account for ninety percent of his arrests, but hunches like mine provide the other ten percent.

I went back to my post and waited. We were supposed to be notified once the convertible had been searched, but we received no word. None.

Then on Saturday evening, at the height of the traffic rush, I saw the yellow convertible heading into Mexico again.

At first we had thought it had checked out all right, and the people at its crossing point hadn't bothered to let us know. My supervisor decided to be sure, though, and sent out a call to find out where the car had crossed back into the States.

In half an hour he had the answer—nowhere. None of the official crossing points had seen the car.

Somewhere along the hundred-mile border, Wilner had found a way to slip across without stopping for a customs check. He was able to drive into Mexico, load the car with whatever contraband he cared to, and return to the United States without worrying about paying duty or fearing arrest. We had to find out where the hole was and plug it up.

A telephone call to the motor vehicles bureau gave us Jack Wilner's name and San Diego address. A twenty-four-hour watch was set up on his apartment, and we went back to waiting. Wilner was away until Wednesday, then he parked his yellow convertible in his carport and went inside.

Except for shopping and normal housekeeping trips, he remained at home until Saturday evening. Then he drove across the border into Mexico while a car filled with customs agents followed fifty yards behind him. I watched the little parade from my post and felt pleased. I was confident we had him hooked and would soon reel him in.

But I was wrong. An hour later the agents returned. They had been trapped in the traffic on Avenida Revolución when he had made a sudden turn near the Jai Alai Frontón.

They had lost him.

I was disappointed, and they were angry. They were certain his maneuver had been deliberate, so they applied for a warrant to search his car when he returned. If they found so much as a marijuana seed, Wilner was in trouble.

I was given special permission to accompany the agents and was on the scene when Wilner returned to his apartment on Wednesday. It was obvious, from the way his jaw fell when they presented the warrant, that he hadn't lost his followers intentionally on Saturday. Until the warrant was thrust in front of him, he hadn't known he was suspected of anything.

We went over his car and found it spotless—literally spotless. It must have been cleaned recently, both inside and out, because even the ash trays were empty. Wilner watched us take the car apart and put it together again, but he wasn't as much at ease as he had been that day at the border. He kept licking his lips and shifting his weight from foot to foot. As far as he knew, the search at the border had been routine, but this certainly wasn't. We were on the scent of something, and he must have known we'd keep after him until we found it.

That's why I was amazed to see him drive into Mexico on Saturday evening. I was even more surprised to see him stop voluntarily at the *aduana* and go inside. We learned later from the agents following him that he'd applied for a residence permit and took care of all the other paperwork necessary for an extended stay in Mexico. He wouldn't be coming back for a while; he was even more frightened than I'd figured.

I thought about Wilner a lot during the following months. In my mind he was the one who got away. In all the time I had been in the customs service, he was the first man who had eluded arrest when I was sure he was a smuggler.

I didn't see Jack Wilner again for over a year, and then I had to go to Mexico to do it. Every spring there's a yacht race from Newport Beach to Ensenada. There are always between three and four hundred boats in the race and they draw a huge crowd to witness the finish. I drove down to see it and found Jack Wilner standing alone not ten feet from me.

I walked over to him and touched him on the arm. "Hi!" I said. "Remember me?"

He gave me a hesitant smile, then it slipped away as he remembered. His eyeballs jerked as he searched the crowd for more so-called familiar faces.

"I just came down to see the race," I said. "Running into you wasn't planned."

That eased his nervousness and he relaxed visibly. We stood side by side and watched the boats. As the day wore on, he became more friendly and told me a little about himself. He was the owner of a small hotel and marina about twenty miles south of Tijuana, and he was in Ensenada to look at a few boats he was thinking of buying. He invited me to stop at his place sometime.

"Did you buy it with your profits from smuggling?" I asked boldly. I wanted to get him to talk about it, and I was sure he never would if I tried to be clever and circuitous.

He smiled with surprise at my directness. "I don't want to sign a statement," he said, imitating a TV villain. Then, after a few moments, he nodded. "Yes, that's how I got the money to buy it."

"You're not smuggling anymore?"

"No."

"That's hard to believe," I said. "You must've been pretty successful to afford a business, and few professional smugglers quit before being caught."

"I'd made up my mind to quit if anyone became curious about me. You people were too curious, so I quit."

We bought tacos from a street vendor and stood eating them.

"In that case, you won't mind telling me how you managed to return to California without being noticed when all the border stations were watching for you," I said.

"No, I don't mind. It was easy. I simply stuck my license plates under my jacket and walked back across the border," he said with a grin. "I was smuggling yellow convertibles, a new one every week."

It's a Lousy World

Bill Pronzini

Colly Babcock was shot to death on the night of September 9, in an alley between Twenty-ninth and Valley streets in the Glen Park District of San Francisco. Two police officers, cruising, spotted him coming out the rear door of Budget Liquors there, carrying a metal box. Colly ran when he saw them. The officers gave chase, calling out for him to halt, but he just kept running. One of the officers fired a warning shot, but when Colly didn't heed it, the officer pulled up and fired again. He was aiming low, trying for the legs, but in the half-light of the alley it was a blind shot. The bullet hit Colly in the small of the back and killed him instantly.

I read about it the following morning over coffee and undercooked eggs in a cafeteria on Taylor Street, a block and a half from my office. The story was on an inside page, concise and dispassionate; they teach you that kind of objective writing in the journalism classes. Just the cold facts. A man dies, but he's nothing more than a statistic, a name in black type, a faceless nonentity to be considered and then forgotten, along with your breakfast coffee.

Unless you knew him.

Unless he was your friend.

Very carefully I folded the newspaper and put it in my coat pocket. Then I stood from the table and made my way through the crowd of fine young men in dark business suits and neatly tacked ties, and the girls in tight, warm wool dresses and short, belted coats. I went out to the street.

The air smelled of pollution. The wind was up, blowing in off the

321

Bay, and rubble swirled and eddied in the gutters. It would rain soon, but the cleansing would be short-lived, and ineffectual.

I walked into the face of the wind, toward my office.

"How's the job, Colly?"

"Oh, fine, just fine."

"No problems?"

"No, no, none at all."

"Stick with it, Colly."

"I'm a new man."

"Straight all the way?"

"Straight all the way."

Inside the lobby of my building, it was cold and dark and still. There was an Out of Order sign taped to the closed elevator doors. I went around to the stairs and up to the second floor and along the hallway to my office. The door was unlocked. I opened it and stepped inside.

Colly Babcock's widow sat in the chair before my desk.

Quietly I closed the door. Our eyes met and held for several seconds, and then I crossed the room and sat down, facing her.

She said, "The superintendent let me in."

"It's all right."

Her hands were clasped tightly in the lap of her plain black dress. "You heard?"

"Yes," I said. "What can I say, Lucille?"

"You were Colly's friend," she said. "You helped him."

"Maybe I didn't help him enough."

"He didn't do it," Lucille said. "He didn't steal that money. He didn't do all those robberies like they're saying."

"Lucille . . ."

"Colly and I were married thirty-one years," Lucille said. "Don't you think I would have known?"

I did not say anything.

"I always knew," she said.

I sat looking at her. She was a big woman, big and handsome—a strong woman. There was strength in the line of her mouth, and in her eyes, round and gray, tinged with red now from the crying. She had stuck by Colly Babcock through two prison terms, and twenty-odd years of running, and hiding, and of looking over her shoulder. Yes, I thought, she would always have known.

I said, "The papers said Colly was coming out the back door of the liquor store, carrying a metal box. They found a hundred and six dollars in the box, and the door jimmied open."

"I know what the papers said, and I know what the police are saying. But they're wrong. Wrong."

"He was there, Lucille."

"I know that," she said. "Colly liked to walk in the evenings. A long walk and a drink when he came home. It helped him to relax. That was how he came to be there."

I shifted position on my chair, not speaking.

Lucille said, "Colly was always nervous when he was doing jobs. That was one of the ways I could tell. He'd get irritable, and he couldn't sleep."

"He wasn't like that lately?"

"You saw him a few weeks ago," Lucille said. "Did he look that way to you?"

"No," I said, "he didn't."

"We were happy," Lucille said. "No more running. And no more waiting. We were truly happy."

My mouth felt dry. "What about his job?"

"They gave Colly a raise last week. A fifteen-dollar raise. We went to dinner to celebrate, a fine restaurant on the Wharf."

"You were getting along all right on the money," I said. "Nothing came up?"

"Nothing at all," Lucille said. "We even had a little bank account started." She bit her lip. "We were going to the West Indies someday. Colly always wanted to retire to the West Indies."

I looked at my hands. They seemed big and awkward resting on the desk top. I took them away and put them in my lap. "These Glen Park robberies started a month and a half ago," I said. "The police estimate the total amount taken at between thirty-five hundred and four thousand dollars. You could get to the West Indies pretty well on that."

Lucille looked at me steadily from her round gray eyes. "Colly didn't do those robberies," she said.

What could I say? God knows, Colly had never been a saint. She knew that, all right. But this time he was innocent. All the evidence, and all the words, weren't going to change that in her eyes.

I got a cigarette from my pocket and made a thing of lighting it.

The taste added more dryness to my mouth. Without looking at her, I said, "What do you want me to do, Lucille?"

"I want you to prove Colly was innocent. I want you to prove he didn't do what they're saying he did."

"I'd like nothing better. You know that. But how can I do it? The evidence . . ."

"Damn the evidence!" Her wide mouth trembled with the sudden emotion. "Colly was innocent, I tell you! I won't have him buried with this last mark against his name. I won't have it."

"Lucille, listen to me—"

"I won't listen," she said. "Colly was your friend. You stood up for him with the parole board. You helped him find his job. You talked to him, guided him. He was a different man, a new man, and you helped make him that way. Will you sit there and tell me you believe he threw it all away for four thousand dollars? Will you just sit there and let them brand him with these crimes, not knowing for certain if he was guilty? Or don't you care?"

I still could not meet her eyes. I stared down at the burning cigarette in my fingers, watching the smoke rise, curling, a gray spiral in the cold air of my office. And I said, "I care, Lucille."

"Then help me," she said. "For Colly. For your friend."

It was a long time before I said, "All right, Lucille. I'll see what I can do."

She stood then, head up, the way it had always been, and the anger was gone. There remained only the sadness. "I'm sorry," she said. "I didn't mean to come on like that."

"Don't be sorry," I said, rising too. "He was your husband."

She nodded, her throat working, and there were no more words for either of us.

They told me at the Hall of Justice that Inspector Eberhardt was out somewhere but that he would be back within the hour. I went across Bryant Street and down a short alley to a coffee shop, and had three cups of coffee and smoked six cigarettes. Forty-five minutes passed.

When I went outside again, it had begun to drizzle. Some of the chill had gone out of the air, but the wind was stronger now. The clouds overhead were black and puffed, ready to burst.

I went inside the Hall of Justice again and rode the elevator upstairs and this time they told me Eberhardt was in. They asked him on the phone if he would see me, and he said he would, and they let me go in then.

Eberhardt was dressed in a brown suit that looked as if it had been hand-washed in lye soap. His tie was crooked, and there was a collar button missing from his shirt. He wore a reddish-blue bruise over his left eye.

"All right," he said, "make it quick, will you?"

"What happened to your eye?"

"I bumped into a doorknob."

"Sure you did."

"Yeah," he said. "You come here to pass the time of day, or was there something? I haven't been to bed in thirty-eight hours, and I'm in no mood for banter."

"I'd like a favor, Eb."

"Sure," Eberhardt said. "And I'd like three weeks' vacation."

"I want to look at an Officer's Report."

"Are you nuts?" Eberhardt said. "Get the hell out of here."

"There was a shooting last night," I said. "Two squad-car cops killed a man running away from the scene of a robbery out in Glen Park."

"So?"

"The man was a friend of mine."

Eberhardt gave me a look. "What friend?"

"Colly Babcock."

"Do I know him?"

"I don't think so. He did two stretches in San Quentin for burglary. I helped to send him up the first time, when I was on the cops."

"Glen Park," Eberhardt said. "That's where they've been having those robberies."

"Yeah," I said. "According to the papers, they've tabbed Colly as their man."

"Only you don't think so."

"Colly's wife doesn't think so," I said. "I guess maybe I don't either."

"I can't let you look at any reports," Eberhardt said. "And even if I could, it's not my department. Robbery'll be handling it."

"You could pull some strings."

"I could," he said, "but I won't. I'm up to my ears in something. I just don't have the time."

I got to my feet. "Well, thanks anyway, Eb." I had my hand on the doorknob before he called my name, stopping me. I turned to him.

"If things go all right," Eberhardt said, not looking at me, "I'll be off duty in a couple of hours. If I happen to get down by Robbery, I'll see what I can do."

"Thanks, Eb," I said. "I appreciate it."

He didn't say anything. He was reaching for the telephone. But he heard me, all right.

I found Tommy Belknap in a bar called Luigi's, out in the Mission.

He was drinking whiskey at the long bar, leaning his head on his arms and staring at the wall. There were two men in work clothes drinking beer and eating sandwiches from lunch pails at the other end, and in the middle an old lady in a white shawl sipped dark-red wine, from a glass held with arthritic fingers. I sat on a stool next to Tommy, and said hello.

He turned slowly, his eyes moving upward. His face was an anemic white, and his bald head shone with beaded perspiration. He had trouble focusing his eyes, and he wiped at them with the back of one veined hand. He was packing one, all right—a big one. And I knew why.

"Hey," he said when he recognized me, "have a drink, will you?"

"Not just now."

Tommy got his glass to his lips, drinking tremulously. "Colly's dead," he said.

"Yes," I said, "I know."

"They killed him last night," Tommy said. "They shot him in the back."

"Take it easy," I said.

"He was my friend," Tommy said.

"He was my friend, too."

"Colly was a nice guy," Tommy said. "They had no right to shoot him like that."

"He was robbing a liquor store," I said quietly.

"The hell he was!" Tommy said. He swiveled on the stool and pushed a finger at my chest. "Colly was straight, you hear that? Straight ever since he got out."

"Was he, Tommy?"

"You're damned right he was."

"He didn't pull those robberies in Glen Park?"

"I told you, didn't I? He was straight."

"Who did pull them, Tommy?"

"I don't know."

"Come on," I said. "You get around. There must be something adrift."

"Nothing," Tommy said. "Don't know."

"Kids?" I said. "Street gang?"

"Don't know," Tommy said. "Don't know."

"But not Colly? You'd know if it was Colly?"

"Colly was straight," Tommy said. "And now he's dead."

He put his head down on his arms again. The bartender came over. He was a fat man with a reddish handlebar mustache. "You can't sleep in here, Tommy," he said.

"Colly's dead," Tommy said, and there were tears in his eyes.

"Let him alone," I said to the bartender.

"I can't have him sleeping in here," the bartender said.

I took out my wallet and put a dollar bill on the bar. "Then give him another drink."

The bartender looked at me, and then at the dollar, and then he shrugged and walked away.

I went out into the rain.

D. E. O'MIRA AND COMPANY, WHOLESALE PLUMBING SUPPLIES was a large two-storied building that took up three-quarters of a block on Berry Street, out near China Basin.

I parked on the street in front and went inside. In the center of the office was a glass-walled switchboard, with a little card glued to the front that said *Information*. A dark-haired girl wearing a print dress and a set of headphones sat inside the switchboard booth.

I went there and asked the girl if Mr. Templeton was in. She said he was at a meeting downtown, and wouldn't be back all day. Mr. Templeton was the office manager, and the man I had spoken to about giving Colly Babcock a job when he was paroled from San Quentin.

I thought about talking to one of the mélange of vice-presidents the company sported, and then decided that they wouldn't have had much contact with Colly. Since he'd worked in the warehouse, I thought it best if I talked to his immediate supervisor. I asked the girl where the shipping office was.

She pointed to a set of swing doors to the left, opposite the main entrance, and I thanked her and went over there and pushed the doors open. I followed a narrow, dark hallway, screened on both sides, and came out in the warehouse. On my left was a long counter. Behind it were display shelves, and behind them long rows of bins that stretched the width of the building. There were four or five men standing in front of the counter, and two more behind it, taking orders. Through an open doorway I could see the loading dock, and out to a cluttered yard where several pickup trucks were parked. On my right was a windowed office with two desks, neither occupied, and another room, jammed with an oblong workbench and dusty cartons of throw-away materials. I went to the office and stepped inside.

An old man in a pair of baggy brown slacks, a brown vest and a battered slouch hat that looked to be as old as he was stood before a narrow counter opposite the two unoccupied desks. A foul-smelling cigar danced in his thin mouth as he shuffled papers.

I waited for a time, but the old man did not look up. Finally I cleared my throat. "Excuse me," I said.

He looked up then grudgingly, eyed me up and down, and went back to his papers. "What is it?" he said, scribbling on one of the papers with a pencil.

"Are you Mr. Harlin?"

"That's right."

I told him my name and what I did, and then I said, "I wonder if I might talk to you for a moment."

"Go ahead and talk," he said.

"Privately, if you don't mind."

He looked at me again. "What about?"

"Colly Babcock," I said.

He made a grunting sound, shuffled his papers again, and then motioned me ahead of him, out onto the dock. We walked along there, past where a blond-haired boy in green coveralls was loading crated cast-iron sinks from a pallet into a pickup truck, and up to the wide double-door entrance to a second high-beamed warehouse.

The old man stopped and turned to me. "We can talk here."

"You were Colly's supervisor, is that right?"

"I was."

"Tell me about him."

"You won't hear anything bad, if that's what you're looking for."

"That's not what I'm looking for."

He thought about that for a moment, and then he shrugged. "Colly was a good worker," he said. "Did what you told him, no fuss. Quiet sort, kept to himself mostly."

"You knew about his prison record?"

"We knew, all of us. Nothing was ever said to Colly about it, though. I saw to that."

"Did he seem happy with the job?"

"Happy enough," the old man said. "Never grumbled or complained, if that's what you mean."

"No friction with any of the other men?"

"No. He got along fine with all of them."

A horn sounded from inside the second warehouse, and a yellow fork lift carrying a pallet of lavatories came out. We stepped out of the way, and the thing clanked and belched past, moving along the dock.

I said to the old man, "Mind telling me your reaction to what happened?"

"Didn't believe it," he answered. "None of us did. I ain't sure I believe it yet."

I nodded. "Did Colly have any particular friend here? Somebody he ate lunch with regularly, like that?"

"Kept to himself mostly, like I said. But he stopped with Sam Biehler for a beer a time or two after work."

"Would it be all right if I talked to this Biehler?"

"All right with me," the old man said. He paused, chewing on his cigar. "Listen, is there any chance Colly didn't do what they say? Oh, sure, I know all about what the papers put down, but a man'd have to be a fool to take half of that."

"There might be, Mr. Harlin," I said.

"Anything I can do," he said, "you let me know."

"I'll let you know."

We went back inside, and I spoke to Sam Biehler, a tall, slender man with a mane of silver hair that gave him, despite his work clothes, a rather distinguished appearance.

"I don't mind telling you," Biehler said to me, "I don't believe a

damned word of it. I'd have had to be there to see it with my own
eyes before I'd believe it, and maybe not even then."

"I understand you and Colly stopped for a beer occasionally?"

"Once a week maybe," Biehler said, "after work."

"What did you talk about?"

"The job, mostly. What was wrong with the company, what they
could do to improve things. You know the way fellows talk."

"Anything else?"

"About Colly's past, is that what you're getting at?"

"I guess it is."

"Just once," Biehler said. "Colly told me a few things. But I never
pressed him on it. I don't like to pry."

"What was it he told you, Mr. Biehler?"

"That he was never going back to prison," Biehler said. "That he
was through with the kind of life he'd led before. That he was at
peace with the world for the first time in his life." He looked at me,
eyes sparkling, as if challenging me. "And you know something?"

"What's that, Mr. Biehler?"

"I been on this earth for fifty-nine years," he said. "I've known a
lot of men in that time. You get so you can tell."

I waited.

"Colly wasn't lying," Biehler said.

I spent a half-hour in the Public Library, in Civic Center, reading
back-dated issues of the *Chronicle* and the *Examiner*. The Glen Park
robberies had begun a month and a half ago, and I had paid only
passing attention to them at the time.

When I had acquainted myself with the reported details, I went
back to my office and called Lucille Babcock.

"The police were just here," she said. "They had a search warrant."

"Did they find anything?"

"There was nothing to find."

"What did they say?"

"They asked a lot of questions," she said. "They wanted to know
about bank accounts and safety deposit boxes."

"Did you cooperate with them?"

"Yes."

"Good," I said. I told her what I had been doing all morning, and about what the people I had talked with said.

"You see?" she said when I had finished. "Nobody who knew Colly can believe he's guilty."

"Nobody but the police," I said softly.

"The police," she repeated, but there was no animosity in her voice.

I sat holding the phone. There were a lot of things I wanted to say, but they all seemed trite and meaningless. After a long moment I told her I would be in touch and then I hung up. The palms of my hands were moist.

I got a cigarette out of my pack. But I was out of matches. I went rummaging through my desk, but there were none there. I put the cigarette back in the pack.

I reached out and put my hand on the telephone. But before I could lift the receiver, the bell rang. I picked it up and it was Eberhardt.

"I was just going to call you," I said.

"I've been trying to call *you* for two hours," he said.

"Something you wanted to talk to me about?"

"Quit trying to hedge," he said. "You know what it is."

"Okay," I said. "Where are you now?"

"Home."

"Can I stop by?"

"If you can get up here within the half-hour," he said. "I'm going to bed then, and my wife has orders to bar all the doors and windows and take the telephone off the hook."

"I'll be there in twenty minutes," I said.

Eberhardt lived on Collingwood, at the foot of Twin Peaks. The house was small and white and comfortable, a stucco job with a trimmed lawn and flowers in neat rows. If you knew Eberhardt, the house was sort of symbolic; it typified everything the honest, hardworking cop was dedicated to protecting. I imagine he knew it, too; and if he did, got a perverse satisfaction from the knowledge. That was the way Eberhardt was.

I parked in his driveway and went up and knocked on the door. His wife, a tiny red-haired woman with astounding patience, let me in, asked how I was and showed me into the kitchen, closing the door behind her as she left.

Eberhardt was sitting at the table, having a pipe, a cup of coffee in front of him. There was a professional-looking bandage over the bruise on his eye.

"Have a seat," he said, and I had one. "You want some coffee?"

"Thanks."

He got me a cup, and then indicated a manila envelope lying to one side of the table. Sucking at his pipe he made an elaborate effort to ignore me then.

Inside the envelope was the report made by the two patrolmen, Avinisi and Carstairs, who had shot and killed Colly Babcock in the act of robbing the Budget Liquor Store. I read it over carefully, my eye catching on one part, a couple of sentences, under "Effects." When I was through, I put the report back in the envelope and returned it to the table.

Eberhardt looked at me then. "Well?"

"One item," I said, "that wasn't in the papers."

"What's that?"

"They found a pint of Kesslers in a paper bag in Colly's coat pocket."

Eberhardt shrugged. "It was a liquor store, wasn't it? Maybe he slipped it into his pocket on the way out."

"And put it into a paper bag first?"

"People do funny things," he said.

"Yeah," I said. I drank some of the coffee and then got on my feet.

"You leaving already?"

"Uh, huh," I said. "I've got some things to do."

"You owe me a favor," he said. "Remember that."

"I won't forget."

"You and the elephants," he said.

I wedged my car into a downhill parking slot on Chenery Street, a half-block from the three-room flat Lucille and Colly Babcock had called home for the past year. I walked through the rain, feeling the chill of it on my face, and mounted wooden steps to the door. Lucille answered on my first knock.

She wore the same black dress she had worn to my office that morning; I had the idea, looking at her, that she had been sitting in the silence of the empty flat, sitting in one chair, for most of the day.

We exchanged greetings and she let me in. I sat in the old stuffed leather chair by the window: Colly's chair. Lucille said, "Can I get you something?"

I shook my head. "What about you?" I said. "Have you eaten anything today?"

"No," she answered.

"You have to eat, Lucille."

"Maybe later."

"All right," I said. I rotated my hat in my hands, staring at it. I had some things I wanted to ask her, but I did not want to instill any false hopes. I had an idea, but it was only that, and too early.

I made conversation for a while, going over again my talk with Tommy Belknap and my visit to D. E. O'Mira. When I thought I could put it in without arousing her curiosity, I said, "You mentioned this morning that Colly liked to take walks in the evening. Was he in the habit of walking to any particular place, or in any particular direction?"

"No," Lucille said. "He just liked to walk. He was gone for an hour or two sometimes."

"He never mentioned where he'd been?"

"Just that he walked around the neighborhood."

Around the neighborhood, I thought. The alley where Colly Babcock had been shot to death was eleven blocks from this flat on Chenery Street. He could have walked in a straight line, or he could have gone roundabout in any direction.

I said, "Colly liked to have a nightcap when he came back from these walks, is that right?"

"He did, yes."

"He kept a bottle here, then?"

"Yes."

I continued to rotate my hat. "I wonder if I could have a small drink, Lucille."

She nodded slowly and went to a squat wooden cabinet near the kitchen door. She bent, swinging the panel open in the front, looking inside. Then she straightened. "I'm sorry," she said. "We—I seem to be out."

I stood. "It's all right," I said. "I should be going anyway."

"Where will you go now?"

"To see some people," I said.

"You'll let me know, won't you?"

"I will," I said. I paused. "I was wondering if you might have a picture of Colly, Lucille? A snapshot?"

"I think so," she said. She frowned. "Why would you want a picture?"

"It might be that I'll need it," I said vaguely. "I have to see a lot of people."

She seemed satisfied with that. "I'll see if I can find one for you."

I waited while she went into the bedroom. She returned a minute or two later with a black-and-white snap of Colly, head and shoulders, that had been taken in the living room there. He was smiling, one eyebrow raised in mock raffishness.

I put the snap into my pocket and thanked Lucille. Then I went to the door and let myself out.

The skies had parted like the Red Sea. Drops of rain as big as hail pellets lashed the sidewalk. Thunder rumbled in the distance, edging closer. I pulled the collar of my coat tighter around my neck, and made a run for my car.

I came inside Tay's Liquors on Whitney Street and stood dripping water on the floor. They had a heater on a shelf just inside the door, and I allowed myself the luxury of its warmth for a few moments. Then I went to the counter.

A young man wearing a white shirt with a green garter on one sleeve got up from a stool near the cash register and walked down to me. He showed teeth. "Kind of wet out there," he said.

No, I thought, it's warm as toast. But I said, "Maybe you can help me."

"Sure," he said. "Name your poison."

He was brimming with originality. I took the snapshot of Colly Babcock from my pocket and extended it across the counter. "Have you ever seen this man before?"

He looked at me. "Cop?" he asked, but his voice was still amicable.

I sighed, and showed him my identification. He shrugged, and then squinted at the picture. His eyes narrowed thoughtfully. "You know," he said, "I might have seen this guy at that."

I did not feel quite as cold as I had when I came in. I had been walking the streets of Glen Park for two and a half hours now. I had been to eight liquor stores, two all-night markets, a delicatessen and six bars that sold off-sale. I had come up with nothing, except possibly a head cold.

The young man was still studying the picture. "Fellow looked like that stopped in here last night," he said. "Nice old bird, too."

"About what time?"

"Eleven-thirty or so."

Fifteen minutes before Colly Babcock had been shot to death in an alley three and a half blocks away. I said, "What did he buy, do you remember?"

"Let's see," the young man said. "Bourbon, I think. Medium price."

"Kesslers?"

"Yeah, I think it was. Kesslers."

"Thanks," I said. "What's your name?"

"Wait a minute," he said. "I don't want to get involved in anything."

"Don't worry," I said. "It's nothing like you're thinking."

A bit reluctantly he gave me his name and his address. I wrote it down in a notebook I carried, thanked him again, and got out of there.

I had something more than an idea now.

Eberhardt said, "I ought to lay one on your chin."

He had just come out of the bedroom, eyes foggy with sleep, hair standing straight up, wearing a wine-colored bathrobe and pajamas. His wife stood beside him.

I held up my hand. "I'm sorry to get you out of bed, Eb," I said. "But this couldn't wait."

He said something which I didn't hear, but which his wife heard. She cracked him lightly on the arm to show her disapproval, and then turned and left the room.

Eberhardt went over and sat on the couch. He finger-combed his hair, and then glared up at me. "What's so damned important?"

"Colly Babcock," I said.

"You don't give up, do you?"

"Sometimes I do," I said. "But not this time. Not now." I told him what I had learned at Tay's Liquors.

He thought about it. "Doesn't prove much," he said finally. "So he bought a bottle there."

"Eb," I said, "if he was planning to hit a liquor store, do you think he would have bothered to *buy* a bottle fifteen minutes before?"

"The job might have been spur-of-the-moment," Eberhardt said.

"Colly didn't work that way. When he was pulling them, they were all carefully planned, well in advance."

"He was getting old," Eberhardt said. "They change."

He was making argument. But he hadn't known Colly. I said, "There are a few other things."

"Such as?"

"The burglaries," I said. "I did some reading up on them. They run in a pattern, Eb. Back door jimmied, marks on the jamb and lock. Hand bar, or something." I paused. "They didn't find any hand bar on Colly."

"Maybe he got rid of it."

"When did he have time? They caught him coming out the door."

Eberhardt wet his lips. I could tell I was getting his interest. "Go ahead," he said.

"The pattern," I said. "Doors jimmied, drawers rifled, papers strewn about. No fingerprints, but it smacks of amateurism, Eb."

He rubbed the beard stubble on his jaw. "And Colly was a professional."

"He could have done the book," I said. "He was neat and precise. He didn't ransack. He always knew exactly what he was after. He never deviated from that, Eb. Not once."

Eberhardt got to his feet and walked to the curtained bay window. He stood there with his back to me. "What do you think, then?"

"You figure it."

He was silent for a time. Then he said very slowly, "I can figure it, all right. But I don't like it. I don't like it at all."

"And Colly?" I said. "Did he like it any better?"

Eberhardt turned abruptly and went to the telephone. He made a call, spoke to someone, and then someone else. When he hung up, he was already unbuttoning his bathrobe.

But at the bedroom door he stopped. "You want to come along?"

"No," I said. "It's not my place."

He looked at me. "I hope you're wrong, you know that."

I met his eyes. "I hope I'm not," I said.

I was sitting in the darkness of my apartment, smoking, when the telephone rang three hours later.

I let it ring a few times, watching the shadows the way I had been, and then I picked up the receiver and said hello.

"You weren't wrong," Eberhardt said.

I let out my breath slowly, waiting.

"Avinisi and Carstairs," Eberhardt said. There was bitterness in his voice. "Each of them on the force a little more than a year. The old story: bills, long hours, not enough pay. They cooked up the idea one night while they were cruising, and tried it out. It worked pretty good; who'd figure the cops for it?"

"I'm sorry, Eb," I said.

"So am I," he answered.

"You have any trouble?"

"Not much."

"What about Colly?"

"It was the other way around," Eberhardt said. "He was cutting through the alley when he saw them coming out the rear door. He turned to run and they panicked. Avinisi got him in the back. When they went to check, Carstairs recognized him from the mug books; they have the rookies reading them through now."

"And they saw a way to get out from under," I said.

"Yeah," Eberhardt said.

"Look, Eb . . ."

"Forget it," he said. "I know what you're going to say."

"You can't help but get a couple of them that way."

"I said to forget it."

"All right. See you, Eb."

"Yeah," he said. "See you." The line went dead.

I listened to the empty buzzing for a time. It's a lousy world, I thought. But sometimes, at least, there is justice.

And then I called Lucille Babcock and told her why her husband had died.

They had a nice funeral for Colly.

They held the services in a small, white nondenominational church on Monterey Boulevard. There were a lot of flowers; roses, mostly, in yellow and red, the way Colly would have liked.

Quite a few people came. Tommy Belknap was there, and Sam

Biehler and Old Man Harlin and the rest of them from D. E. O'Mira. There were faces I didn't know, too; the whole thing had gotten a big play in the papers.

Surprisingly, unless you knew him, Eberhardt was there as well. And, of course, Lucille. She sat very straight on the wooden pew in front of the coffin, next to me, and her eyes were dry. She was some fine woman.

We went to the cemetery afterward, quiet and green with wide-pillared gates in Colma, and listened to the words and watched them put Colly into the ground. When it was done, I offered to drive Lucille home, but she said no, there were some arrangements she wanted to make for gardening and for a headstone with the cemetery people, and that they would see to it that she got home all right.

I rode alone with the driver of the big, black hearse back to the church on Monterey Boulevard. Eberhardt was waiting there with his car. I walked over to him.

"I don't like funerals," he said.

"No," I said.

"What are you going to do now?"

"I hadn't thought about it."

"Come on up to my place. My wife's gone off to visit her sister, and I've got some brandy there. Maybe we'll get drunk."

I got in beside him. "Maybe we will at that," I said.

Only
So Much
to Reveal

Joan Richter

When the police left—the two who had come from Nairobi by car
and the two Africans who had walked over from the police station
across the river—Matua locked up the main house and went to his
quarters behind the line of pepper trees. He added a few more pieces
of charcoal to the cook fire which had burned low during his absence, fanned it into a new flame, and put the pot of meat and beans
back to cook again. Then he sat down on the stone steps to think.

Overhead the sky was a clear blue, with puffs of high white clouds.
If he raised his eyes he might see the tops of the flame trees that grew
down by the river, their scarlet blooms and broad green leaves ob-
scuring the orange tile roof of the local police station just beyond.

Black or white, the police were the same, swollen by the authority
their uniforms gave them into thinking they were bigger men than
they really were. His friend Tano was no different. Since Tano had
become a policeman there was no kindness in him, none of the old
good-natured laughter. Only when his heavy boots were undone and
set aside, and a freshly brewed bowlful of *pombe* began to gurgle in
his stomach and flow in his veins, did Tano's face soften, his lips curl,
and laughter fill his mouth. But still not in the old way.

Today Tano had not come as a friend. Like the other three with
him, he had come as the police, with his boots on. One lunge of a
boot and a man would fall to his knees. Matua had seen it happen

339

many times. And always it made the last meal he had eaten fight in his stomach.

The first time was in his village many years ago when he and Tano were boys. The police were all white men then and they came in their boots and uniforms, with their truncheons swinging at their sides. They were looking for a man. Matua could no longer remember of what crime the man had been accused, but he remembered how he and Tano had watched from the shadows of one of the huts as the man was found, kicked, beaten, and finally dragged away.

Matua shook off the recollection and leaned back against the stone of the step, sighing. Things had changed, but not in the way he had dreamed of. Independence had come and now Africans wore police uniforms side by side with Europeans. Tano was one of them. It bothered Matua more to see an African kick an African.

Yet today there had been a timidity about Tano that surprised him. It was the same with the other man who had come from the station house across the river, but Matua's quick mind found an explanation. The two black men were ill at ease in front of the big red-haired Englishman from Nairobi whose uniform was more elaborate than theirs and who had arrived by car with an Indian policeman as his driver. The Englishman's face was puffy and discolored, with streaks of purple in his cheeks. Rusty brows frowned over hard blue eyes and a bushy mustache twitched about his wet mouth like the tassels on a ripe ear of maize. The Indian wore a starched Sikh turban instead of the regulation hat and stared at Matua with bright hard eyes, but he too was silent as the questioning began.

"When was the last time you saw the Bwana alive?" the Englishman asked.

Matua opened his mouth but did not speak. Long ago he had learned it did not serve an African of his station to acknowledge how well he understood the white man's language. Feigned ignorance allowed one to say less and learn more. His silence was rewarded. The question was repeated, as he had hoped, in Swahili.

"After dinner," he answered. "The Bwana said he did not want anything else, so I went to my room to sleep. It was no later than nine o'clock."

"What noises did you hear during the night?"

Had he heard something? Some small cry? Or perhaps even a

scream. How could he be sure? It might have been a tree toad or an owl or the wild screech of a civet cat thwarted in its search of prey. Perhaps what he had heard had been only the sound of his own snoring. But his answer to the red-haired European showed none of his uncertainty. "I heard nothing," he said.

"Nothing!" The mustache twitched, the bloodshot cheeks reddened. "How could you not hear some sound? Look at this!" They were in the sitting room then where kapok lay in heaps on the floor and clung in clumps to the sisal rug that Matua had brushed and swept only yesterday. A white powder clouded the border of polished wood. Every seat had been slashed, every piece of furniture overturned and ripped apart. In the bedroom it was the same—the mattress in pieces, the pillows in shreds, feathers lying like fallen leaves around the room, as in a henhouse after a cockfight.

"My house is behind the trees." Matua pointed out the window. "It was very cold last night." It was true—he had even wished for another blanket. "My window was shut. I heard nothing."

The Indian turned to the Englishman, his head and turban moving as one plastered unit, his sallow face sly. "They sleep and it is as good as dead. But I think this one lies."

Matua gave no sign that he understood the English-spoken aside, but an old anger leaped in his stomach. It was eased a little when he saw the look that Tano gave the Indian. In it was his own hidden hatred, and once again he felt united with his friend, because together they were seeing in that sallow face the countenance of all the Indians at whose shop counters they had been cheated and abused.

Long ago the British had brought Indian laborers to East Africa—hundreds of them, and their families—to work on the railway. A few returned to their homeland, but the others settled along the coast of East Africa and inland. They became shopkeepers and merchants and gained control of all the commerce and trade in East Africa. In small villages and towns the Indian *duka* was the only shop. In large communities *dukas* were side by side, connected like beads on a string by hidden passageways, where prices were set and word was passed when an African buyer appeared. If the price in one shop seemed too high it did no good to go to the one next door. The price was fixed and inflated, down the line, for everything—rice, tea, sugar, cloth, thread, a single needle. It is easy to learn to hate a man who will give you only half the amount of rice your money should buy, when half is not enough to feed your family, and the coin in your hand is all the money you have.

The British policeman scowled at the Indian's comment, but made no reply. Matua had learned early there was no love between them either. The policeman turned to Matua and continued his questioning.

"When did you return to the house?"

"At six-thirty this morning."

"Is that your usual time?"

"Yes."

"But you did not ring up the police station until fifteen minutes after seven. Is that correct?"

"It is correct."

"Why did you not call immediately? What were you doing from six-thirty to seven-fifteen?"

"I was making scones."

The mustache twitched and the words that came from the moist lips were punctuated with spittle. "What are you talking about? Scones! Your master had been murdered!"

"I did not know the Bwana was dead. I did not go into the bedroom right away."

"Why not? Did not this mess tell you something was wrong?"

Matua shook his head.

The Indian took a step forward. "Do not shake your head! Speak!" The Swahili command was an explosion of garlic breath in Matua's face. "You are taking time to think up some lies!"

Matua swallowed but looked straight into the Indian's small black eyes. "I do not know what you mean by lies. It is I who called the police." Matua glanced at Tano to see if he would support his statement, but Tano was staring straight ahead. The Englishman spoke, angrily, "I want to know when you discovered the Bwana was dead!"

"It was six-thirty when I came into the house, by the kitchen door. Always I go to the sitting room to open the curtains, but this morning with the scones to make I did not go. I would do it later, while the scones were in the oven, after I had brought the Bwana his first cup of tea.

"It was seven o'clock when I took the tea tray down the hall to the bedroom. The door was closed. I knocked and went in. It was dark and I set the tray down on the small table inside the door and went to open the blinds. I stumbled over something lying on the floor. 'Bwana,' I called, but there was no answer. I backed away and turned on the light. The Bwana was lying on the floor dead."

"How did you know he was dead? Did you touch him?"

Matua frowned. "He did not need touching for me to know. There were many wounds and much blood. He was dead."

"When did you call the police?"

"Then." The answer was almost the truth. There was no need for him to say that he had run from the house first, to his own room, that he had sat on the edge of the bed shivering with terror and wondering what he should do, that he had even thought of running away.

But why should he run? He had done nothing. Where would he go? His village was far away and he did not have enough money for the bus fare. And what of the tea tray he had left in the Bwana's bedroom? And the scones still baking in the oven? He could not leave without cleaning the kitchen, or when the police came—and he knew they would come sometime—they would know he had been in the house and had run away. They would think he was the one who had killed the Bwana and they would come after him to his village. They would track him down as though he were nothing more than a wild pig.

Matua had covered his face with his hands, had tried to shut out the pictures forming in his mind of his children clinging to one another in the shadow of their hut, of his wife standing with the other women, watching as he was beaten and dragged away. It had not been the sight of the dead Bwana that had filled him with terror, but of the *panga*, lying next to him, its broad blade caked with dried earth and newly clotted with blood.

"I telephoned the police station where my friend Tano works. Tano was not there, but the others came. They took the body away and told me not to clean the room. Now you are here." He did not have to tell anyone about how he had almost run away. There is only so much that a man has to reveal of himself to other men.

"And the *panga*? Where is that?"

"They took the *panga* when they took the Bwana." He thought again of the knife as it had lain beside the dead body. Every African owned a *panga*, sometimes two. They were protection in the forest, a hoe in the field, an ax for splitting bamboo or chopping firewood, a knife to cut a pawpaw in half and scrape out the seeds. All alike, with their solid wooden handles and broad blades, they could be bought at an Indian *duka* for fifteen shillings each. One was hardly recognizable from another. But a man knew his own *panga*, just as a man knew his own woman.

"The *panga* was mine," Matua said, and saw the Englishman lift his head and look at him. The Indian looked too, and so did Tano and the African policeman beside him. "I had worked in my *shamba* yesterday, hoeing beans. When I was done I left my *panga* standing outside the door to my room, with the earth still on it. It was there when I went to sleep last night, but it was gone this morning. I would like to have my *panga* back when the police are through with it."

"Of all the bloody nerve!" the Indian exclaimed. "He'd like to have his *panga* back!"

The African policeman beside Tano stepped forward and spoke for the first time. Matua did not know his name, but he had seen him with Tano once in a while in town. "A *panga* costs fifteen shillings. It is Matua's right to have it back."

"It's a murder weapon, you idiot!" the Indian shouted.

"What will be done with it when the investigation is over?" Tano asked quietly.

"How should I know," the Indian said.

"You know." Tano's voice was louder now. "You will take it! And then you will sell it to someone for *more* than fifteen shillings. The *panga* is Matua's. It will be returned to him."

The hate that gleamed in Tano's eyes warmed Matua. Once more they were boys together.

"Enough of that," the Englishman commanded and turned his attention to Matua. "You heard no one come to your house last night?"

"I heard nothing."

"What was the murderer looking for?"

Matua frowned, not certain that he understood. "I do not know what you mean."

"The murderer was looking for something. Why else would he have done all this?" The Englishman nodded at the ruined furniture.

"I do not know. Perhaps it was money."

"But didn't the Bwana keep his money in the bedroom safe?"

"Yes, but I do not think there was very much money there. It is the end of the month now and the Bwana always went to the bank on the first day."

"Whatever was there is gone," the Englishman said.

"The Bwana said it was not a very good safe. That is why he did not keep much money."

"What did he keep in the house?"

Again Matua frowned. "I do not understand."

"The murderer wanted more than what he found in the safe. He tore up this whole bloody place to find it. What was it? What was he looking for?"

Matua shook his head. "I do not know."

The questioning went on for a while longer and then suddenly it ended. Matua was glad, because there was no more to be said. The Englishman told him to clean up the house. The landlord had been informed of his tenant's death and already had someone interested in renting the house. They would be coming from Nairobi tomorrow.

Matua rose from the step and went to look at his cook fire. He had begun to smell the sweet odor of the beans and meat cooking together and he realized he was hungry. He was thinking how good it would be to have someone to share his meal with when he heard a footstep along the path on the other side of the pepper trees. He was not certain whether it was real or his imagination. And then all at once his breath froze in his chest. Not until that instant did he realize that if the murderer had not found what he was looking for, he might come back.

"*Jambo*," came a greeting through the trees.

"*Jambo*," Matua replied, his heart beating like a trapped bird in his chest.

"*Habari gani*, how are things?"

Matua felt his heart quiet. He recognized the voice. "Ah, Tano. You have smelled my meat and beans even from across the river."

They sat on the steps and ate with their fingers, dipping balls of cooked cornmeal into the stew. They spoke of unimportant things at first and then Matua asked, "What do the police think about the Bwana's murder? Do they know who did it?"

"A robber."

"A robber? But who?"

"How can they know who? He did not leave his name."

Matua frowned. He did not like Tano's joke. "But the police are clever. They have ways of finding things out."

"What things? What can be found out in the house? Have you discovered something?"

Matua shook his head. "I have discovered nothing. I only think it strange that the Bwana was killed with my *panga*, but that another knife was used to do the rest."

"And how do you know that?"

"The blood would have been gone from my *panga*, so would the earth left from my bean patch, if it had been used to open up the mattress and to rip the cushions."

Tano looked at him strangely, his eyes narrowing. "And what do you think is the meaning of that?"

Matua shook his head. "I do not know. Perhaps the murderer is someone not comfortable using a *panga* for very long. What was done to the furniture took a long time."

Tano frowned. "That is a good thought, Matua. I am sure the English policeman from Nairobi did not think of it. Tell me, though, why did you tell him the *panga* was yours? You do not need the fifteen shillings that much."

Matua looked up from the bowl. "Why should I let the Indian have it?"

Tano shrugged. "But that is not why you spoke of it."

"It is better I tell the police it is my *panga* than if they find out later. There would be trouble."

"How could they find out? One *panga* is like any other."

"There are differences. And the police are clever." Matua paused, realizing he had been talking about the police as if Tano were not one of them. "Besides, it is easier to tell the truth than it is to lie. A lie can be forgotten. But the truth never."

Tano laughed and sucked the juice of the meat off his fingers. "Why then did you not tell the truth about what the murderer was looking for?"

Matua raised his head, startled. "What do you mean?"

"You have said it is easier to speak the truth than it is to lie. So why lie to me, your old friend?"

"I do not know what you are talking about, Tano."

"A long time ago when you first came to work for the Bwana, when the Memsab was still alive, you told me they showed you diamonds—diamonds the Bwana had taken from the Congo which, if they were found, would put him in jail. That is why they had to be kept in the house, carefully hidden. But where, Matua? Where did the Bwana hide the diamonds?"

Diamonds. Matua heard Tano say the word again and thought to himself what a fool he had been to have forgotten. Too late he saw that Tano had caught the look of recollection in his face.

"Now you remember!"

"I have not thought of them for many years."

"Well, think of them now. Where are they?"

Matua frowned—only a fool or an old man could forget something he once knew. Why is it that I cannot remember? The Memsab once spoke of them to me, and so did the Bwana. They said that some day if the coffee crop failed there would be the diamonds. But it is not the kind of thing for a European to tell a servant. Why was it I had to know? And why was I such a fool to boast about it to Tano? But that was long ago before Tano wore the uniform of a policeman.

"Come, Matua. We are old friends. Tell me where the diamonds are."

"I do not know where they are." Matua spoke with impatience, looking straight into Tano's eyes. Then he reached for the empty bowl and took it to the outside faucet to rinse it clean. "I must go back to the house now. There is much to do, with new people coming tomorrow."

Tano rose. "I will help you. Perhaps while you clean you will begin to remember. Perhaps together we can find them. Lend me one of your shirts, Matua. I cannot return to the police station looking like a houseboy."

Matua looked at the starched uniform and the polished black boots and at the new gold watch that gleamed on Tano's wrist. He did not think the job of a policeman paid so well. Without a word he went into his room to get Tano the shirt he had asked for. He wanted Tano to go, to leave him to his cleaning, but he would not say this because Tano would think he wanted to be left alone so he could find the diamonds. And in a way that was so, but not for the reason Tano would think. Just as clothes were in the closet, meat was in the refrigerator, and money was in the safe, the diamonds too were somewhere. But they were not his, so he had not thought of them. What would he do with a handful of diamonds? What good had they done the Bwana?

While Matua swept and dusted and carried the stuffings of furniture out to a rubbish pile in the garden, Tano examined the furniture, probing into corners with a shiny knife he had taken from his trouser pocket.

Once Matua called to him. "Help me with this rug, Tano. I cannot clean it in here. I must put it outside on the line and beat it."

With a flick of his wrist Tano sent the bright knife into the wooden arm of a chair where it landed upright and quivering. Matua pretended not to notice. Since he had become a policeman a *panga* was not good enough for Tano. But what good was a small knife like that? It could not hoe, nor could it chop down a bamboo tree. Matua bent over the rolled-up rug while Tano took his end.

"The safe in the bedroom—" Tano started to say as they heaved the large rug over the wire line outside the kitchen door. "Why did the Bwana not keep the diamonds there?"

"The safe was not strong." Matua squinted against the sun slanting through the curtain of pepper-tree leaves and looked over the rug barrier between them. How could Tano be so sure the murderer had not finally found what he had been looking for?

They went back into the house and with the rug out of the way it was easier to clean the sitting room. Tano helped him carry some of the broken furniture out onto the veranda and stack it in a corner. They took the mattress to the rubbish pile. Then Matua put on his sheepskin footpads and began skating over the wooden floors, rubbing in the coconut oil that made the wide boards gleam.

"I am thirsty after all this work," Tano said as he came upon the cupboard where the Bwana kept his whiskey. "Let us have a drink."

Matua shook his head. He liked *pombe*, the African beer of his village, but he had no taste for the white man's whiskey.

"What is this?" Tano held up a small green bottle. "I have not seen this kind of whiskey before."

Matua looked across the room at the bottle Tano was examining. "It is not whiskey. It is something called ginger ale, to be mixed with whiskey. When the Memsab was alive that is what she and the Bwana would drink, with a little ice. But afterwards the Bwana did not want anything but whiskey."

"Fix me a drink, Matua. A drink like the Bwana used to have. Pretend I am the Bwana of the house now and you are my servant."

Matua looked at him. "I will fix you one drink. And then you will go. You are keeping me from my work. There is more to clean if new people are coming tomorrow. Perhaps if I have the house to their liking they will ask me to stay and work for them." He took the bottle of ginger ale and the whiskey from Tano and started toward the kitchen.

Tano called after him. "I will have my drink and I will stay while you clean the rest of the house. I am not satisfied that you do not know where the diamonds are."

Matua turned around. "I have told you I do not know. The Memsab and the Bwana spoke of them once, a long time ago. And never again. What good would they do you anyhow?"

"Diamonds are worth a lot of money, Matua."

"Who would give you money for them?"

"Merchants in the bazaar."

"Indians."

Tano shrugged. "If I have diamonds and I want money for them, I must go to who has money and who wants diamonds. Yes, Indians."

Matua shook his head. "They would cheat you and then they would report you to the police."

Tano threw his head back and laughed. "You forget, Matua. I am the police."

Matua smiled sadly. "Yes, sometimes I do forget." He turned then and went into the kitchen and took two tall glasses from a side cupboard. It was automatic. Whiskey and ginger ale belonged in two tall glasses. One for the Memsab and one for the Bwana. But that was a long time ago. He put one glass back on the shelf and went into the pantry to the refrigerator for some ice.

He reached for the small tray on the right. That, too, was automatic. Always the tray on the right. Why never the other? He stood for a moment staring into the open coldness and felt a small smile move on his lips. He reached for the tray on the left and carried both trays into the kitchen and put them on the counter near the sink. The refrigerator would need cleaning too.

Tano was leaning in the doorway, fingering the blade of his small knife, watching Matua thoughtfully. "What you have said about the Indian merchant is true. If *you* would go to him with the diamonds he would report *you* to the police, but he would not tell them you had brought him many diamonds—only one or two. But one or two would be enough to put you in jail for a long time. And the Indian would have all the rest."

"Why do you say this to me?"

"Because I want you to know that without me to help you with the diamonds they will do you no good."

"And what makes you think that with your help they would do me good? What good did they do the Bwana? I do not need your advice, Tano."

"And what do you mean by that?"

"I mean that if I knew where the diamonds were I would not touch them. And if they came into my hands I would get rid of them."

"You are either a fool or a liar!"

"Perhaps a fool, Tano, but I do not lie. Now here is your drink." Two ice cubes tinkled against the glass as he held it out.

Tano took it from him with his left hand, but his right hand shot forward, pointing the knife. "If I learn someday that you have lied to me, Matua, that the diamonds are already yours—"

Matua stared into the eyes of the man, who as a boy had been his friend, and then looked deliberately at the clean blade of the knife in his hand. He was not afraid. Tano would not hurt him. Two murders in the same house would cause the European policeman with the mustache like the tassels on a ripe ear of maize to become suspicious. Perhaps he was suspicious already. Matua had admitted that the *panga* used to kill the Bwana belonged to him, but what of the other knife, the knife that had been used to slash up the furniture. To whom did it belong? The Englishman could not be the fool that Tano thought him to be.

Their glances met over the point of the knife and Matua found himself wondering if the uniform could be blamed for the man. He did not think the Bwana had minded dying. He was not young any more. He had grown old quickly after the Memsab's death. That Tano had killed him was a great misdeed, but that he had used an old friend's *panga* was the greater misdeed.

Tano raised the glass to his lips and took a long swallow. "It is good. Why do you not have one?"

Matua shook his head. "I have work to do," he said and turned to the sink. He emptied the two trays of ice cubes there and let water pour over the cubes. As they became small he got rid of them by sweeping them down the drain with his hands. He let the water run as he rinsed the trays and set them aside to dry. Later, after he had cleaned the refrigerator, he would fill the trays with fresh water and put them back in their place. For a while it would still be automatic for him to reach for the tray on the right, never to touch the one on the left. But now he realized that it did not matter any more.

Beside him Tano made a noise as he sucked up the last of his drink and then tossed the ice cubes into the sink.

Matua turned his head away as he reached for the faucet to flush down the last two cubes. He smiled to himself. It had been a good hiding place.

Who's Got the Lady?

Jack Ritchie

Bernice Lecour moved the enlarged color photograph of the "Patrician Lady" a bit closer to her easel. "That enigmatic smile. The Eternal Mysterious Woman."

"Frankly," I said, "I think she's simpering."

Bernice shrugged. "Perhaps. I understand that they had awful teeth in those days and didn't dare grin from ear to ear like our modern beauty queens."

I glanced at my watch. "I have an appointment at Customs and after that I'll drop in at Zarchetti's and steal the rubber stamp."

"Wouldn't it be simpler just to go to some shop and have a duplicate made?"

"Simpler, yes. But I want the imprint to be absolutely authentic under a microscope. The police will undoubtedly visit Zarchetti looking for one particular stamp and I want them to find it."

Bernice picked up a magnifying glass, studied a corner of her almost completed copy of the "Patrician Lady," and then carefully applied another stroke of amber. "Have you ever stolen anything before?"

"Only the X-rays."

And that had occurred in Paris three weeks ago. I had been alone with Monsieur André Arnaud in his office completing arrangements for the American exhibition of the "Patrician Lady" when he had been called out of the room.

He had been absent a considerable time and I had found myself wandering idly about, examining this and that, and eventually opening a filing cabinet. It was there that I found the X-rays of the "Patrician Lady."

I had been mildly startled that they were not under lock and key, but upon further reflection I realized that while the "Patrician Lady" herself might be worth a few million dollars, her X-rays were intrinsically of little value. They were probably not even referred to more than once every two or three years.

No one would possibly want to steal them.

But then I had pondered upon Bernice's enormous talent as a copyist and the fact that we would both be a great deal happier with a large sum of money, and it was at that moment that my plan was born and very rapidly outgrew its swaddling clothes.

I slipped the X-rays under my coat and when Arnaud reappeared I was all innocence and admiring a Rubens sketch upon the wall.

And now Bernice darkened a dab of sienna on her palette. "During his lifetime, the master painted eighty-seven portraits—one hundred and twelve of which are in the United States." She surveyed her work and sighed. "If I had lived in his time and been a man, I too would have become immortal."

"I prefer you mortal and in this form," I said. I looked at my watch again. "I'm afraid I'll have to go now, Bernice. My appointment with Amos Pulver is at three."

She lifted her eyes momentarily from the canvas. "About the Renoir?"

"Yes."

"What have you decided?"

"It's authentic."

She grinned. "What did you do? Flip a coin?"

I kissed her. "Goodbye, Bernice."

I arrived at the Amos Pulver townhouse a few minutes before three. The others were already there—Louis Kendall, of the Oaks Galleries, and Walter Jameson, who fancied himself an authority on Renoir.

Two months previously Pulver had purchased a Renoir—or what purported to be a Renoir—at the annual Hollingwood auction. The price had been forty thousand and Pulver had been satisfied—until last week when he had read a magazine article concerning art forgeries while in his dentist's waiting room.

Pulver had immediately assembled the three of us to pass on the authenticity of the painting and we had each had the canvas for several days of study.

Now Pulver bit the tip off a cigar and surveyed us. "Well?"

Louis Kendall spoke first. "In my opinion your painting is a forgery."

Jameson regarded Kendall coldly. "You are mistaken. The painting is an original Renoir. There is no question about it."

Amos Pulver turned to me. "What's your verdict?"

I considered a moment and then said, "Your Renoir is absolutely authentic."

"Ridiculous," Kendall snapped. "Any fool can see that the canvas is simply a pathetic attempt to imitate the Renoir dry style."

Walter Jameson raised his favorite eyebrow. "What do *you* know about Renoir's dry style. I've written six articles on that alone."

Amos Pulver waved a hand. "The hell with his dry style. All I wanted was an official vote and I got that." He removed three checks from his wallet and passed them out. "But I still wish the vote would have been unanimous."

Pulver let Kendall and Jameson leave, but he detained me.

He mixed two bourbons and sodas. "I don't know a damn thing about paintings and couldn't care less. But everybody I know is collecting and I don't want to be left out in the cold with nothing to talk about."

He handed me my glass. "Tell me, do you experts really know what you're doing when you look over a painting?"

"Your bourbon is excellent," I said.

Pulver sipped from his glass. "I read that the "Patrician Lady" is being shipped here for exhibition in the Vandersteen Memorial Wing of The National Art Center."

"A cultural exchange," I said. "France allows us to view her pictures and we are allowed to admire them."

"This one's worth a few million," he said with a touch of reverence. "The greatest painting in the world."

"Yes," I said. "It would appear so."

"I hear they're taking a lot of precautions? Since you're the Vandersteen Wing curator you must be well informed as to that."

I nodded. "The painting is being transferred by ship. It will be inside a specially constructed case—insulated, cushioned, and air-conditioned."

"I mean they're really guarding it. I hear that at least four armed guards are with it twenty-four hours a day. I understand that when it gets here there will even be a marine guard."

"With loaded rifles," I said. "Two of them will be stationed beside the painting at all times when it is on exhibition."

He admired the security of the operation. "I'll bet a thing like that is impossible to steal."

"Virtually impossible," I said. "And if things go well, the American public will next see 'Winkler's Brother.' "

Pulver thought about something else. "When the 'Patrician Lady' gets here, will there be a regular parade down the Avenue? I heard something about drum and bugle corps, baton twirlers, and maybe a couple of Shriner marching bands."

"I'm sorry," I said. "At the last moment some spoilsport canceled those arrangements."

He brightened a bit. "Well, anyway there will be quite a big ceremony at the Center, won't there? The governor's going to speak?"

"He will attempt to. But I'm afraid the acoustics are terrible."

When I left, I stopped at the first public phone booth and called Hollingwood. "You won't have to give Pulver his money back. The vote was two to one."

"Good," Hollingwood said. "But I was positive it was an original anyway. I'd stake my reputation on that."

"Nevertheless," I reminded him, "you did take precautions."

"I know," he said. "You'll get your check in the morning."

I took the subway to Zarchetti's Art Supply Shop. In the third floor storeroom I chatted idly with one of the clerks—as is often my habit —while he uncrated newly arrived supplies.

Zarchetti marks his goods in two ways—most of them with an ordinary paper label imprinted with his name, his address, and the inked price of the item. However, on certain other objects—raw canvases, for instance—he uses a common rubber stamp wetted with indelible ink.

He once explained to me that art students, being what they are, often remove labels from the cheaper canvases and paste them over the labels of the more expensive ones—thereby escaping past unlearned clerks with treasures worth five times their purchased price.

I watched the clerk consult his price list, adjust the wheels of a stamp, and affix the marking to a canvas—*Zarchetti's Art Supplies. 218 Lincoln Avenue. $10.98.*

There were at least half a dozen similar stamps lying about on the tables and I found the opportunity of slipping one of them into my pocket. I doubted if it would ever be missed.

That evening after dinner I read that Bernice had just received second prize of $1,000 for one of her paintings at the Raleigh Exhibition. It had been for a canvas entitled "Scylla Fourteen." According to the newspaper article, it consisted of a canvas painted a solid primary blue with just a hair's brush of orange in one corner. It impressed one of the judges as "A bold venture into the fastness of the unknown—the firm vertical strokes exemplifying the inexorability of the exploding universe. And yet there remains the contradictory, the insistent, unrhymeable orange to contribute a human shriek against the inflexible mathematics of existence." I read that twice.

At eight-thirty, I took a taxi to the National Art Center, let myself in, and went to my office. I unlocked the large bottom drawer of my desk and removed the zipper bag with my tools and materials. At one of the janitor closets in the hall, I picked up a ladder and carried it with me to the Vandersteen Wing. Its large east gallery, like the rest of the building, was closed to the public at five.

It had been selected for the exhibition of the "Patrician Lady" and for the occasion all other paintings had been removed. The room had been thoroughly redecorated and painted, and during the process I had taken the pains to secure one of the buckets of wall paint the workmen had used.

The painting was to be hung in a small alcove at the far end—a recess approximately twelve feet wide and four feet deep. Attached to the ceiling at its entrance was a flexible metal lattice, now rolled up somewhat like a window shade. During the hours when the painting was not on exhibition, the device would be lowered and locked to the floor, thereby securely shutting off the "Patrician Lady" from the rest of the room. In addition to that, two armed marines and sundry French and American security agents would be stationed at all times just outside the alcove.

I examined my work of the previous evenings and again verified that all of it was undetectable to the eye.

Within the alcove itself, to one side, I had drilled a series of holes in a four-foot circle, installed powder charges, and primed them. I had further chiseled a groove from the circle to the ceiling. My wiring extended up this groove to the ornate molding and followed behind it to the rear of the room and down again to the dry cell batteries and to one of the three push-buttons I had installed behind a heavy, almost immovable, settee.

Using patching plaster to cover the grooves and holes and applying new paint to new paint had concealed my work entirely. I had followed a similar procedure with the installation of the smoke bombs and the charge placed at the metal shutter above the alcove.

So far I had installed two smoke bombs directly inside the alcove, two in the ventilator system, and one in the wall midway down the room. I thought that one more directly opposite the latter would be sufficient for my purposes.

There was little if any danger that Fred, the night guard, would hear me at work. I had ascertained that he made but one inspection trip every three hours and then retired to the couch in his cubbyhole in the basement. He there set his alarm for the next round and promptly relapsed into a deep and unshatterable sleep. It was a routine for which he should have been fired, but for the present I found his habits convenient.

I put on my rubber gloves, picked up my chisel and rubber mallet, and went to work. When I finished the opening it was approximately five inches deep and four in diameter. I inserted the last smoke bomb and the small explosive charge. When I pressed one of my pushbuttons the charge would shatter the plaster immediately in front of the bomb, allowing the smoke to pour into the room.

I wired by contrivance, created the channel to the ceiling molding, and was in the process of splicing to one of my main circuits when I heard the soft voice behind me.

"How are you doing?"

I very nearly fell off the ladder.

However I recovered and turned. "Bernice, *must* you do that?"

She grinned. "I just came to see if you were done."

"How did you manage to get into the building?"

"Darling, you forget that our keys are common property."

I finished the splicing and descended the ladder. "By the way, Bernice, you've been keeping a little secret from me. I had to read that you took second prize at the Raleigh Exhibition. How did you manage to find the title 'Scylla Fourteen?' "

She flushed faintly. "I opened the dictionary twice at random. It's the only intellectual way to do things these days."

I began mixing my patching plaster. "Truly a fine painting, Bernice. A bold venture into the fastness of the unknown—the firm vertical strokes exemplifying the inexorability of the exploding universe. And yet there remains the contradictory, the insistent, unrhymeable orange to contribute a—"

"Oh, shut up," Bernice said.

I finished my plastering and cover painting and removed my gloves. "Everything is quite ready now, Bernice. While the governor is speaking, I shall wander casually through the crowd to that green settee and reach behind it.

"When I press the first button, there will be a small sharp explosion. This will destroy the mechanism holding up the metal gate and it will roll down, isolating the 'Patrician Lady' from everyone in the room, including the two marine guards.

"When I have seen that accomplished—perhaps a second or two later—I will press the second button. This will immediately activate my six smoke bombs. And when the room is sufficiently dense with smoke and confusion, I will press the third button. This will blast open a hole in the alcove—an opening large enough for a man or a woman to crawl through. While carrying a painting, of course."

Bernice nodded approvingly. "And the hole leads to the storage room behind the alcove and the window to the alley will be open?"

"Exactly."

She became thoughtful. "Do you have to wait for the ceremony and all those people to be present? Wouldn't it be much easier if just a few of you were here? The French officials and the guards?"

"No, Bernice. In that event there exists the possibility that the entire incident might be hushed up. And for our purposes we want as much publicity as possible."

"Do you suppose they will suspect that you had anything to do with it?"

"I rather doubt it. If they *dare* to admit any suspicion, it will probably be directed toward the workmen who have been cluttering up the place the last few weeks."

I looked down the long room to the alcove and smiled. "Bernice, one of the advantages of being the curator of an art museum is knowing the collectors with money—and how much the unscrupulous ones will pay for what they want."

The "Patrician Lady" arrived by armored car the next afternoon. Her escort consisted of half a dozen automobiles containing uniformed police, plain-clothes men, French and American secret servicemen, and the delegation of French officials led by Monsieur Arnaud.

Two squads of United States marines followed closely in a two-and-a-half-ton truck.

After a brief exchange of introductions and handclasps, the entire entourage marched to the east gallery of the Vandersteen Wing.

The crate containing the "Patrician Lady" was there disassembled and she was presented to view.

A sheet of unbreakable glass protected her from crown to spleen. It was my opinion that once she was mounted in the alcove, the thousands who viewed her would see little more than the ornate frame and the glare of glass. However they would all probably depart satisfied, having seen the emperor's clothes.

Arnaud and two of his assistants carried her carefully into the alcove and presently she was in place. Two of the marines immediately took parade rest positions just outside the recess.

I slipped the rubber stamp out of my pocket and concealed it in the palm of my hand. "Excuse me, gentlemen, I believe the 'Patrician Lady' is a fraction of an inch off horizontal."

When I grasped the painting, my fingertips pressed the stamp firmly on the backing of the portrait. I was certain no one had seen what I had done.

I stepped back. "There. Now everything is perfect."

Later that afternoon I managed to slip away to Zarchetti's for a moment and return the stamp. I did not think it had been missed.

At seven-thirty in the evening the Vandersteen Wing was filled to overflowing with selected first-nighters, all of whom gazed reverently in the direction of the alcove. They were not as yet allowed to approach closer than twenty feet.

The governor arrived at eight and mounted the small platform set up before the alcove. There were any number of introductions and credits—apparently anyone who had touched the "Patrician

Lady" 's crate demanded his moment of recognition. Even I, as curator of the gallery, was required to deliver a quota of words.

When I finished I left the crowded platform to make room for the mayor and his introduction of the governor.

I made my way slowly through the assemblage to the rear of the room. I put on my gloves, stood next to the green settee, and my fingertips hovered near the push-buttons.

At five minutes after nine, the governor finally rose and smiled at the audience.

The moment was appropriate. Everyone's attention focused upon him.

I pressed the first button.

The report from the top of the alcove—much like a rifle shot in close quarters—followed immediately. The heavy mesh roll clanged down its full length to the floor, instantly separating the "Patrician Lady" from every person in the room.

The marines were startled out of their parade rest and apparently the governor's initial thought was one of assassination. His hand instinctively explored his chest for hints of a cavity.

I pressed the second button.

The noise of the six explosions were minutely staggered by the echoes against the walls and my smoke bombs spewed forth their grayish-white vapor.

Within a matter of moments complete confusion and the lack of visibility reigned.

I pressed the third button.

The explosion this time was considerably louder as it created the hole in the alcove.

I felt my way blindly into the adjoining room—more or less flowing with the general exodus.

The air here was almost clear and I watched with interest as men in various uniforms dashed in for a breath of fresh air and then back into the east gallery. Most of them had drawn revolvers.

The governor was one of the last to leave the east gallery, possibly because he had the farthest to travel. But I did not see the marines. Apparently they remained true to their posts and I could not escape a sense of national pride at their indomitability and staying power.

Eventually I heard the tinkling of glass as windows in the east gallery were smashed and the smoke bombs tossed into the alley.

After half an hour the smoke in the big room had dispelled sufficiently so that I could reeenter. Several dozen guards and officials were gathered at the iron grate, either peering through its lattice work or attempting by brute force to raise it. Evidently it had jammed.

I also noticed several uniformed policemen inside the alcove. Apparently they had entered via the storage room and the hole my explosion had created.

A Lieutenant Nelson of the Metropolitan Police organized the strong backs and after mighty groans of exertion the gate was finally raised approximately four feet.

We stooped and entered the alcove.

The "Patrician Lady" appeared unharmed, if a bit askew.

Arnaud's hands fluttered anxiously. "She is unharmed. I *think* she is unharmed."

Lieutenant Nelson pointed to the hole in the wall. "The way I figure it is that the one who was supposed to steal the painting crawled through there right after the last explosion. But either he lost his nerve, or the smoke got too much for him, so he just backed right out again and left by the open window in the next room."

Arnaud removed the painting carefully from the wall and examined it.

"Let me take a look at her," I said.

He clutched the "Patrician Lady" to his chest. "Monsieur, she is *mine*."

"Sir," I said sternly. "*I* am the curator of this gallery and you are on American soil."

It was with great reluctance that he allowed me to remove the painting from his hands.

I examined the front of the painting and then turned it over. I stared at the backing and then closed my eyes. *Oh, no!*

Quickly I turned the painting back over and attempted to rehang the *Patrician Lady*. "There is absolutely nothing wrong with her, gentlemen. *Absolutely* nothing."

But Arnaud snatched away the "Patrician Lady." He peered at the backing too—as did everyone else in the alcove.

They all saw the blue-inked stamping, but it was Lieutenant Nelson who had the nerve to read the words aloud. "Zarchetti's Art Supplies. Two-eighteen Lincoln Avenue. Fourteen dollars and ninety-eight cents."

He rubbed his jaw and stared at Arnaud. "Are you people *sure* you shipped the original to this country?"

Arnaud was pale. "Of course we shipped the original." He looked at the stamping again. "I do not understand," he said plaintively.

We all stood silent with thoughts that were probably exemplified when Lieutenant Nelson finally spoke. "Suppose they *switched* paintings while all the commotion was going on and nobody could see?"

None of us said anything and so he continued. "I heard that some of these art forgers are real masters. They can age the paint and the canvas so that *nobody* can tell the difference. Not even an expert." He cogitated further and then brightened. "But like all crooks, they slipped up on a little thing. They missed seeing that Zarchetti label on the backing when they put the whole thing together."

"Don't be ridiculous," I said coldly. "This is the *original* 'Patrician Lady.' Isn't that correct, Monsieur Arnaud?"

He was still pale and now he regarded the painting with a trace of suspicion. "I do not remember seeing this dent in the frame."

"The explosion," I said hastily.

But Arnaud was not listening. We all allowed him thoughtful and respectful silence until he came to a decision. "There is only one way to be positive. I will send for the X-rays in Paris. A clever forger may possibly delude even the best of experts, but he cannot fool the X-ray. He could not possibly duplicate every nuance of the paint—its thickness or thinness in strategic spots. And he certainly could not duplicate what is behind the paint—the microscopic individuality of every thread on the original canvas."

Arnaud turned to me. "Mr. Parnell, lead me to a telephone."

In my office we put through a call to Paris and waited on the open line. After a considerable interval, one of his subordinates evidently returned to the phone.

Arnaud listened and appeared about to faint. But he pulled himself together, issued further sharp orders in French, and then hung up. "Some idiot of a file clerk has misplaced the X-rays of the 'Patrician Lady.' However, never fear. I have given the command to ransack the files ruthlessly. The X-rays shall be found."

But, of course, they never were.

One week later a distinguished panel of twenty French and American art experts met in convocation to study and pass upon the authenticity of the "Patrician Lady."

After a month, the results of their examination were made public. Twelve of them pronounced the work to be truly the original. Six declared that it was a clever forgery. And two maintained that it was a clumsy forgery.

The governor took it upon himself to publicly proclaim his faith in the majority opinion and he was backed by the State Senate, 64 to 56. The vote was strictly along party lines.

The "Patrician Lady" returned to France. However Paris announced that it had canceled plans to replace her with "Winkler's Brother."

My appearance was thoroughly muted by a false beard and dark glasses. Further, I wore a black wig and spoke with a slight French accent.

Though I had met Mr. Duncan a number of times, I felt positive that he did not have the slightest inkling of my real identity.

I began putting the money into my suitcase. Two hundred thousand dollars—none of it in bills larger than one hundred—is quite bulky.

Duncan stared at the painting, his eyes awed, and yet triumphant. "So it really *was* stolen."

"Monsieur," I said. "I know nothing about the stealing. Absolutely nothing. The 'Patrician Lady' merely came—accidentally—into my hands."

He smiled knowingly. "Of course." His eyes went back to his new possession. "Millions of fools will look at that copy in Paris, and all the time *I've* got the original."

"You understand, of course, Monsieur," I said, "that you may show the painting to no one else. No one. It is for your private enjoyment. If it were discovered that you possess the original 'Patrician Lady,' the authorities would take it away from you and even put you into prison."

He nodded. "I'll keep it under lock and key. No one will see it. Not even my wife will see it!"

I could understand the last precaution. She was currently his fourth and might prove vindictive in any divorce action.

I closed the suitcase. "Goodbye, Monsieur Duncan. You are indeed fortunate to have a million-dollar painting for only one fifth of that sum."

In my taxi I sat back and relaxed. So far Bernice Lecour had made six copies of the "Patrician Lady" and I had had no difficulty in disposing of them as originals.

Perhaps Bernice and I could have stolen the authentic "Patrician Lady," but then the police of the entire world would have joined the search for the thieves.

It was much safer this way—merely to create the suspicion that she *might* have been stolen, and to capitalize upon it.

I thought that now Bernice and I deserved a vacation. Brazil should be interesting.

Perhaps we would not return.

Hey You Down There

Harold Rolseth

Calvin Spender drained his coffee cup and wiped his mouth with the back of his hand. He belched loudly and then proceeded to fill a corncob pipe with coarsely shredded tobacco. He scratched a match across the top of the table and holding it to his pipe, he sucked noisily until billows of acrid smoke poured from his mouth.

Dora Spender sat across the table from her husband, her breakfast scarcely touched. She coughed lightly, and then, as no frown appeared on Calvin's brow, she said, "Are you going to dig in the well this morning, Calvin?"

Calvin fixed his small red-rimmed eyes upon her, and as if she had not spoken, said, "Git going at the chores right away. You're going to be hauling up dirt."

"Yes, Calvin," Dora whispered. Calvin cleared his throat, and the action caused his Adam's apple to move convulsively under the loose red folds of skin on his neck. He rose from the table and went out the kitchen door, kicking viciously at the tawny cat which had been lying on the doorstep.

Dora gazed after him and wondered for the thousandth time what it was that Calvin reminded her of. It was not some other person. It was something else. Sometimes it seemed as though the answer was about to spring to her mind, as just now when Calvin had cleared his throat. But always it stopped just short of her consciousness. It was disturbing to know with such certainty that Calvin looked like something other than himself and yet not know what that something was. Someday though, Dora knew, the answer would come to her. She rose hurriedly from the table and set about her chores.

Halfway between the house and the barn a doughnut-shaped mound of earth surrounded a hole. Calvin went to the edge of the hole and stared down into it distastefully. Only necessity could have forced him to undertake this task, but it was either this digging or the hauling of barrels and barrels of water each day from Nord Fisher's farm a half mile down the road.

Calvin's herd of scrub cattle was small, but the amount of water it consumed was astonishing. For two weeks now, ever since his well had gone dry, Calvin had been hauling water, and the disagreeable chore was becoming more unpleasant because of Nord's clumsy hints that some form of payment for the water would not be amiss.

Several feet back from the edge of the hole Calvin had driven a heavy iron stake into the ground, and to this was attached a crude rope ladder. The rope ladder had become necessary when the hole had reached a depth well beyond the length of any wooden ladder Calvin owned.

Calvin hoped desperately that he would not have to go much deeper. He estimated that he was now down fifty or sixty feet, a common depth for many wells in the area. His greatest fear was that he would hit a stratum of rock which would call for the services of a well-drilling outfit. For such a venture both his funds and his credit rating were far too low.

Calvin picked up a bucket to which was attached a long rope and lowered it into the hole. It was Dora's backbreaking task to haul the bucket up hand over hand after Calvin had filled it from the bottom of the hole.

With a mumbled curse Calvin emptied his pipe and started down the rope ladder. By the time he got to the bottom of the hole and had filled the bucket, Dora should be there to haul it up. If she weren't, she would hear about it.

From the house Dora saw Calvin prepare to enter the well, and she worked with desperate haste to complete her chores. She reached the hole just as a muffled shout from below indicated that the bucket was full.

Summoning all her strength, Dora hauled the bucket up. She emptied it and then lowered it into the hole again. While she waited for the second bucketload, she examined the contents of the first. She was disappointed to find it had only the normal moistness of underground earth. No water seeped from it.

In her own fashion, Dora was deeply religious and at each tenth bucket she pulled up she murmured an urgent prayer that it would contain more water in it than earth. She had settled at praying at every tenth bucketload because she did not believe it in good taste to pester God with every bucket. Also, she varied the wording of each prayer, feeling that God must become bored with the same petition repeated over and over.

On this particular morning as she lowered the bucket for its tenth loading, she prayed, "Please God, let something happen this time . . . let something really and truly happen so I won't have to haul up any more dirt."

Something happened almost immediately. As the rope slackened in her hands indicating that the bucket had reached the bottom, a scream of sheer terror came up from the hole, and the rope ladder jerked violently. Whimpering sounds of mortal fear sounded faintly, and the ladder grew taut with heavy strain.

Dora fell to her knees and peered down into the darkness. "Calvin," she called, "are you all right? What is it?"

Then with startling suddenness Calvin appeared, literally shooting out of the hole. At first Dora was not sure it was Calvin. The peeled redness of his face was gone; now it was a yellowish green. He was trembling violently and had trouble breathing.

It must be a heart attack Dora thought, and tried mightily to suppress the surge of joy that swept over her.

Calvin lay upon the ground panting. Finally he gained control of himself. Under ordinary circumstances Calvin did not converse with Dora, but now he seemed eager to talk. "You know what happened down there?" he said in a shaky voice. "You know what happened? The complete bottom dropped right out of that hole. All of a sudden it went, and there I was, standing on nothing but air. If I hadn't grabbed aholt of the last rung of the ladder . . . Why, that hole must be a thousand feet the way the bottom dropped out of it!"

Calvin babbled on, but Dora did not listen. She was filled with awe at the remarkable way in which her prayer had been answered. If the hole had no more bottom, there would be no more dirt to haul up.

When Calvin had regained his strength, he crept to the edge of the hole and peered down.

"What are you going to do, Calvin?" Dora asked timidly.

"Do? I'm going to find out how far down that hole goes. Get the flashlight from the kitchen."

Dora hurried off. When she returned, Calvin had a large ball of binder twine he had gotten from the tool shed.

He tied the flashlight securely to the end of the line, switched it on, and lowered it into the hole. He paid out the line for about a hundred feet and then stopped. The light was only a feeble glimmer down below and revealed nothing. Calvin lowered the light another hundred feet and this time it was only a twinkling speck as it swung at the end of the line. Calvin released another long length of twine and another and another and now the light was no longer visible, and the large ball of twine had shrunk to a small tangle.

"Almost a full thousand feet," he whispered in awe. "And no bottom yet. Might as well pull it up."

But the line did not come up with Calvin's pull. It stretched and grew taut, but it did not yield to his tugging.

"Must be caught on something," Calvin muttered, and gave the line a sharp jerk. In response there was a downward jerk that almost tore the line from his hands.

"Hey," yelled Calvin. "The line . . . it jerked!"

"But, Calvin," Dora protested.

"Don't Calvin me. I tell you there's something on the end of this line."

He gave another tug, and again the line was almost pulled from his hands. He tied the line to the stake and sat down to ponder the matter.

"It don't make sense," he said, more to himself than to Dora. "What could be down underground a good thousand feet?"

Tentatively he reached over and pulled lightly on the line. This time there was no response, and rapidly he began hauling it up. When the end of the line came into view, there was no flashlight attached to it. Instead, there was a small white pouch of a leatherlike substance.

Calvin opened the pouch with trembling fingers and shook into his palm a bar of yellow metal and a folded piece of parchment. The bar of metal was not large but seemed heavy for its size. Calvin got out his jackknife and scratched the point of the blade across the metal. The knife blade bit into it easily.

"Gold," said Calvin, his voice shaky. "Must be a whole pound of it . . . and just for a measly flashlight. They must be crazy down there."

He thrust the gold bar into his pocket and opened the small piece of parchment. One side was closely covered with a fine script. Calvin turned it this way and that and then tossed it on the ground.

"Foreigners," he said. "No wonder they ain't got any sense. But it's plain they need flashlights."

"But, Calvin," said Dora. "How could they get down there? There ain't any mines in this part of the country."

"Ain't you ever heard of them secret government projects?" asked Calvin scornfully. "This must be one of them. Now I'm going to town and get me a load of flashlights. They must need them bad. Now, mind you watch that hole good. Don't let no one go near it."

Calvin strode to the battered pickup which was standing near the barn, and a minute later was rattling down the highway toward Harmony Junction.

Dora picked up the bit of parchment which Calvin had thrown away. She could make nothing of the writing on it. It was all very strange. If it were some secret government undertaking, why would foreigners be engaged in it? And why would they need flashlights so urgently as to pay a fortune for one?

Suddenly it occurred to her that possibly the people down below didn't know there were English-speaking people up above. She hurried into the house and rummaged through Calvin's rickety desk for paper and pencil. In her search she found a small ragged dictionary, and she took this with her to the kitchen table. Spelling did not come easy to Dora.

Her note was a series of questions. Why were they down there? Who were they? Why did they pay so much for an old flashlight?

As she started for the well it occurred to her that possibly the people down there might be hungry. She went back to the kitchen and wrapped a loaf of bread and a fair-sized piece of ham in a clean dish towel. She added a postscript to her note apologizing for the fact that she had nothing better to offer them. Then the thought came to her that since the people down below were obviously foreigners and possibly not too well versed in English, the small dictionary might be of help to them in answering her note. She wrapped the dictionary with the food in the towel.

It took Dora a long while to lower the bucket, but finally the twine grew slack in her hands, and she knew the bucket had reached the bottom. She waited a few moments and then tugged the line gently. The line held firm below, and Dora seated herself on the pile of soil to wait.

The warm sunlight felt good on her back, and it was pleasant to sit and do nothing. She had no fear that Calvin would return soon. She knew that nothing on earth—or under it—could keep Calvin from visiting a number of taverns once he was in town, and that with each tavern visited time would become more and more meaningless to him. She doubted that he would return before morning.

After a half hour Dora gave the line a questioning tug, but it did not yield. She did not mind. It was seldom that she had time to idle away. Usually when Calvin went to town, he burdened her with chores to be done during his absence, coupling each order with a threat of what awaited her should his instructions not be carried out.

Dora waited another half hour before giving the line another tug. This time there was a sharp answering jerk, and Dora began hauling the bucket upward. It seemed much heavier now, and twice she had to pause for a rest. When the bucket reached the surface, she saw why it was heavier.

"My goodness," she murmured as she viewed the dozen or so yellow metal bars in the bucket. "They must be real hungry down there."

A sheet of the strange parchment was also in the bucket, and Dora picked it out expecting to see the strange script of the first note.

"Well, I declare," she said when she saw that the note was in English. It was in the same print as the dictionary, and each letter had been made with meticulous care.

She read the note slowly, shaping each word with her lips as she read.

Your language is barbaric, but the crude code book you sent down made it easy for our scholars to decipher it. We, too, wonder about you. How have you overcome the problem of living in the deadly light? Our legends tell of a race living on the surface, but intelligent reasoning has forced us to ridicule these old tales until now. We

*would still doubt that you are surface dwellers except for the fact that
our instruments show without question that the opening above us
leads to the deadly light.*

*The clumsy death ray which you sent us indicates that your scien-
tific development is very low. Other than an artifact of another race it
has no value to us. We sent gold as a courtesy payment only.*

*The food you call bread is not acceptable to our digestive systems,
but the ham is beyond price. It is obviously the flesh of some creature, and we will exchange a double weight of gold for all that you
can send us. Send more immediately. Also send a concise history of
your race and arrange for your best scientists, such as they are, to
communicate with us.*

Glar, the Master

"Land sakes," said Dora. "Real bossy they are. I've a good mind
not to send them anything. I don't dast send them more ham. Calvin
would notice if any more is gone."

Dora took the gold bars to her petunia bed beside the house and
buried them in the loose black soil. She paid no heed to the sound of
a car coming down the highway at high speed until it passed the
house and wild squawking sounded above the roar of the motor. She
hurried around to the front of the house, knowing already what had
happened. She stared in dismay at the four white leghorns which lay
along the road. Now Calvin would charge her with negligence and
beat her into unconsciousness.

Fear sharpened her wits. Perhaps if she could dispose of the bodies
Calvin would think foxes had gotten them. Hastily she gathered up
the dead chickens and the feathers which lay scattered about. When
she was finished, there was no evidence of the disaster.

She carried the chickens to the back of the house wondering how
she could best dispose of them. Suddenly, as she glanced toward the
hole, the answer came to her.

An hour later the four chickens were dressed and neatly cut up.
Ignoring the other instructions in the note, she sent the bulky parcel
of chicken down into the hole.

She sat down again to enjoy the luxury of doing nothing. When she
finally picked up the line, there was an immediate response from
below. The bucket was exceedingly heavy this time, and she was
fearful that the line might break. She was dizzy with fatigue when

she finally hauled the bucket over to the edge of the hole. This time there were several dozen bars of gold in it and a brief note in the same precise lettering as before.

Our scientists are of the opinion that the flesh you sent down is that of a creature you call chicken. This is the supreme food. Never have we eaten anything so delicious. To show our appreciation we are sending you a bonus payment. Your code book indicates that there is a larger creature similar to chicken called turkey. Send us turkey immediately. I repeat, send us turkey immediately.

Glar, the Master

"Land sakes," gasped Dora. "They must have et that chicken raw. Now where in tarnation would I get a turkey?"

She buried the gold bars in another part of her petunia bed.

Calvin returned about ten o'clock the next morning. His eyes were bloodshot, and his face was a mottled red. The loose skin on his neck hung lower than usual and more than ever he reminded Dora of something which eluded her.

Calvin stepped down from the pickup, and Dora cringed, but he seemed too tired and preoccupied to bother with her. He surveyed the hole glumly, then got back into the truck and backed it to the edge of the mound of earth. On the back of the truck was a winch with a large drum of steel cable.

"Fix me something to eat," he ordered Dora.

Dora hurried into the house and began preparing ham and eggs. Each moment she expected Calvin to come in and demand to know, with a few blows, what was holding up his meal. But Calvin seemed very busy in the vicinity of the hole. When Dora went out to call him to eat, she found he had done a surprising amount of work. He had attached an oil drum to the steel cable. This hung over a heavy steel rod which rested across the hole. Stakes driven into the ground on each side of the hole held the rod in place.

"Your breakfast is ready, Calvin," said Dora.

"Shut up," Calvin answered.

The winch was driven by an electric motor, and Calvin ran a cable from the motor to an electric outlet on the yard lightpost.

From the cab he took a number of boxes and placed them in the oil drum.

"A whole hundred of them," he chuckled, more to himself than to Dora. "Fifty-nine cents apiece. Peanuts . . . one bar of gold will buy thousands."

Calvin threw the switch which controlled the winch, and with sickening force Dora suddenly realized the terrible thing that would soon happen. The creatures down below had no use or regard for flashlights.

Down went the oil drum, the cable screeching shrilly as it passed over the rod above the hole. Calvin got an oil can from the truck and applied oil generously to the rod and the cable.

In a very short while the cable went slack and Calvin stopped the winch.

"I'll give them an hour to load up the gold," he said and went to the kitchen for his delayed breakfast.

Dora was practically in a state of shock. What would happen when the flashlights came back up with an insulting note in English was too horrible to contemplate. Calvin would learn about the gold she had received and very likely kill her.

Calvin ate his breakfast leisurely. Dora busied herself with household tasks, trying with all her might to cast out of her mind the terrible thing which was soon to happen.

Finally Calvin glanced at the wall clock, yawned widely, and tapped out his pipe. Ignoring Dora he went out to the hole. In spite of her terrible fear Dora could not resist following him. It was as if some power outside herself forced her to go.

The winch was already reeling in the cable when she got to the hole. It seemed only seconds before the oil drum was up. The grin on Calvin's face was broad as he reached out over the hole and dragged the oil drum to the edge. A look of utter disbelief replaced the grin as he looked into the drum. His Adam's apple seemed to vibrate, and once again part of Dora's mind tried to recall what it was that Calvin reminded her of.

Calvin was making flat, bawling sounds like a lost calf. He hauled the drum out of the hole and dumped its contents on the ground. The flashlights, many of them dented and with lenses broken, made a sizable pile.

With a tremendous kick Calvin sent flashlights flying in all directions. One, with a note attached, landed at Dora's feet. Either Calvin was so blinded by rage that he didn't see it, or he assumed it was written in the same unreadable script as the first note.

"You down there," he screamed into the hole. "You filthy swine. I'll fix you. I'll make you sorry you ever double-crossed me. I'll . . . I'll . . ."

He dashed for the house, and Dora hastily snatched up the note.

You are even more stupid than we thought [she read]. *Your clumsy death rays are useless to us. We informed you of this. We want turkey. Send us turkey immediately.*

Glar, the Master

She crumbled the note swiftly as Calvin came from the house with his double-barreled shotgun. For a moment Dora thought that he knew everything and was about to kill her.

"Please, Calvin," she said.

"Shut up," Calvin said. "You saw me work the winch. Can you do it?"

"Why, yes, but what . . . ?"

"Listen, you stupid cow. I'm going down there and fix those dirty foreigners. You send me down and bring me up." He seized Dora by the shoulder. "And if you mess things, I'll fix you too. I'll really and truly fix you."

Dora nodded dumbly.

Calvin put his gun in the oil drum and pushed it to the center of the hole. Then, hanging on to the cable, he carefully lowered himself into the drum.

"Give me just one hour to run those dirty rats down, then bring me back up," he said.

Dora threw the switch and the oil drum went down. When the cable slackened, she stopped the winch. She spent most of the hour praying that Calvin would not find the people down below and become a murderer.

Exactly an hour later Dora started the oil drum upward. The motor labored mightily as though under a tremendous strain, and the cable seemed stretched almost to the breaking point.

Dora gasped when the oil drum came into view. Calvin was not in it. She shut off the motor and hastened to the drum, half expecting to find Calvin crouching down inside. But Calvin was not there. Instead there were scores of gold bars and on top of them a sheet of the familiar white parchment.

"Land sakes," Dora said, as she took in a full view of the drum's contents. She had no idea of the value of the treasure upon which she gazed. She only knew it must be immense. Carefully, she reached down and picked out the note, which she read in her slow, precise manner: *Not even the exquisite flavor of the chicken compares to the incomparable goodness of the live turkey you sent down to us. We must confess that our concept of turkey was quite different, but this is of no consequence. So delectable was the turkey that we are again sending you a bonus payment. We implore you to send us more turkey immediately.*

Glar, the Master

Dora read the note a second time to make sure she understood it fully. "Well, I declare," she said in considerable wonder. "I declare."

Too Many Sharks

William Sambrot

The sea was placid, glinting blue and lovely under the early morning sun. Allen Melton inhaled deeply, not looking at Marta, his wife, knowing her lazy gray-green eyes were taking in his smoothly tanned body, flicking boredly, uninterestedly over the bunched muscles, like oiled cables, rippling under his skin. His jaw tightened and with an effort he kept his narrowed eyes out toward the reef where the pelicans wheeled in slow graceful circles.

"It ought to be good hunting out there today," he finally said, directing his words to Jim Talbot, who sprawled, angular, graceless, on the already hot sand at Marta's feet. He swung quickly, catching Marta off guard long enough to see the swift glance that passed between her and Jim. For a split second her defenses were down and he saw the naked unashamed passion in her eyes.

His throat swelled with thick bitter rage. The urge to slam the deadly long-shafted barb he held into her body, between her firm rising breasts, was shockingly overwhelming. He fought himself, bending his close-cropped head down, to hide his face from her. She'd always been able to read his thoughts. Too bad he'd never been able to reciprocate. But at last he knew. So it was Jim Talbot. Good old lifelong pal. Always at hand, ready to make it a threesome, or a fourth—and ready to make it two whenever Melton wasn't around.

He fiddled with the controls of his spear gun, seeing Marta spitted on the long shaft, twisting and turning, the bubbles streaming from her lovely lying mouth, drowning under the warm green waters far out near the reef where the pelicans and gulls soared about, slipping down now and again to snatch up a silvery wriggling fish.

"We've been here two weeks, now," Marta was saying, not very convincingly. "And every day you've been out there, shooting fish underwater. Why not stay on the beach, for once?"

He looked at her, his hard eyes traveling slowly over the supple rounded length of her, knowing at last the passion she was capable of, wondering why she'd never responded to him. He was suddenly weak at the thought. *All these years . . . with Jim . . .*

"Yes," he said slowly, "I suppose I have been neglecting you—but then, Jim's been good company, hasn't he?" He bared strong white teeth in a savage grin at Jim.

Talbot had the good grace to flush. His glance slid over to Marta and he straightened, one sun-bleached brow cocked. "Someone had to fight off the wolves," he smiled faintly, "while you were out spitting half the fish in the ocean."

"Al never does things by halves," Marta said lazily. She crossed tanned legs and settled back in her canvas beach chair. "If it's skiing, he spends six days on a cross-country tour. If it's grizzly, he'll beat the brush for weeks—"

"I get what I'm after," Melton said softly.

"But do you, dear?" she answered coolly.

"I'll bet," Talbot said, smiling his intimate smile at Marta, "he's making love out there to a mermaid."

"Not if there's anything swimming around he can spear," Marta said casually. "Making love interferes with a man's sport, doesn't it, Allen?"

"It interferes with a lot of things," he said. He turned to Jim Talbot. "How about it, Jim, coming out on the reef with me? You agreed to take a stab at it at least once before we leave."

"Well, I hadn't planned—" Jim hesitated, glancing again, covertly, at Marta.

"I imagine Marta can get along without you for at least an afternoon," he said pleasantly. Marta looked at him, and the alarm leaped into her face. Her eyes changed color. *She knows*, Melton thought, and again he grinned, tightly, thinking of Jim and Marta alone on the tiny deserted island a few hundred feet offshore, making love wildly —Marta with an abandonment she'd never shown him. It had been the merest chance that he'd decided to come in early, yesterday. And sliding along in the pirogue, he'd glimpsed the motion in the rank grass of the island and put his powerful glasses on them . . .

"What's the matter, Jim—not afraid of underwater spear-fishing, are you?" He punched Jim playfully in the shoulder, forcing himself to hold the punch, but even so, Jim's lean frame rocked backward. He draped an arm negligently over Talbot's shoulder and faced Marta, conscious of the contrast they made. Melton over six feet, narrow-hipped, big-chested, his eyes dark chips of ocean blue. Talbot lean and stringy, weak-jawed, ill at ease in a bathing suit—but not on a lonely island . . .

He had a sudden absurd impulse to swing Talbot off his feet, to hold him, easily, above his head, with all his muscles flowing and bunching, to throw him a great distance, or squeeze him in a bone-crushing grip, forcing him to cry out before Marta, proving he was the lesser man.

Instead, he said, "Nothing dangerous about spear-fishing, Jim. Even the kids hereabouts do it. Fifteen-year-old boy out there yesterday speared a sixty-pound jewfish."

"Why the sudden urge for company?" Marta said. She bit her lips and looked out toward the reef. "Looks as if there's something big out there," she added. "All those birds. Won't a school of fish bring —sharks?"

"Probably," Melton said easily. "They don't bother you. Just sit still and they'll pass." He turned to Talbot. "What say, Jim? It's a lot of fun—good clean fun."

Again Talbot reddened. He swallowed and nodded lamely. "Yes, I did promise we'd go out before . . ."

"Good!" Melton waved an arm toward the boathouse. "Might as well get started now. I've got an extra set of gear in the pirogue—and lunch, too." He tightened a big hand around Jim's biceps. "I'll have you out over the reef in twenty-five minutes, and believe me, Talbot, it's something you'll never forget."

"Jim—Allen." Marta was on her feet as, reluctantly, Jim fell in beside Melton. They stopped. "Be . . . careful," she said, and as they nodded and turned to go, Melton knew she'd been speaking to Talbot. It was good advice. A lot of things could happen out there on the reef, with six or seven fathoms of emerald water overhead. A lot of things . . .

On the way out to the reef Melton explained how to use the expensive French portable aqualung. He pointed out the valves which controlled the flow of compressed air to the mask and, last—as the pirogue bobbed over the farthermost reef, away from the other underwater sportsmen—he showed him how to charge and cock the long-barreled speargun.

"Nothing to it, really," he said, his cold eyes traveling slowly over Talbot's bony body and riveting at a spot between his breastbone. "The gun works on compressed gas. It has killing power up to about ten feet." He slipped on his fins and hoisted the oxygen apparatus onto his shoulders. "Be careful in which direction you point that thing," he said. "You could kill a man with that spear—without half trying."

They went down together, sending a fine stream of bubbles up through the clear water, Melton moving powerfully, easily, like a sleek seal. Talbot kicked awkwardly, his skinny legs looking even thinner with the giant fins dangling on his feet. Melton's jaw tightened. What in hell attracted Marta to him? What did she see in this skinny nonentity to bring all her hidden fire aflame so that shamelessly, in broad daylight . . . ?

He swallowed and gripped the gun tightly. A gaudy parrotfish flashed past, and then another, and another. Soon a whole stream of fish, myriad flashing bits of colors, like a suddenly shattered rainbow, whirled past, faster and faster. The big schools of fish that had been feeding about the inward reef were coming toward them, as though driven before a strong wind. And then, shadowy in the distance, he saw the ominous bulk of a great blue shark, with lesser sharks tagging behind. He watched the sixteen-foot slab of muscle and killing power slide along, slashing and tearing at the big jacks, and hastily he flipped toward Jim. He touched his shoulder and smiled as he felt the flesh crawl. He put his face mask against Talbot's.

"Remain perfectly still," he shouted. He saw the whites of Talbot's eyes rolling about as he watched the shark dwindle into the soft green distance and vanish. He felt something bump and slide down his side and he pulled away, looking down. It was Talbot's gun, dropping from his nerveless fingers. He'd forgotten to attach the gun to his wrist with the cord provided for that purpose.

He leaned close again. "Talbot," he said, "can you hear me?" Talbot nodded and made violent gestures, up to where the bottom of the boat made a dark blob against the film of crystal that was the surface.

Melton shook his head, savoring the fierce exultation that came with the knowledge of what he was about to do. There would be no up for Talbot, not ever. Here, on the brilliant coral reef, he would pay for usurping the role that only he, Melton, in the sight of God and man, had the right to play. He would close those mocking eyes, stop the ears that had heard her whispered lies, shut the mouth that alone could shout aloud his shame.

An accident, he would say. He'd spotted a big jewfish, pointed it out to Talbot, and somehow, as they'd both swum toward it his gun had discharged. A regrettable accident. One of those things that happen to even the most careful and experienced of hunters.

But Marta would know.

His teeth bared behind the mask. *Marta would know* and that was the sweetest revenge of all. Abruptly he put his mask against Talbot's, seeing the alarm in his eyes.

"There's going to be an accident," he said calmly. "Nothing pleasant—like making love to Marta on a lonely island—"

He choked, trembling, and Talbot grabbed him, his hands cold and slippery, his lips moving, speaking, wildly, hastily.

"Don't! Please—don't!" he shouted, his mask pressed close to Melton's, eyes fixed, wide with reflected horror at what he saw in Melton's eyes. "It's true—but why kill me? I'm not the only one." His clutching hands pawed at Melton's hard body, trying to fend off the coming death. *"What about the others?"*

Mechanically, without volition, Melton kicked him away, brought up the gun and pulled the trigger. He watched the slim needle-pointed dart smack into Talbot's body, just above and to the left of the breastbone. A perfect bulls-eye. He waited, watching the spurting line of red that trailed up, up to where the crystal surface film lay.

It wasn't true. He watched the thin line of bubbles break, flow, break, become scantier and finally cease. What Talbot had said wasn't true. It was only a desperate man's final attempt to escape the death he'd seen glaring out of Melton's faceplate.

He crouched over the still body, holding the shoulders, his brain cold, rigidly under control. There were no others. Talbot was the only blot on his manhood, the only one who'd held her close. The only one . . .

He knew he should be going up, taking the body. To wait too long might look suspicious. But still he remained, fighting to reassert himself. All the mountains he'd climbed and conquered; the rivers swum; the animals, cunning and treacherous, he'd overcome. He'd proved he was a man, over and over again. Big, rugged Allen Melton, sportsman, he-man, married to a lovely passionate woman. Too passionate. He should never have taken so many trips. Should never have stayed away for so long a period at a time. He wasn't running from her, from her unquenchable thirst—not at all. It was just his nature to want to pit his strength against everything tough and brutal in the world and beat it. He was man enough for her or any woman. Man enough . . .

He stooped, cradled the cold slippery body in his arms, and kicking strongly, headed up. He stared into the white face so near his. *"I get what I go after."* *"But do you, dear?"*

Then suddenly the fish were streaming back, frightened hordes fluttering about, bumping into him, as they fled along through the green clear water, and abruptly he realized his terrible danger. He'd waited too long. The shark was returning, smelling the blood, Talbot's blood, which still streamed slowly up, a bright red ribbon of smoke curling toward the surface. He dropped the body, seeing in the dim distance the onrushing bulk, looming larger and larger.

For a wild immeasurable instant he tried to remain motionless, defying gravity, remaining suspended between heaven and hell. But slowly, slowly, he began to sink, following the gently twisting body, with the damnable red ribbon enveloping him, impregnating his hair, his swimsuit, with the lurid scent. Every instinct cried out to swim, to thrash his powerful legs and speed up, up to the crystal surface and safety. But his brain, cold and logical, fought back. Don't move. To move is instant death. And still he sank, down, down.

The great shark, a narrow torpedo shape of sheer destruction, pivoted slowly and faced him, waiting for a movement to explode it into biting rending motion.

Melton's glance slid down, and there, glinting with metallic highlights, directly below the slowly settling body, lay Talbot's spear gun, undischarged, with the long needle-pointed spear still in it. In that instant, he made his decision. With a powerful kick he moved desperately for the gun. Out of the corner of his eye he saw the swift motion as the shark catapulted toward him.

Frantically he pumped toward the gun, a scant few feet from him. Just as he reached it, Talbot's body settled onto it, emitting a steady stream of red, rocking to and fro, and then, he heard the sudden *thuck!* and saw the quick stream of bubbles rise as the breathing tube on Talbot's body discharged the spear gun.

He crouched there in the eternity of a second, staring at the white dead face, hearing again the last words those stiff lips had spoken, realizing, at the end, their truth. He still had his knife, but he made no move for it. There were too many sharks. The ocean, the world, was full of them. Glittering-eyed, sharp-toothed creatures of insatiable appetite. Too many sharks.

He crouched there, all his defenses gone, waiting . . .

Christopher Frame

Nancy C. Swoboda

Christopher Frame looked out the window of his little shop at the rain. It was just after five in the evening and people with umbrellas and colorful raincoats hurried to get home from work. That's all they ever did anymore, he thought. They hurried through their jobs and they hurried through life, and there was no time for pride left in either one. He stirred up the gray lumps of coal in the tiny fireplace until they glowed orangy-red against the blackened grate and returned to his work at the big desk.

The building was incongruous on the modern downtown street. It was two stories high, not too wide, and was sandwiched in between two impersonal-looking steel-and-glass structures. Across the top of the door and big window on either side was an old-fashioned sign in raised brass letters. All it said was FRAMES. For over eighty-two years his father and then Christopher Frame had been in the business of photography—mostly restoration, tinting and oils, and framing. The coincidence of the name had made a descriptive trademark for their work.

Now Christopher was alone at both his job and his life. He lived in the back rooms of the old building and used the barny upstairs for storage and supplies. The ancient brownstone structure had been his home, his world for thirty years. At fifteen he had become his father's apprentice, the same year his mother died, and the two Frames had moved to their place of work to live. When Christopher was thirty his father died, leaving him sole owner of an expensive piece of real estate upon which rested the sum total of his existence.

The rain had settled into a steady drizzle and the gray afternoon was fast darkening into evening. Christopher made himself some tea and toast and studied the picture before him on the desk. He had

387

been looking at it, pondering over it ever since that Mr. Walters had brought it in four days ago. It was a very old photograph of a family outing—on a picnic, probably, but it was badly faded and dog-eared. Mr. Walters wanted it restored and done in oils as a present for his wife. It seemed the picture was of her side of the family and she was very sentimental about such things. Naturally, he entrusted Christopher Frame to do an excellent job. He had even selected a beautiful old gold-leaf frame to finish it off.

And finish it off, Christopher could not do. Briefly, Mr. Walters had mentioned his wife had blue eyes and that her hair was fair when she was a child. But the rest of the people—what of them? Eyes? Hair? What color were their clothes? How blue was the sky? In the background he could make out what looked like a lovely little town with a church spire spearing the clear day, but it was faded, and the family group in the foreground posing on the hillock blurred into various degrees of white outlined and accented in brown.

Pride and perfection went into each piece of his work, and now that picture restoration was so popular it bothered Christopher not to be able to reproduce the photographs faithfully. Most of them were in brown or sepia and the people who brought them in had no idea, of course, of any coloring, since they were either too young or not even born. He enjoyed creating oil tones for his subjects, but he felt he was misrepresenting the true past somehow. How few craftsmen were left. No one took time anymore—or cared. It was like the difference between some of the beautiful old gold-leaf and hand-carved frames he had stored upstairs and the impersonal and uninteresting modern frames he shuddered to use on his work.

He stirred up the fire and added a bit of coal and then went to the big high-ceilinged room at the back of the shop. It was furnished as a bedroom in massive old mahogany pieces and a big fourposter with a patchwork quilt. It was a man's room, but it was warm and cheery—old-fashioned. He had the picture with him. He propped it up on the dresser opposite the foot of the bed and then settled himself on top of the quilt for a nap. The timer he used for developing was on the nightstand close by. He set it for one hour and then lay back to contemplate the troublesome photograph. If only he could be there . . . just long enough to see the true picture, the colors. What a wonderful thing it would be. He dozed off to the measured ticking of the timer.

The combination of something prickling in his ear and an awareness of a bright light brought him back from a heavy sleep to a groggy consciousness. He opened his eyes and looked straight into a stand of lush green grass and above it a horizon of china-blue sky. He was lying on his side under a tree, and it was a beautiful warm sunshiny day!

Cautiously, he rolled over and sat up. The air smelled of sweet clover and the sound of a steeple bell floated lazily in the soft summer breeze. He was on a hill overlooking a neat whitewashed village that nestled against a patchwork quilt of farm land and green slopes. He sat in sheer ecstasy sniffing the clear heady air, but laughter and voices startled him back to the realization that he was in a strange place and an even stranger situation.

Slowly Christopher Frame stood up and peered around the tree. His mouth fell open and a look of shocked disbelief washed over his face. In front of him, living, breathing and posing was the fleshly counterpart of the picture on his dresser! The photographer, his back to Christopher, was placing his subjects and instructing them to stand very still for the camera. The colors were so vivid in the summer sunshine! Christopher stared at the group and memorized as much as he could and then made notes in the little book he always carried. Surely he was dreaming, but perhaps it was some sort of telepathy coming to him from the picture caused by his anxiety to know more about the faded print.

Just as the little girl in the group spied him a loud ticking started in his head and exploded into ringing bells. The picture before him blacked out, and when he could see again he was looking at the ceiling of his own room and the timer had gone off. He sat up on the edge of the bed and glanced at the picture. What a realistic dream, he thought, chuckled and patted the small notebook in his breast pocket. He decided to get to work on the reproduction while the scene was still clear in his mind. If not accurate in detail, at least this work would be inspired.

He stood, stretched, and then on an impulse, reached for the little book. It was warm from being so close to his body. He opened it and drew in his breath. On the page in his neat script was a detailed description of the photograph. In his excitement the book dropped from his trembling hands to the floor. As he stooped to pick it up he saw the green blades of grass caught in the heels of his shoes. Dizzy, with a feeling of strange elation, he sat down again on the bed. Gingerly, he picked up the timer and examined it. It was the same one he had used for years. There was nothing unusual about it now. He put it back on the nightstand and for a long moment stared at the single dial that stared back at him like a benign Cyclops.

The import of his experience left Christopher confused. He hovered between reality and whatever level of consciousness it was where he had been. Slowly he moved from his bedroom to the outer regions of the old building. The coals were now gray ashes in the grate and the rain had stopped. Nothing was different about the familiar surroundings. He opened the front door and took a breath of the cool rain-washed air. Everything outside was the same, too. He liked his street best at night. The electric signs winked against the steel-and-glass buildings and made the cold impersonal structures appear cheery and friendly.

So often it seemed to him that this place was a fortress from within whose walls he could look out and see lovely old stone shops razed and new modern steel-and-concrete monsters thrown up, people hurrying faster each day to skim over their work and hurry home to start all over again. In a way Frames was a monument to the past and he intended that his work would continue in the fine tradition of his heritage.

Many nights as they warmed their feet by the small fireplace Christopher's father told of the days when it took weeks to turn out one piece of furniture and how most things you bought lasted a lifetime, how men were craftsmen and artisans instead of hurried workers. The pictures, the very old ones that people brought in, made those days seem even more real and desirable to Christopher. After his father died he gathered the walls around him even more closely and worked hard at his profession. He longed for the companionship of a wife, but he was too old-fashioned to be attractive to women, or so he thought. He made himself content in his work and the security of the old building.

The air helped clear his head and he felt free of the lingering cobwebs of his dream. But *was* it a dream? Blades of grass and a detailed description written in his notebook were tangible facts. Anxious to translate all he had "seen" into the photograph he put aside any further speculation and set to work.

The sun was casting a rosy glow on the pale-gray building across the street when he finished. It was like looking through the gold-leaf frame into the real scene. The vividness with which he had reproduced the picture astounded him. He gazed at the distant church spire and the little village barely visible beyond the smiling group and he felt a faint nostalgic longing. Excitement overcame the melancholy and he lifted the receiver to call Mr. Walters to tell him the picture was finished. Then he realized it was only dawn—much too early. He decided to lie down for a short nap, and after affixing his trademark to the back of the picture he went to his bedroom. With a moment's hesitation he set the old brass alarm clock instead of the timer.

The day was uneventful. Mr. Walters was pleased with the restoration and framing of the photograph, but not overly impressed. Of course, he wasn't aware of Christopher's strange experience. There was a steady stream of customers, but he didn't handle them in his usual meticulous manner. His mind was preoccupied with other thoughts. He kept going over what had happened to him. It had to be real. There was no grass for miles around and one didn't write as clearly or as coherently in one's sleep as he had done in his little notebook. He knew he would try to make it happen again—now, after closing, and he knew just the picture he would use.

It seemed an eternity until five o'clock. He locked the front door and paused to watch the hurrying parade of people running for buses, rushing to parking lots, all fleeing from work after skimming through the day. Well, he had done the same thing today, too, but this was an exception. It threatened rain again. Christopher started a small fire in the grate, turned off all but the desk lamp and hurried to his bedroom.

Propped up on the dresser, just as he had done with the first one, was another old photograph. It was of a group of young men posing on a wooden sidewalk in front of a glass-fronted store. How many times Christopher's father had told him about all of those eager young fellows and the fine times they had. They, his father included, were all apprentices at various shops, learning a trade for board and room, and sometimes a little extra if they worked especially hard.

Cautiously, he set the timer for one hour and lay down on the bed. Perhaps he would wake up in the town square opposite the store. How strange it would be to see his father as a very young man. In spite of his excitement he did fall asleep, but when the timer rang he was still in his own room and with no knowledge of having been any-where at all. The picture remained inviolate on the dresser. Disap-pointment and doubt sapped the benefit of any rest he gained from the short nap.

He sat up most of the night brooding in front of the fire. Why hadn't it worked? The circumstances were almost the same. Maybe it had to be a past of which he had no cognizance. The desire to go back—even more, to prove or disprove the reality of so doing—over-whelmed him. He looked at his pocket watch. There was still time before dawn, and he was a bit sleepy. Carefully he sorted through the file of old photographs waiting to be restored and chose one brought in by a Mrs. Nellie Hampton. He knew nothing of or about her other than that she was a customer.

Again, he placed the picture on the dresser and set the timer at one hour. He studied the faded old print from his bed. It was evi-dently a party in someone's backyard. There were Japanese lanterns crisscrossed from the porch to the trees, long tables of food, and a smiling group in their best dress standing stiffly on the porch steps. But wait! He jumped up and examined the picture more carefully. There must be something that he could bring back with him—proof of his actually having been there. Ah! That was it. The porch railing had gingerbread spindles topped off by little round wooden balls. He could snap off one of those easily. Quickly he lay back on the bed and after a final look at the picture he closed his eyes.

It was the swaying motion that awakened him—along with the dis-comfort of the wooden slats in the swing. He was on the porch facing the side yard away from the party in a big chair swing suspended from the ceiling by two stout chains. In front of him, plain as day, was a railing made of ornate spindles topped with little round wooden balls! He stood up and walked slowly to the corner of the porch and peered around the side of the house. As before, the group in the picture posed, waited for the photographer to dismiss them and then moved from the steps back to the festivities.

He was there! He looked at himself. In pants and shirt-sleeves he was not too conspicuous, for several of the men had taken off their coats and were pitching horseshoes. He walked nonchalantly down the steps and stayed close to the bushes where he could watch this wonderful old-time party. He was tempted to sample the food. The smells that wafted over to his nose in the balmy air made his mouth water. There was chicken and pie and home-baked rolls and a small crock of freshly churned butter. To the side was a tub full of ice surrounding a big gallon tin of fresh-strawberry ice cream.

"Hello. Would you like something to eat?" The soft voice startled him.

Christopher Frame whirled around and looked into the bluest eyes and sweetest face he had ever seen.

"Wha—? Oh, thank you. No, I've—I've already eaten."

"You're new, aren't you? My name is Sarah Phillips."

She looked at him with such genuine interest that on top of the headiness of being here he felt a strange new sort of dizzying elation.

"Er, yes. I've just arrived in time for the party."

"I'm glad you could come, Mr.—I'm sorry. I didn't catch your name."

"Christopher . . . Christopher Frame."

"What part of the country are you from?"

Although she still regarded him with interest, he could see that she was curious about his appearance.

"I—I'm a photographer. I travel a lot."

"Will you be here long?" Her golden curls shone in the sun.

"I don't think so. I'm not sure."

He looked at her hard and tried to fix a picture of her in his mind. Then the loud ticking started in his head.

"Mr. Frame? Are you all right?"

"Yes, but you must excuse me. I want very much to stay, but I must go now."

"I'm sorry you have to leave. I hope we'll meet again." A tiny frown crossed her brow.

"And so do I, Miss Phillips . . . Sarah. Goodbye."

The ticking was deafening now. He had to hurry. He walked rapidly out of sight around the side of the house. He barely managed to snap off a little wooden ball from the railing before the bell rang.

He was lying on his back when he awoke. The first rays of sun shone through the window to cast a pinkish hue on the ceiling. He was afraid to move, afraid to leave behind the last wisp of the world he had found but could not hold on to. Then he remembered the railing. Perhaps he did hang on. Slowly he closed both hands. Nothing. Despair engulfed him, not only for losing the past, but for losing Sarah Phillips.

He had been the victim of his own vivid dreams—dreams that had opened the flood gates to yearnings he had kept quietly within himself for so long.

He stood up and walked over to the picture. She was there, smiling out at him, but the faded print obscured her simple beauty. How foolish, he thought, to fall in love with the past and then with a girl who was part of it. Well, at least Mrs. Nellie Hampton would have an imaginative restoration when he finished. With a sigh he started for the front of the building. Getting to work would help a little. He stopped and looked at the timer. Perhaps he should get a new one. Then he glanced at the bed, looked again and cried aloud. Hidden by the busy pattern of the patchwork quilt was a little round wooden ball!

Clutching the picture and the precious little piece of the past, a euphoric Christopher Frame staggered out to his desk and sat down heavily. It was all true. He had actually gone back into time prescribed by the old photos. Then a terrible thought crossed his mind. Just how long would he be able to go back? What if the timer broke? Tenderly he put the picture back on his desk and turned on the bright light. He studied Sarah's dear face through a magnifying glass, and suddenly he knew what he would do.

All day he worked hard to complete as much as he could. Pride and integrity still governed his actions despite the wild thoughts that whirled in his head. Anyway, he wanted to be good and tired by nightfall. As was his custom, he closed for an hour at lunchtime. He went to the second floor. Everything was neat, catalogued and in order. He browsed through the small storeroom, where all of the old family heirlooms were kept. Admiringly he ran his hands over the carving in the high-backed chair, held a cranberry glass goblet up to the light, studied the inlaid mother-of-pearl design in the graceful little secretary. Today any of these objects would be priced beyond the average person's reach. In the past such fine things were commonly available. It made him tingle to think of working among such artisans as those who considered doing no less than their best in every detail.

By closing time he was satisfied with his accomplishments and he was really very tired. He looked out the front window as if he hoped to see something other than the usual five o'clock rush, shrugged and turned away. Carefully he took the picture from his desk, glanced around once more and went to his bedroom. It was almost like a rit-

ual now. Again he placed the old photograph on the dresser—just as
it had been the night before. Sarah was still there, smiling out from
the past.

Beyond the picture he could see himself in the dresser mirror. His
hair was rumpled and his shirt was flecked with oil paint and developing chemicals. Quickly, for he felt a great weariness overtaking
him, he put on a fresh shirt and combed his hair. Then with trembling hands he set the timer for one hour. He was tempted to set it
for a longer period, but he was afraid to upset the pattern. With a
nervous little sigh he stretched out on the bed and shut his eyes
tightly.

From far away he could hear her calling, and then closer—almost
in his ear. He felt his head cradled in something soft and crinkly.
Slowly, he opened his eyes and gazed into the face of a very worried-
looking Sarah Phillips. She was holding his head in her lap.

"Christopher! Mr. Frame? Are you all right?"

"Sarah!" He started to get up.

"Now, just be still for a bit. You didn't look well when you rushed
off around the side of the house. That's where I found you."

"Found me?"

"Yes."

"I—I guess I must have let the heat get to me."

"Do you feel able to get up now? I can get you a glass of cool lem-
onade."

"No, I'm fine." Regretfully, he left the haven of her lap and stood
up. "I'd feel better if we could walk a little."

He had to know if the realm of the past extended beyond the
house, the backyard party, the smiling group on the porch steps. He
offered Sarah his arm and she took it with a shy, pleased smile.

They walked out to the front of the house. It was all there—the
tree-lined street, the big whitewashed homes. They strolled slowly,
deliciously, and he couldn't begin to absorb the richness of the surroundings. Two blocks over, they came to the town square, lushly
green and manicured, surrounded by charming little shops in stone
and wood buildings. This was where he wanted to be. Oh, if
only . . . then he heard the ticking start.

"Sarah, I've decided to settle here. Would—would that please
you? I mean, well . . ."

"Yes, Christopher, it would. I'm very glad . . . but you have that strange look again. Perhaps we've walked too much."

"Perhaps we have. Let's go back to the party. But Sarah? Just for a time, hold my hand—and don't let go for anything."

She looked frightened and the ticking in his head was deafening now. He could feel the firm pressure of her soft hand holding his. At last, they reached the house and went around to the back. Just before the bell went off he tightened his grip on Sarah's hand and shut his eyes.

It was three days before anyone called the authorities' attention to Christopher Frame's unannounced absence. Several of his customers with pictures promised them by the faithful Mr. Frame became concerned and two detectives were sent to check up on him. They found nothing amiss in the building, nor did they find any trace of Chistopher Frame.

One of the officers discovered the picture on the dresser. "Hey, Charlie. Come in here. Want ya to see this."

"What's up?"

"See this picture? Just so's you'll know who we're looking for. Must be a relative of old Chris's from way back. Sure looks just like him."

"Which one?"

The detective pointed a big finger at the faded print. "Here. This one—holding hands with the girl on the porch."

Obituary

Paul Theridion

Reporter Bartholomew Schreiber and copyreader A. T. Ropos were fated for a bad end.

As city editor I knew them well: they were like chemicals, harmless apart but dangerous together.

Schreiber, who covered general assignments, was a big overgrown guy, mostly blubber, who had developed physically in all directions but not emotionally.

I could sometimes get great results from Schreiber by appealing to his pride. He was after all a Yale man and regarded his professional preparation as superb. But his performance was erratic, although it had once or twice come within a hairbreadth of a Pulitzer Prize.

We are a medium-sized newspaper with a copy desk of four—three scissors-wielding copyreaders directed by our news editor and charged with grooming our copy, locally written and off the wire, and devising headlines. All had gone reasonably well until copyreader Clem Lotho decided to turn in his eyeshade and pencil and retire under the publisher's penurious pension plan.

With newspapers folding so often these days, we had our pick of candidates and the managing editor chose Ropos, who had read copy for some prestigious dailies and was a Harvard man to boot. We called him familiarly A.T. because, as his personnel record indicated, the initials were mere ciphers bestowed upon him by whimsical parents who did not believe in name-calling.

He was a bony elf with a shock of fiery hair, bushy eyebrows and a wild mustache that covered his mouth and most of his chin. He regarded language, for all its lacy texture, as tangible as wrought iron, and was determined to guard it to the death against the insidious corrosion of change and the drastic battering of abuse.

When Ropos joined the staff he brought his scissors with him. I had never seen their like in a newsroom. They were eighteen inches long, nickel-plated, and forged of Solingen steel. He kept a small honing stone in his drawer on the rim of the great horseshoe of the copy desk. Each morning before starting work he would stroke the stone expertly along the edges of his scissors as the light danced on the gleaming blades.

It was a hoary custom on our paper for all the takes on a story to be pasted into a long sheet by the reporter who wrote it. When I passed a story to the news editor, I could see the eagerness with which Ropos awaited the copy. With one hand he would brandish his shears, taking snippets out of the air, while with the other hand he waved his soft black copy pencil frenziedly like a maestro conducting Wagner in a blazing concert hall.

The first time Ropos operated on Schreiber's copy was the initial skirmish in what quickly became all-out war. The story, actually not up to Schreiber's usual standard, was a maudlin feature about a little blind girl who lived in a hamlet near the city. Her rustic neighbors had taken up a collection to dispatch her to the surgical wizards of the Mayo Clinic, where it was hoped a miraculous cure would be effected.

Schreiber was watching apprehensively over the platen of his old L.C. Smith as Ropos seized the copy from the news editor.

"Aha!" Ropos cried as his dark little eyes alighted on a blemish. "General consensus of opinion, eh?" His pencil slashed all but consensus from the redundant phrase. "Clutched her dolly to her left chest, eh?" His pencil made it the left side of her chest. Then he shook his head and mumbled, "Drivel," as his sharp blades pierced the copy, causing Schreiber to clutch his abdomen. An irrelevant paragraph fell into the wastebasket like an excised appendix into a surgeon's slop bucket.

As Ropos bent over his work, the copy pencil twitched, darted, glided and stopped at last.

"Aha!" said Ropos as he patted the now subdued copy.

Then he scribbled an ironic headline which fit perfectly.

Later, as the presses rolled, our ancient building shook and so did Schreiber. When the copy boy handed Schreiber the paper with ink still moist, the reporter blanched as he read his truncated prose in 9 pt. Times Roman.

Schreiber strode to the copy desk, where Ropos was admiring his handiwork.

"Beastly butcher!" Schreiber cried.

"Scrofulous scrivener!" Ropos retorted, his scissors *en garde.*

"Harvard harpy!" Schreiber countered, his pudgy fists clenched.

"Yale yahoo!" the elf replied.

Had the news editor and I not restrained the two, the inevitable tragedy would not have been deferred. I judge that Schreiber's copy was the better for Ropos' surgery, but it was the little man's sadistic glee accompanying the operation which consistently infuriated the reporter.

For a while I hoped some benefit might result from the conflict. Schreiber was obviously trying harder. Before handing in a story, he would apprehensively scan it for errors in usage, grammar or punctuation.

As for Ropos, his obvious devotion to editorial excellence inspired the forgotten wretches on the copy desk who now felt they could hold their own in their eternal struggle with reporters.

But tragedy struck when both the news editor and I were in the paper's grubby lounge having our morning coffee after depositing a dime apiece in the publisher's collection box. As witnesses related the story to me later, Schreiber took from his desk drawer a short piece of copy he had been tinkering with for weeks and which he would hide whenever anyone approached.

The city room was a hushed arena when Schreiber stalked from his desk holding the story, and confronted Ropos at the copy desk.

"Let's see you cut this," Schreiber said belligerently as the smiling Ropos took the copy, his scissors snipping the air in anticipation.

But as Ropos read, his smile faded, and holding his shears at port he turned to face Schreiber, who had drawn a revolver and fired point-blank at the little man's chest.

Animated by a sense of outrage, Ropos sprang from his chair, his shears *en avant.* He plunged the scissors into the reporter's heart and the two adversaries sank in death to the city-room floor.

Who was the victor of this tragic battle? Perhaps the answer was in the faint smile that clung to Schreiber's lips as the reporter lay prone, his life claimed by the blades that had mutilated so many of his progeny.

For clutched in Ropos' hand was the story which said tersely:

A. T. Ropos, 49, copyreader for the *Bugle*, was shot to death at 10:30 a.m. today in the newspaper's editorial office by reporter Bartholomew Schreiber, 42, who was in turn stabbed to death by the copyreader.

Schreiber's story, which required only a headline supplied by the news editor, was run without a word changed.

Ransom Demand

Jeffrey M. Wallmann

Frances Bartlett sat in her husband's easy chair, her big hands clasped loosely in her lap, a plumpish auburn-haired woman in her late thirties, wearing a quilted robe over her pink nightgown. She was watching the *Today* show on television after having packed the children off to school, but this particular morning she wasn't relaxing as she usually did. She was worried.

She wanted to know what had happened to Paul.

Her husband was supposed to have been home sometime after 2 A.M. last night, after his flight from Chicago landed. Frances had awakened at three-thirty from the instinct bred of ten years' marriage to a sales manager, and had tossed and fretted in the dark for an hour before calling the airlines. A clerk at the check-in counter told her the plane had arrived on time, but that she'd have to wait until the business office opened to learn if her husband's name was on the passenger manifest or if he had transferred flights. Sorry. Touched slightly by hysteria, Frances had phoned long distance to the hotel at which Paul had been staying; he had checked out the previous evening without leaving any messages. Sorry . . .

She hadn't been able to sleep the rest of the night.

At least there hadn't been a crash, she told herself as she sat watching the television. She'd have heard about it if there had been, and surely she'd have been notified if there'd been an accident or Paul had gotten sick and was in a hospital. It was probably nothing, a mix-up of some kind. But it wasn't like Paul not to let her know. Where was he? Oh God, where was Paul?

401

She glanced at her wrist-watch. Another hour and she'd phone the airlines office, and if they couldn't help her, she'd wait until the next flight from Chicago, and if he wasn't on that, she'd . . . Frances shivered, not wanting to think about what she would have to do then. The police, Paul's boss, the publicity and questions and embarrassment; the prospect seemed too dreadful for words.

A commercial began, and she went to the kitchen for another cup of coffee. She was stirring it absently when the phone rang. She set the cup down and hurriedly picked up the receiver of the extension phone near her.

"H-Hello?"

"Mrs. Bartlett? Mrs. Paul Bartlett?"

"Yes. Who is this?"

"We have your husband, Mrs. Bartlett." ·

"What?" she said blankly. "What?"

"We have your husband," the voice repeated.

"What? You have Paul? How?"

"This is a ransom demand. Now do you understand?"

"Oh, my God . . . !" Frances sucked in her breath, trying to steady herself with her free hand. She knocked over the cup, coffee spilling across the counter; she never noticed it. "Paul, is he all right?"

"He's fine. He'll stay that way only if you do what I tell you."

"Let me speak to him. Please, let me—"

"No. Listen to me, Mrs. Bartlett, and listen closely." The man's voice was low and flat. "We want ten thousand dollars in unmarked bills, nothing over a twenty. Is that clear?"

"Yes, but I don't have—"

"Hock your jewels if you have to, but get ten thousand together by noon if you want to see your husband alive again. Take the money in a lunch pail—the old kind with the round top—to McKinley Park. You know where that is?"

"Downtown," she answered quickly. "It's downtown."

"Right. There's a statue of McKinley in the middle of it. At exactly twelve-thirty, walk along the north path and put the pail beside the third bench from the statue. Got that? Third bench, north side."

"I—I'm afraid I don't know which is north."

"The side facing Woolworth's. Then keep on going and don't look back."

"I won't. Twelve-fifteen, third bench, facing Woolworth's," she re-
cited numbly. "When do I . . . I see Paul?"

"Tomorrow night."

"That long? Can't you . . . ?"

"Don't call the police, Mrs. Bartlett. We'll be watching you, and if
you try to double-cross us, you'll never get another chance."

"I understand. But can't you let him go sooner? Please, can't you?"
And then she realized that she was talking into a dead receiver; the
man had hung up. She stood holding the phone for another moment,
still stunned, and then slowly replaced it with mechanical delibera-
tion.

"No," she cried out to her still, empty house. *"No!"*

Frances had been unable to sit still since she'd returned from
McKinley Park. Now, with school over and her children playing in
the yard, she paced aimlessly through the house, the phone serving as
the base of her wanderings. She would walk to the living-room window and move the drapes aside to peer out; then let them drop to
pace through the hall and up the stairs, gazing abstractedly into her
bedroom, hers and Paul's; down to smoke a cigarette and drink a cup
of coffee, only to leave it half finished; return once more to stare at
the phone, occasionally touching its bright plastic.

She knew she would carry this day alive and painfully fresh in her
mind for a long time. She wouldn't forget her initial panic, when
she'd almost called the police, followed by her longer, cold dread of
the chance she'd be taking if she did. She wouldn't forget how frantic
she'd been at the bank, closing out the accounts and cashing most of
their bonds, or how acutely she'd had to control herself when she'd
left the pail and simply kept on walking. Or now, despairing, hoping
she'd done right and praying Paul would be released unharmed. She
kept asking herself why? They weren't rich or famous—only an average, middle-class family like millions of others. Why had they been
picked?

The phone rang again. She ran to it, clutching it.

"Hello? Hello?"

"Honey?"

"Paul!" Tears of relief welled, blurring her vision. "Oh, Paul, are
you all right?"

"A little tired, but otherwise I'm okay. What's the matter?"

"Where are you?"

"Philadelphia."

"Philadelphia?"

"Sure. The meeting just broke up; it lasted longer than I thought."

"Meeting?" Frances felt dazed and bewildered. "Paul, I-I don't understand. What meeting?"

"This new accounts thing that came up at the last minute. I tried calling you last night to tell you I had to go, but the line was always busy, as usual. Didn't you get my wire?"

"No, I didn't. You mean you're all right?"

"I told you, I'm okay. Just what's going on, anyway?"

"You mean you . . . you weren't kidnaped?"

"Kidnaped!" Her husband laughed. "What makes you think I was kidnaped, for God's sake?"

Frances thought about the phone call and the ransom demand— then she thought about the ten thousand dollars and she fainted.

Lew Sieberts lounged in his swivel chair, tapping his thick fingers on the battered oak desk, impatient for his shift to be over. He was still amazed how smoothly the job had gone, and every once in a while he'd have to look in the third drawer of his desk just to be sure the pailful of money he'd picked up on his lunch hour wasn't a figment of his imagination. Man, if he had to get fired, this was the kind of severance pay to leave with; the job was proving to be the best he'd ever had, even if the shortest. He'd stick around to pocket his regular severance tomorrow morning, but then he was getting out of town before that Bartlett guy returned. To New York City, maybe—it had the action, and he could get so lost there he'd never be caught. Yeah, New York sounded real good . . .

The teletype across the room began to chatter. When its bell rang, Sieberts went over to it and tore off the flimsy. It read:

BLTMR XLT1960 JS DL PD KANSAS CITY MO 6/21 340P XXX CAROLE WILSON 424 MAXWELL CT BLTMR MD 467 9073 XXXX MUST GO TO SPRINGFIELD FOR TWO DAYS STOP UNEXPECTED BUSINESS SORRY STOP DONT WORRY LOVE PETER STOP END XXXX

Sieberts sat down again, studying the message. It was very similar to the wire Bartlett had sent yesterday. He leaned back until he could see out of the dusty window of the telegraph office and smiled faintly, wondering if he could pull the same trick twice in a row. Well, twenty grand was twice as much as he had now . . .

He swiveled around and picked up the phone, dialing the number printed on the telegram. The line buzzed and then a woman's voice answered.

"Mrs. Wilson? Mrs. Peter Wilson?" he said to her. "We have your husband . . ."

The Mother Goose
Madman

Betty Ren Wright

Only one thing distinguished the letter—that was the start of the te ror—from the twenty she had already opened. The others were a dressed to Juvenile Editor, Webster Publishing Company. This or said, Mrs. Julia Martell, Editor of Children's Books.

Julia noticed the distinction, but took no pleasure in it. She pre ferred anonymity in her job, which consisted chiefly of saying No t people. As a rule she barely glanced at the letters, but turned at once to the manuscripts which accompanied them. The letters were likely to tell too much, to paint too clearly the desperate beginner, the frustrated housewife, the poverty-stricken mother.

She slid a single sheet from the envelope. *Dear Miss Muffet*, the letter began, and she sighed, anticipating a cute approach. *Under separate cover please find my contribution to your line. It has been planned with you in mind and no one else. I hope it proves useful. If not, you will hear from me again. Sincerely, J. Smith.*

She glanced over the packages, looking for one addressed in the same hand as the letter. It was there, stamped *Fragile* and *Handle With Care* in a half-dozen places.

Fred Thompson stopped beside her, his arms full of art boards, and looked at the markings with amusement.

"Must be worth its weight in gold."

"Then it's not worth much," Julia said dryly. "Feels empty."

She slipped off the wrappings. There was thinly spread excelsior inside the box, with a feathery scrap of black showing through. She moved the excelsior aside.

407

Her first reaction was disbelief. But there it was: the spider's black hairy body drawn up over folded legs, the tremulous gathering of defenses as the excelsior was shifted. Then the legs moved.

"Oh!" she exclaimed. "Oh, *no!*"

She recoiled, because of her dread of all crawling things, while Fred slammed the heavy art boards down on the spider.

The brightly lit drugstore marked the beginnings of home. She stopped there every evening on her way from the bus to pick up a paper, to buy a pint of ice cream, or to reorder the eyewash that made her hours of reading possible. Possibly she liked the store because it reminded her of the one in which she had worked during her college days—the days before she had met, married, and been rejected by Ted Martell. Certainly her feeling about the place had nothing to do with the clerks and pharmacist who, big-city fashion, came and left with monotonous regularity.

Now she waved her prescription at the white-coated man in the back of the store, laid the slip on the counter, picked up a newspaper, and dropped a dime beside the prescription.

"Anything else?" the man called to her.

"No," Julia said, but with some reluctance. The cheerful store was especially soothing after the unpleasantness of the afternoon.

Partly, of course, it was the fuss everyone had made that disturbed her. There was Fred, his eyes showing more concern than his comments, which consisted mostly of consigning all practical jokers to damnation. Then the copyreaders and secretaries who had conjectured about Miss Muffet and her spider until it was time to go home. Even Mr. Webster had come in, curious about the excitement in the usually subdued editorial offices.

She hated their attention, which threatened to break through barriers she had built around herself. It wasn't easy to maintain those barriers. She knew that according to psychologists it was not only difficult, but wrong. Yet for her it was the only way. Having given herself, really given herself to the last, foolish degree, and having had the gift returned without thanks, she could not take a chance again. She would therefore depend on no one. It was part of the bargain she had made with herself in the months after her husband had left her.

But it was more than the attention of her fellow-workers that had upset her. She considered that as she left the store and hurried down the block to her own apartment building. And it was more than the fact of the spider—actually, harmless. She was disturbed because in her determination to avoid every possible entanglement she had failed. There was, somewhere, a person who called himself J. Smith who, she intuitively felt, hated her with a very real hate. She, who had tried so hard to remain aloof from all feeling, was caught in the entanglements of another's deep emotion.

She lifted the door of her mailbox and took out a handful of letters. Bills. Two invitations to spring book conferences. A letter from her aunt in Bangor, writing to thank her for a birthday present.

And an envelope addressed to Mrs. Julia Martell, Editor of Children's Books.

She put the other letters into her bag, opened the door of the automatic elevator, and stepped inside. She opened the envelope, almost eagerly. It was the same kind of paper, she saw that at once, the same thin hand. But she also saw that the salutation was different.

Dear Miss Humpty Dumpty, Did you enjoy my first submission? Expect another one soon.

The elevator lurched upward. Julia put out her hand to the emergency Stop button, but hesitated, did not touch it. The elevator slowed, halted. The doors opened and she faced her familiar hallway with its muted light, gray carpeting, lilacs on the table. She stepped out and waited for her heart to stop its violent thumping.

Humpty Dumpty had a great fall—

It wouldn't be in the elevator, or here in the hallway, where one of the other tenants might be the victim. But it might be inside her apartment, or possibly—

She turned into the shadowed ell that led to her own door. If she had been stepping along at her usual brisk pace, it would have been a very bad fall, but caution had slowed her steps. As it was, she stopped at once when the wire barely brushed her left ankle. Then she sat down, hard and without dignity, because her knees suddenly failed her.

It was a thin, gray wire—the same shade as the carpeting—stapled to the paneling on either side of the corridor, about three inches above the floor. A foot away it could not be seen.

After a moment Julia stood up, took a white linen handkerchief from her bag, and draped it over the wire as a warning to anyone else who might be coming in. Inside her apartment, she looked carefully in the bedroom, the kitchenette, the bath, the closets. Then she came back into the living room and called the police.

The next morning, she took the manuscript rejection files into the small conference room and closed the door behind her. If, as the police believed, her correspondent was a disgruntled and fanatic amateur writer, she would determine his identiy herself. The handwriting was distinctive—unfinished loops on the ascending letters, a slanted cross on the *t,* narrow *o*'s. She would recognize it.

There was only one letter in the file from a J. Smith—a barely legible scrawl which apparently accompanied some childhood reminiscences and was signed, *Jack Smith, age eighty-nine.* The letter was two years old.

Patiently, Julia moved back through the file to its starting point. The lieutenant had warned her that J. Smith was probably a pseudonym, and common sense told her that the writer, even though he had taken no pains to disguise his handwriting, would hardly sign his own name to what would be evidence against him.

She was halfway through the third drawer, when the door opened and Fred came in.

"Any luck?"

She shook her head, then looked up, startled, into his grin.

"Everybody's guessed what you're doing in here," he said. "And at least six people volunteered to help your secretary sort your mail this morning . . . Didn't find a thing."

Julia bit her lip. "I wish they'd just forget it," she said. "The whole thing is silly. I wish *everyone* would forget it."

Her tone was sharper than she had intended, and his reply matched it. "What's eating you?" he asked, and it was as if the question had been there for a long time, waiting to be asked. "Just why—why don't you want people to care about you? Is that a crime in your book?"

They stared at each other.

"End of conversation," Fred said, after a long moment of silence. "Full stop. Now—how about dinner at Charlie's tonight—all the spaghetti you can eat and extra meatballs on request?"

"No, thanks."

"We can discuss politics; who's going to win the pennant this year."

"Thanks anyway."

Afterward, staring at the closed door with a feeling close to shame, she thought how pleasant it would have been to have said Yes. He was a nice fellow, fun to be with, gentle in a way her husband had never thought of being. If she were just the kind who could forget and start over . . . At once she was hurtled back to the months after Ted had asked for a divorce. This was the hell one invited by caring for someone—endless days punctuated with pain when sharp little slivers of the past forced their way into the present. Endless, unspeakable nights. She would never take a chance on going through such a period again.

It was late afternoon before she had completed checking the last file. Nowhere had she come across handwriting like the writing in the letters. The day had been wasted. And she should have been able to do the job, she scolded herself, much more quickly than she had. The trouble was that it had been impossible simply to glance at the letters and put them aside. J. Smith was there somewhere; she found herself searching out the emotions of the writers, smiling at the timid jokes, responding to every question and request for advice.

Her secretary looked in to say she was leaving, but Julia remained at the conference table. As she had gone through the files she had taken out every letter that held a reference to Mother Goose. These were stacked before her in a neat pile, ready to be checked again.

There were letters criticizing the rhythm of the old verses, and letters praising the Webster Company's two-volume edition. There were letters asking the meaning of a particular poem, or offering an explanation of another. One of them was written in an uphill hand on stationery headed Ravensfoot Sanitarium, Belden, Colorado, and was dated February eleventh. Julia found it quite moving.

Dear Editor: I am sending you my original Modern Mother Goose Rhymes for Modern Children. During my illness I have passed many hours making up these little poems which, I feel, would have appeal for today's child. I am allowed to sit up for a half-hour every day, and during that time I have copied the poems by hand. I don't mention this to gain sympathy, but to show you how deeply in earnest I am about the value of the verses. Thank you for your consideration.

The letter was signed, *Dorothy Kesselman.* A note indicated that the standard printed rejection letter had been sent on February sixteenth.

Julia picked up the phone. "Will you get me the Ravensfoot Sanitarium in Belden, Colorado, please?" she asked the late-duty operator. "I want to speak to the doctor who is caring for Dorothy Kesselman."

She waited, fingering the letter, until the operator called her back. Then she listened without comment. When the operator had finished speaking, she thanked her and asked her to call Detective Schwarz at the police station.

"This is Julia Martell," she said when the lieutenant answered. "I think I have something for you to look into. A Dorothy Kesselman sent us some original nursery rhymes two months ago, and we returned them with our regular rejection letter. She was ill with advanced tuberculosis, and she died the day she received the letter. The hospital, in Colorado where she was a patient, says her husband, Adolph, moved to this city after his wife's death."

It was spring without question when Julia got off the bus that night and walked up the block. Children skipped like wraiths in the twilight. And in front of the old brick houses near the corner, jonquils poked yellow heads above their green. Julia looked at the narrow windows of the houses and wondered about the people behind them. Were they happy? Were they lonely? Had any of them ever noticed her as she returned night after night?

At the drugstore, one of the girls who worked part time was behind the counter. Julia collected a paper, some magazines, and her medicine, which was wrapped and waiting for her.

"How are you tonight?" she said, and was aware that the girl stared in surprise at the greeting. "It's spring," she added, foolishly.

Outside again, she felt as if she were ill and the greeting to the clerk had been a symptom, ominous as a first sneeze. The air crackled with the pain, the yearnings, the disappointments and the delights of all who breathed it. She shook her head, but could not shake away the awareness. Yet she knew she had to. The whole city was storming her barriers now, and she had to keep it out.

She walked faster, trying not to hear the children's shouts, the mutterings of old people on their front stoops, the soft laughter of couples passing by. When she reached her foyer, she tried to pass the mailbox without looking into it. But she could not ignore the envelope's whiteness, seen through the little slot in the box.

Dear Miss Peep-Peep, the letter said. *I don't know if you are much of a swimmer or a mountain climber, but it doesn't matter. The name fits—or soon will. This is my last submission, one which you have earned by your sympathy, your compassion, and your understanding. Sincerely, J. Smith.*

She read it again. Then, frowning, she crossed to the elevator and rode upstairs. She traversed the corridor with a slow, gliding step designed to reveal any invisible obstacles, and when she opened the door she stood back a moment before going inside.

It could be anything this time. She had never heard of Peep-Peep.

The living room appeared as she had left it. She looked around the rest of the apartment, then with her coat still on, took her *History of Mother Goose* from the shelf and thumbed through the index. It was there—a short riddle-rhyme about a star:

> *I have a little sister, they call her Peep-Peep;*
> *She wades the waters deep, deep, deep;*
> *She climbs the mountains high, high, high;*
> *Poor little creature, she has but one eye.*

The telephone rang. Julia picked it up and heard the voice of Lieutenant Schwarz.

"You can relax, Mrs. Martell," he said. "We've got your joker. Picked him up right after you called us. The husband of the Mrs. Kesselman who wrote you—he admitted it right away. Went off the deep end after his wife died. He says she worked for six months on the poems she sent you, and you didn't even— Well, he seems to think that if you'd sent a word of encouragement instead of a form letter, it would have made a difference. She was practically staying alive for your answer, according to him, and when it came—she just gave up."

Julia leaned back. "Yes," she said, "I understand you, Lieutenant. But it wasn't fair, was it? I mean, to put all that responsibility on me—"

The lieutenant sounded uncomfortable. "He says he wrote a letter that should have tipped you off," he said. "He knew he was going to be caught at this, but he didn't care . . . I'm sorry, Mrs. Martell. Anyway, you don't have to worry any more."

"Do I know him?"

"Could be." Lieutenant Schwarz seemed relieved to get off the delicate subject of motive. "At least, you've seen him. He's the pharmacist in the drugstore just down the block from your place."

Julia returned the receiver to its hook and sat for a moment without moving. Then she picked up the bottle of eyewash from the coffee table and unwrapped it. Her handkerchief was lying on the table, and she poured a little of the solution on the cloth. The spot widened and then, as she watched, the dampened area shredded and dissolved. Through the small round hole, she saw the wood of the coffee table turn yellow.

Poor little creature, she had but one eye. Julia looked around the room that had been for a long time her cheerful, safe retreat. Then she picked up the telephone directory and began turning the pages.

"Fred," she said a moment later. "This is Julia. Are the spaghetti and meatballs still available? I think I'd like them very much."

The Green Fly and the Box

Waldo Carlton Wright

A fly buzzed under the edge of the blue blind. It sounded like a plane diving toward the woods, at once near and then far away down the valley. Hanford lay without breathing, knowing if he did it would hurt deep down in his ribs, the way the pain had flared up with the blast of the shotgun.

There had been an accident. Of that Hanford was sure. Just where or how was still back there, in the blackout; but now he felt fully awake and light enough to float.

Cautiously he tried to open one eye, to watch the fly, knowing it sat on the window sill preening its wings. It had come to lay nits in his insides, hasten the decomposition of the body he had dragged around the fields and barn. His body had served him well, making a living of a sort on the old farm, finding joy in being alive but never becoming a capable farmer.

The morning light carried the same urgency that disturbs a seed buried in the ground. He was too young to be lying idle in this box with the white satin lining. His son Shean needed a guiding hand; and Betty was still young enough to marry again. It hurt just to think of that.

Now over the edge of the box he could see the fly. It was a female, large and green. Her wings glistened in the wedge of sunshine under the blind, near enough to swat. He reached out swiftly.

The motion lifted him clear of the box and he found himself floating. It was a bit awkward at first, moving like a cloud. It was smoother than using a crutch, the way he had hobbled around after

415

he broke his leg when his first tractor turned over on the side hill.

He was drifting toward the wall and closed his eyes, expecting a bump. Instead he passed through it, just as if there were nothing there. Outdoors in the sunshine he circled the catalpa tree, riding a merry-go-round of nothingness.

The second time around he saw the couple drawing up in a large sedan, parking by the garden gate. Now he realized it was the purring of their car on the hill that had wakened him. He swung back under the fretwork of the porch to see who they were.

Then from the henhouse his son Shean appeared, carrying two buckets of eggs. Hanford must remember to caution his son to clear the nests at least twice a day in this heat.

By rolling on his side, still hearing the blowfly buzzing inside against the glass, Hanford recognized the visitors, his wife's sister, Elizabeth, and her husband, Matt Burr. Coming to the wake, no less.

"Mother's expecting you, Aunt Bess, in the living room," Shean said, setting down the buckets of eggs. Hanford noted the yellow seal on the back of Shean's blue sweat shirt: Future Farmers of America.

The woman spread her arms to embrace the boy. "What a horrible thing to happen," she said.

The lad pulled away, pushed back his stubborn mop of red hair, and motioned the woman toward the kitchen door.

Elizabeth's husband covered the embarrassment by reaching for one of the buckets of eggs. "Let me help you put these in the refrigerator," he said.

"I can do it, Uncle Matt." Hanford's son picked up both buckets and headed for the cellar.

"I'd like to see how the apple trees are coming along, the ones you set out the last year you were in high school," Elizabeth's husband called after him.

As Elizabeth opened the side door and passed inside, a gust of air blew Hanford from under the porch so that he hung, light as the fluff of a milkweed pod, over the woodshed.

Elizabeth's husband, waiting for Shean to come out of the cellar, reminded Hanford of the centurion who had told Jesus he was accustomed to ordering men around. Born in a Brooklyn ghetto, he had learned to climb over other men's backs, until he was head of his own Somerset mills—master of all, except in his own home.

Shean came out of the entry carrying Hanford's shotgun in the crook of his arm. Shep, the collie, uncoiled from under the lilac bush, his tail wagging like the metronome Betty kept on the top of the parlor organ. Shean led the way, up the path by the blighted cherry tree, toward the leaning silo and the old red barn, and Hanford wondered why neither of them looked up to see him hanging in the air, right smack over the weather vane.

The sheep dog turned his nose skyward and sniffed. Then, to show his disdain of men who floated around instead of walking like normal critters, the dog raised his leg and watered a patch of dandelions.

At the barnyard, Shean's heifer moved out from under the straw stack to lean her muzzle over the rail for the boy's caress, and Shean said, "She's due to freshen any day now, Uncle Matt."

Matthew Burr reached out to pat the heifer's neck, but she drew back, shaking her head and watching them. Floating around the stack, Hanford chuckled to himself about the heifer drawing away instinctively from Elizabeth's husband.

"But why a Jersey?" Burr was asking.

"You sound like my old man," Shean said. "Don't you know it pays to raise the butterfat over four percent?"

"Well, now, that makes sense," Elizabeth's husband said. "What have you done to modernize the barn?"

"Come and I'll show you the surge milker and the stainless-steel storage tanks," Shean said.

They passed under the overhang, into the stalls. Hanford preferred not to try to wedge in, to hear what Burr would say about the new stanchions and the water cups. His son had bought these against his advice, going deeper and deeper in debt, and somehow Hanford no longer felt a part of all this.

He began to get the hang of floating in air. The trick was wishing to be someplace, hard enough, and resting in space, doing nothing, like floating on your back when swimming. Up here he could hear anything they said.

"My old man felt he could strip the cow's udders better by hand, more cream, the way his folks had done in Ireland all their lives." Shean's voice bounced out the entry and slithered soft-toned off the stone wall by the watering trough.

"But your mother—she was on your side, wasn't she?" Burr's voice was prodding, researching, firming up the facts, to lay them one-two-three on the intercom. You standardize this, you automate that. So, the Problem stands resolved.

They were outside again, walking right under him past the watering trough, heading for the orchard. There the old trees had died out, and Hanford had sawed them down singly with a one-man crosscut for firewood. His son had laid out the new orchard on the same west side of the ridge, as a 4-H project, with the help of the county agent.

Hanford had been against the project. Milk was a money crop, and cows returned strength to the soil. The new orchard would have to be sprayed with all those new poisons that killed the curculio and leafrollers and checked the powdery mildew. Poisons soaked into the soil and in time would seep into the well and creep into the home vegetables. Science can go too far, his Scanlon grandfather had told him as a boy, when they went up Sunday afternoons to salt the sheep.

"My old man loved this place, just as it was; just as his father and grandfather had struggled here," Shean was saying. He walked in long high-stepping strides, the way a farm boy learns to clear the furrows left by the spring plowing, carrying this stride with him all his life.

"It's just as if he were out of step with life," Burr said, the way he would explain why it was necessary to let one of his accountants go now that the employee was over fifty and wages were handled by one machine, even the check writing.

Elizabeth had written to Betty about these time savers her husband had made at the Somerset mill, but his wife had never complained to Hanford or even hinted he was out of step with this thing called progress. That was why he had kept on believing in her, loving her, feeling her warmth smother some wildness in his heart, nights on the old farm.

Below him, the boy and man walked down the center row of the young trees. Every now and then his son would stop to examine the fruit, rubbing a green Rome Beauty with the sleeve of his blue shirt.

"They're beginning to show color," he told his uncle.

"How often do you have to spray them?" Burr asked.

Hanford couldn't catch the number of times Shean mentioned. Sliding along above the tops of the trees, brushing his stomach on the soft green leaves, he could feel the chalky coating rub off on him, the way powdered lime sifts right through your shirt, smarting your chest.

Up here, higher than the ridge, it looked like a toy farm, with its old log house, red barn, and the black and white specks of the Holstein herd grazing along the creek. The clover held back the soil from washing into the valley. The cows enriched the land, giving back measure for measure to maintain the balance. It was a slicker accounting with time than any of Burr's data-processing machines could attain. Life here was simpler, mocking all the furor of pouring more steel, shaping it into pistons and gears, refrigerators and cars, speeding up the looms, sealing more packages, capping more bottles. The nonsense of it made Hanford laugh out loud.

At the rumble of Hanford's voice, Shean glanced up between the trees. For a moment he thought his son saw him floating there.

"The thunderheads are building," he told Burr. "We'd better take a shortcut to the house."

"I distinctly heard something," Burr said, frowning up at Hanford as if ordering him to come down from his perch and be a man again. Burr had often told him, "You'd make more in a year working for me than you will on this old farm the rest of your life."

No, no, you tried that before, dangled other offers through my wife's sister. Now you'll try to lure my son away—unless he's got some of my Irish rebel blood in his gizzard.

"I can get you a good job at the mill, you know." Burr was taking quick military strides down the field, half stumbling over the cross contour lines left by the plow, trying to keep up with the boy.

Shean walked ahead, the shotgun bobbing in the crook of his arm. From across the field came shrill barking. A rabbit jumped clear of the pine woods, headed toward them. The boy brought the gun to his shoulder. At the blast, dust spurted almost in the rabbit's nose. It swung down the field, leaping high to clear the clumps of clover, disappeared into the woods. The sheep dog came running from the woods toward the gun, his tongue lolling, expectant of picking up a limp rabbit.

"You missed," Burr was criticizing his son, just as he would the first time Shean let a faulty gadget slide by him on the inspection line.

Hanford knew better. Shean had purposely missed the rabbit, merely wanted to scare it out of the clover. He gets that hate of killing wild things from his mother.

Hanford watched Shean break open the barrel, ejecting the red plastic shell. Then he blew through the breach, the way he had been taught. You don't have to explain twice to an Irishman to keep your gun at the ready.

They had come to the stake and rider fence that separated the clover from the corn field. Hanford banked lower on the current of hot air that flowed down the ridge, to hear what would be said. This was the spot where he last remembered carrying the gun. Was it yesterday or a week ago? Or beyond time? But it was here. He was almost sure.

"This is where I found him yesterday," Shean said, as if that were on his mind when he aimed in front of the rabbit.

"Right at this spot?" Burr asked, staring at the brown spot near the rails. He would have to know the facts exactly.

"It wasn't as if he didn't know how to crawl over a fence." Shean handed the gun to Elizabeth's husband. "Hold this while I take down a rail."

"Do you suppose the trigger caught?" Burr asked.

It seemed terribly important to Hanford to hear what his son would say, but just as Shean crawled over the rail lightning struck a tree in the woods. The blast pushed Hanford aside, sent him tumbling down the hill on a current of hot tangy air. When he recovered himself, floating over the Holsteins, Hanford bounced upward, fluttering the bulges that were his arms, like wings. By now the rain was falling through him, and Shean and the man were running past the vegetable garden, toward the fan doorway of the farmhouse.

Hanford floated after them, finding it breathless to keep up, feeling something was being washed out of him, the way water leeches the salts out of the soil, eroding it, leaving it fallow.

They had gone in ahead of him and closed the door. He knew they were gathered in the parlor and that his wife Betty would have raised the blind only after she was sure the lid was on the coffin.

Hanford slid noiselessly through the plaster chinks, between the old logs that his grandfather had laid up when he first settled here a hundred and fifty years ago, retreating from the potato famine in Ireland.

Elizabeth sat in the rocker by the window, facing Betty, who stood by the door as if keeping watch over the coffin. Burr had slid into Hanford's captain's chair, an heirloom of a Scanlon. Burr's feet were stretched out to relax after the climb around the old place. Shean wasn't in the room. He must have gone up to the barn to see whether the Jersey heifer had dropped her calf.

Instead of sliding back into the coffin through the black lid, Hanford rested on a strand of cobweb along the ceiling above the mantel. The strand was soft and springy and from here he could watch them all, even hear their breathing. From the way Elizabeth's finger knocked the ashes from her long cigarette into the blue jardiniere, he knew his wife's sister had something that had to be said before the lad came in, now her husband was there to witness.

"Matthew will buy the place," she said, and then looked up quickly at the corner of the room, as if she had seen Hanford lying there on the cobweb. She shrugged as if she felt a chill, then brushed her hand over her eyes to fan away the puff of smoke coming from her nose.

Betty sat down quickly, the way the legs of a calf sag when the butcher hits it with a sledgehammer between the eyes. He had seen her collapse that way once before, when lightning struck the old barn just after haying. Grain and hay, even the herd, everything but the house, had gone up in flames. It was the summer she had been carrying Shean.

Hanford eased his leg over the cobweb to relax. He suddenly felt tired to death, wanting to stretch out in the chair where Burr lolled. The man was waiting for Betty's reaction to his offer to buy the farm. Betty and the boy would move into the city. Shean could have a job on the inspection line, the way he had offered it back there at the fence, holding the gun that had somehow been part of this meeting, while the lad crawled over.

"The way of the world is change," Burr was saying. "The trick is to move ahead of the changes."

That must be how he thinks, that change is everything, always for the better. Hanford shook his head but knew they would not look up to him for guidance. He was just an old-fashioned farmer, proud of his acres. However lean, the land had still supported him, his wife and son. Until the accident, that was.

The female blowfly was again zooming around the room, dipping and buzzing, protesting at being shut out of the coffin. She sounded heavy with eggs, the nits that would assure Hanford's decomposition.

"You'll be better off living in a small house in Somerset." Elizabeth snuffed out her cigarette on the edge of the blue jar and dropped the butt among the dried pussy willows, to indicate it was all agreed, settled.

The door swung open and Shean stood outlined like a back-country Blue Boy in a frame. Raindrops trickled off the mop of red hair and his face was splotched with mud.

"Ma, Betsy's had her calf. Isn't that great?" Still grinning, he turned to Elizabeth's husband. "You must come up and see it."

"No, thanks. We've got to be going shortly," Burr said, sitting up straight, the way he brought a meeting of his board of directors around to a decision.

Elizabeth reacted to her husband's cue, first glancing at the coffin and then turning to face the lad. "Matthew will see that you get ahead at the mill. It might even be yours someday."

Hanford rolled over on his side on the cobweb, to watch his son's face. Shean seemed unable to grasp what was being spread out before him by his rich uncle.

The collie wedged by Shean, turned once, then stretched out at Betty's feet. The gesture seemed to ask, And what about me? Who'll feed me?

"I wouldn't like working in your mill," Shean said. "This is my farm. This is where I belong."

"For shame, Shean," Betty said. "Matthew only wants to help us, not take the farm."

"The farm is not for sale." His son's eyes seemed fixed on the black lid of the long box in the corner, as if he were making a vow.

"Well, think it over and if you change your mind . . ." Elizabeth's husband stood up. His head bobbed into Hanford's ribs. Then the visitor brushed a cobweb from his bald head and strode decisively through the door.

Good-bye, good-bye. Hanford almost fell off the cobweb laughing for joy. His son was every inch an independent Irishman.

Betty lingered behind for a moment. She stroked the lid of the box lightly, then drew the blue blind down to the window sill like a curtain falling on the last act.

When she had gone, Hanford listened for the revving of the car motor. Its departure rattled the windowpanes like the rumble of distant thunder. The green fly took up its frustrated hum, reminding him of its urgency.

Hanford could feel the open spaces, cleansed by the rain, like a cool draft when he opened the door of the egg refrigerator. He could still hear the priest kneeling beside him, mumbling the words of the last rites. Then he remembered his own mumbling, his thick tongue, his smoldering fire. He had been drinking all day in the barn, not even bothering to milk the cows. He had spent the egg money for a little fun, to forget with a jug of Irish whiskey, the best.

Just as it was getting dark, Shean had driven in. The lad had wasted the whole day at a meeting of the county apple growers association down in Bedford. He had insisted Hanford go with him, right then, up the ridge where the new orchard would be. What angered Hanford most was the crazy fool buying a thousand more four-year-old red Delicious on bank credit, through the word of the county agent, putting him deeper in debt. It didn't make sense to Hanford.

As they walked they quarreled. At the stake and rider fence, his anger mixed with the whiskey. He clouted his son across the mouth, knocked him into the corn stubble. Flames of rebellion to a changed way of life, all he had worked for, roared through his mind, licked out at the cause of all his frustration. He remembered aiming the gun at Shean's chest. The lad grabbed the barrel and hung on, pleading. There had been this yellow blast and Hanford felt his ribs cave in, the way they had done when the tractor fell on him.

Somehow he had expected to wake up in hell. Or maybe, if he had been absolved, crowned and alone, sitting on the ridge of a cloud, wearing a white robe, sipping stale beer from a golden mug, his blunt fingers trying to pick out "Londonderry Air" on an Irish harp. Instead, this heaven was more like an extension of memory, linking him with the living, forever near those he loved on this old farm.

World weariness seeped through him into the open spaces left by the rain. He was falling into a bottomless sleep. Feet first, drawn out like a wisp of smoke, he slid slowly into the long black box, feeling the satin brush his cheek like Betty's hand in the night: *Now go to sleep, Hanford my love, my Irish prince.*

Just before oblivion, he remembered to push up the edge of the lid with one toe. That way the female blowfly could wedge in, lay her nits, assure the return of his body to the soil that had formed him.

The Blue Rug

Mitsu Yamamoto

"That guy there would be perfect."

I looked up from the equation I was checking at the two men standing in the doorway of my lab. One was Jamison, a vice president in charge of PR and advertising. The other I knew right off was some creative type—he was wearing a vicuna sweater, brown corduroy pants, and no tie. This turned out to be Reg, Reg of The Rug.

But the rug came later. Now Jamison was patting me on the arm and saying, "Don, here, is one of our think-men. Does most of his chemistry behind his desk."

Reg looked about thirty, a very trim thirty, with an eager manner and big smile. I felt myself warming toward him though I knew he was some Madison Avenue nuisance. "What's this experimenting by remote control?" he asked, motioning to my desk.

"Not completely remote," I said. "I figure it out, my assistants set it up, we run the experiment, it flops, they wash the glassware, and I'm back at my desk with a pencil."

Jamison frowned slightly. "Now, come, Don, the zinc purifier was all yours."

Reg ignored him, just shook his head at me, and said, "For the commercial, Don, you're going to have to get in there and lower the Bunsen burners yourself."

I noticed he was calling me Don already, but it just reminded me of a guy I knew in the Army. Same kind of heartiness. He was the first in our outfit to buy it. "Commercial?" I said.

Jamison interposed hastily. "Now, Don, you've heard we're planning some institutional advertising on TV, burnish up the image a bit. And Reg is in charge—writer, director, everything."

"And I want an actual Parkson chemist," Reg said. "But we'll use an actress for the housewife part."

"But I'm no actor," I objected.

Reg laughed. "You don't have to be. With that studious look, confident manner—you're type-cast."

So I was on TV, or almost. Reg planned four commercials, using a kitchen and a lab like mine. We packed tons of Erlanger jars and glass tubing off to a West Side studio. I tried to get the equipment set up in a way that would make some kind of sense, but Reg said it didn't matter, it was only background. But he spent an hour sighting the shots of the burners painted with Parkson's newest stove paint.

The man who really fussed around was the lighting director. He found too much glare from the glass everywhere. Then my hair was too dark, he claimed, and absorbing too much light, so up went another spot to counteract it. I stood under the hot lights, in a blue lab coat, feeling like an ass. But Reg loved it all and poured out energy, running, shouting, calling shots, moving us around, and interviewing girls for the housewife's role as they turned up.

At the end of the first day, I was completely beat from just standing around and moving on cue, so Reg took me back to his apartment for a drink. I expected to see the typical bachelor apartment of a bachelor who earned forty thousand dollars a year—the going price for top TV commercial writers, Reg told me to my annoyance. But Reg's apartment was all Reg.

In the living room were only three large dark-blue couches, end tables, a bar, a hi-fi and a pale-blue rug. The rug measured about 16' by 16', perfectly plain except for the middle which had a dark-blue intertwined design that was hard to make out from the doorway. All the furniture bordered the rug, but some dark-blue cushions were thrown around on it.

"Now, laddie, life can begin," Reg said, throwing off his coat and going to the bar. "Two belts of Scotch for two needy men." He looked over at me in the doorway. "Well, come on in."

I pointed to the rug. "You mean it's for walking on? With shoes?"

Reg laughed. "With shoes—at first. I have a cleaning service that comes in regularly once a month."

I stepped on the rug and it was like walking with pillows strapped to your feet.

Reg watched me with a delighted grin. "It's got to you, hasn't it? You want to walk around in your socks or, even better, barefoot, don't you?"

I nodded sheepishly and took off my hat, my coat, and then my shoes. The rug felt even better. It was soft, it was sybaritic, it was damn near tranquilizing. "It's great, great," I murmured, feeling like all the feather beds in the world were underfoot.

Reg kicked off his shoes and handed me my drink. "Now you come to Phase Two. You want to sit down on the rug." He plopped himself down and leaned back against one of the couches. "You want to stretch out, maybe even lie down and feel good all over, the way your feet feel. Right?"

"Right, but I just had this suit pressed." But I found myself sitting down on the rug and leaning back against a couch, like Reg. I tasted my drink—it was very high-class Scotch and I knew this more as a chemist than a drinker, since my salary didn't run to it. I relaxed and watched Reg, now stretched toward the middle of the rug, tracing the dark-blue pattern there with a lazy finger. "Is there a Phase Three?" I asked.

Reg smiled again and said, "Phase Three is when she says"—here he reared back on his heels and stared at the blue design in simulated surprise, saying in a girl's voice—" 'Why, it's a picture with people or something.' Then she looks closer at the people, the two people who seem to be entangled with one another."

I took another sip of Scotch. "*She* says?"

Reg sighed. "Don't be stupid, laddie. Do you think I poured five thousand dollars into a custom-made rug for guys like you to rub their socks into?"

"Five thousand dollars for this rug?"

Reg finished off his drink. "And as Mother Nature is my judge, it's been worth every cent."

"Mother Nature, huh?" I heaved myself forward and crawled two steps until I was looking down at the dark-blue design. I studied it very carefully, beginning with the woman's leg on the man's shoulder and ending with the splayed fingers of the man's right hand. Automatically my hand reached up to receive the second drink Reg was passing me. I crawled back to my position against the couch, the concern for the crease in my trousers a thing of the past.

"That," I pronounced, "is the most real, the most delicate, and the only piece of wool pornography I have been privileged to see." And I drank to it.

Reg nodded happily, his good-looking face aglow. "But that's only half of it. That stuff is Art. Right out of the *Kamasutra*. This husband and wife down in the Village made it to order for me. He was a designer and she was a weaver and they copied it right out of some scholarly Oriental art book." He sighed reminiscently. "And they went off to Mexico on the five thousand, and my rug and I went on to glory with countless, countless beautiful girls."

I interrupted this reverie. "But Kinsey says women are not particularly stimulated by pornography."

Reg sat up. "First, let us stop calling it 'pornography.' It's art. Famous Indian art. Second, yes, Kinsey said that, but no one can *actually* know that about *every* girl."

I crawled back to the design, to take it in again. "I admit I'd love to have this rug around the house, but I'd hate to spend all that money and find Kinsey right about most of the girls most of the time."

Reg had brought the Scotch bottle with him last time, and now he crawled over with it and refilled my glass. "No, laddie, you got it wrong. I don't expect the little girl to be all shook up by this." Here he stroked the woman's right buttock. "What I expect is just what's going on here. We are having a discussion about sex; nay, more, we are having a discussion about copulation. Did you ever bring a girl around to the topic this fast? And at the same time have her down on the floor with her shoes off and a sensuous desire to stretch out just because the rug is so soft?"

I shook my head admiringly. "I drink to two rugmakers in Mexico and to a great dirty mind beside me," I joked.

Because for me, it was just a big joke. I was in the market for marriage. I had a good job that I liked and I was getting tired of chasing around. I wanted my own girl and I wanted three sons. I was simply ready for *the* girl. But I could appreciate the Madison Avenue approach that Reg made with his rug, an approach that worked time after time, I heard later at the TV studio. The girls knew it was a big blatant joke and try-on, but they loved it—it was so fantastic—and besides the rug was soft and Reg had a lot of charm.

The first commercial was set to roll on Tuesday. At ten Reg was still turning down girls for the housewife part. The same agent always cast for him and usually there were no problems, but this time the girl had to match up with me. I'm dark, so they wanted a blonde. I'm six feet, so they didn't want a girl under five feet three. I have rather sharp features, so they wanted a kitten-type girl. And to balance my voice, which tends to be fast and a little bossy, they wanted a smooth, olive-oil-sounding girl.

Sarah "Sally" Larsen turned out to be that blond olive-oil kitten. Reg hired her after one look and her first sentence to him, "I'm trying out for the Parkson commercial." The casting agent had matched us perfectly from a physical viewpoint, and Sally turned out to be sweet and intelligent. By the time we had wrapped up the third commercial, I was in love with her. By the end of the fourth, I had told her, just to get her used to the idea.

Of course, everybody liked her. As soon as she came on the set, each man started doing his job like a pro—from the sound mixer to the kid keeping the camera cables from getting tangled. We all wanted to look good in front of her. All of us, including Reg.

During the week we made the commercials Sally, Reg, and I were like the Three Musketeers. But we never went to Reg's apartment. He had to save his rug as a surprise for any new girl, so we all went to a new bar and a different restaurant each night. And the question loomed early: I wanted Sally, Reg wanted Sally, who did Sally want?

We kicked this question around for the next two months. I went back to my lab at Parkson's, but the three of us were in constant touch by phone and dates in the city. I watched the commercials every chance I got, just to see Sally's eyes light up when she looked at her stove burners painted with Parkson's paint. I knew Reg had been pressing Sally to come to his apartment for dinner, but she had been in New York only six months and was a little afraid of his smoothness. I told her about Reg's rug—just as a warning without having to say it was a warning against Reg—which was probably a mistake, for the idea of the rug intrigued her. But I kept telling myself I had something intriguing too, an offer of marriage. I didn't realize how much I was in love with her until one morning at eleven I found myself leaving the lab and rushing home to look at a Parkson commercial that I had seen twenty times over. Then I knew I *had* to marry her.

The Christmas holidays were terrible. Sally spent them in Ohio with her family and Reg was invited to the Bahamas. I spent a lot of time at the lab, including evenings, but I determined that next Christmas I would spend double that time at home with my own wife, planning the house we would build on some beautiful wooded land I had bought near Parkson's.

I made so many plans for Sally and me that I could scarcely take it in when she told me. At home she had given us a lot of thought and decided it wasn't fair to keep me dangling. She wanted to be married and possibly to me, but not yet. So one of her New Year's resolutions was to enjoy herself in this New York period while she was still the girl every man in the room turned to look at when she entered. She would begin by accepting Reg's invitation to dinner at his apartment that Sunday.

I went home and got drunk by myself. The last thing I remember is explaining to the umbrella stand, "I want to marry her, so I don't get the girl. Reg doesn't want to marry her, so he does." It took me two days to really sober up and by then it was Friday. Friday before Sunday. Sunday, which would be the end of my dream of a wonderful life with Sally.

I always think best at a desk, with a pencil in my hand. So now I made myself a hearty breakfast, took the phone off the hook, and went into my study. I sat down at my desk and took up a pencil. I put a scratch pad in front of me and then I began to think about my problem. A scientist starts out by absorbing the facts about his field and training himself in its technics. This makes him a technician in his field. When he learns to direct his mind, to *think*, to solve problems in his field, then he becomes a scientist. And I was a scientist with a problem. I sat at my desk and thought throughout most of Friday. At midnight I went to bed, only to wake up at four in the morning. I had some milk and went back to my desk. By nine o'clock Saturday morning I had solved my problem, and I went back to bed for a nap until it was time to call Reg.

I finally got hold of Reg at his apartment about six that evening after calling regularly all afternoon. I made my voice a little unsteady and said, "I want to talk to you about Sally. She . . . she tells me you two have a date tomorrow."

Reg was embarrassed by the emotion he could detect in my voice, but said heartily, "Well, sure, laddie, but I'm going out this evening. And tomorrow is out. How about lunch next week?"

But I insisted it had to be this evening, letting my voice rise some-what. So Reg finally agreed to my coming to his apartment around midnight, promising to cut his date short. I hung up with satisfaction.

I got into the city about eight and bought the pink, sweet liqueur that Sally was fond of. I had dinner alone and went to a French film. I was pleased to notice I was detached enough to enjoy the movie, though every now and then I became conscious of the weight of the liqueur in my lap. From eleven to midnight I drank. Reg was an ex-pert in estimating how drunk a man was—it was part of his job en-tertaining clients for his agency, getting them happy without making them unmanageable. So I had to draw a fine line between being alert and being sloppy enough to convince Reg.

Reg answered the door quickly when I rang and I caught the shadow of annoyance that passed over his face when he saw me steadying myself against the door frame. He didn't want to talk about Sally, he didn't want to see me, and, most of all, he didn't want to contend with a drunken, aggrieved friend.

I held out the liqueur. "It's for Sally. She likes it." I sat down abruptly on the floor, still holding the bottle.

"Okay, Don, take it easy," Reg said. "I'll put some coffee on."

"No, wait," I commanded loftily. "I was going to knock the beje-sus out of you. But that . . . that too degrading for Sally. Jus' want you to know you ruined my life."

Reg sighed. "Oh, come on, Don. Sally and I'll see one another for a while and that'll be it. She's not *really* interested in me. It's just the New York bit. You'll see."

He left me sitting on the floor and went to make the coffee. I didn't bother taking off my coat, but opened the liqueur and care-fully dribbled it over the blue rug. I emptied the last of the bottle over the entwined figures and rubbed the sticky pink liquid into the wool with my foot.

I looked up when I heard Reg gasp. I saw him fight for control of his feelings and gain it. He was tight-lipped as he set the coffeepot down on a table. "Okay, Don. You're drunk and unhappy and think you have a right to be. Maybe you have. I don't see it that way."

I stood looking down at the pink mess I had made of the two dark-blue figures. "She was my girl," I said. I tried to slur it drunkenly.

"Go home. We have nothing to discuss. You think this"—he

waved his hand at his stained rug—"will prevent Sally from coming. But you're wrong. It's not even a delaying action."

I looked up at Reg and smiled inwardly. I hadn't been mistaken in him: the value I had assigned to him in my equation was correct. He was coldly furious but determined.

"I intend," said Reg, spacing his words, "to clean this rug and have Sally to dinner tomorrow as planned. Or today, I should say. There's an all-night drugstore at Times Square and they must have something I can use. So, take off, back to your test tubes."

I sagged and started toward the door. Reg watched me. At the door I turned and passed my hand over my forehead. "Reg, I . . . I . . . you've got to understand how this has hit me. I can't believe I've done this childish thing." But my eyes glinted with pleasure as I saw how the thick fibers of the rug had absorbed the liquid, leaving small beads of stickiness to catch the light and glisten.

"Well, you sure did," said Reg, with a little less hardness in his voice. "I only hope they don't have some kid on duty at the drugstore who won't know anything." He went to the closet for his coat.

I turned the knob of the door. "Oh, just ask him to give you carbon tet."

Reg's expression softened slightly. "Carbon tet?"

"That's right," I said. "Carbon tetrachloride." Then I let myself out and walked for about an hour in the cold dark. After a while it began to snow.

On Sunday evening at eight o'clock Sally called me from a hospital. She was almost hysterical, so I drove as fast as I dared into New York. When she saw me hurrying through the hospital lobby, she flew into my arms and started to cry. I knew she was in my arms to stay.

"Oh, Don, it was awful, awful. I was supposed to come for dinner, but he didn't answer the door. I got the super because we could hear the hi-fi going."

"And Reg was . . . ?" I prompted.

Sally lifted a tear-streaked face to mine. "He was lying on the floor unconscious. And in the ambulance, he died!" Her voice began to rise. "Reg died!"

I gave her a little shake. "Get hold of yourself, Sally. Tell me what happened."

"The doctor said he poisoned himself. Besides he was drinking beer and the alcohol made him absorb it faster. Oh, Don, he was all blue." She shuddered.

"Reg poisoned himself?"

Sally gave a big sigh. "This is all so ugly I'll never forget it. He was cleaning his rug, that loathsome rug you told me about. Cleaning it for my benefit. There was a bucket and brush beside him. The doctor said it was carbon tet poisoning."

She began to tremble and I held her close. My Sally. "Never mind. I'll take you home now. It was just an accident. An ordinary mistake. Could happen to anyone."

She let me lead her out of the hospital, but stopped on the sidewalk and looked up at me through the snow. "Just an ordinary mistake—that's what's so terrible. If he wanted a cleaning fluid, why didn't he ask you what to get? You're a chemist, you could have told him."

"That's right," I agreed. "I'm a chemist, I could have told him."

Then I drove her home.